The Posthorn Inn

GRACE THOMPSON

The Posthorn Inn

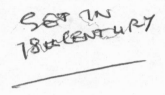

SET IN 18th CENTURY

BARRIE & JENKINS
LONDON

First published in 1991 by Barrie & Jenkins Ltd,
Random Century House, 20 Vauxhall Bridge Road,
London SW1V 2SA

British Library Cataloguing in Publication Data
Thompson, Grace
The Posthorn inn.
1. Title
823.914 [F]

ISBN 0-7126-4593-4

Phototypeset in Linotronic Baskerville by
SX Composing Ltd, Rayleigh, Essex

Printed and bound in Great Britain by
Mackays of Chatham PLC, Chatham, Kent

To all those library assistants
who have been so generous with their time
and help

SET IN
18th CENTURY

Chapter One

Pitcher Palmer stood outside the entrance of his alehouse watching the road leading to the town of Swansea. He was waiting for the letter-carrier. The wind was strong and, as the edge of the tide was close by, the wind was wet with spray. It blew through his Welsh flannel shirt and made him shiver. But he did not move, apart from glancing back towards the corner of the road leading up to Newton and, occasionally, up above his head to the window where his wife Emma often sat to watch the activities of the village.

He stepped towards the doorway, to be hidden from her view. The letter he was expecting was one he did not want her to see. Emma was his partner in almost everything, but his hopes of turning the alehouse they owned into an inn where people could eat and stay overnight, he wanted, for the moment, to keep to himself.

Pitcher was not a large man, but there was a look about him that suggested strength. His eyes, constantly moving – as if watching for the slightest hint of a way of making money, some said – were small and of that blue which sometimes shines green. He was dressed in a pair of brown wool-cloth trousers and the shirt which had been made by Emma from the Welsh flannel she bought annually in the Pontypridd market. A waist-coat of velvet, once his best but now relegated to morning wear, was faded and spotted with stains and he knew that Emma would be furious with him for wearing it outside to be seen by passers-by. She insisted that if he wore it at all, it was to be in the cellar. 'It's very important to keep up appearances, Pitcher.' He smiled as he imagined her saying it.

The roar of the waves bustling in filled his ears. Even louder was the crash as they touched and exploded in white cascades over the walls of the small houses that had stood defying them for years. Each wave sent echoes, reverberating in harsh counterpoint to the next, making boats bob and sway along the shore, irritable at being disturbed. Pitcher shivered and leaned in the direction from which Barrass would come with the post, in the hope of hearing the clopping of the pony's hooves above the noise.

With three daughters, each needing a husband, Emma had persuaded Pitcher to make her a parlour instead of the bedrooms to rent out that he so badly wanted. Now, with one daughter married, there were still the twins. He sighed, doubting if he could persuade Emma to listen to his plans. But there was no harm in starting enquiries. And perhaps, if he could show her what he had in mind, and what it would cost, her good business sense would come to the fore and she would let him have his way.

He was rewarded at last by the sound of the post horn being blown by the letter-carrier as he turned the corner, and moments later, by the sight of him appearing in the distance; leather bag across his shoulders, body bent against the gusting wind. Other riders had approached and passed him as he had waited, but Barrass the letter-carrier was easily recognized by the red waistcoat he wore, even if he had not sounded the horn to warn of his arrival. The dark-haired young man riding towards him saw him waiting and waved a greeting. His wave was so enthusiastic that Pitcher guessed that the letter he waited for had arrived.

'Quick, boy, let me put it out of sight before Emma comes down.'

Barrass delved into the leather bag and handed the white, folded pages to him.

'Not supposed to do this you know. I'm supposed to give them intact to Kenneth for sorting,' Barrass said, accepting Pitcher's payment for his letter and placing the money in the leather bag. But his smile gave a lack of seriousness to the words. Despite the many differences in their situations and their ages, they were friends.

'Take the bag to Kenneth and Ceinwen then, and come back for some food before you set off around Gower. It's a chill morning and you'll need a good packing before you go,' Pitcher said.

He shouted for Arthur, the potboy, to get from the cellar and start frying bread and some eggs 'for Barrass and yourself',

2

while then he opened his letter.

Arthur, a thin individual, bony-jawed and with an Adam's apple that did a jig at the slightest prospect of trouble, listened to the words with disbelief. He was constantly hungry and he quickly abandoned the bottles he was sorting and sprang up the cellar steps to do as Pitcher asked. A hot breakfast, and Barrass to keep him company while he ate, that was a rare treat. He passed a table on which a large platter stood. Under a vinegar-soaked cloth the remains of a cooked ham sat issuing a tempting aroma. Pitcher was still at the front door, Emma and the girls were safe upstairs. He quickly cut two generous slices which he intended to fry with the bread and the eggs, and hurried to where the large frying pan was hanging. Trotting along beside him was his dog, who seemed like an appendage, rarely more than a few yards from his master's feet. The dog seemed to share Arthur's grin as Barrass left them to hand the letters to Kenneth and Ceinwen to sort.

'Arthur, come here at once.' Emma called down the stairs from the door of the dining room. She tapped her foot impatiently while Arthur put down the pan and hid the ham he had stolen, and ran up the stairs. When he appeared, anxious-eyed, his Adam's apple wobbling nervously in his throat, she waved fussily for him to close the door.

His shoulders drooped as he prepared for a telling off. Frowns crisscrossed his young face as he tried to think of the reason for any complaint. She couldn't have known about the ham. Could she? Pitcher often said she could see through walls and hear a mouse sneezing above the sound of the quarrymen. To his relief, Mistress Palmer smiled at him.

'What's going on, Arthur?' she said in a conspiratorial whisper.

'Going on, Mistress Palmer? What d'you mean?'

'Pitcher's been like a drunk on a frozen pond since he left his bed. Unable to stand still. He's waiting for something, a letter maybe?'

'Potboy I am, not his assistant, Mistress, begging your pardon. How would I know what's going on?'

'Because there's never a thing that goes on here without you knowing. What letter did he send?'

'Bills, that's all I ever see. Demands for people to pay their

3

debts and demands for him to pay his. Nothing of interest ever comes from the post.'

The outer door closed and they both looked towards the door to the stairs as the sound of Pitcher's approaching feet was heard.

'Go you, I'll talk to you later.' Emma dismissed Arthur with a wave of her fat hand and began to stack the used plates that were still on the table from the family's breakfast. Pitcher and Arthur met in the doorway and Emma pushed past them both and called for the servant to come and clear away.

'Use the bell, Emma,' Pitcher said as they all staggered in confusion. She did and he covered his ears with his hands.

'Not to deafen me, Mrs Palmer!' he said irritably.

'I want a word, Mr Palmer!'

Pitcher glanced at Arthur as the boy ran thankfully down the staircase back to the breakfast he had been asked to cook. But he was given no sign that suggested Emma had made him talk.

'Mistress Palmer,' Pitcher said firmly. 'I wish you would not stop the boy working. I give him a task to do and you call him up on some excuse. I wish you would leave below the stairs to me, I really do.' He always found it wise to begin an interview like the one he was expecting with an attack.

'Pitcher, dear,' Emma softened her tone. 'I was concerned about you, standing out there waiting for your letter in the cold morning air and you with only an old waistcoat between your goose-pimpled skin and the wildness of the wind.'

Pitcher shuffled nervously, wondering how much she knew and how he could explain about not telling her about his enquiries before.

'It's come, has it?' she asked. 'The letter?'

'What letter? What are you talking about?'

'You know very well what letter, dear Pitcher. From London, was it?'

Pitcher knew when he was beaten.

'All right. It isn't as if I wasn't going to tell you, I just wanted a few facts before I discussed it, that's all.'

'Of course you wouldn't keep anything so important as – that letter – a secret from me. See it, can I?' She held out her hand and Pitcher reached into his pocket and handed it to her.

4

'How *did* you know about it?' he asked. 'Just out of interest, like.'

'I didn't, until now,' she replied as her eyes scanned the page. 'But why else would you be standing half-frozen staring along the road waiting for Barrass if it wasn't a letter of some importance?'

Pitcher laughed. Polly, the small, thin, pale-faced servant, came apologetically in and stacked the dirty china on to a tray. When she had departed, Pitcher hugged his wife, burying his face in her curled hair.

'Too smart for me you are, Emma.'

'And don't you forget it,' she hugged him back, her breast heaving with laughter. 'Now, what are we going to do about this dream of yours, Pitcher? Seems to me that you won't settle until you are the keeper of a grand, important and profitable inn.'

'I thought to call it The Posthorn Inn. That's supposing we get permission for the change.'

Emma thought for a moment, staring up at the ceiling as if for inspiration.

'– Mistress Palmer of The Posthorn Inn, Mumbles – Yes, Pitcher, that sounds very well, even if the post horn is only sounded by Barrass riding on Kenneth's pony!'

Later that day, while the table was being prepared for dinner guests by Polly, assisted by her sister Seranne, on loan from Ddole House, Emma was in the parlour listening to the complaints of her two daughters.

'Mamma, you really expect us to manage without any new clothes for the summer?' Daisy almost shouted. 'But last year's are so soiled and ragged, we couldn't be seen in decent company wearing them. I swear, Mamma, you'd be shamed never to re-cover if we went to visit our friends in last year's faded clothes!'

Pansy dropped the waistcoat she was embroidering and stood beside her twin. She had never been so thoroughly vain as Daisy, but even she found it hard to understand how her mother could ask such a thing of them.

'We wore them in the house long after they had passed their usefulness as visiting clothes, Mamma,' she added.

'Anyway, I've promised the best of them to Seranne and Polly to cut down for themselves and the servants.' Daisy said the

5

words as if they would end the argument completely.

'Then you'll have to tell her you've changed your mind,' Emma retorted.

With the income from the alehouse, supplemented by the activities of the boats bringing illegal wines and spirits and tobacco from the continent, Pitcher and Emma had been able to give their three girls a comfortable life. Violet, Daisy and Pansy had attended the very best school and had made friends with, if not the richest, at least some of the more respectable of the local families.

Twice each year, Mistress Gronow, the seamstress from the town, visited and brought with her samples of cloth from which the girls ordered new clothes. They needed morning dresses, day dresses, walking and riding clothes, hats and shawls, as well as the more ornate gowns for the many parties and dances they were invited to attend.

For Emma, it was all a wonderful, unimagined success. Her own beginnings had been small and rather poor, but with Pitcher goaded on to better and better objectives, they had succeeded to the stage where she had appointed herself the decider of good taste and opinion for the village. She irritated a number of her one-time friends, and was a fount of irrepressible mirth for many more, but most accepted her and tolerated her fine ways, considering her to be a harmless, and often kindly, oddity.

Now, her patiently learnt manners and careful speech were forgotten as she reminded her girls of how fortunate they were compared with most of the families in the village and around about.

'You should be pleased to help your father after what he's done for you,' she shouted, her red face growing ever redder, her plump figure seeming to swell with the gases of pure rage.

'Mamma,' Pansy warned, 'don't distress yourself or you'll have a fit!'

'I think that having taught us to accept a certain standard, you have no right to ask us to abandon it on some silly whim of Father's!' snapped Daisy, always the least tolerant of the twosome.

Below them, attending to the feeding of himself and Barrass, between attending to the wants of two early customers, Arthur glanced nervously at Pitcher. The alehouse keeper was begin-

6

ning to sigh with shortening patience. As Arthur watched, Pitcher's control finally exploded. He hurried from the bar-room, where he had been adding wood and attempting to draw the fire into an even brighter blaze, and ran two at a time up the stairs.

Leaving their almost empty plates, Arthur and Barrass followed to listen shamelessly at the foot of the stairs.

'What is going on, Mistress Palmer!' Pitcher demanded, bursting into the parlour. 'Do you want to provide entertainment for the whole village with your rankling? No one is drinking down there for fear of missing a word!'

'Dadda, is it true? Do you want us to go about wearing clothes ragabonds would be ashamed to own?' Daisy said before her mother could gain the breath to reply.

'We have to go carefully for a month or so until certain things are paid for, yes.'

'But we can't do without clothes! We can't! Mamma, tell him!'

Confused as to whose side she was on, Emma murmured something unintelligible and looked at her husband.

'I have some expenses which means that temporarily, my dear daughters, we will all have to cut back on outgoings. Outgoings is, temporarily, out!' Pitcher explained.

'We've been brought up used to the good things of life, and we have friends who are likewise blessed. Dadda, you *must* find a way for it to continue or,' Daisy paused to give her words their full effect, '– or, you'll have to send us away, so we don't have to face the disgrace.'

'You just come-along-a-me one day, miss, and see how most families live. Then tell me that doing without a few dresses and frills will disgrace you!'

Both girls lowered their heads, knowing that for the moment their father must have the last word. The soft, ladylike sobs coming from their mother assured them that their pleas would be argued favourably at a later and more advantageous time. Daisy sat and frowned and Pansy returned to her sewing.

Outside on the landing, two faces were pressed against the door of the dining room, looking out. Polly, kneeling below Harriet, her eyes wide in the thin, drawn face, covered her mouth with a slender hand to stifle her giggles. Harriet stuffed the corner of the gingham work apron that covered her black and white uniform between her large, strong teeth.

'Mistress Lady-until-roused-Palmer has a voice fit for selling shellfish to sailors in a storm, hasn't she?' Harriet whispered.

In the parlour, Pitcher, his arms around the shoulders of his daughters, drew them to the window which looked out on to the street below. Percy the stableboy was helping as a carriage was turned, its horses being backed into the narrow entrance of his stables. The occupants, a young woman and a young man, and another couple, possibly the parents of one of them, had alighted and stood looking over the sea. The ladies were huddled in shawls, the gentlemen wore thick coats which had additional cloaks attached around the shoulders.

'Come for the fresh sea breezes,' Pitcher explained. 'They'll be wanting a meal and some warm, clean beds soon. But where will they go for them? Back into town! I want them to stay, daughters. Stay and spend their money here, in our alehouse.'

Emma and the twins were both watching the tall, handsome young man, and all three were thinking of the advantages of having others like him spending the night under their roof. Unconsciously, Emma patted the straying hairs around her shoulders, tidying them into the wig she wore. There was more to consider than money. She had two daughters still to find husbands.

'Your father knows what's right, my lovely girls,' she said softly. 'He'll do his best for us all.'

For once, Daisy did not argue. Her eyes were following the progress of the foursome walking along the edge of the tide, her intelligent mind considering the prospects her father had outlined.

Pitcher did not know for certain that Arthur had told Emma of his plans, but he cuffed him anyway as he ran down the stairs to where the potboy and Barrass had hurriedly returned to their food.

'What's that for?' Arthur protested.

'You know very well!' Pitcher replied. 'Now hurry and clear away that mess and get back to your work in the cellar!'

Harriet, the sister of Carter Phillips the local carrier, came down the stairs. She had been hired to assist with the dinner party. She joined Arthur and Barrass as they collected the pewter plates and mugs to take to the kitchen. She took the plates from Barrass and looked up at him with a smile.

'Let me do that, Barrass, there's plenty for you to do today, walking all over Gower with important letters. Wish I could come with you,' she sighed, and Barrass returned the smile, his dark eyes moist with yearning.

'Best you stay here, where Mistress Palmer pays you, that's something I can't do,' he said.

'Paying is not always in money,' she whispered with a secretive wink.

It had been Barrass's intention not to see Harriet again, but he remembered well how she abandoned all inhibitions and pretence of primness once they were alone. To Arthur, he had declared her the most exciting woman he had known.

'At eight of the clock tomorrow, shall we meet and you can tell me all the day's adventures?' she whispered. 'And perhaps have a few more?'

He nodded, ashamed of his weakness but unwilling to deny himself the pleasures she offered.

Barrass left the alehouse and walked to the grassy bank on which the house of Kenneth and Ceinwen stood. It was whitewashed and roofed with thatch. Windows gleamed in the morning sunshine, the curtains, a bright and cheerful yellow, were opened and tied back to let the light into the small dark rooms within.

The door stood open, defying the wind that still gusted, but which was weakening as if the receding tide were persuading it back towards the distant horizon, to torment other places. A sack of potatoes that were sprouting into growth, and a box of sad-looking green leaves, stood near the door and Ceinwen was serving a couple of women who had come to buy. There were eggs too, both duck and hens' eggs, soiled and with straw sticking to them, plus a dish of curd cheese to which pieces of chopped, dried garlic had been added. The last of the day's oysters were displayed, having been brought by Olwen, the fisherman's daughter, on her way to her work.

Barrass pushed his way past the shoppers and went into the room which Kenneth used as his office for the deliveries of the Gower mail. A fire burned in the hearth and from a pan hanging over it came the smell of boiling fish.

'Your dinner, Kenneth?' Barrass asked, nodding towards the simmering pan.

'Preserve me from that! No, it's fish that Spider couldn't sell. Ceinwen is boiling it for the fowls.' He stood up and reached to take a thick, leather-covered ledger from the shelf near the window. 'It's very late you are, boy! And don't blame the postboy from Monmouth. I saw you going into the alehouse early enough. What d'you find to keep you so long there, boy? That Harriet again I'll be bound.'

'Pitcher offered me food and I find that harder to resist than women,' Barrass smiled.

Barrass was a tall, strongly-built young man. Barely seventeen, so far as anyone could tell, yet with shaving already a daily necessity. His body was broad and he stood several inches taller than Kenneth. His shock of wiry dark hair, which he allowed to grow unrestrained, gave the impression of several more inches. Dark eyes shone with enthusiasm and confidence in the young face and stood in contrast to the worried and anxious expression of Kenneth.

They both pored over the ledger for a while, checking that all the letters for delivery had been correctly entered, and the monies due noted correctly on both Barrass's notebook and the page of the ledger.

'Seventeen letters, quite a large number for a Wednesday,' Kenneth commented.

'Yes, and as widespread as they possibly could be!' Barrass groaned. 'Why is it that the Rector of Rhossili always has a letter on the same day that there are some for Oxwich on the south coast?'

'It's the way of the world for poor folk like you and me,' Kenneth said lugubriously.

The Royal Mail arrived into Swansea three times a week brought by Ben Gammon, the sixty-year-old postboy, who brought it from the last leg of the London to Carmarthen relay from Monmouth. The mail continued via Brecon to Carmarthen, being met at each point by other postboys who carried it to some of the larger towns. With the postboys travelling some ten miles in each direction, the network of deliveries and collections usually resulted in a letter reaching London in five days.

Ben Gammon arrived in the Swansea sorting office, which was situated in a building at the side of The Voyager Inn, at six o'clock in the evenings of Sunday, Tuesday and Friday, and on the morning following his arrival, Barrass rode in from Mumbles and collected the ones for Mumbles and Gower. He then waited for the letters to be sorted by Kenneth and Ceinwen and, as soon as they were ready, set off on foot to walk around the peninsular.

On this particular Wednesday, Barrass was fortunate enough to be offered a lift by a carter. Seeing the cart approaching him, heading the same way, he had waved hopefully and run as the cart with the two large horses pulling it had rumbled to a stop.

As the cart drew near he had been dismayed to see that the driver was Carter Phillips, someone he would have preferred to avoid. If he had recognized him before waving to him, Barrass would have hidden until he had passed.

'Ho there, Barrass,' Phillips called and he reached a hand to help pull the young man aboard. 'I'm going as far as the Rhossili Rectory if you've a mind to ride with me.'

Barrass was torn between being grateful for the ride and dreading the way that conversations with Carter Phillips always turned to the need for a man to take a wife, Carter Phillips's sister Harriet being the main contender for that privilege.

They stopped at a small village to gather the firewood they were to collect for delivery at the Rectory close to the sea. Carter Phillips accepted Barrass's help to load the cart as a matter of course and again Barrass wished he had recognized the carter in time to avoid him. He climbed back on to the heavily loaded, flat cart with the apprehensive certainty that he would also be expected to assist with the unloading, and he wondered if the acceptance of the ride would in fact lose him time rather than gain it. It was definitely more energetic than walking the full distance! As the cart once more stopped and Carter Phillips looked from him to the load of wood, his eyes filled with expectancy, Barrass was convinced he had made a mistake!

'Spare a while to help me unload and I'll be sure to put a good word in for you with my sister,' the man coaxed, seeing the unwillingness in Barrass's face. He did not know that a good word for Barrass to Harriet was hardly necessary. If he knew how well

I already know Harriet, he'd bury me under these logs! Barrass thought, staring at the huge, muscular arms of the carrier.

'I'll be late,' Barrass said reluctantly, and with a lack of truth. Carter Phillips, whistling cheerfully, seemed not to hear. Barrass groaned as a log of roughly sawn timber was thrust into his unwilling arms. "I have to be at Port-Eynon before nightfall.'

'And so you will be. I'll take you there once we've finished here, and, what's more, you're invited to a fine supper tomorrow night that Harriet will cook for you. Now, how does that sound?'

Barrass was comforted by the sight of two burly men on their way up the hill from the Rectory, obviously sent to help them.

'Very well,' he sighed, 'but remind me to refuse if you offer me a lift again!'

The carter laughed good-naturedly, and felt Barrass's strong arms.

'Good training this'll be, my friend. For one day, perhaps, you and I will be partners in this carting business.'

Barrass did not reply. The suggestion was clear, the man was offering a partnership – and his sister for a wife! But the thought of spending his life alongside Carter Phillips, struggling with heavy loads for people who considered themselves his betters, did not appeal.

He left the carter at the top of the hill leading to Oxwich, and checking on the letters still to deliver before the place where his overnight accommodation was arranged, found himself with an hour or two to spare. April was too early in the year to bathe with any degree of enjoyment, yet he went into the tide. He found the surge of the foaming water invigorating and after a while, surprisingly warming, as he splashed and swam. The bubbling foam seemed to have gained heat in its pounding of the rocks below the church.

He knew that the poor lodgings Kenneth paid for, for him to spend the night, would not have hot water for the wooden tub which always hung, green with disuse, on the outside wall.

The food would be mean too, a dish of potatoes and stringy vegetables left from the previous harvest, and a small amount of stewed meat. Bread to mop up the juices, if he were fortunate enough to have any, and perhaps a piece of hard cheese. He wondered how much Kenneth paid the old couple but did not ask. The food was not important, and the bed, in a lean-to behind the earthen walled cottage, was no worse than the room in which he slept at Kenneth and Ceinwen's.

He was frequently invited to stay for food at houses he passed, although he had been too long poor himself readily to take advantage of the people who spared the little they could in exchange for the news he could pass on. But by accepting a little from a few cottagers, he usually managed to keep hunger at bay. In this way he became a welcome sight, one who brought a little of the outside world to the small villages as he passed through, without beggaring them with demands for food and drink.

The sound of his horn, blown as he reached the village green, or the crossroads close to a small group of houses too small to be given that appellation, brought riotous movement. Excited children came first, then women and the old. Then men, and dogs, and even the occasional pig ran out to greet him. He would pass on messages received during his long walk, and hear news of the happenings, both happy and sad, in the small community, before departing on his way.

On the following day he returned to Mumbles, stopping when requested, to collect letters to be sent on their way to London, or to others in the locality for a small fee. Rain had begun with the break of day. He was used to the changes in the weather, and carried a waterproof, leather cloak, but he still hated the rain. If there was one thing likely to reduce his spirits, it was a soaking. It wasn't walking with the water dripping from his hair and darkening the colour of his clothes and the leather bag that he disliked, it was the aftereffects, when he arrived at the end of his journey with practically everything he owned completely soaked.

Living without a real home, having only the use of the cold and damp room behind Kenneth's house, he had the daunting prospect of trying to dry his coat and trousers. Having few items of clothing, he could not manage if they took days to dry. He frequently put on clothes that were still wet from the previous day's rain. Barefoot throughout his childhood, his boots were some he had found abandoned on a village midden and were distorted from their original shape, stiff and uncomfortable. They felt far worse when they were cold and wet too.

It was a Thursday, the day when Kenneth made his excuses

to his wife, explaining to her that Thursdays were always long, and Barrass needed his help to finish in reasonable time. Barrass hated Thursdays. Kenneth went to visit Betson-the-flowers in her cottage along the green lane, for an hour of love and attention. Barrass was his alibi and therefore could not go home until Kenneth did. A rainy Thursday was as much as he could bear!

They met at the end of the green lane; Barrass was early and Kenneth was late. Barrass had attempted to make a tent of his cloak, and he sat in it, a picture of abject misery.

'I don't care what you say, Kenneth,' he shivered as the ex-letter-carrier greeted him. 'I am not sitting here for a further two hours while you warm yourself in front of Betson-the-flowers's roaring fire!'

'But, boy, you promised me if I let you take my job and carry the letters for Gower you'd keep quiet about Thursdays!'

'Keep quiet I will, but sit here I will not!' Before Kenneth could argue further, Barrass stood up, water pouring from the cloak in a torrent on to the grass around him, and added, 'Going to the alehouse I am. I'll come home in good time, but not until I'm dry, warm and fed!'

'The letters, boy! You mustn't go astray with the letters!' Kenneth called, but Barrass did not hear.

Squelching along the muddy lane, sliding and grasping at trees to save himself falling, he went to the village and, avoiding passing Kenneth's house, went into the alehouse and called for Pitcher.

Pitcher came and after a look at his bedraggled figure standing tall and large near the fire, already steaming in the heat, he called for Arthur to fetch spare clothes.

'There won't be much here to fit you, boy,' he laughed, comparing their different height and build; he being several inches shorter than Barrass, his shoulders far narrower, 'but at least they'll be clean and dry.'

Barrass followed him up the stairs to the room where Pitcher's family ate. No company was expected so the table was simply laid for four; Pitcher, Emma and the twins. While Pitcher barred the door, Barrass dragged the unwilling clothes from his wet body and rubbed himself dry on the towels Emma had sent with the spare clothes.

'Thanks Pitcher,' Barrass sighed as he pulled on the ill-fitting, but warm, dry clothes. 'I'd have been going out in wet clothes for days after a soaking like I've had today.'

'Ceinwen dries them for you surely?'

'No, I have to hang them in the room where I sleep at the back of the house, and hope for a warm night.'

'You don't sleep in that old lean-to at the back, where they used to keep wood?' Pitcher half smiled, expecting Barrass to jeer and share his laugh. Instead, the young man nodded.

'I don't mind, but drying clothes is a problem. When has it not been!' he added bitterly, thinking back over the homeless years of his childhood.

'But in the evening when you eat, surely you could put your things around the fire?'

'I spend the evening when I leave here, in the lean-to. It's there that I eat. Now Pitcher, don't sound off like the blowhole up on the cliffs,' Barrass warned, 'like a grampus with a headache! It's grateful I am. At least I don't have to live out in the fields or on the cliffs, like I did before I started helping Kenneth with the letters. Grateful I am,' he insisted.

'How much do you earn, boy?' Pitcher asked when they were down in the bar again, seated in the inglenook close to the roaring fire. 'When the week ends, what do you have in your pocket?'

'I don't want to complain, Pitcher.'

'How much, boy?'

'Well, Ceinwen has to take for my keep, and for the daily meal, so it's about one shilling.'

'The man deserves to be hanged! There's you doing all the tramping and traipsing around, and with a shed to sleep in that's far worse than places where people house their pigs! Disgraceful, that's what it is.'

'I'm glad of the chance to work for the post, Pitcher. It's only for a while, just to show the postmaster in Swansea that I'm good and reliable and honest. One day I'll be a postboy and carry the letters on a horse from Swansea to Monmouth and back. That is my dream, Pitcher, and I don't want you to do anything to spoil my chance of living it.'

'If you should live long enough,' Pitcher muttered. 'Hanged he should be. Hanged!' Pitcher wondered if the postmaster would allow the situation to continue if someone were to tell him what was happening.

'You won't complain to Kenneth, will you?' Barrass said.

'No, boy, I won't complain – to Kenneth.'

Pitcher was thoughtful during the rest of the evening. When Barrass set off for supper with Kenneth and Ceinwen, his eyes followed him, frowning slightly with the idea he had been considering. He was thinking of the advantages to his trade if the post were to be collected here, at the alehouse, instead of the small cottage on the bank.

Chapter Two

After delivering the basket of oysters to Ceinwen, Olwen, the daughter of Spider, the fisherman, walked up the steep hill away from the beach towards the woodland above. She was a small figure, thin legs revealed below the lifted skirt of her woollen dress. Her freckled face was already tanned with the sun, her untidy hair blowing around it was spangled by the glow of the morning into an aureole. Her hair had once been long, and having burnt it trying to make it curl, she had cut it in the hope that a more mature style would give her the appearance of a woman instead of a child.

From the wood, her way led along the green lane on which Betson-the-flowers lived. Olwen saw that the curtain, a signal which told her visitors whether or not she was occupied, was open. Olwen saw the door open and paused to spend a few moments talking to the young woman.

The differences in the two people were many. Olwen was small, looking years younger than her fourteen years. She had blue eyes that sparkled with innocence and the joy of life, and full lips that seemed always looking for an excuse for laughter.

Betson-the-flowers was so named for her love of the blooms that always filled her room in the old cottage of which only one room was habitable. She used flowers that were given to her by her many visitors to hide the shabbiness and precarious condition of her cottage. With the roaring fire she kept lit even through the months of summer, the flowers and the polished and shining windows, she gave the old place a magical air.

Betson was taller than Olwen, her hair was long and a rich red. She always wore black, with just a few touches of colour. She dressed habitually in long flowing skirts of varying lengths, one over another to give layers. The layers continued to the shirts and shawls and head covers she wore. Most of the clothing had been discarded by others, who railed at the sight of Betson, wearing clothes they had no further use for and turning them into items of great attraction with her innate skill.

'Are you off to work, Olwen-the-fish?' she asked as the girl hesitated.

'Yes, I work for William Ddole at Ddole house.'

'I know. I know most of what goes on hereabouts,' Betson smiled. 'I know you don't walk past my cottage very often. Want to talk to me, do you?'

'I – er – of course not !' Olwen longed to ask her how she made herself so attractive that so many men from the village and further afield risked their wives' wrath and found an excuse to call on her, give her money as well as flowers, pay for coal and wood to be delivered, supplying between them the means for her to survive in comfort without any apparent way of earning money. Perhaps Betson-the-flowers could teach her how to make herself look older. But now, looking into the dark, quizzical eyes of the woman, she lost her nerve.

'I'm going to look at the corner of the wood to see if there are any violets still in bloom, for my mother,' she extemporized.

'Find some ragged robins,' Betson smiled. 'They will tell you who you'll marry.'

'I know who'll be my husband,' Olwen replied, blushing and wishing she had not spoken the words.

'Ask the ragged robins.' Betson's voice was slow and she smiled deeply. 'Take some flower heads, give them each a name. The first to open will be the one you'll marry.'

'I must go, Florrie will shout if the work is delayed.' She waved and ran off.

'Come and see me again, little fishergirl,' Betson called after her.

Olwen did not run for long. She glanced up to the woodland where she knew she would find the plant to which Betson had referred. It was nonsense of course. But her feet refused to take her in the straight line to Ddole House. She looked at the sun, weak and enshrouded with a mist but rising in the sky. She was late. But another few moments wouldn't make Florrie shout any louder. Picking up the skirt of her dress, she ran to the damp corner and picked her way through the hazel and birch trees and looked at the pretty, pink, ragged flowers she had come to find.

She picked the heads and holding them in a row between her

left forefinger and thumb, she said, 'Arthur, the potboy, Tom, the soldier, Barrass, the letter-carrier.' She ran away from the trees and, afraid now of the lateness of her arrival, she hurried on, down the drive and to the kitchen door of Ddole House and a day spent working in the busy kitchen.

She looked the epitome of a beautiful country girl as she burst through the door. Her face was glowing, her eyes sparkled with health and good humour. To her surprise, Florrie was dressed, not in her prim grey-striped flannel dress, but her black one over which her voluminous cook's apron was tied. Of Seranne, who was paid for the role of cook, there was no sign.

'Where have you been, girl? There's the breakfast things not washed yet, Seranne has failed to arrive and me with a meal to cook for the master and three guests!' Florrie hardly gave Olwen time to remove her cloak and put on an apron before pushing the empty water buckets into her hands. 'Go and fill these and be quick about it.'

Olwen went to the yard and working the pump as if life itself depended on it, filled them in a rush and hurried back to the kitchen. She was not frightened by Florrie's outburst as she would have been a few weeks ago, used as she now was to getting a scolding to be followed moments later by a sudden kindness.

The morning was filled with preparations for the meal, which would begin at three, and end when the men had settled the business they had met to discuss. Bream, freshly caught and delivered early by Olwen's brother, were already baking in the large oven and would be followed by a saddle of lamb. Assorted sweetmeats were already prepared and a syllabub, well spiced and flavoured with French brandy, was cooling on the window-sill. When they had only the vegetables to prepare, and they were allowed to stop for a while to eat the food Florrie had prepared for them, and luxuriate in a drink of good strong tea, Olwen looked at her flowers. The one she had named for Barrass was slowly opening its forked petals.

She knew Barrass loved her best of all, but she also knew that he did not keep his heart free of others. Three girls in the village had produced babies, each one claiming him to be the father. One was the daughter of Pitcher and Emma at the alehouse, and although Violet had since married Edwin Prince, a wealthy farmer, everyone knew that the child was not her husband's, but Barrass's.

Olwen was convinced that her youthful, not to say childish, appearance was to blame for Barrass's reticence. She would make him forget all the rest once she was accepted as a woman and not a little girl. She put the flowers back and took another thick crust of the bread remaining on the table. If she ate plenty, surely that would increase her size?

It was as if, out of her thoughts, she had conjured up Barrass. As she had filled her mouth with the crust, there was a knock at the door and it was opened to reveal him standing there, filling the space with his height and width, and swelling her heart with the warmth of his smile. His appearance lightened the day more than the sun that had just broken through the thin veil of cloud and had entered with him.

'Barrass!' she ran to greet him and felt his arms around her, one of the rare times when she felt glad to be small. When she was with Barrass she was more sure of herself and confident. It was easy then to forget her lack of inches, and the way everyone referred to her as 'the little girl belonging to Spider and Mary-the-fish'.

'Florrie? Where is Seranne today, you aren't supposed to be the cook as well as the housekeeper now, are you?'

'She isn't here, that's for sure. But where she is I can't tell you. Forgotten the time, lolling about in that bed of hers no doubt. At the alehouse yesterday fit as you like, now she'll complain of feeling ill.'

'Not reliable, is she?' Barrass took the ale Florrie offered and sat near the fire to drink it.

'She wouldn't know the meaning of the word!' Florrie snapped. 'If you pass her house, will you knock and tell her what day it is, supposing she cares?'

'I'll go, Florrie,' Olwen offered at once. 'Go like the wind and be back before you've missed me.'

'All right, I know how you like to escape from the house for a while. But don't be long, mind!'

Putting a fresh bowl of water ready for washing the few mugs and plates from their light meal, Olwen hurriedly found her cloak. If she were quick, she might be able to walk a short distance with Barrass.

She hurried from the house as Barrass began to walk up the drive. She watched hopefully as he reached the gate; if he turned to the left, then he would be walking in the same direction as herself. At the gate, he stopped and waited for her.

'I heard footsteps behind me, and guessed it was you,' he smiled.

'I was afraid you wouldn't wait.'

'Of course I'd wait. I don't see you often now you are a working girl. But I thought I'd better get out of sight from the kitchen in case Florrie thinks I'm encouraging you to waste time. Going to the house of Seranne and her family, are you?' He began to walk as she reached his side. 'I'm going that way too. Not that there's a letter for that family, I doubt if they can read!'

'Of course they can read!' Olwen defended. 'Taught by their mother. She worked at The Ship and Castle, and did the accounts until she was drowned, poor thing.'

'She and her husband died together, didn't they, in a boat involved in the smuggling?'

'Leaving five children to fend for themselves. No storm or anything, they left the ship with a fully loaded boat and it just broke up and sank. They drowned before anyone could get to them. And don't say it was justice, Barrass!' she added sharply. 'We all know how you feel about the smuggling!'

'I wouldn't wish that to happen!' he protested. 'Besides, I've helped, haven't I? That makes me as involved as all the rest. Once you have become a part of something like the nightboats, you can't ever be free of it.'

They reached the small field in which a once neat cottage stood amid the chaos of partly prepared ground, and the relics of outhouses in the process of being rebuilt. A stream ran down, close to the walls of the house; in it the long fingered leaves of the water crowfoot were already sending up a few pale, buttercup-like small flowers.

A rat ran across their path as they walked through the open gateway. Chickens scattered at their approach and a goat stared but continued chewing, its baleful eyes accusing and unfriendly. A dog tied to a post watched the rat pass close to its paws as casually as he might watch a bird fly past, then he raised his head a little and gave one lethargic bark to announce their arrival.

Olwen walked to the doorway and looked inside, curiosity making the errand a pleasant one. The Morgan family were well-known, but only through their occasional visits to the village. No one was invited to call, and the attitude of the family did not encourage anyone to visit uninvited or try and make friends with any of them. It was surprisingly neat, but the smell of mildew and dampness caught at her throat and she did not enter when a voice invited her to do so.

'Seranne?' she called. 'It's me, Olwen, come to see if you're all right, sent by Florrie who's worried.'

'Worried that her dinner won't be cooked more like!' Seranne came out of the house, coughing and holding a hand to her chest. 'I'm sick, tell her that will you, and say I'll be back to work just as soon as I can stand without my knees giving way.'

'Is there anything you need?' Olwen asked. She looked at Barrass; the girl was obviously in need of a doctor.

'I am passing the house of the doctor, shall I ask him to call?' Barrass suggested.

'No need. I get this cough each winter but it passes as the sun gets stronger. Nothing he can do except send me a bill for medicine that's foul to take and which doesn't ease the pain.'

As their eyes became accustomed to the dark interior viewed through the open door, they saw that Seranne's two brothers were there, sitting at a table, drinking from large pewter mugs. One of them turned around and waved his mug at Barrass and called,

'Stay for a quaff of ale, will you, Barrass-the-post?'

The prospect of sitting in that dark, mouldering room was not one that appealed to Barrass. He shook his head as if in regret.

'I am already late and some take pleasure in complaining,' he excused. He looked again at Seranne, leaning on the door and trying to steady her breath to hold back her coughing. 'If there is nothing I can do?'

Seranne looked across the field as if waiting for someone.

'Our sister Vanora will be back presently. Gone to gather some coltsfoot leaves to boil. With some sweet honey, that will help take away my affliction.' The last words were lost as she once again succumbed to violent coughing. Her brothers took no notice of her distress.

'I have to run, or Florrie will have me busy 'til midnight!'

Olwen and Barrass moved away, both relieved to be distancing themselves from the unhealthy family and the house that smelt of poverty and neglect.

'No wonder their sister Polly always looks so sickly,' Olwen whispered.'The place is worse than a swamp.'

Barrass thought of the pale, thin girl who worked for Pitcher and Emma and nodded. 'I think they are unlikely to improve unless they move from that dreadful place. Living under the skies would be safer.'

Olwen looked thoughtful. 'The place isn't that dreadful. Tucked in the corner of the field with the stream so conveniently close, it would be a lovely place to live, if those brothers would do something to improve it.'

'Fancy the job of sorting them, do you?' Barrass grinned. 'I'd have thought you've enough to do, with working for the Ddoles, helping your mother with her wool and spending time with your father and Dan and their fish!'

'I haven't time, and I wouldn't fancy spending too many hours with those brothers. Make me nervous they do.'

'Olwen, I have to go. Run back now and tell Florrie what you know. Come and see me at the alehouse tomorrow night if you can, and we'll talk. It's not easy to find time now, is it?' He bent and kissed her lightly on her warm cheek and turned quickly to continue his round.

She watched him go, large, strong and so dear to her. The sun glinted on the horn which was tied across his shoulder. That, and the red waistcoat, worn to tell everyone who he was, seemed to have separated them from each other. She longed to follow him, walk the lonely miles at his side, regain the special friendship they had until recently always enjoyed. If she couldn't have his love yet, then she would settle for a return to that companionable warmth they had shared for so long.

When he had passed from her sight, without even a final wave, Olwen reluctantly set off back to Ddole House. With Seranne obviously unable to work, it seemed unlikely that she would finish work early enough on the following day to go and see Barrass. She kicked irritably at a tuft of grass that was high above the rest and ran back to face her busy day.

For a while, it seemed that Barrass had accepted what she had always known, they were partners for whom marriage was the inevitable conclusion. But somehow he was more distant now than when he had been a homeless beggar, excluded from every house, surviving on what he could beg from the kind-hearted villagers.

Behind her, the brothers of Seranne stepped out of the doorway and watched her go. Morgan Morgan was seventeen and Madoc Morgan two years older. Since the death of their parents in the boating accident, their sisters had treated them like naughty but lovable children. Polly, who was fifteen, worked for Emma. Seranne was almost thirty and had had a succession of jobs. She now cooked for Ddole House, when she was well enough to walk the distance from her home. Vanora, although not the eldest, had taken charge of the family. The brothers did little work, being adept at finding reasons for not completing the many jobs they were set, but none of the sisters thought to complain, even when they knew that the brothers had earned money and not given a contribution to the running of the home.

Now, they threw down the dregs of their ale on to the earthen floor and put the mugs on the table.

'Best we have another go at this shed,' Morgan sighed. 'Else we'll never get them chickens comfortable and in a mood to lay.'

The chickens for whom the henhouse was planned lived in the house and were clucking around the doorway in the hope of a few crumbs. Vanora had begun to tire of finding one or two perched beside her when she woke in the mornings and had tried to persuade the others that the chickens and the goat should be partitioned off from the one room in which the five of them lived and slept. As usual, Madoc and Morgan willingly agreed to do the work, but no progress had yet been made.

The brothers saw Vanora coming back with a basket filled with the leaves of coltsfoot to make a healing brew, and at once began banging with enthusiasm on the partly built henhouse. As soon as Vanora had gone indoors, they dropped their tools and sidled off to find something less energetic and more fun.

They returned several hours later with three squealing piglets.

'Madoc! Morgan!' Vanora screeched in dismay, her tall, thin figure stretched in outrage as she glared at her brothers. 'Where d'you think we can keep them? In with the rest of us?' It did not occur to her to ask where they had obtained them.

'Only for a while, until we finish the henhouse. We thought that hens, well, they don't bother us much, and if we used the shed for pigs, well, there's food for the whole of next winter, or a fine profit for us on the market.'

What Madox said seemed to make sense to Vanora's tired mind. She had been awake for three nights disturbed by both sisters' coughing, and she was too weary to argue or even try to find a convincing way of saying no.

'Just make sure that place is finished before Sunday comes. Or you'll be finding pigs where your bed ought to be and your bed outside!' she snapped in rare anger. Then she went to prepare another dose of the soothing coltsfoot brew for Seranne.

Olwen hurried back to the kitchen of Ddole House and looked apprehensively at Florrie, expecting a telling off for being so long, but when she explained about Seranne's illness and the unlikeliness of seeing her for a few days, the woman just nodded and arranged for one of the stableboys to take a basket of food to the family.

'Anyone called while I was away?' Olwen asked with a sly wink at the girl they all called Dozy Bethan, who was dreamily washing pots at the sink.

'Only Daniels the Keeper of the Peace,' Florrie replied and the girls shared another look of understanding. It had become apparent to them both that there was nothing so guaranteed to put Florrie in a pleasant and amiable mood as a visit from Daniels.

Daniels, the local Keeper of the Peace, was a tall, smartly dressed widower with five children who seemed to be an admirer of Florrie; a regard that was reciprocated by their worthy housekeeper. He took his work seriously and was known to be determined to seek out and arrest those local families involved in smuggling. For this reason he was feared and few would call him their friend. But to Florrie, who had enjoyed many cups of illegal tea and several bottles of the best French brandy without a qualm of conscience, he was a way of transforming her life from the servant of the Ddoles, to being a respected and comfortably situated wife.

Florrie had been the cook at Ddole House for many years, and recently, after the death of Mistress Dorothy Ddole and the departure of their daughter, Penelope, for London, had been promoted to the position of housekeeper. Today, because of the absence of Seranne whom William Ddole had chosen to take her place in the kitchen, she was once again relegated to the task of cooking the meals.

The meeting which took place at Ddole House that afternoon consisted of Markus, the blind man; Edwin Prince, who was married to Pitcher's daughter, Violet; John Maddern, a visitor from London, and William Ddole himself. William waited until his guests had eaten before beginning to discuss the business reasons for their meeting.

'I have to tell you that for a while, my house can't be used for our – activities,' he said, refilling the glasses of his friends with more brandy. 'Daniels is a regular visitor here, now he and Florrie are walking out. He isn't a man to turn away from a hint of suspicion and he certainly isn't a man to ignore what he sees.'

'Does this mean that we have to find another permanent place?' Edwin asked. 'It isn't easy. All the people we trust are already helping.'

'Florrie told me today that she and Daniels will marry. I doubt she will continue working for me, although she has not yet said so. Daniels has five children and I suspect Florrie, efficient as she is, will be kept busy enough caring for them.'

'So, once Florrie is gone from here, Daniels won't be such a regular visitor?'

'So I presume. I can't see the man seeking my company, nor I his. He is far too pompous for me,' laughed William. 'And so fussy about his appearance he makes me feel unwashed!'

John Maddern stood to find a light for his cigar from the fire with the aid of a spill. He was neatly dressed in fashion rarely seen in the area. His complexion was dark, foreign-looking and his deep set, dark eyes made many people nervous in his presence. He lived in a house once owned by William's secretary and was looked after by Bessie Rees when he was in the village, but his business, selling and buying properties for clients, kept him mostly in either London, Bristol or Bath. When his cigar was drawing he said, 'This matter is urgent. Is there no one who will help us for this next landing?'

'Pitcher might find room for a few extra parcels,' William said. 'But not as much as I usually hide.'

'You can use my cellars.' Markus spoke for the first time. A rather taciturn man, he seemed to criticize every time he made a comment and now sounded as if he were irritated and forced into offering the solution. 'I shall be in Bristol, my family need my assistance with some business matter. Will that do?'

'Thank you, Markus. But the servants – ?'

' – are trustworthy. They have all been with me since – since this damned accident robbed me of my sight.'

'Thank you,' John echoed. Like many, he was embarrassed when Markus spoke of his affliction.

'What shall we do to keep Daniels out of the way?' William asked, 'use Florrie?' He smiled at the others. 'A woman can usually be trusted to keep a man occupied.'

Florrie was not involved in the small-scale smuggling that went on at the local beaches, but, having lived in Ddole House since a child, she was obviously aware of the activities of others.

'I only hope that marrying Daniels doesn't make her transfer her loyalties,' Markus warned, 'or he might find himself widowed for the second time.'

'She wouldn't risk harming me,' William said confidently. 'My family have treated her well.'

The plans for the forthcoming arrival of goods from France were finally complete and only when the men stood to leave, did William ask the question that he had been wanting to ask since John Maddern had arrived from London earlier that day.

'My daughter, John, is she well?'

'You would be pleased at how easily Penelope has fitted into London life, William,' John assured him. 'Your daughter is leading a full and exciting life. I called to see her before I left so I could have the latest news for you. She begs me to give you this letter.' He took from his pocket a folded sheet sealed with sealing wax and addressed to 'My Dear Father', in Penelope's handwriting. 'I should have given it to you the moment I arrived, but hot and weary from travel, I selfishly thought only of water to wash and clothes freshly laundered. I'm sorry, William.'

William forced himself politely to see his guests out before opening the letter. John was riding down to the village to talk to

Pitcher and Emma at the alehouse. Markus was returning to his dark, gloomy house on the cliffs near Longland. William smiled as he opened the two page epistle, imagining confirmation of John's words that the girl was happy and content.

The letter made the smile fade. Contrary to John's words, Penelope begged him to allow her to come home. She hated the noisome city of London and said her life there was full of tension; the people, and especially the men who drove carts and poor conveyances through the streets, were frighteningly aggressive and impatient, and at times, quite abusive with their tongues. 'Such manners you would never believe,' she ended, 'so please, dear Father, if you love me and care for me as I know you do, please give me permission to return home.'

William closed the pages and threw the letter from him. How was a man supposed to cope with a wayward daughter? He closed his brown eyes for a moment and remembered how easy everything had seemed when his wife Dorothy had lived. She would have known how to deal with Penelope. He had failed miserably. He sat at the desk that he had bought for his wife and wrote a reply, insisting that she stayed with his friends until she married or at least until Barrass the letter-carrier did!

It was on account of Barrass that Penelope had been sent away, and until that young man showed some sign of settling down to one woman, he did not feel able to risk having Penelope back home, where he was not capable of watching her every move. But oh, how he missed her. Losing her company so soon after the death of Dorothy had been cruel.

He wondered how John Maddern felt. John had proposed marriage to Penelope, who had turned him down. If only they would find love for each other, he sighed. Penelope could return and his life would not seem so empty or lacking in love. He folded and sealed the letter and addressed it with a shaking hand. He sent for Bethan and handed her the letter.

'Please to hand this to Barrass should he call. If he doesn't come, then take it to the house of Kenneth for the next collection for Swansea.'

He watched as the slow, sleepy-looking girl who nevertheless did a generous week's work, felt behind her for the door handle before sliding around the door and curtsying, then closing it behind her. He wondered vaguely why she always had difficulty finding the door handle, standing with her hand waving in-effectually about before clasping it in obvious relief.

His thoughts turned again to his daughter, who had managed the house after her mother's death and run it so smoothly he had hardly seen the servants. He remembered that time with regret; gliding through his days with everything he wanted always ready for him without the need to ask. Guests accommodated and given warm beds and good food without him having to worry about how it was all achieved.

In less than a week, his daughter would be reading the words he had written. He hoped he had shown love for her in his reply, as well as determination that she should not, for the moment, return.

Edwin Prince was in no hurry to reach home. Violet was not a loving wife and since the birth of the child, had been even less enthusiastic to greet him after an absence. He rode slowly, allowing his mount to choose the pace, moving towards the Longhouse which he had converted into a spacious home for his bride. Behind the house were stables and, to his wife's disgust, large, solidly built piggeries, which disguised the storerooms below ground level where the packages from the illegal boat cargoes were hidden.

When he reached his house, he still did not hurry to go inside, preferring to stable his horse and walk down to the distant buildings, intending to make sure he had sufficient space for what he had promised to store. It was broad daylight but no one would have been suspicious at seeing him visiting his pigs; eccentric behaviour was soon accepted as normal for people with wealth, he had learnt.

Llewellyn, who was feeding them, came to meet him.

'Sir,' he said with anxiety in his eyes, 'sir, there are piglets gone missing. Three of them. Taken from the sties I believe.'

Edwin was angered by the theft, not for the cost of the piglets although that did not please him; but the thought of someone entering the newly constructed buildings and perhaps seeing something of the additional work that had gone into them troubled him.

He could hardly go to the Keeper of the Peace and complain! Thoughts of Daniels putting his long, elegant nose into the pigsties did make him smile though. He imagined the man's dismay at finding dirt, and worse, on his highly polished boots. The look of polite agony as he tried to cope with the smell. But should the man's sharp eyes note the slightest unusual thing, he knew that Daniels would never give up searching for something more, and would not rest until the real reason for the new piggeries were uncovered. He looked around uneasily as if Daniels were already watching him, and abandoning his plan to examine the hidden storeroom he went into the house.

In Olwen's house there was much excitement. The arrival of a pig had puzzled, thrilled and amused them all, although she could not imagine who had sent it. Mary and Spider were pleased that although the gift was anonymous, it seemed likely that Olwen had an admirer besides Barrass and that was what they had hoped would happen. Their pleasure at the surprise arrival, which they had found tied to a tree on a length of brightly coloured yellow ribbon, was greater because of that supposition. Mistress Powell, who shared their house, was laughing at the animal's antics and remembering years long ago when she had a pig at the end of her own garden.

Olwen had arrived home after her long day at Ddole House to be met by the sounds of an offended piglet who was objecting to being fenced in, between boxes that Spider and Dan used for taking fish to market. The little creature seemed to be angry at being able to smell fish and not finding any to eat.

'He is starving!' Olwen protested. 'Mamma, can't you find him some food?'

'He has already swallowed all the milk we had, what vegetables I could spare and most of the bread. If he doesn't admit to being full soon, there will be nothing left for us!' Mary laughed as she dropped crumbled cake in front of the small pink snout. 'He's also upturned the bucket of water, tripped up Dan and your father, terrified the chickens and muddled my wool so it looks like the work of a mad woman!'

They managed eventually to make him safe behind a temporary barricade, and when the animal had settled for the night, with a disgruntled expression on its face, Olwen sat watching it, tickling the hairy skin and smiling with delight.

Mary and Spider hoped that whoever had sent it would fill

Olwen's heart with kind and loving deeds and encourage her to forget Barrass.

Olwen was wondering how soon she could go and find Barrass to tell him about the surprise arrival.

Chapter Three

Olwen rushed home on the day following Barrass's invitation to meet him at the alehouse, her fingers in the shape of a cross, her mouth whispering a prayer. 'Please God, don't let Mam say I can't go.'

She knew her brother Dan and her father still treated Barrass the same as they had always done, but her mother certainly did not seem pleased on the occasions Olwen had told her she had been talking to him. Would she stop her going to meet him?

Olwen was tempted to lie, but hesitated, knowing that it was highly unlikely she would get away with it. Mam sold fish, and during her walks around the village pushing the small wooden cart, she gathered information more efficiently than Dadda's nets caught the sewen and salmon, mackerel and mullet that gave them their living!

Perhaps there was something about Barrass she did not know? Mary might have heard gossip about yet another baby on the way wanting his name. She frowned as she considered the girls rumoured to keep company with him. Perhaps Harriet had persuaded him into her bed? Having hurried, to allow plenty of time to clean herself and go and meet Barrass, Olwen began to dawdle as soon as she reached the vicinity of her cliff-top home. She diverted from the worn path and spent a while searching for flowers.

The countryside around was so beautiful. Willows showing new greeny-yellow leaves, birches with their purple shoots, the oaks making patches of rust as they clung to their last year's leaves which had refused to budge even with the wildest and most determined wind. Under the trees were daffodils, streaking the ground like runaway sunshine.

Celandines and dandelions were beautiful and richly coloured and the daisies were like forgotten snow among the fast growing grasses, but they would fade fast. It was violets she searched for and gathering a few from a mossy bank, their stems small as their flowering season drew to an end, she added a surprise hoard of primroses and tied them with a length of ivy stem, to carry home.

Work on the new room for Enyd and Dan to make their home was in abeyance, the fishing having to come first, and spare time not easy to find. The walls were high but the roof was still to be completed, and it seemed to Olwen as she approached the house that the plan for it to be finished and furnished in time for Enyd and Dan's wedding would not be accomplished.

Her mother, Mary, was sitting outside the cottage in the last of the sun. Olwen was surprised; it was rare to see her mother's hands idle. Tied to a bush by a length of rope which allowed him sufficient freedom to explore the garden was Olwen's youngest brother, Dic, who was nine months old. He began chortling when he saw her approaching and she ran to pick him up and hugged him.

Giving the flower posy to Mary, Olwen asked, 'Mam, can I go to the village, just for a little while? It's so long since I talked with anyone except Florrie and Dozy Bethan who takes so long to think of an answer you can take a nap in between!'

'I hoped you would settle to help with the shawls, Olwen. I need to have a good pile of them for the Fair in three weeks' time. People will be less inclined to buy them as the weeks lead us into summer.'

'Oh Mam, just for a little while.'

Mary rose from the small stool on which she had been sitting and Olwen saw she had been peeling rushes to make rush lights. She had not been idle after all.

They used tallow candles and occasionally the sweeter smelling beeswax candles, like most people. But Mary, always cautious, liked to have a supply of rush lights in case the cost of candles became a burden on her purse. They used to make their own candles, and the boring task of dipping, cooling and redipping the wick into the hot wax had been Olwen's. She had been relieved when her father said they could buy them from the candle maker who called with a supply at regular intervals. Olwen remembered the task and sighed inwardly with relief that the work was no longer required.

'You can go,' Mary smiled, then laughed at the way her

daughter's face fell into a scowl when she added, 'but only if you promise to dip these in fat for me before you go to bed.'

'Oh Mam, it's a-w-f-u-l tedious!' But she agreed.

She called at the house of Kenneth, to see if Barrass had returned with the letters for forwarding to Swansea, but there was no one there. The side window, through which people could hand in their letters, was open but the door was firmly closed.

Crossing the road alongside the beach, she went to the door of the alehouse and looked inside. The room, in spite of the candles and lamps, was less bright than the fading daylight outside, being full of smoke. Arthur was frantically trying to get rid of it by waving a piece of sacking.

'Wet wood,' he explained as Olwen ran in and taking the sacking from him put a metal square across the top of the chimney opening to draw the smoke upwards. In a few moments the room was clear.

'Thanks, Olwen, I didn't think of the draw-er,' he said. 'Come to see Barrass, have you?'

'Is he here?' she asked, coughing against the last wreaths of smoke that drifted slowly out of the open door. 'I went to Kenneth's house but there is no one there.'

'Kenneth and Ceinwen have gone with Enyd to buy more material for the wedding,' Arthur explained with a disapproving sniff. 'Fancies herself she does, that Enyd. I hope your Dan can afford to keep up with her grand ideas.'

'She'll soon forget the fancies her mother has for her once there's a couple of children to feed and only a fisherman's money to manage it on,' Olwen said.

'Having the dress made by Mistress Gronow, she is. Won't have anything her mother can make,' Arthur added, his thin face frowning. His eyes rolled and he nodded up towards the living rooms of the alehouse. '*She* encourages her, mind.' He referred to Emma, who considered herself the wise woman of the village when it came to the way things should be done.

'Mam is making my dress and arranging the flowers for my hair for that day,' Olwen said. 'So grand I'll be, you won't know me.'

'I'd know you anywhere,' a voice said, and she shrieked with delight at seeing Barrass enter, still with his leather bag across his shoulders, and his post horn in his hand, the waistcoat of red, made for Kenneth, stretched across his wide shoulders. 'How are you, is work at Ddole House enjoyable?' he asked. 'And what's this about a piglet?'

'Barrass, you know! And I wanted to show you and tell you myself!'

'I'll come to see him soon.'

His arms didn't wrap around her when she ran to him but touched her shoulders lightly, charging her with a shock as severe as cold water. She nodded, bewildered and embarrassed at the chill formality of his greeting. His attitude was worsening. She shivered. There must be another woman.

Arthur handed him a mug of ale and he moved away from her and sat, easing the bag slightly from his shoulders and drank the reviving drink.

'Where's Kenneth, then?' he asked. 'Supposed to be here to take these letters from me.'

'You'll have to talk to me instead, there's no escape, Barrass,' Olwen joked, but the light-hearted tone of the words hid the suspicion that Barrass had forgotten his invitation, and was less than pleased to see her.

She felt uneasy, a sensation she had rarely felt with the tall, handsome young man, three years her senior. Picking up the dusty-looking white dog from near Arthur's feet, she buried her face in the rough fur, wishing she hadn't come, wishing the time could miraculously race on to the day when she was accepted as an adult, or run backwards to the freer, more relaxed days of childhood. Anything but this uneasy, over-polite strangeness.

'I had supper with Carter Phillips and Harriet a day or two ago,' Barrass said, addressing her obliquely, his dark eyes not quite meeting hers. 'Cooked a fine plaice, peppered and covered in capers,' he added.

'My Mam says a woman only uses strong flavours to cover up bad cooking!' Olwen retorted, and smiled ruefully as the other two laughed.

Dejected, her longed-for meeting with Barrass unaccountably ruined, Olwen put the dog down and walked to the door.

'I have to go,' she said. 'Mam wants me to help with rush lights, and I'll be cooking the meal. A better one than what you had at Harriet's table for sure!' was her departing remark.

*

'You're treating her unkindly, aren't you, Barrass?' Arthur said when the girl had left them. 'Always been your friend she has, even when you had no others.'

'She feels too protective towards me, she doesn't want any other friend except me,' Barrass said, his expression stiff. 'Spider thinks it would be kinder for me to keep away, give her a chance to meet other, younger people. More innocent than me I think he means. That was why he and Mary sent her to work for the Ddoles, to get away from me.' He smiled when he said it, suggesting it was a cause for amusement, but Arthur saw in his eyes a sadness that belied the gesture.

'Olwen *is* very young,' Arthur conceded.

'But I'm very fond of her. I miss her company, miss her funny ways. But I can't disagree with Spider and Mary. They love her too and I can see how they wouldn't want her to become too fond of someone like me, with three children in the village each demanding to be given my name. I'll have to stay out of her life and let others seek her out and enjoy her friendship.'

Arthur shrugged.

'No point me trying to walk out with her,' he said in his high-pitched voice that made the vicar sit him with the sopranos in church. 'She'd rather kiss my dog than me!'

The sound of a cart approaching led them to the door and they saw Kenneth and his wife Ceinwen struggling down with arms filled with parcels. Their daughter, Enyd, sat waiting to be helped down, a pouting look on her haughty face.

Arthur and Barrass were pushed aside as Emma came out to greet the family and inspect their shopping.

'Got plenty of lace, have you?' she demanded. 'You can't have too much lace for a wedding. And ribbons! Did you remember the ribbons?' Emma followed Ceinwen across the road to the bank on which her house stood. Behind them went Kenneth and his daughter, then Barrass, who was removing the leather postbag from his shoulders.

Barrass stood for a moment at the foot of the grassy bank, looking up along the path that Olwen would have taken back to her cottage. He felt as lost without her as she obviously did without him. But Spider had to be obeyed. After all, how could he even think of giving his love to a beautiful child like Olwen? He was older in far more than years. He had no right to besmirch her perfection with his grossness. Not Spider's words but clearly the essence of his 'request' for Barrass to discourage her. He had not dreamed it would be so hard to do.

The wedding of Olwen's brother, Dan, and Kenneth's daughter, Enyd, took place on a Sunday. The village went to the morning service as usual, but reassembled later for the ceremony.

For Olwen, the day began early. She had to go to Ddole House to attend to the routine tasks that even after the most fervent pleas of the vicar could not be neglected. She helped Seranne, now fully recovered from her sickness, as the cold platters were arranged for luncheon. She and David, one of the stableboys, helped Bethan with the fires, carrying up extra coal and logs to feed the fires that would burn in both bedroom and living room, besides the big cooking fire in the kitchen.

All the servants were being given a few hours of freedom to attend the wedding, once they had accompanied William to morning service and completed the tasks necessary to make his day a comfortable one. In between the chores, they discussed what they would be wearing. Excitement at the rare opportunity to dress in their best gave a flush to even Seranne's pale face. Only Florrie was absent. She was walking to the church with Daniels, his sister and his five children, showing the village they were 'walking out' and that a wedding was also on their minds.

Olwen raced home and hurriedly changed into the cotton frock her mother had patiently made, to which old Mistress Powell, who spent her days in the chimney corner of their living room, had added small bows of pale lemon ribbon.

She had no mirror in which to view herself in her finery, but twirled and enjoyed the sensation of the full skirt flaring about her thin legs, held out by the frilled hem. For her feet she had borrowed the shoes, hand-sewn from coarse linen, her mother had kept from her wedding day.

'Don't put them on until you reach the church, and take them off the moment you come out, mind,' Mary warned as she tried them for fit on Olwen's dainty feet.

'Don't worry, Mam, I'll want them for my own wedding one day.'

Baby Dic was not left out of the preparations. Mary had sewn bells on to ribbons for him to wear on his wrists and ankles, and he sat, shaking them experimentally, chortling at the merry sound.

Olwen smiled as she added wild flowers to her shiny fair hair, imagining the day when she would walk through the church gate, past the graves and into the dark, strange-smelling old church to stand beside Barrass and become his bride.

She picked up the posy Mary had made for her to carry, then put it down again to re-adjust her hair. Unseen by Olwen or her mother, baby Dic crawled determinedly towards it, and when she bent to pick it up again, she saw him chewing happily on the fresh blooms.

'Mam! Dic has ruined my posy!' Olwen wailed. 'And us with no time to make another!'

Mary took the half demolished flower arrangement and, with her clever hands, swiftly restored it at least partially to its former neatness. Pushing Olwen impatiently in front of her, afraid they were late, Mary scooped up the baby and stepped out into the sunshine of the May afternoon. With a hasty goodbye to Mistress Powell, the three of them hurried down the path to the village.

Spider and Dan had already left. Olwen imagined them sitting in the chilly church, excited but anxious too, Dan hoping he wouldn't stumble over the formal words, Spider wondering where Mary and the baby were. They would be listening for the sound of the congregation arriving, wishing they could stand at the doorway to see them sooner, but sticking to their seats and pretending to be calm. A great swelling of love for her father and Dan filled her heart and made tears sting and cause her to blink.

As they approached the road outside the alehouse, they heard the mumble of voices and saw that most of the village had congregated to walk together to the church. As if they had been waiting for them to arrive, the family of the bride began to move slowly off. Enyd with her father, Kenneth. Ceinwen close behind and supported by her soldier son, Tom, fortunately home for the occasion from his army posting.

Enyd wore muslin, but her dress was of several layers, each one embroidered and touched with colour. The veil, also muslin, was embroidered to match. Palest blues and greens and lemon seemed to float about her as she walked beside her father. Her long, dark hair seemed to emphasize the almost fairy-like quality of her appearance.

As she fell into step behind her, Olwen saw that Enyd's usual disapproving look had remained and spoilt the illusion of utter happiness the more distant view suggested. Behind the bride, looking even larger than usual, Ceinwen had chosen a skirt of dark blue over which a loose top flowed and flapped in the breeze from the sea on their left. She wore a hat with a flower-covered brim which threatened to fly away every second, and she used both hands to hold it a prisoner to her head.

In natural order, relations of the bride and groom followed on, and with a few sightseers making up the tail, the procession made its way along the road beside the sea, past the harbour and to the church door. A few unnecessary touches to the bride's dress and headdress and a few useless attempts to make Ceinwen's untidy hat behave, and they stepped inside. Olwen, Kenneth and Enyd waited in the porch until the rest had found their seats and the organist had found his place. Notes of the chosen hymn, wrong notes and dust were produced by the organist in equal quantities.

Emma and Pitcher, followed by their twin daughters, Daisy and Pansy, were among the last to settle. They walked down the aisle of the ancient church as if *they* were the people the rest had come to see. Emma was wearing a colourful, full and flowing skirt and a blouse over which she had thrown a silky scarf but, seeing Betson-the-flowers outside wearing something very similar, she had discarded the scarf as if it were a badge of shame and it was now sticking out of Pitcher's pocket, like a guilty secret.

Olwen looked for Barrass, and saw him when she had almost given up hope, standing in a corner at the back of the church. Then her heart leapt painfully with dismay. Beside him was Harriet, the Carter's sister. Why wasn't he near her family? He was their friend, wasn't he, not Harriet's, who, according to her mother, was free with favours and unfussy about choosing whom should receive them! The thought made her want to run out of the church and hide where she couldn't see them together, where she could pretend he was truly her own.

She wasn't aware of much of the actual service and hardly

looked at the couple apart from sharing a brief smile with Dan. She was waiting for the moment when she could turn and look once again at Barrass. Perhaps this time he would be alone, although this she doubted.

Was he content with Harriet for a companion? Had he sought her out? Or – as she fervently prayed – was Harriet forcing her company on him and him trying to escape?

Throughout the simple service her movements and the responses she gave to the comments around her were automatic, she heard her voice as if it were the voice of someone else. When they walked out through the church, her eyes at once turned to the corner where she had glimpsed Barrass and Harriet. They weren't there! In an agony of determinedly hidden impatience, she walked sedately behind Enyd and Dan, and out into the sunshine.

The procession re-formed, but this time, Dan walked with his bride, and behind them Olwen, Tom and their parents. Then others joined as they saw fit. On impulse, Olwen took Dic from her mother's arms, his bells jingling in time to their steps. The rhythm seemed to represent music and they began to sing, the waves beside them an accompaniment. Hymns they had just sung came naturally to them, but Olwen knew that before the day had finished, the songs would be earthy and audaciously aimed at the newly married couple's first night together. She hoped her father wouldn't send her away.

Emma turned once or twice to check that her daughters' appearances were perfect, and, seeing Arthur talking to Pansy, she waved her hands at him and told him to return to the alehouse and prepare for the guests' arrival.

'Really, Pitcher,' she whispered, 'that boy's becoming too familiar. You'll have to talk to him.'

'I'll talk to him as soon as we get back, my dear,' Pitcher promised, as he had promised several times before, and put it from his mind immediately.

Several families who had not intruded on the marriage ceremony were waiting for them outside the alehouse. Two unwelcome sights met Olwen's eyes. Unmarried Bessie Rees with her unmarried daughter and granddaughter, and Ivor the builder and his wife, with their unmarried daughter with her child.

Both girls claimed that Barrass was the father of their

daughter, and Olwen hated seeing them. A reminder of Barrass's affection for those girls and others, and a reminder of her own immaturity always depressed her. To add to her dismay, Emma and Pitcher's daughter Violet Prince was there too. Although married, Violet too admitted that the baby was not her husband's but Barrass's. Olwen threw down the now untidy posy and, hidden from sight by the crowd, kicked it to a scattering of fallen petals and green leaves among the pebbles and stones of the road.

She watched as the new bride walked over to the girls and waved her wedding ring in front of them. Emma took the opportunity to lecture the twins on the dangers of succumbing to the weaknesses of desire.

Daniels the Keeper of the Peace was there and he held Florrie's arm as he paraded with his five, beautifully dressed children. The girls wore dresses of flowered material covered with cream, lace-trimmed pinafores. The boys were in knee-length trousers and high socks, and coats of soft woollen material. The party looked, to most eyes, rather ostentatiously apparelled for the wedding of a fisherman and his girl. He had intended to stay only a few minutes after the service, but his children were enjoying the spectacle and Florrie was meeting and talking with so many friends, he agreed to stay a while longer.

'After all, my dear,' he said proudly, 'I want everyone to see what a handsome family we will make, just as soon as you and I follow the example of Enyd and Dan.'

Florrie smiled up at him, admiring his splendid, well-groomed, almost noble appearance, but the words which he wanted to hear, that his eyes pleaded to coax from her, would not come. He wanted her to agree to go with him to see the vicar and name the day for their marriage. But she could not. She knew she would be a fortunate woman to have Daniels for a husband, but something made her hesitate; there was a formality, a stiffness about him that augured badly for her future happiness.

She tightened her grip of his arm, smiled lovingly up into his eyes, but was glad of the crowd around her, needing to be a part of the mass, fearing that the day when she married Daniels she would be cutting herself away from them all. The people who were her friends would not be considered suitable company for her once she was Mistress Ponsonby Daniels.

Smiling but impatient to leave, Daniels was persuaded to stay 'just a while longer', time and again, using the children as an excuse. Florrie was pleased when the children gradually slid off the cloak of hesitancy and joined with others of their ages to have fun. With luck Daniels would be persuaded to stay for the evening's entertainment. It would surely do the children no harm to share in the laughter and gaiety. To Florrie's eyes, they lacked the spontaneous vivacity of children.

Although the sun was not strong, adding a brightness but little warmth, the crowd ate outside, going in to fill their plates with the food provided by Ceinwen, Mary and Emma plus several of the villagers, and coming back outside to sit on chairs provided or on the sea wall, where they could look across at the two islands of Mumbles Point, the inner one joined by an arch of rock to the mainland.

Olwen avoided Tom, Enyd's brother. She had once been frightened by his urgent kisses and his thrusting body and was afraid that even a smile might persuade him she had changed her mind about her lack of interest. He wore the red uniform decorated with white and touches of gold proudly but held no attraction for her. She hoped ruefully that he might take Harriet into the deep grasses and keep her away from Barrass.

Rather than lessening, the crowd increased as the afternoon faded to evening, and with the tide happily accommodating them by working its slow way back and back, to extend the beach, they began to move from the outside of the alehouse on to the sands.

Olwen had searched in vain for Barrass. He had finished his Sunday deliveries early, she had learnt that from Kenneth. So what was he doing, and more important, was he with Harriet? In the pretence of looking for Enyd and Dan, she went into the alehouse and through the bar-room to the room beyond. He was sitting at the top of the cellar steps, a book in his hand, a candle helping to light the pages.

'Barrass? Why aren't you enjoying the celebration?' she asked, relief flooding through her like a breach in the sea wall. 'You aren't ill?'

He looked up and smiled. How could he tell her that avoiding her, and being watched by Spider and at the same time chased by both Harriet and her brother, Carter Phillips, was more than he could cope with?

'I was on my way to get more ale from the cellar,' he lied, putting aside the book he had been reading. 'Arthur is kept so busy I offered to help.'

'Arthur is helping to build a bonfire on the sands,' she said. 'Why don't you come as well?'

'Best I stay here, in case Pitcher needs a hand,' he said. 'Go you, and I'll try to come out later, when there's less demand for drink.'

'If I wait for that I'll wait for ever!' she laughed, but she left him, puzzled by his attitude but unwilling to ask him to explain.

As darkness fell, some people left the crowd, to return wearing more comfortable and practical clothes, and as the last of the day faded, and torches and lanterns were lit and spread around the area, Carter Phillips drew a long, enticing note on his fiddle and dancing began.

The new steps learnt by Emma's three daughters and others with such diligence were attempted by some but soon abandoned. The dances were impromptu and followed no set pattern, but then Carter Phillips didn't play a recognizable tune, so no one cared, except Emma, who disapproved of anything not done 'properly'.

Mary, with Dic wrapped close to her in a Welsh shawl, danced with her long-legged husband. Emma stayed at the edge of the crowd and tutted as the music refused to fit with her carefully executed steps as she brought an unwilling Kenneth to partner her. Olwen refused all invitations to join the throng; she was waiting for Barrass.

Dozy Bethan was there but Harri, the young man who had for a time walked out with her, ignored her. He worked for Markus and his attention was fully on Polly, the shy, thin little servant who worked for Emma. Bethan did not seem unduly worried, even when she was told by Polly that Harri had 'given her up' several weeks ago!

'He's got black teeth,' she told Olwen in her slow way. 'Never liked black teeth.'

Seranne and Polly were dressed alike, as they did whenever possible to show kinship. Over their black serving dresses, they had on their best aprons, with full, deeply frilled *broderie anglaise*

43

straps that went across their shoulders and down their backs to join with the waist strap and the long, frilled ties. They wore their hair loose, enjoying the feeling of their unrestrained tresses folding themselves around their shoulders and falling down their backs.

During a lull in the dancing, Seranne began to sing, her sweet voice silencing the crowd magically, but before she reached the end, she succumbed to a bout of coughing, and Dan finished the song for her. Olwen was horrified to hear a murmur of voices speak of the fear that the morbid lung disease was likely to rob Seranne of her life before she reached thirty, in a few months' time. Seeing them together, Olwen realized that the disease was probably present in Polly too and she shivered.

Olwen wandered among the laughing people, friends all of them, some young and having fun and many old and content just to watch and remember. Why was she forced to waste her life watching, waiting for others to realize she was a young woman, when it could be taken from her as early as Polly's tender years? Why wouldn't Barrass see that, small as she was, she was old enough to be his girl?

Using two lengths of wood taken from the pile gathered to feed the fire, Spider did a sword dance, his long gangly legs thrashing about and his toes touching the ground with surprising lightness between the crossed sticks. Then Dan joined in, singing a sailors' working song and the two of them danced together, shadows moving beside them so the scene was one of comic fantasy, with the tall, thin men dancing accompanied by their mocking shadows. Firelight danced too, sending spasms of light across the sweating faces of the entertainers and laughing audience.

When the two men finally fell exhausted to the ground, Barrass appeared beside them with ale to revive them. Olwen ran to him, and as the music began, insisted he danced with her. Not for Olwen the centre of the stage. She pulled Barrass away from the brightness of the fire into the surrounding shadows.

'Olwen, I have to go,' he said, obviously ill at ease. She dropped her thin arms to her side and looked up at him, her eyes alone recognizable on the shadowy face fired from within with challenge.

'Why, Barrass? Why are you behaving so badly? I thought we

44

were friends for ever?' she said, trying to hold back the temptation to cry.

'Things change. We grow up and with every month that passes we become different people,' he said. Then she saw him glance up and her father was there, still panting a little from his exertions.

'I think your mother is looking for you, Olwen,' Spider said, and taking her hand, he led her back through the noisy crowd, to where Mary sat with Ceinwen and Emma.

Spider glanced back and Olwen turned in time to intercept a silent exchange between them. She saw Spider, from his very stance showing displeasure. He frowned at the boy, and Barrass shrugged as if to say, 'what can I do?' She knew in that moment that Barrass's attitude was due to pressure from her parents. They had told him to stay away.

Pushing her father angrily, she ran from the friendly camaraderie of the beach and up the path to her home. Ignoring the enquiries about the party from Mistress Powell who was dozing in the corner, wrapped in several woollen blankets and wearing a thick nightcap that half hid her face, she ran upstairs. Throwing herself on her narrow bed, she sobbed as silently as she could into the wool-filled pillow.

On the beach and around the front of the alehouse the celebrations continued late into the night. When Dan and Enyd tried to sneak away, they were seen and the shouted remarks calling them back became more and more lively. Florrie had managed to keep Daniels with her by flattery and cajoling, although his sister had taken the children home to their beds.

Pitcher kept the ale flowing, Carter Phillips and Oak-tree Thomas kept the music wailing into the night sky and somehow, the dancers found the energy to continue to jig to the strains of barely recognizable melodies.

It was after midnight when Olwen remembered that with their room still unfinished, Dan was bringing his bride to his own bedroom. They would be sharing the room next to hers. She had not slept and was certain no one had yet come in. Wide awake and angry with herself for running away from the rare opportunity to dance and laugh and spend the night hours with her friends, she tiptoed past Mistress Powell, who was emitting gentle puffing snores, and left the house.

She could hear the sounds of the revellers as soon as the door closed behind her and, determined to enjoy what was left of the night, she hurried towards the steep path.

A sound stopped her, and suddenly fearful of whom she might meet at such a late hour, she dropped to the ground behind a bush of blackthorn and waited. She shivered in the night air. Having left her warm bed and without adding more than a thin shawl, the keen breeze pressed against her and slid through her clothes with ease.

It was hooves she heard first, the slow, almost melodic regularity that was usually pleasant and soothing becoming threatening as they came closer and closer to where she was hiding as they headed inland. The hoof fall and the swish as the animals' legs pushed through the grasses built up into a menacing, overshadowing fear. The first one was led by David, the boy who worked in William Ddole's stables. Percy, from Pitcher's stables, came next and other ponies and donkeys followed without men to guide them, obediently following the heels of the leader.

When the donkeys and ponies were passed, men, women and a few children followed, each one with either a bag or a barrel over his shoulder. Olwen crouched lower, pressing herself to the grass and shutting her eyes tightly. She knew what was happening but did not want to learn anything about who was involved. To be ignorant could mean your life saved. She did not move until the silence had been unbroken for several minutes.

She went to sit beside her mother, Ceinwen and Emma Palmer, who were all tired but shared Emma's determination to watch over her daughters until they were safe in their beds.

'It's at times like these,' Emma was telling Mary, 'when common sense is abandoned in pursuit of dangerous pleasures! It's when everyone is intent on "having fun" that girls forget their need to be strong against the demands of the flesh.'

Olwen's shivers made her stop.

'There's cold you are, Olwen!' She tightened her lips in obvious suspicion.

'Go to the fire and warm yourself or we'll have to go home before Enyd and Dan,' Mary said, rubbing her daughter's hands with her own.

'Take my shawl,' Emma said. 'Dancing has me so hot I think I'll melt if I don't cool off a little.'

Leaving the three women sharing the confidences of friends, Olwen walked disconsolately through the laughing crowd. She didn't stop to talk to those who called out to her, wanting to sit beyond the blaze of firelit merrymaking, and ponder her own situation. She was doomed to be treated like a child for ever, she was convinced. Just because, like her mother, she was small, and looked less than her age, people believed that her heart and her mind were young too.

She stood in the shadows, away from the circles of people around the fire, and gradually realized she was not alone. This time there was no fear, this was not the smugglers about their night-time journeying. She looked around and saw someone sitting on a rock, arms hugging knees, the face directed towards her. She could not decide whether the figure was male or female, old or young, until the voice gave her a clue.

'Hello, why are you standing alone when so many friends want your company?' the young man asked.

'Who are you?' Olwen demanded.

'Cadwalader.' he replied, unfolding himself, his black cloak unwinding itself like wings from around him. He came to stand beside her, small, pale-faced in the weird light, eyes deep set in shadows, a streak of white hair showing clearly on one side of his dark head.

'I know you are Olwen, daughter of Peter the fisherman, known as Spider,' he surprised her by saying. Having taken her hand briefly, he returned to his previous position, rewrapping his cloak around him to ward off the chill of the hour.

To Olwen, he seemed to be a part of the rock, carved by the wind and the sea. He had taken it for his own. He wasn't perched there, a temporary appendage, but was in possession. As the fanciful thought entered her head she trembled, for a moment believing the stories about the fairy people who came from the sea and coaxed young girls back to their watery kingdom.

'Do you think I might ask a favour?' the young man asked. 'On so short an acquaintance I realize it's hardly polite, but I would appreciate some food and a sip of ale. I have not eaten for more than a day and my stomach is complaining of neglect.'

Olwen walked back through the crowd and collected a platter which she filled from the remains of the feast. For a moment she hesitated about returning to the strange young man and eventually persuaded Polly to go back with her.

Cadwalader was still where she had first seen him, but he jumped lightly down at her approach and greeted her friend Polly with a politeness that was at odds with his appearance. He was obviously a wanderer, taking food where and when he could, perhaps working for a while at one place before moving on.

He began to eat the moment the platter was placed in his hands, but continued to watch Olwen in a disconcerting way, ignoring the newcomer. Olwen felt flattered by his obvious admiration, but took Polly's hand and backed away asking him to return the platter when he had finished the food.

'You have an admirer. I could sense it even though I could barely see his face,' Polly giggled as they returned to Mary and Spider. 'What an adventure.'

They did not see him again. Soon after they had supplied him with his supper, the crowd realized that Enyd and Dan had succeeded in getting away. Allowing the couple the customary time alone, the party slowly subsided and people began to drift homeward.

With Mary carrying a sleeping Dic, and Spider having to be helped to stay on the steep path, Olwen went home. The image in her mind that made her lips curve in a smile, was of Barrass, frowning down at the squatting form of the dark-eyed Cadwalader. The idea of Barrass being made to feel a jealousy as acute as hers for him and Harriet kept her awake until the crowing of their cockerel warned her that it was time to rise and begin another day.

Chapter Four

With the details of the improvements necessary before he could apply to change his alehouse to an inn, Pitcher went to see Barrass. Although Barrass was still a very young man, not yet eighteen so far as anyone could guess, Pitcher and the boy were friends. It was Barrass who had helped him when he had built the parlour that Emma had so desperately wanted to entertain her daughters' friends. Now Pitcher knew that if he could persuade him, Barrass was the one to help him now.

Friday was the day the boy was free from the deliveries of Gower letters and early in the morning, Pitcher went to the back of Kenneth's house and found him, sitting on the edge of the narrow, heather-filled mattress on the floor of the outhouse he was allowed to use. A dish from the previous evening that had contained cawl was on the floor, the contents revealed by the few chicken bones that had been the basis of the broth. To Pitcher it showed clearly the minimal care Kenneth and Ceinwen gave the boy in return for all his long hours of walking across Gower.

Barrass looked embarrassed when Pitcher opened the door and stared at the poor accommodation Kenneth had given him.

'This is worse than I thought, boy! How can Kenneth let you live like this?'

'It's better than the cave that was my last home,' Barrass smiled. 'At least I know where I'll sleep each night. There's many a day when I haven't known where I would curl up.'

Pitcher silently decided to talk to Emma and try to persuade her to allow Barrass to sleep at the alehouse. Angry with Kenneth, but saying nothing to show it, he invited Barrass to eat a breakfast with Arthur the potboy.

'There's something I want to discuss with you,' he said, 'but first you'll eat your fill.'

When the food had been cooked and Barrass, Arthur and the dog had eaten all they could manage, Pitcher put his proposal to

Barrass, while Arthur listened.

'I need some more building work done,' he began. 'Emma and I plan to make this place into a fine inn that will attract the wealthy businessmen and their families. I want to persuade them to stay here instead of going back to the town for their bed and their food.'

'There are other places in the village where they can find a good, warm bed. Why d'you think they would stay here?' Barrass asked doubtfully.

'Because, situated where we are, they will see us first!' was Pitcher's joyful reply. 'And because, sitting here close to the sea where they wish to wander and breathe deep of the fresh, salty air, with Arthur neat as a bud in a smart uniform, and the improved stables showing the care we'll give to their animals, they will look no further. What d'you think, boy?'

Arthur's Adam's apple jigged anxiously.

'Wear a uniform?' he asked in his high-pitched, girlish voice. 'You didn't say nothing about that, Pitcher!'

'Made by Emma and in colours we shall choose together,' Pitcher reassured him, patting the bony shoulder.

As Arthur went doubtfully back to his work, Pitcher and Barrass wandered through the rooms of the house and outhouses, discussing the possibilities. Between serving customers, Arthur joined them, listening but adding little to the discussion. He hoped that Barrass would come back to live at the alehouse. They were good friends and he would greet a return to the sharing they had once enjoyed with delight but the thought of having to wear a uniform and suffer the tormenting remarks of others brought doubt on the suitability of the scheme.

Before the day ended, Pitcher and Barrass had drawn a plan of sorts and copying it neatly, Pitcher prepared to take it together with his accounts books, to discuss the loan with the bank in town.

'Tomorrow,' he told Barrass, 'when you go into town to collect the letters, I will ride with you and start this idea going.' He grinned as he glanced at the still worried Arthur. 'And I'll bring some patches for you to choose your colours, you and Emma. What about black and white with frilled aprons like the maids?'

'Pitcher! It's bad enough that I talk like a girl without you making me dress like one!' Arthur complained.

'I thought a touch of gold, being as how you want to call the place The Posthorn Inn,' Barrass suggested.

'Fancy colours, and I go off with the first band of strolling players that pass through!' Arthur threatened, and was relieved to see the other two laugh. 'But a modest amount of gold might be suitable,' he conceded thoughtfully.

'But what we really need,' Pitcher said as they prepared to pack away the plan so far made, 'what we must decide on, is a way to make us more popular with everyone, not just the visitors come to look at the sea. They come in the spring and summer; we need to survive the dark months as well.' His sharp eyes glanced at Barrass to see how his suggestion was received, and said slowly, 'Now, if we were to use the inn as a receiving office for the Royal Mail instead of it going to Kenneth's old house – now that would bring people here day after day. Attract them like Betson-the-flowers attracts wayward husbands, that would.'

'But there's no chance of Kenneth giving up the letters.' Barrass was alarmed. 'And beside, if there were changes, I might lose my work. No Pitcher, don't think of changing things, or I will lose out.'

Pitcher said no more. He could see that the poorly paid and thankless task Barrass performed for Kenneth was important to him. It was the nearest the boy had ever been to stability. And besides, all his life, Barrass's dream had been of carrying the King's Mail. But Pitcher railed inwardly against the way Kenneth and Ceinwen treated the boy, and the seed was sown for changes, even if he did not have Barrass's support at present. What he had in mind would benefit them both.

Later that evening, when Barrass had settled to help Arthur in the busy bar-room, Pitcher went up to talk to his wife. Emma rarely came down in the evenings. She preferred to pretend that the bar-room, with its noisy drinkers, storytellers and occasionally, songsters, was a world apart. It was a place where they earned the money to live comfortably and give their daughters the best of everything but, to Emma, it was something of which she was ashamed.

Despite her grand ideas and her pretence that she had begun somewhere more grand than the dilapidated shack behind Fishermen's Row, Emma had a brain for business. She had seen at once that changed to an inn, the building would be a finer and more profitable place. Now, Pitcher's half-held thought of applying for the inn to be a collection place for the Post appealed strongly.

'A first step would be for us to allow Barrass to sleep here,' Pitcher said hesitantly. As he expected, Emma raised her doubts loudly and long.

'Have that lecher in my house? Under the same roof as our beautiful girls? I tell you, Mr Palmer, you try my tolerance cruelly. *No!* You've persuaded me otherwise in the past, but I had not a moment's peace while he was here. Creeping up the stairs he'd be, ravishing those poor girls. No, Mr Palmer, not for a single night will I allow it.'

'But think, if he is already here, perhaps stopping on his way from Swansea with the mail to break his fast, the idea of cheating Kenneth wouldn't be so disloyal. It's we who are his friends, Emma, and it's a short step from stopping off to eat and stopping off for us to sort the letters.'

Emma wasn't convinced, but Pitcher knew her well enough to know she would think about his words and gradually see the strength of them.

Olwen was awake long before she needed to rise. She listened to the droning voice of her new sister-in-law complaining about the lack of a home, the boredom of her life so far from the village, and, Olwen guessed, about everything else besides. She could not hear Dan's whispered words but knew he was pleading with Enyd to be patient, that it would be different when they had their own room, but Olwen suspected that things would never be right for Enyd: she was doomed to live a discontented life, whatever Dan did to try and please her.

It was Friday she realized as she roused and considered the day ahead. Olwen hated Fridays. There was no possibility of seeing Barrass. Not only was there no possibility of a delivery of a letter to Ddole House, Friday was a day on which she had to begin early and work until late, having many extra jobs to do for Florrie in preparation for the weekend. She dragged herself out of bed, the only consolation being that Dan and her father were usually out before her and the fire would be blazing and both water and gruel warmed for her.

Mistress Powell was dozing in her corner, and barely opened a wrinkled eye when she passed. She stopped to fasten the blankets firmly around the shrunken shoulders and hugged the old woman affectionately, then went to dish out a bowl of gruel for herself.

After eating, she went first to look at the simple sty her brother had made for the newly arrived pig, wondering why Morgan Morgan and his brother Madoc had given it to her. It pleased her to see him trotting to greet her and she scratched its pink back and laughed at the expression of pleasure on the small, snouted face.

She saw Madoc and his brother slipping through the woods as she set off to work, although they did not see her. Under their coats were suspicious-looking bundles and she felt a moment's pity for the family who had to live by thieving and occasionally, begging for food. Perhaps she ought to go to the damp old cottage and thank them?

Running across the fields toward Ddole House, her thoughts flew ahead of her to the tasks waiting for her there. Water to be brought in. That was always her first occupation with the small comfort that at least it warmed her, carrying the heavy buckets across the yard and into the kitchen.

Besides water for cooking and washing the seemingly endless dishes, water was needed for bathing and washing. William insisted, as his wife had insisted before him, that each of the servants bathed once each week, taking turns to get in the soapy water in front of the kitchen fire while the rest waited their turn.

Her first surprise of the day was finding that the buckets and the big container that was heated by the fire were already filled.

'What happened?' she asked Florrie as she removed her cloak and reached for her coarse apron.

Florrie pointed to the window and outside, Olwen saw a figure she half recognized. The young man was thin, his legs encased in black, ragged trousers that ended in thick woollen socks and worn down boots. A cloak round him concealed most of him, but his hair, black, but with a white streak to one side, brought memory flooding back. It was Cadwalader, whom she had met on the beach, the night of Enyd and Dan's wedding.

'What is he doing here?' she asked.

'Came early and offered to work in return for food to break his fast,' Florrie explained. 'He's swept the yard so clean the mice will want to move out for fear of starving!' she added. 'He'll be well fed, Olwen. See to it, will you?'

Curious, Olwen invited the man inside.

Seeing him closely and with the benefit of daylight, she saw that he was sturdily built, but with arms that were short and hardly reaching beyond his waist. His neck too was thick and almost nonexistent, giving him the appearance of a carving, a shape that was unfinished, not intended to run and move freely. She remembered thinking that he was a part of the rock on which he had been sitting and smiled guiltily at her unkind opinion. Yet there was a beauty about him, and a suggestion of strength and gentleness that was appealing. Olwen knew he was watching her closely and with admiration, but his eyes were set deep in fathomless shadows. She could not see them at all clearly yet knew they were friendly and smiling.

When he had eaten, and finished the work he had contracted to do for Florrie, he didn't go away, but sat cross-legged on a wall pillar, his possessions in a bundle beside it, and watched the comings and goings of the busy house. Olwen took him food when they paused to eat their midday meal, but he said little, just smiled with those deep set, dark eyes and touched her hand briefly in appreciation of her kindness.

He was still there when the Keeper of the Peace arrived for his almost daily visit. This time, however, he had not called simply to enquire after Florrie's wellbeing.

'I have a report,' he announced in his pompous manner, 'of some missing pigs.'

Behind her, Olwen heard the gasp of dismay from Seranne and her own voice was trembling with fear as she answered,

'I – I found a piglet wandering, lost, and have him safe at home.' She had decided immediately that the pig which had been a gift from Seranne's brothers was one of the missing ones, and hoped she would be able to get home to warn her parents of what had happened before Daniels reached them and was told a different story. 'A very young piglet,' she added. 'Would it be one of those you are looking for?'

He questioned her closely about when and how she found it and with every answer, Olwen became more frightened. Now she would have to go and warn her mother. It was unlikely that her answers would be remotely the same.

Daniels went to talk with William Ddole and Olwen, her face a picture of dismay, asked Florrie, who was about to follow him for a few private words, if she might go home for a short while.

'Of course you may not!' Florrie's usual amiable mood when she had spoken with Daniels had not yet materialized. Desperately Olwen reached out a hand for her cloak. She had to go. If it meant losing her place, then it was too bad. To lose her job was the least of her choices. If she were found to be in possession of a stolen pig, she would be sent to gaol. She trembled as she thought of the horror of it.

A voice close beside her whispered, 'Don't worry, little Olwen. I will go and tell your mother everything you told the constable. There's nothing for you to fret about.' Taking up his cloth-wrapped bundle he had propped against the pillar, he smiled, bowed and was gone.

She was white-faced when she returned to her work and Florrie asked her if she were ill.

'No, just a passing discomfort, that's all.' She managed to smile and only then stopped to wonder why she felt certain that Cadwalader, a stranger, would help her as he promised. She had fed him twice. No reason for her to trust him, but she did.

Daniels talked for a surprisingly long time with William Ddole. Florrie waited for him to return to the kitchen and had placed a glass for his ale and a plate of cake for him to eat. When he eventually came back into the warm kitchen he asked more questions, both of Olwen and Bethan, the sleepy kitchenmaid. His questions became conversational so Olwen was disarmed.

'The wedding was a fine day out, so well victualled too. I do believe all the village enjoyed it,' he said, smiling kindly at Olwen. 'Such a pity that William Ddole your master missed all the fun.'

'Yes, but perhaps the amusement wasn't for the likes of him, sir,' Olwen said, then a sharp kick on the ankle made her stare in amazement at Bethan. She had no idea the girl could move fast enough to surprise her with a kick of such ferocity.

'Dreaming you were, Olwen,' Bethan said in her slow way. 'Why, I even danced with the master myself. Fancy you forgetting he was there, him and that Master Edwin Prince and his gentleman friend from London, er – John – er – '

Belatedly, Olwen realized that William might have given the wedding as his alibi for other more dangerous activities.

' – John Maddern. Of course! Sorry, Mr Daniels. I don't know what I was thinking of. I remember clearly now. Master William danced with Bethan and made us all laugh for the size of him and the lack of size with her! Spent a long time talking to the bridal pair too, and gave them a gift of money.' She hoped her embroidered tale matched somehow with what her employer had said.

Daniels left, after having a few private moments with Florrie, and he stared doubtfully at both Olwen and Dozy Bethan as he stepped through the door, a solemn figure; tall, smartly dressed, a half-feared representative of the law.

'I hope you two realize how important it is to tell the truth to a man in my position?'

'Oh, yes, sir,' the girls chorused. Olwen thought the activities of the day had been so far from the truth that she doubted her own name!

'Thanks,' she whispered to Bethan after the man had gone. 'He quite lulled me into talking as if to a friend.'

Bethan sniffed, rubbing a hand across her face in slow disapproval.

'And they calls me dozy!' she muttered, the only time she had hinted that her nickname was known to her.

Seranne seemed untroubled by Daniels' questions, getting on with her work, and overseeing the work of others with no sign of anxiety. She had told Olwen of the two piglets her brothers had brought home but hearing the Keeper of the Peace tell them of the theft of three piglets from Edwin Prince seemed not to worry her. She sang as she worked, stopping once to sip from the bottle of white horehound medicine Florrie had made for her, to ease her coughing.

When Daniels had gone, Seranne suddenly stopped singing, begged Olwen to cover for her and pelted off in the direction of her shabby home as if her heels were dogged by demons. Olwen watched her go, skirts held high not to impede her progress, and knew for certain that the calmness Seranne had shown in front of Daniels was the result of experience; the Morgan brothers had probably given Seranne, Polly and Vanora many such frightening moments.

Cadwalader returned a few hours later, but this time he did not ask for food or work. He sat where he had before, on the pillar at the end of the wall, and waited until Olwen came out for water.

'I spoke to your mother and she understands fully. I waited until the Keeper of the Peace arrived, and chuckled to see him carrying the piglet away, trying to prevent it from touching his nice clean clothes,' he reported in a whisper.

He smiled, his eyes deepening, yet giving his face a brightness; the promise of fun slowly revealed in his hitherto serious expression. He helped Olwen back with her filled buckets and with another strange bow, departed.

Soon afterwards, Seranne returned, pale, breathless and exhausted. In sympathy, knowing they both suffered the same uneasy fears, Olwen offered to stay longer and finish the work usually done by the cook.

'Go you,' she said, 'Bethan and I will see everything is fit for the morning.'

Bethan nodded apathetic agreement.

During the following days, several gifts appeared at Olwen's door. Rabbits, a few pigeons, a hare and even a pheasant, plucked of its fine feathers and placed like a wedge in a corner of the door, all arrived overnight and welcomed by Mary without suspicion. No one who loved Olwen would place her in danger twice, she thought erroneously. Olwen saw the pleased expression on her mother's face and knew that if she told her whom she suspected of bringing the food, the smile would fade. The Morgans were hardly the sort Mary would choose for her daughter to marry.

Barrass disliked taking letters to Markus, the blind man who lived in a dark, unfriendly looking house on the cliffs. The man rarely went out, and when he did, he was unapproachable and surly. The house itself seemed to reflect the man's personality and although a strong young man and afraid of little, Barrass shivered as he approached it. The package he had for Markus on this Thursday had been given to him to deliver by the man who lived at Penclawdd on the north coast.

The man had also given Barrass a feed of cockles gathered on the beach and cooked in an outhouse behind his home. These Barrass had eaten for his midday meal, washing them down with a mug of ale in a small alehouse near the forge at Llanrhidian.

He was tired, wanting only to walk back to the village, hand in the letters, his notebook and the money he had collected, and settle to rest on his lonely bed. But as well as having this letter to deliver, he knew that, being Thursday, he would have to kill time until he met Kenneth at the house of Betson-the-flowers in the green lane. Wearily he walked past Olwen's cottage and along the path high above the sea.

The watchman stepped out as he approached Markus's gate and demanded to know his business. Handing him the letter and sitting to wait while the watchman went to get his fee, Barrass felt in his pocket for the letter that had come for himself on the previous day. It had been read many times since he had first opened the seal and unfolded the pages, but the excitement as he began to read was still enough to make his heart stumble in its beatings.

When Penelope Ddole had been found with him in the old coach at Ddole House, their interrupted loving caused her father's face to redden with rage and immediately afterwards Penelope had been sent away. She now lived in London with Gerald and Marion Thomas, friends of her father. The intention had been to separate her from Barrass and in this they had succeeded – but for the post.

In little more than a week after her arrival in the city, Penelope had written to Barrass care of the Swansea sorting office and he had written back, addressing the letter to her care of Coakley's Coffee House for her to collect. The letter held in his hand was the third he had received and in it she declared her intention of writing to her father and pleading to be allowed home.

Soon, dear Barrass, we will be together again and then nothing will separate us.

She had signed it with her flourishing signature and below it had added a kiss.

He stared at the letter, imagining her sitting at some unknown desk, hiding the words from those who were caring for her, and then hurrying to hand it in to the post office for delivery to him, some 200 miles away. He sat beside Markus's gate and in his mind he was composing a reply, suggestions of what she should say to persuade her father.

He imagined too how it would be when they were reunited. He even rehearsed the words he would speak. His brown eyes were starry in the fading light and a half smile curved his lips.

'What are you dreaming about now, Barrass? Which woman is it this time?'

He jerked out of his reverie and saw Olwen standing beside him, hands on hips, bending over in obvious disapproval. He hurriedly hid the letter and stood up to greet her.

'Olwen, why are you here so late?'

'I saw you pass the house and guessed you were on your way to deliver a letter to Markus. Waiting for his reply, are you?'

'Maybe there'll be a letter to take in return, but it's the fee for delivering the letter that keeps me sitting here.'

'That and the letter you read so dreamily. You don't open letters and read other people's secrets, do you, Barrass? But what other explanation can there be? Surely no one would be writing to you?'

'The letter was for me! You know I would never open the Royal Mail! And – ' he added quickly, 'you must promise to say nothing. If you talk it will get someone into trouble.'

'That someone being – ?' she asked.

'No one to concern you.'

She went to him and slipped an arm around him. Hardly reaching his broad shoulder, she smiled up at him sweetly, but Barrass knew there was something she had to say and it would not be pleasant.

'Has my father told you to keep away from me?' she demanded, the smile still intact. 'Me, almost sixteen and with a father who treats me like a child?'

Barrass laughed. 'Almost sixteen?'

'Well, has he?'

'Spider loves you and wants only what is best,' he said, pulling away from her.

'What he *thinks* is best for me! Only I *know* what I want!

59

Barrass,' she pleaded, 'don't push me out of your life. Friends, aren't we?'

'Friends we'll always be, Olwen. But I'm older and Spider thinks it best if you make friends who are your own age. Being my friend seems to prevent that. I – I promised him not to encourage you to think of me as anything more than an acquaintance you have all but outgrown.'

'That was why he and Mam sent me to work at Ddole House. I knew it! And you encouraged them!'

She hit out at him, her thin arms flailing wildly and he laughingly held her close to stop the blows landing on him. He bent his head and felt her warm face against his neck and they stood there for a while, each taking comfort from the closeness, each unwilling to end the contact.

It was only when the servant returned with payment for the letter that Barrass slowly eased the girl away from him. He placed the coins in his bag and, with an arm around Olwen's shoulders, walked slowly back to her home. As they came in sight of it, he moved away from her and she looked up at him pleadingly.

They stopped, hidden by a freshly-leaved hawthorn on which blossom buds showed and he kissed her gently on the cheek, his arms wrapping her close to him. She was very dear to him, but her father was right, he was not worthy of her love.

Wriggling suddenly against him, she reached out and with her hands holding his curly head, she kissed him firmly and childlike on his lips before running off across the flattened grass to her open door. It was several minutes later that he missed Penelope's letter.

Daisy and Pansy, the Palmer twins, had always been inseparable. Daisy was the more confident of the two and it was she who led the opinions of the twosome. Occasionally, Pansy would protest at something Daisy said or did, but mostly she would follow her sister without protest. But of late, Daisy noticed that there was less and less enthusiasm when an invitation was received to attend a party or a dance. Pansy preferred to sit at her sewing, something her twin could never understand.

On this afternoon, Emma was out visiting friends, Pitcher had driven her, and the girls were alone in the upstairs living room above the alehouse bar. They were both sewing. Daisy was making embroidered chair backs for their sister, Violet. The cloth would hang over the backs of Violet's new velour chairs to prevent grease and dirt from the heads that rested there from soiling them. Pansy was making a neater job of embroidering a waistcoat, the small stitches building up a pattern of subtle greens and greys on a deeper green cloth.

When Pansy disappeared, Daisy did not become curious for a while, presuming her sister had gone to use the closet. When several minutes had passed, she put down her sewing, glad of the excuse to abandon it for a while.

All was quiet outside the parlour door, and she slipped down the stairs and into the passage behind the bar. Peeping through the half open door she saw the bar-room was empty, the few customers having chosen to sit outside in the weak sunshine. Whispering voices led her to the door of the cellar, which was raised to reveal stone steps leading down to where her father stored most of his supplies.

She hesitated. Apart from games when she had been a child, she and her sister had never ventured down the cold steps into the even colder cellar. Her mother had made it clear that the business did not concern them, the money made there was all that they need concern themselves with. So why was the sound of her sister's voice coming from there?

Pulling her shawl closely around her shoulders, she stepped warily down the stone steps, her slippered feet not making a sound. Pansy was sitting on a wooden crate which had been upturned. Beside her, talking to her in whispered tone that to Daisy's ears sounded companionable and familiar, was Arthur. Arthur's dog was on Pansy's lap and was enjoying the caresses of both of them. A lantern standing close by lit the trio, surrounding them in a glowing nimbus.

'Pansy!' Daisy said in a coarse whisper that made the couple spring apart like the jaws of a trap. 'What are you doing here?'

'It's the dog,' Pansy said at once, and her sister had the strong feeling that the story was a prepared and rehearsed one. 'It's the dog, he has a splinter in his paw. I came to help Arthur remove it.' By the time she had finished telling her reason, her tone had changed from shocked embarrassment to one of haughty control.

'Removing a splinter would be better done in the bright light of the sun, not feeling around in candle and torch light in the cellar,' Daisy said. 'Come on, get out of here before Dadda comes back. He won't believe your story either!' she added pointedly.

While her sister jumped down from the crate and hastily brushed down her woollen skirt to remove any dust, Daisy looked around her. The cellar was different from how she remembered it. It was smaller, less frightening. The walls, instead of being a dark grey stone, were whitewashed and clean. The floor was cobbled and surprisingly free of litter. In one corner, beside a huge barrel in which the dog obviously slept, was a bed. It was of sacking filled with heather, showing the indentation of Arthur's body. There was a cover too, one made of linen, ragged at the corners, that had once been on her and Daisy's bed.

She didn't follow her sister when she and Arthur made for the steps, but walked to the end of the cellar where, she remembered, the room had continued with a lower ceiling. So this was where the illegal goods were hidden. Her sharp eyes noticed the slight gap between the wall and one of the pillars. The end had clearly been partitioned off. It was not only the uncertain memory of childhood plus growing up into a new concept of size that made the place appear to be smaller. It really had shrunk.

Daisy had always known about the smuggling, but had accepted it as a part of life that did not concern her. Now she thought about the danger and felt a surprising warmth and love for her father, who had risked so much to give them a comfortable life. She was smiling as she climbed back up into the brightness of daylight after her sister.

Daisy didn't return to the drawing room. Let her sister wonder for a while about how she would deal with her discovery. Befriending a servant like Arthur would make their mother very angry. She had no intention of telling Emma about what she had seen in the cellar, but best to let her sister worry a little. That way she'll be extra nice to me for a while at least, she smiled. Perhaps even give me that brooch of hers I so admire.

She stood at the doorway of the alehouse, another forbidden thing to do, and looked out at the sea and at the small houses nestled so dangerously close to it. Almost touching the tidemark, their walls were green and patterned with seaweed and the small crustaceans that depended on the twice daily tide for nourishment. A group of people was sitting watching the boats being prepared for their next voyage, and others were standing looking up towards Kenneth's house, waiting for the arrival of Barrass with letters and news from his travels.

So that was why the alehouse was empty. Everyone gathering for gossip that came with the Post. She pushed the door closed, unreasonably angry with the disloyalty of the customers who had left their tables to stand and wait at Kenneth's door. Further down the road, small groups of people were heading towards the house on the bank. They had been waiting at other establishments, supping ale to while away the time before the arrival of Barrass.

She watched as Barrass came into view, his red waistcoat visible long before he was close enough to be recognized. Stepping outside, she saw people gather around the bottom of the bank below the receiving house. Kenneth opened his door and stepped out to stand importantly waiting for the letters to be handed to him, his nose raised as if to compensate for his lack of height.

Ceinwen followed behind him and it was she who took the bag and the notebook in which Barrass had reported all his transactions. Kenneth talked with Barrass for a few moments then, while the boy went inside to be given a drink, Kenneth took his customary place and began to tell his audience the news brought back by the letter-carrier.

Barrass returned, mug in hand, to prompt him, but it was Kenneth who told the news, acting out some of the reports passed to him by Barrass. Ceinwen came out with trays of small cakes and fancies to sell, and the people who sat listening to Kenneth's performance and discussing the few items of gossip Barrass had brought, chewed the cakes and sweetmeats, passing money into Ceinwen's willing hands.

At the corner of the alehouse the wind whipped Daisy's hair into a dark cloud. The coldness of the air was unnoticed as her mind filled with thoughts and ideas that excited her making her unaware of the discomfort. What if the letter-carrying could be taken from Kenneth who didn't deserve it anyway, and brought to the alehouse? People would wait there, take food from their tables instead of buying Ceinwen's offerings. Even those who habitually waited at other eating establishments might prefer to wait at the place where Barrass arrived with news and letters.

Her rather severe expression softened as she imagined the scene. A comfortable place, warm and with good food and ale easily available would make people gather and, more importantly, stay, until Barrass came with the letters. He would sit among them and entertain them with his gossip while they ate Pitcher's food and drank Pitcher's ale. They wouldn't have to stand in all weathers and listen to the self-important pronouncements and opinions of Kenneth!

Unaware of how closely her thoughts matched those of her father, she ran in to talk her ideas over with Pansy.

'Not that it would involve us,' she explained to her sister, who had returned industriously to her sewing, but with tension in her straight back and tight jaw. 'But it would bring in more custom and that means we might not have to lose our clothing allowance after all!'

Pansy's answers and comments were vague. Daisy considered beginning over again but decided not.

Pansy was thinking about the possibility of Arthur losing his place. She was unaware of what Daisy was telling her, waiting for her to finish so she could ask for her promise not to tell.

'You won't tell Mamma, I mean about me going down the cellar?' Daisy asked anxiously. 'It isn't that I mind. Mamma's punishments are hardly severe. It's for Arthur's sake I would rather she did not know. It was nothing but a kindness for a poor animal on my part, but Mother will not understand. If Arthur loses his place it will be his home as well as his work. What would he do?' Pansy looked at her sister and saw that she had not listened to a word of her pleading.

'Daisy, my dear?' she questioned. 'Do you agree?'

'I think I will talk to Dadda this evening,' Daisy replied.

'What? About Arthur? Daisy, you cannot!' Pansy stood up in alarm.

'No, sister dear. About another matter entirely.' Daisy smiled.

Chapter Five

When Barrass rode back from Swansea with the letters a few mornings later, Pitcher was waiting for him. This time, it was not a letter Pitcher was anxious to see, but Barrass himself.

'Barrass, I want to talk to you. Come-along-a-me and get some food inside you, then spare me a while before you set off.'

Barrass gladly agreed. The breakfasts served to him by Arthur were large and nourishing.

He took the postbag to Ceinwen for sorting and took pleasure in refusing her offering of ale and a crust of bread.

'Pitcher has invited me for food,' he said. 'Arthur has it cooking already. Damn, I think I can smell it from here.'

'Don't dawdle, boy,' Kenneth warned. 'There's a letter for Llanmadoc and that means you go the long way round.'

Barrass groaned. What was it about that village that it attracted men of business who wrote frequent letters? Small farms and a church was all that was there!

When he had eaten his fill, Arthur left them and Pitcher sat beside him near the smoking fire.

'Emma and me, we want you to come back and live here,' he said. 'It's not right, you living in a damp old place and walking all the miles you do. There's the food too. You know how much store Emma holds for a full belly. She wants you to live and eat with us. You can share the cellar with Arthur.'

'Emma does?' Barrass was surprised, knowing how much Emma had hated the idea of him being under the same roof as her daughters. 'But why, Pitcher? What's changed her opinion of me?'

'Her opinion hasn't changed, boy,' Pitcher laughed. 'She still thinks you a danger to any young girl with a less than downright ugly face. You won't be allowed upstairs in her living rooms, just the cellar and yard. And the bar-room should you ever feel like helping out.'

'I still don't see why – ' Barrass frowned, his dark eyes lighting up at the thought of a dry bed, meals to satisfy his large appetite and best of all, some company to share the hours between work and sleep. He looked at Pitcher and saw the man was uncomfortable. 'You haven't told me the full story, have you?' he questioned. 'I just know there must be a reason for Emma's agreement.'

Pitcher looked at the young man, then nodded as if coming to a decision.

'I want to tell you something of my plans, but I beg you to keep a still tongue once you know of them.' When Barrass nodded, he went on, 'Me and Emma think to try and take the Post Office arrangement from Kenneth. He doesn't deserve it, not doing any of the work himself and paying you less than an idiot could earn mending roads.' He waited to see the reaction. Barrass looked surprised but he did not interrupt.

'Seems to me that instead of people standing out in all weathers for their letters and the news you bring, they would be better served to wait in here with ale and some food to comfort them while they wait. Emma and me, we thought to go and see the Deputy Postmaster in Swansea and ask him to write to London on our behalf. There you have it. Well, what's your opinion?'

'Pitcher, you can't take from Kenneth and Ceinwen!'

'I've been awake half the night pondering over it, and I can't think of a single reason why not!'

'Just – take his living from him?'

'It's you who does the work, boy, you and Ceinwen. Kenneth just puffs on his pipe and struts importantly and gives the impression he does it all.'

Barrass stood to leave, a frown darkening his features.

'I have to go. I'll think about it while I travel, but I don't feel that it's right, Pitcher.'

'One more thing. I might not have thought to do anything even though the idea was in my mind, but d'you know, my daughter, Daisy, came to me with the same idea? Yes, she and I thought along the same lines! And her a young lady brought up to look pretty and not much else besides. Surprised me proper she did. I never thought a daughter brought up by Emma would ever have the brains to see a business opportunity as sharp as that one.' He followed Barrass to the door. 'Goes to show, doesn't it? The idea must be a good one if me and my empty-headed daughter came up with the identical thought?'

When Barrass went back to collect his bag, he could not meet Kenneth's eye. Although the idea was not his, just knowing of what Pitcher planned made him carry the guilt of it. He set off with a solemn expression and for the first time hated the prospect of the long miles ahead of him. He felt the need to sit and think about Pitcher's words and decide how his own conscience would deal with the idea.

He had no delivery for Ddole House, but it was his intention to go there first. He had to see Olwen and retrieve the letter she had undoubtedly stolen from him. If William Ddole saw the message from his daughter, Penelope would undoubtedly suffer further punishment. The letter made clear her intention of seeing Barrass again as soon as she were allowed to return home. William Ddole would make sure she stayed away for even longer than he now intended.

When he had missed the letter, soon after leaving Olwen on the cliffs near her home, he had searched the cliff path between where he had missed it and the gate where he had sat reading it. To and fro he had gone until long after the light had faded, forgetting about the letters on his shoulder and forgetting his arrangement to meet Kenneth near the green lane.

The watchman at Markus's house came out suspiciously and demanded to know what he was about. When Barrass explained that he had lost a letter, the grumpy man had helped him search. Far beyond the path, inland across the small fields they wandered. There was only a slight breeze but they made certain the letter hadn't been lifted and dropped beyond the vicinity of the tree-lined path. They found a kerchief torn and ragged, a dead rabbit and a shoe, but no letter.

Barrass had slept badly. He wondered if somehow the letter would reach William Ddole and planned his response to the man's accusations. It was as morning approached that he came to the conclusion that Olwen had taken it. Relief, then anger stirred in him and he wanted to rise then and go and face her, demand she return it. He wished he had done what he had promised, and destroyed it. Like the other two, he had planned

67

to keep it beneath his mattress so he could re-read them all.

When he arrived at Ddole House there was an air of abandonment about the place. The kitchen door was shut and there was no sign of activity. Barrass began to fit the silence with the loss of the letter and thought that William had gone storming to London to demand tighter control over Penelope. The explanation was simpler.

'Master Ddole has gone to Bristol on business,' Dozy Bethan told him. 'We've been given some spring-cleaning to do then we can relax a little. *That* makes a change in a busy house like this! Seranne and Florrie are in town replenishing the stores, Olwen has been given the day to spend as she will. Tomorrow is my turn and I think I'll just have a lazy day,' she said slowly. 'Best to take things easy while you can.'

Barrass was angry. He did not have the time to go searching for Olwen, he had to get on with his journey. It would be tomorrow before he would be back in the village, another day to worry about the whereabouts of the damaging letter.

After reaching Llanmadoc and delivering the letter, he was offered a ride and late afternoon found him in Port-Eynon, with hours to spend worrying about who was examining the note meant for him only.

The accommodation arranged for him was poor and he defiantly turned away from it and asked at one of the houses for a bed and a meal. The meal was fish, but better cooked than at his usual lodgings, and well served by an attractive woman, Charity, whose husband was out with the boats.

Charity made it clear that she did not sleep well alone and Barrass, unhappy and worried as he was, took little persuading to slide into her bed and comfort her. When he eventually slept he did not dream about Penelope being confronted by her angry father, but of the soft, welcoming body of the fisherman's wife.

He was jerked from his slumbers by Charity shaking him.

'The tide has turned, he'll be here soon!' she warned, and without a morsel to break his fast or a sip to ease his dry throat, he was wrapped in a kiss full of passion and promise, then pushed out through the door into the cold morning.

He still hadn't given much thought to Pitcher's proposal and when he returned to Kenneth's house later that day, he handed in the letter bag and walked away from the direction of the ale-

68

house, not ready to discuss it. He went straight to the cliff path intending to search for Olwen.

She was on the grass at the edge of the cliffs, kneeling admiring the flowers that abounded amid the short grasses and low shrubs. For a moment his anger left him and he stood watching her, admiring her innocent beauty. She looked up and saw him and smiled, her wide eyes as blue as the bugloss that flowered in June. The freckles that covered her face so delightfully in summer were already apparent.

'Barrass, come and see,' she said and he bent down beside her.

As excited as a child, she pointed out the boldly blue spring squill and the less bright bugle. Sheepsbit also blue peered shyly just above the grass and nearby, the almost unnoticed ground ivy. She pressed the leaves of the wild thyme for him to smell its strong fragrance and found a clump of the sage-like wild clary for him to admire. Forgetting his mistrust of her, he marvelled with her at the miniature beauty so casually displayed about them.

He had considered his tactics and began by telling her that he was indeed in touch with Penelope.

'She was so distressed at being sent away from her home and all her friends,' he said, 'that she needs to keep a contact. Her love for me is only loneliness and unhappiness,' he added. 'I would hate her to be in trouble for writing to me, wouldn't you? You are her friend too. I have to find that letter to make sure her father doesn't see it.'

Silently, Olwen felt in the pocket of her full, cotton skirt and handed him the letter.

'I wanted to read it but I couldn't. If it was talk of your loving, I couldn't bear to know,' she whispered.

They were silent for a while, neither knowing what to say. Then Barrass put the letter safely inside his coat and began to talk to her about Pitcher's intentions to take the postal deliveries from Kenneth.

'Kenneth offered it to Dan you know,' she told him. 'When Dan married Enyd, he had the chance never to go to sea again, but the sea is what he wants. Enyd knows that now.'

'You don't sound angry? Don't you think it's wrong of Pitcher to cheat Kenneth out of his living?'

69

'No, Barrass, I don't! Kenneth cheats on you. He gives you as little as he can and makes you do all the work. Ceinwen breaks the law and serves drink from the back window of her house. He cheats on Ceinwen too,' she added, looking at him with a bold, provocative stare. 'Him going to the green lane to see that Betson-the-flowers whenever he can. No, Pitcher is right to try and take the post. I wish him luck!' She concentrated on a flower she had just picked for a moment or two, then went on, 'You want to be someone important, don't you, Barrass? Well, to be important you have to be determined and even a bit ruthless. William Ddole wouldn't hesitate to take something from someone else if the need and opportunity were there.'

'Olwen!' Barrass said in surprise.

'This would mean you'd have a fairer share of the money from the letters, wouldn't it? Pitcher is a more honest man than Kenneth?'

'Well, yes, he is, but – '

'Then it's Pitcher you should trust. Be bold, and do as Pitcher says if you want to rise in the world.'

'Olwen, you constantly amaze me,' he said.

'Surprises in plenty you'll get from me, once you accept that my childhood is over!' She snuggled against him and slid her arm around his waist as they walked companionably back.

They separated before they could be seen and Barrass prepared to go down the path to the village.

'Do you love her, Barrass?' she dared to ask. 'Would you marry Penelope Ddole if you could?'

'No chance,' he said lightly, 'saving myself for when you grow up, aren't I?'

'Don't tease me!' She bent and grabbed handfuls of grass which she threw at him before running through the open door of the cottage. He watched her go, a smile on his face as she lifted her long skirt revealing bare feet and legs as thin as lace-makers' bobbins.

The coach from Bristol was lurching badly, throwing William Ddole and his fellow-travellers first one way then another. The roads were bad after the winter mud and frost and so far, the stretch over which they were passing had not been repaired. Ruts in the surface were soft with the recent and continuing rain, yet deep enough to threaten to roll the coach far enough to dislodge those unfortunates riding up on top. He was tired and the sudden uncomfortable jerks as the coach leaned and then righted itself made his neck ache. Dozing fitfully, he found this journey interminably long.

When the way became less bumpy, an elderly woman who sat opposite him stood and prepared to use the coach pot that stood between the seats. William sighed, took out his handkerchief to attempt to block out the smell that emanated from the foul contraption. He saw by glancing around at the faces, the efforts of others to hold their breath until the copper lid was safely back in place, the inserted china bowl safely hidden from sight.

Outside, the weather reflected his mood, rain and gusting winds making it impossible to allow any fresh air into the coach. The windows were steamy and even if it were daylight, he would have been unable to see anything to break the monotony of his ride. The passengers had at first been prepared to chatter, but lethargy and tiredness soon discouraged them, the effort required too much for more than the occasional politenesses.

He imagined the journey from the coach terminus in Swansea to his home in Mumbles. Another uncomfortable ride. As always at this stage of a journey home, he wondered why he had left, and half promised himself that it would be the last time he would travel so far. But business frequently called him away and sometimes, Ddole House was so large, so empty, that he had to find a reason to escape from it.

The house was well-run, although, with Florrie threatening to leave and marry Daniels, another change was likely. Dozy Bethan and young Olwen managed well enough. Seranne was a capable cook, even if she lacked Florrie's flair. He was well blessed with his staff, but they did nothing to hide the emptiness.

He missed his wife, who had died so recently. He still wore the black mourning clothes that the villagers thought an extravagance but which gave him inexplicable comfort: the clothes and the constant visits to her grave, which he covered with any flowers he could obtain.

He bitterly regretted sending his only daughter, Penelope, to live in London. At the time, with his wife so recently taken from him, he had lacked the confidence to deal with the matter of her affair with the local boy any differently. Now there were only servants to welcome him back. He sighed, adding a little more to the opaqueness of the coach windows. Servants weren't enough.

The coach clattered to a stop in the courtyard of the Coaching Inn in Wind Street, and he stretched his stiff limbs preparing to dismount. The old woman in the corner had fallen asleep and he left it to the guard to waken her, sliding past her spread-eagled feet and avoiding touching the unpleasant coachpot as he stepped down on to the rough, cobbled surface.

The rain continued, determined, he thought irritably, to make the day as unpleasant as possible up to the final moment. He ran into the inn leaving the servants to fetch his luggage and went to buy himself food and drink. David was waiting at a table near the fire, a glass of ale in front of him, his hat on a chair beside him.

'Master Ddole, sir, glad I am to see you. What a day! What a journey you must have had!'

William allowed the boy to chatter, while he sat before the fire and allowed the welcome warmth gradually to ease away the stiffness of the journey.

He did not stay long, tempted as he was to ask for a bed for the night and delay his arrival until the following day. David brought the small carriage to the door of the inn and William sank into the soft, leather seats, hoping the roads were not blocked, or deeply muddied. He had no fancy for any more delays or other trouble this night.

He was met by Seranne, who had stayed past her usual time to greet him.

'Food is ready and hot as you'd wish, sir,' she said, as she followed him through to the dining room, where a cheery fire glowed. 'A warm meal will be what you need after a journey like that.'

'Have you ever travelled on a coach, Seranne?' he asked.

Seranne shook her head reproachfully. 'Sir, what would I be doing riding on one of those things? I've never been further than I can comfortably walk!'

When he had eaten, Seranne put her coat on to go home.

'You had a visitor this afternoon,' she told him. 'I said she was to come back tomorrow and not before nine.'

'A visitor? Who would that be?'

'Says she's from Bristol, sir, and come about the job of housekeeper.'

'From Bristol you say? But who – ? Good heavens, Seranne. I spoke to a lady there only hours before I set off. How did she arrive before me?'

'I sent her to find a bed with Bessie Rees, although I doubt she'll be very comfortable,' Seranne added.

Too tired to vex himself with the answers he went to bed and forgot about it until the morning.

Florrie was there when he rose the next morning. He felt refreshed and over his melancholy. He took the list she had written down, names of those women who had applied for the position she was about to vacate.

'I think it should be you who chooses, not me,' he smiled. 'How can a mere man know what to ask, and how to evaluate the answers?'

'Best you see them at least,' Florrie said. 'You will know well enough those whom you can't abear to have in your house.'

Looking down the list, William asked to see Bessie Rees.

'She looked after Henry Harris your secretary well enough until he died,' Florrie reminded him, 'and now looks after John Maddern when he is here. But the house is small, and there's never been any entertaining to fluster her.'

William interviewed the elderly woman and saw at once what Florrie's words implied; Bessie had not the confidence. He thanked her kindly for attending and for giving a bed to the visitor from Bristol. Then he asked Florrie to send in the next on this list.

'Daniels's sister!' he exclaimed, looking at the list. 'But it's bad enough having your fiancé himself wandering in and out of my kitchen, without his sister come spying inside my home!'

'I did hint, sir, that she might be lacking in experience,' Florrie smiled. 'Best you see her though, to show there's no unhealthy concern over her brother being who he is, sir.'

Harriet, the sister of Carter Phillips, was also rejected as both Florrie and William considered her 'too flighty'. Carrie, the one-time maid was also turned down as she had a small child, by Barrass, and even the thought of that young man made William resentful. Barrass was to blame for Penelope's sojourn in London.

Finally there was only the woman from Bristol, whom Florrie had kept waiting until the last, convinced that she was the only likely candidate.

'The lady is called Mistress Annie Evans,' she told William. 'A widow of a sailor. She has run a respectable house where young and old rent rooms, and she has cooked for them and provided warm, clean beds. Or so she tells me, sir,' she added cautiously. 'She has letters confirming that, but none of the signatures are known to me.'

'Write letters to them asking for assurance if you please, Florrie.' William rubbed his eyes wearily. All this nonsense was not for a man to do. Oh, how he missed the unnoticed efficiency of Dorothy. He was not meant to be a widower so young. He stretched his long legs, and walked around the room while he waited for Mistress Annie Evans to be shown in.

He was startled by her youthfulness. Her hair was light brown and was fashionably styled in a loose halo pushed back and fastened at the centre with a small, twisted pigtail of a bun. Her lashes and eyebrows were thick and gave the impression that her eyes were small. When she smiled, her eyes shrank even further in creases of accustomed good humour.

When she spoke it was in quiet, modulated tones and at once, William knew that this woman would be the one to organize his life and allow him to forget the problems that occurred from day to day. He hardly knew what to ask her, and it was Florrie who drew the information that Annie Evans was forty-two and had no children, that she was free to start at once as she had sold her business in Bristol, having the desire for a change of scene.

'As I intend to leave in a month or so,' Florrie said, 'I suggest she works with me and learns how you like things done, sir.'

William agreed and he rode out to talk to Edwin Prince, relaxed, knowing that the irritation and misery of so many household changes would soon be a thing of the past. Annie Evans would take all the strands of his daily life into her small, yet capable hands.

As requested, Florrie wrote to the people whom Annie Evans had given as referees and asked for confirmation of their remarks. She felt sad as she did so, resenting the woman who was to replace her. She had worked at Ddole House since she was twelve, starting as a kitchen maid and learning from the various

74

cooks that had come and gone, until, when they were again without someone to organize the kitchen, she had stepped into the position and had never been asked to leave it. When Dorothy Ddole had died and Penelope had been sent to London, she had slipped just as easily into the role of housekeeper.

The four letters finished and sealed, she placed them on the small table near the kitchen door with several others written by William, to wait for Barrass's next visit. Next, she had to make ready a room for the new arrival. Annie would have to use Penelope's room until the day she herself left to marry Daniels, the Keeper of the Peace.

The thought thrilled her. At forty-five she had given up all hope of marrying. Yet there was a residue of regret. The work here was hard, the hours long, but she suspected that looking after Ponsonby Daniels and his five children would be harder and after a few exciting months, thankless.

She shook off her apprehensive mood and went into the kitchen to check on the day's activities. Behind her, as the kitchen door closed, the cloaked and hooded figure of Annie Evans re-entered the house and picked up the four letters and, slipping them into her capacious pocket, left the house.

Annie smiled deeply as she hurried along the drive and made for the house of Bessie Rees. Good fortune was smiling on her without doubt. She had booked a seat on the coach for Swansea, choosing the town at random. Then, as she sat sipping tea and waiting for the time to take her place, had heard William Ddole talking and revealing his need for a housekeeper.

His loneliness and unhappiness were apparent and the look of him pleased her. She would soon make herself indispensable to him and who knew what would come after that? The previously booked seat had enabled her to arrive before him and make the appointment to be interviewed without delay.

Having decided to take the business of the Gower letters from Kenneth, and persuading Barrass to agree, Pitcher then had no idea how to set about it.

'Seems we'll have to wait for something to happen,' he said to Emma one evening a few weeks after his discussion with Barrass. 'Wait for something to happen that we can take advantage of.'

75

'Such as what, Pitcher?' his wife asked, raising her eyes from her sewing to look at him curiously. 'What sort of "something"?'

'I don't know and that's the vexing part. I just have to hope that something will happen and that we are sharp enough to grab the opportunity it offers.'

'You could offer Barrass the use of a pony for his travels,' Emma suggested. 'Specially if you want him to help you with the building work. That way he'd be a partner to you and less of a partner to Kenneth.'

Pitcher went to look at the stables and decided that he needed to buy a small Welsh cob, a sturdy animal that could cope with the weather and the terrain and carry Barrass with ease. He found one easily enough after a word with Edwin Prince, who seemed to have dealings in many and varied trades. He rode the cob back, and after stabling it, called at the room behind Kenneth's house and left a note for Barrass to call on him at the earliest moment.

'Come-along-a-me, boy,' he said when Barrass appeared. Curiosity widened Barrass's brown eyes and raised his thick eyebrows.

'Not news of a change already?' Barrass asked in a whisper.

'A beginning, boy, a beginning,' Pitcher smiled. He walked to the stable yard and opened the door of a stall to reveal the horse. 'There you are, Barrass, and she's yours. Now what d'you think of that? Jethro he's called.'

'Mine? But – why?'

'Not such a generous gift. I want you to have some time and strength left at the end of your day to work with me on the changes to the alehouse,' Pitcher confessed. 'Go on, boy, try him out, you'll find him a comfortable and good-natured ride.'

Not waiting to be asked twice, Barrass saddled the horse and with a shriek of joy, rode off along the road which led around and up to the cliffs where Olwen lived.

'Olwen!' he called, knowing that at such a moment, she *had* to be there to share it. Mary came out followed by Spider, and they admired both the horse and the generosity of Pitcher in providing it for his use.

'Not providing him,' Barrass almost shouted. 'He's mine! Jethro is mine! Where's Olwen, I must show her.'

'Not yet back from her work,' Mary said.

Disapproval showed in Mary's face and she glanced at Spider anxiously. Barrass knew they couldn't refuse, not today, not when he had such joyous news to share with her. 'I'll go and meet her then.' He looked at Spider, only a slightly tilted head showing that he was asking permission.

'Go you,' Spider nodded. 'Olwen will love to meet your new friend.' Behind him stood the tall smiling figure of his son, Dan, with Enyd on whose young face a scowl deepened. Good fortune for others was not something she could celebrate. Mistress Powell stepped from between them, her wrinkled face lighting up at the boy's obvious delight. They all waved him off as he remounted and set off, cheering him as if he were an adventurer setting off for dangerous places.

Barrass saw Olwen strolling down the green lane, a bunch of bluebells in her arms, and when he stopped near her, the smell of the flowers rose to meet him and became a part of her, the sweetness and freshness of the early summer becoming the perfume and newness of her youth and beauty.

'I have a friend who would like to meet you,' he smiled, his voice thick with unaccustomed emotion. She was a part of this perfect day, the joy and excitement of Pitcher's gift embodied in her welcoming smile. 'Meet Jethro, my own horse, given to me by Pitcher.'

As he had guessed, Olwen's excitement matched his own and she hugged the gentle-eyed animal and Barrass in turn. A tirade of questions burst from her and he laughed as he tried to answer them all.

'Come on, today your father won't object to my giving you a ride.' He lifted her up on to the animal's back and mounted behind her. A click of his tongue and they were off, along the lane, across the fields, startling flocks of pigeons that were feeding on newly germinated peas and beans, laughing as they answered the shouted comments of friends.

Along the cliff path they rode, not fast as the path was unsafe in places, but to Olwen they seemed to be flying, her hair streaked out behind her like a banner held by a warrior riding off to war. They went down on to the beach called Longland to the west of the village, and then, excitement took all three of them in its grip and the horse was given its head. They raced across the hard sand, turning and racing back. The horse, firm and sure-

footed, gave them a smooth ride, apparently enjoying the freedom as much as its riders.

Returning to the cliff path, Barrass slackened the reins and
allowed Jethro to walk. Olwen was leaning against him, the
smell of her had changed to send wafts of the sea breezes up to
him, clean, fresh and bewitching. It was with regret that he dismounted and helped her down outside the white-painted cottage on the cliffs, where her parents waited for her. Handing her
back to them was a wrench.

He returned to the stables and a smiling Pitcher.

'Thank you. I have never had a more wonderful gift,' Barrass
said.

'The idea was Emma's,' Pitcher said, brushing the gratitude
aside. 'Tomorrow when you go on your round, we'll see how
much it helps.'

Barrass stayed at the stables for a long time, caressing Jethro,
whispering to him, his heart threatening to burst with the happiness of the day. He had never owned anything apart from the
clothes he wore, and the generous gift from Pitcher had surprised and uplifted him.

But it was thoughts of Olwen, pressed against him, laughing
up at him, sharing his moment of happiness as they rode across
the sands of Longland that filled his mind as he drifted into sleep
that night. In his dreams they rode together while Spider and
Mary nodded their approval, and he was transported out of the
shabby, damp room to the cliffs where the sun shone and everyone laughed with them and wished them well.

Chapter Six

Pitcher began drawing plans of the alterations as soon as he knew clearly what would be required by the licence office. The walls to come down were marked and lines drawn where new ones would rise.

'The yard and wall at the side of the stables must stay, I think,' Barrass said as Pitcher stared at it wondering about an extension. 'The boys use it for playing "Fives" and I think they would move to another drinking house if we deprived them of it.'

'I agree,' Pitcher smiled, 'and damn me for not thinking of it myself!'

The wall was fronted by a flat piece of ground that had once been the floor of a store. It made an excellent court on which to play the game, which involved hitting the ball against the wall with a hand, which was usually protected by a glove or with material wound around it. For youngsters of less than three up to grown men, the wall was a popular and busy place. Barrass was right, the participants who collapsed with exhaustion and had to be revived by drink from Pitcher's cellars would move somewhere else, and that would be a loss of good will as well as good money.

'I did think to include a shovel board in the plans, Barrass,' Pitcher mused, 'but have decided that the space could be better used. Some, they say, are longer than three feet by thirty, though that I doubt.'

'The smaller penny boards are popular now in London, or so the travellers tell us. Why not add one of those, they take up only a smallish table?'

'Perhaps we'll ask someone travelling to London or Bristol to buy one for us.'

'The stables will need a lot of changing,' Barrass said, looking at the narrow opening that required the wagoners to reverse in before returning to town. 'We'll have to make more room and widen the entrance so they can drive in and turn in the yard.'

'It's all in my plans,' Pitcher assured him. 'Storage under a low roof for temporary callers as well as flat carts; hay barns and warm stalls; the visitors will have the best, Barrass, the best.'

Sitting at the window of her parlour looking down at the two men below, Emma sighed. Only just clear of the dust and rubble of the recent building of the parlour, she had now to face weeks of it again. Dust and mess threatening her precious new furnishings, and the noise which made it extremely difficult to entertain. She patted her wig and tucked in a few stray ends and went down to join them.

'I want you to promise that it will be completed before the summer ends, Pitcher,' she pleaded. 'There's no point in getting it done then finding the travellers you hope to attract are all ensconced in their own home for the winter.'

'Before summer's end, Emma, I promise you that,' he smiled. 'Just so long as you don't dawdle about the choice of furnishings for the rooms we will be letting.'

'Ivor Baker has already been given the order to make chests of drawers and small tables for the rooms. It isn't me who's slow, Mr Palmer!' she added with an offended tilt of her head.

Emma and Pitcher's twins were not only unmarried; they had not even followers to boast of. Daisy was popular, seeming to receive plenty of invitations which she sometimes refused to attend unless her sister, Pansy, were invited too, but Pansy seemed reluctant to go to the parties and musical evenings that friends arranged. She seemed content to sit at her sewing, or take a gentle stroll along the shore, and even – horror of horrors – sit with the parlour door open listening to the activity in the bar-room below.

The recently built parlour was intended to improve things. With a decent room to withdraw to after a meal, Emma hoped that the increase in social gatherings she could now arrange would bring a selection of suitable young men for the girls to meet. Now, the fresh building work with its inconveniences had put a stop to it all for weeks, perhaps months.

It was only the strong possibility of better trade once the work was completed that stopped her from screaming in frustration.

The grand carriages were bound to stop and spill respectable and eligible gentlemen at their door. Better than the assorted carts and wagons that stopped at present. She smiled as she imagined the scene, a double wedding with the twins dressed identically in gowns bought from London with the money the alehouse would earn.

Pitcher, seeing the tranquil expression on his wife's face, smiled back at her and was startled to receive a scowl and a warning to 'hurry yourself!'

It had become a habit that the alehouse encouraged entertainment of a higher quality on several evenings of each week. Dan, Olwen's brother, had a fine tenor voice and he was paid with food and drink to sing for the people who gathered to hear him. Occasionally, Oak-tree Thomas played the fiddle and sometimes danced around crossed swords in a parody of the delicate and nimble footwork of the experts.

So it was with interest that Pitcher listened to the stranger who came to him and offered to play, dance and sing for his supper.

'My name is Cadwalader,' the small, dark-haired man introduced himself. 'I play the harp exceedingly well and dance a little. My voice is not unpleasant and I have a repertoire of some length.'

'Come at seven, we shall soon see if you boast untruthfully,' Pitcher smiled. 'The complaints fly faster than compliments with my regulars!'

Cadwalader left the bundle which included his Welsh harp at the alehouse and went to sit on the beach watching the sun setting in a red blaze over the horizon. The glow settled around him as he sat hugging his legs, his black clothes set afire by its brightness, the white streak in his black hair strikingly clear. Dan found him there, and recognized him from the day of his wedding party.

'You are passing through, again?' Dan asked curiously.

'I have been no further than the town of Swansea,' Cadwalader said, his hand reaching out in greeting. 'This place called me back although I have no business here. Except,' he added with a smile, 'except the promise to entertain at the alehouse of Pitcher Palmer this evening.'

'You sing?' Dan asked, interested. When the man nodded, he

said, 'Perhaps we can exchange a few songs?'

'How is your voice, high or low?' Cadwalader asked and to-gether they sang a few of their favourites and began rehearsing to sing a duet, Dan's tenor swelling and rising above the sound of the waves accompanied by the deeper tones of Cadwalader.

Pitcher, standing at the door of the alehouse with Barrass, nodded approval.

'Seems we have a new asset to our evenings,' he said.

'But who is he and where does he come from?'

'Who cares as long as people come-along-a my place and listen to him?'

Pitcher told everyone he met to spread the word of a new talent that would be performing on the following Thursday night. He knew that above all, except perhaps the excellence of his ale, the local people enjoyed a singer. Dan had increased his trade and perhaps Cadwalader would do the same. Thursday would be a busy night and well worth the food that was all Cad-walader asked for in return for his songs.

With the pony to make his journey easier, Barrass still stayed overnight on his thrice-weekly journey around Gower, but on the second day of each round of visits, he finished early. On Thursdays, this did not suit Kenneth.

'If you don't keep your promise, boy,' Kenneth whispered angrily as the letters were being sorted by Ceinwen, 'I shall have to think again about letting you do the work!'

'Who would do it for the money you pay me?' Barrass said, although his heart was pounding with the dread that Kenneth would do as he threatened and give the job to someone else. 'I cost you very little, with Pitcher feeding me more often than not. And I'm sure you can come to some other arrangement for meeting Betson-the-flowers.'

'Hush, boy! Got ears that are a cross between a buck rabbit and an excise man, Ceinwen has!'

'So change the subject in case she heard what I'm saying,' Barrass warned and smiled inwardly to see the man glance ner-vously towards the door.

'All right, but only for this week. With the summer coming on you can surely find a way of losing a few hours of an afternoon once a week!' The words were spat angrily out of a barely opened mouth. 'Think about it, boy.'

Barrass had thought about it and knew that the time he wasted could be used helping Pitcher with the new building work. With the aid of occasional labour, they had already made good progress. The walls were built of rocks brought from the nearby quarry, rolled down with little effort into the back of Pitcher's yard. Even small children helped with this for no fee except an occasional cake from Emma's kitchen, treating it as a game, chasing the stones after setting them free at the top of the slope, and shouting with glee.

At Ddole House there was tension. Annie Evans, who was to replace Florrie as housekeeper when that lady left to marry Daniels, was gradually persuading the other servants to take instructions from herself rather than Florrie. Florrie, who was still unwilling to give a date for her marriage to the Keeper of the Peace, relinquished her authority reluctantly and there was constant friction.

Olwen always seemed to be in the middle of it all. Seranne told her to fill the water buckets as the boy was not to be found, but she was stopped before she could get to the pump by Annie insisting she brought coal instead. Then as she struggled up the stairs with coal, Florrie stopped her and told her it was not her job to carry coal when she was paid to work in the kitchen and deal with food, and sent her to Edwin Prince with a note from William Ddole.

'It's enough to drive me into the ground, twisting and twirling one way then another,' she muttered to Bethan as she took off her coarse apron and gathered her cloak around her small form. 'How d'you manage to stay clear of their silent arguments?'

'I'm so slow that Annie Evans has given up on me.' Bethan smiled her slow smile and Olwen wondered how much of the girl's slowness was genuine and how much a way of avoiding too much work. Then she saw Bethan struggle to gather up the dried peas that had fallen on the floor and decided that the slowness made extra work and was indeed natural.

Both girls would have been worried if they had been able to listen to the conversation in William's study close by.

'But it's so unfair to you, sir,' Annie was saying softly. 'You having to pay the wage of two housekeepers. I know enough of

83

the way you like things done now to manage very well without the advice of Florrie. If she is to marry, then wouldn't it be kinder of you to tell her she is no longer needed here and she can go with a happy heart?'

'I suppose I hate change and there have been so many in my life of late,' William said.

'You won't notice anything, except perhaps a few pounds left over at the end of every week from the money you allow,' Annie said.

'You think Florrie is extravagant? My wife did not find her so?'

'Not extravagant, your comfort and the good food you enjoy are not to be criticized, but there is an unnecessary excess of people here. For one man to be taken care of takes only a few dedicated and devoted people, sir.'

'I do not wish any of the servants to be without work.'

'Work would be found for them, sir. But Bethan does very little for the money you pay her, and she has her keep which, in this house, means she is well fed and comfortable. I think she should go.'

'Bethan? She has been here since she was nine or ten!'

'And does no more work than she did then, sir. The little she does manage can easily be accomplished by Olwen.'

'No, Annie. I do not wish you to make changes, not yet.' William stood up from his desk and walked to look out of the window. 'I want to settle and feel that the stream of my life is flowing gently once more, not battering the rocks in a fierce waterfall, startling me constantly with its unexpected change of direction. Let things be.' He turned and she was standing close to him, her small eyes strangely attractive, her thick brows combed upwards in strong, furry lunettes. She smiled as he sharply turned away.

'I'll tell Seranne there are five for dinner, sir,' she said as she glided quietly out of the room.

She met Florrie as she stepped out into the passageway and beckoned to the woman to follow her. They went into the dining room, where the fire was laid but not yet set alight.

'Master Ddole is becoming concerned about the expense of your staying,' she said in an undertone, as if confiding in a friend. 'He will say nothing, yet, but I thought that, as you have

84

been so helpful to me I should warn you. Have you and Daniels arranged a day for your wedding?'

'No, we haven't, and Master Ddole gave me to understand there was no hurry,' Florrie said. She was flustered. The wedding was something she had not yet become convinced about and every step towards it added to her consternation. But perhaps she was being unfair, taking a wage for the work she now only partly did. 'Perhaps I should have a word –' she said.

Annie shook her head.

'I think he finds it hard to involve himself in the running of a household, which is after all work for a woman. Every query reminds him of the loss of his wife, and the absence of his daughter. Best we don't add to his distress.' She smiled, and put an arm around Florrie. 'We can sort this out without upsetting him, I'm sure.'

Olwen went through the fields towards the enlarged Long House where Edwin Prince lived with Violet and their baby daughter, Gabriella. Olwen did not like calling at the house. Gabriella was not Edwin Prince's child. Violet had not hidden the fact that the baby had been fathered by Barrass. Seeing the child and knowing it was proof of Barrass's love for Violet, was like the reopening of a tender wound.

To Olwen's dismay, the baby was outside in the mild air, swinging in a cradle that Ivor Baker had made for her, under a beech tree not far from the back door of the house. She could not resist a glance at the sleeping child.

Gabriella was wrapped in layers of clothing and under several blankets and embroidered covers. Her tiny head peeped out of a cotton bonnet, which was embroidered with pink and yellow flowers. Olwen searched the round face for recognition of the features of Barrass but could find none.

'What do you want with the baby, Olwen-the-fish?' a voice called and she saw Mistress Rees shaking a mat near the bank of the stream which ran near the garden's edge. The mat was thrown over a bush and Mistress Rees joined her in admiration of the child.

'There's a beautiful grandchild for Emma and Pitcher,' the woman cooed. 'So proud of her they must be.'

'It's Barrass's child!' Olwen said defiantly.

85

'But Violet Palmer *is* the mother. There's no doubting the mother now is there? But show me the baby that can prove who fathered it!' she laughed.

'And how is your daughter and *her* baby?' Olwen asked, hands on hips, half expecting to receive a swipe for her impertinence. But Mistress Rees smiled wider and said, 'Lovely she is, and none the worse for not being able to claim a father. I brought up Carrie without a man to help me and I'll help Carrie bring up little Maude too.'

Olwen handed her the note for Edwin Prince and walked slowly back to Ddole House. Seeing Barrass's baby and hearing news of another of his love-children, Maude Rees, had saddened her. How could she keep Barrass with so many girls willing to love him?

To her further dismay, she met Blodwen Baker as she reached the drive leading to the house. Blodwen was carrying sticks she had gathered in the wood nearby and with her, held firmly and closely to her was her baby, Beryl. Another child who, it was claimed, had been fathered by Barrass.

Olwen remembered helping Barrass to hide from Ivor Baker's wrath when he had been told of his daughter's condition. Having seen baby Gabriella Prince and heard news of Baby Maude Rees, she could not face seeing Blodwen's baby Beryl. She turned and ran up the drive and closed the kitchen door behind her as if she had been chased.

The kitchen was empty apart from Annie Evans.

'Don't pretend with me, Olwen,' Annie surprised her by saying. 'I saw you dawdling as if you had no work to finish, then run to appear breathless at the door as if you had run every inch of the way!'

'But I didn't – I wasn't trying to trick you, I – ' a sharp cuff under the ear that sent her flying across the room cut off the words.

'Don't think you'll be able to cheat on your work with me like you can with Florrie.' Annie's small eyes glittered, yet, to anyone watching, she still appeared to be smiling. Olwen threw off her cloak and forcing herself to hold back tears, went to the sink where a pile of dishes waited to be washed.

'The dishes are Bethan's job,' Annie said in a soft, gentle voice, 'you must fetch the coal.'

It was very late when Olwen had finished her day's work to the satisfaction of Annie Evans. Florrie had been given time off to spend with Daniels and his family, and Annie had found more and more work for both Olwen and Bethan. Tears were close as she walked into the small overfull room where her mother waited for her, a bowl of hot food prepared. She did not talk about her unhappy day, but ate the food, and then prepared to go to bed.

A sound outside made her listen attentively. Then her shoulders drooped. Whoever the visitor was, it would not be Barrass and there was no one else who would cheer her. Aware gradually of a stillness in the room, she looked up and saw that her father and mother were smiling, staring at her expectantly.

'Mamma?' she frowned. 'What is it?'

'Go outside and see,' Spider said, reaching for Mary's hand and holding it in his own.

A strange sound reached Olwen's ears and curiosity overcame her lethargy. Opening the door she followed the repeated sound and saw, in the sty Dan had made for the piglet, a young nanny goat. The little creature bounced with excitement as she approached, glad of company after being taken from its family.

'Mamma! Dadda! Is it mine?' Olwen shouted, bending to pick up the struggling form. 'It's beautiful. But where did it come from? Is it safe to keep it? It's a-w-f-u-l small.' She looked from one smiling face to another as she pressed her face against its roughness. Then a thought struck her. 'If it's from Madoc we'd be better off taking it to Daniels without delay.' Her face saddened at the thought of losing it; already she had begun to love the coarse-coated little animal.

'It's all right,' Spider assured her. 'It's a gift from me and from Barrass, who insisted you needed a replacement for the stolen piglet.'

'Dadda, thank you for the loveliest present I have ever had.' She walked the goat on a rope for a while, then went to put the goat into the pen, playing with it for hours, laughing at its sudden jumps and playful antics. She regretfully left it when Mary insisted she went to her bed, and turned repeatedly to look at its rather haughty nose squeezing through the wooden bars of the gate, and the eyes begging her to stay a while longer. Sleep shied away from her like a frisky and spiteful horse. In the room next to hers she could hear Enyd and Dan murmuring softly and the presence of them, so close, yet apart from her by both the flimsy wall and years of experience, made her feel the loneliness that an animal to care for did not alleviate. If only she could talk to Barrass, tell him how much she appreciated his thoughtfulness, talk to him about Annie's unkindness. He would make her feel better.

The house gradually melted into silence but she was still unable to relax and let the darkness claim her. The thought of how few hours were left before she had to rise and begin her day only added to her inability to sleep. In desperation she left her bed and went down the ladder to find herself a drink.

'I'll have a sip too if you please, Olwen,' a voice whispered and Olwen filled another cup and gave it to Mistress Powell who was sitting in the corner near the dying fire.

'I hope I didn't wake you,' Olwen whispered back. 'I couldn't sleep and thought if I came down and had a drink and got a bit chilled, the bed might be more tempting.'

'You didn't wake me. The night is long and lonely and I'm glad of you breaking up the hours,' the old woman said.

'Then I can stay a while?'

'Something is worrying you, Olwen?'

'Only the prospect of miserable times ahead.' She sounded so world-weary that chuckles emanated from the blankets wrapping Mistress Powell.

'Oh, I know you think it funny, but it's true. Once Florrie leaves Ddole House and we have that Annie Evans to deal with, life will be utterly miserable. She's a-w-f-u-l mean.'

'I seem to remember you said the same about Florrie when you first started work there.' Mistress Powell chuckled again.

'Florrie is a bit of a bully, but she is kind deep in her heart. But this one! Duw, she's going to be a trial and that's for sure!'

'Will you look for another place?'

'Not much chance of that. Besides, I can't risk having no job. Mam needs what I bring for when the weather is too fierce for Dadda and Dan to go out in the boat. It's little enough, but it helps.'

'This Annie Evans, are you sure she will be staying? Perhaps William Ddole will prefer to find someone else?'

'She'll show him how well she runs the place but not how she treats us to do it. And she'll throw out any of us who won't follow her. There's no chance of him knowing what she's really like, once Florrie's gone.'

'Don't be unhappy, Olwen, you're too young to be anything but content, and confident of the future. Look for another way of earning the money you bring back each week. Put up with this Annie Evans but keep your eyes open for something else. You never know what's around the corner.'

Olwen climbed back up to her bed but slept only intermittently, hearing the birds begin to sing as dawn woke them, and listening as Dan went down the ladder. Soon she would not even have Enyd and Dan near her during the long nights. Their room was finished and they would be sleeping there as soon as the fire had warmed the walls.

She was wide awake when Spider and Dan set off down the steep path to their boat, and heard her mother stirring the fire and murmuring softly to baby Dic who always woke the moment his mother did. Yet Mary had to shake her awake when it was time for her to get up and set off for Ddole House.

There were only three letters for Barrass to deliver on the way back home that day. One was addressed:

'To Blind Markus, so patient in his affliction.
The house on the cliffs, above the gut,
approaching Longland Bay, out of Swansea.'

That one would be the last. Another was addressed:

'To my friend Ponsonby Daniels,
whom God protect and preserve,
Keeper of the King's Peace,
at the village of Oystermouth
near the town of Swansea.'

The third was from Penelope Ddole and was addressed to her father at Ddole House.

Barrass pressed the letter against his cheek, imagining the hands of Penelope leaving a hint of her for him to capture. He longed to open it but that was something he dare not do. He hoped it contained a plea to her father to allow her to come back home, and silently prayed that the words would have the desired effect.

He went first to the house of Daniels, where he was surprised to see Florrie.

'Left Ddole House already?' he asked. 'Does this mean you have a day named for your marriage?'

Florrie shook her head and he saw that she was far from tranquil, nor was she pleased as was usually the case, to discuss her forthcoming wedding.

'I have just washed and dressed five unwilling children, prepared for them food which they refused to eat. Now I have the cheerful task of entertaining them until midday when there will be another battle to wash and feed them. The idea,' she went on as he stood unable to think of a way to reply, 'is for me to spend a few days here getting to know them. The trouble is,' she lowered her voice and half closed the door behind her, 'the trouble is, Barrass, the more I see of them the more I dislike the lot of them and at the moment, that includes Daniels!'

Barrass was smiling as he continued on his way. Conversations, opinions or revelations like that one were the fermentation of his day and added a zest which made the journeys far from boring. He wondered idly about the time he would marry. He had some money now, in Pitcher's keeping. Not much, but it was a start on the long road to respectability, and a home and a wife of his own. The road would be a long one because people would have to forget his early years before they could see him as anything but a ragged-arsed beggar.

He still felt certain that he and Violet Prince would have made an excellent couple, and with Penelope he would have been more than content. But if even Spider, a simple fisherman, discouraged him from seeing his daughter, what chance did he have of finding himself a wife whose ambitions were as high as his own? Although the prospect frightened him, he thought that one day he might have to go away, start again in a place where his past was whatever he chose to tell people it had been.

He spent the night with Charity, whose loving was a welcome interlude in a long ride. She turned him out before the dawn took the chill off the air and he rode disconsolately towards his first stop, idly wondering why he had succumbed to the temptation of sharing her bed, knowing as he did that he would have hours of the early morning to fill, with an empty belly for company.

At Ddole House he was offered no ale, and hungry and thirsty he rode across the fields towards the house of Markus. He stopped to look at the sea below him and admire the beautiful blue which was reflected from the sky above. Shadows of small clouds touched the water with a mysterious mottling but did nothing to detract from the brightness of the day or the feeling of excitement that comes with some calm days in summer. The wind was benign, almost nonexistent, soothing and without the threat of storms that was often felt even in its mildest caress.

He heard voices and turning to the left, saw two oyster boats making their way east to Horsepool Harbour. The voices seemed close and he could almost hear the words being casually spoken in the still air.

The fishing boat also making for the village was easily recognized as that belonging to Spider. His son, Dan, stood near the mast, singing, his voice coming clear and magical to where Barrass sat astride Jethro. He waved and shouted, and the figures on the boat waved back and shouted for him to join them at Pitcher's alehouse later. Smiling, Barrass pulled up Jethro's head from the grass he was munching and turned towards Markus's house, his last call.

The watchman stepped out as Barrass dismounted at the gate and held his hand out for the letter.

'I'll fetch your money,' the man said, and Barrass leaned against the gate and prepared for the usual long wait. But the man returned almost immediately. 'Go in, he wants a word with you,' he informed Barrass. 'I'll take charge of your horse.'

The house seemed like walking into a cave after the brightness of the afternoon. Being blind, Markus had no need of light and he seemed to resent supplying it for others; he kept the curtains closed and rarely allowed the wall lights to be lit, complaining of 'the foul smell of burning fat'.

Markus was sitting in a deep armchair in a corner of the room. He grunted a greeting as Barrass entered. A boy came in and handed Barrass a glass of strong beer and he was invited to seat himself. He sat on the edge of the chair to which Markus had gestured and sipped noisily at the drink. He knew the man's hearing was acute and the sound would enable him to know exactly where he was.

'I need your help, boy,' Markus said, looking in his direction. And Barrass's heart sank.

It was what he dreaded most, the demand, for demand it was, no matter how it was worded, that he help with the boats that came at night. He could not refuse, knowing that if he did, he would be considered to be against the men who arranged the smuggling. That could easily lead to his death. They had little patience with those who did not support them.

'What do you want me to do?' he said, hoping the dismay at being asked did not reveal itself in his voice for the keen eared Markus to hear.

'On Thursday night, one of the clock, bring your horse,' Markus said.

Barrass put down the emptied mug and muttering his agreement, hurried from the house.

Because of his gloomy concentration on the night's work to come, Barrass did not notice Olwen standing at the side of the path until she called to him.

'Barrass,' she shouted, 'I do believe you're asleep and letting Jethro carry you home without even a nudge to guide him! Come at once and see my new friend! Oh, Barrass, thank you for her, she's so beautiful and hairy and I think of you every time I see her.'

'Beautiful and hairy? Is that how you see me then, Olwen-the-fish?' he laughed, caught up at once in her excitement.

As always, he was pleased to see her. She lightened his mood and made him feel that the world was a truly wonderful place. He loved her, he knew that and the sight of her certainly warmed him, but not in the way he suspected she wanted him to love her. But he could not, must not feel for her the passion he had experienced with Violet and Penelope. She was not yet a woman. He admitted he had come close to it on one or two occasions, but had reminded himself of his protective role and held back. But seeing her wiped the gloom of his meeting with Markus from his mind, cleaning it like a wet cloth on the windows of the alehouse, letting in the light of day after a storm had covered them with salt and dirt.

'You look full of good cheer,' he smiled, dismounting from the patient Jethro and walking beside her.

'Who wouldn't be after receiving such a gift! And besides, Dan is singing on Thursday night at the alehouse and Dadda has said I can go,' she smiled. 'If only Annie Evans will let me finish early!'

'Is she plaguing you, Olwen?'

'So much that if someone doesn't marry me soon, I will have to look for another place.'

He laughed and ruffled her fair hair.

'And who would have you?' he teased and saw from the slight tightening of her lips that he had been unkind. 'Who would dare, with me to face if they even thought of taking you from me!' he added hoping his joking tone would ease her dismay.

'I will see Cadwalader there,' she said, her pertness touching him with fresh realization of her youth and his love for her.

'Then I will certainly be there too, so I can make sure he behaves,' he said. 'And as for Thursday, why don't you ask William Ddole himself, I'm sure he will not be unkind?'

'Ddole House won't be a happy place to work once Florrie leaves,' she sighed. 'I think this Annie will send us all packing and bring in people she chooses for herself.'

'I suppose that is understandable,' he said. 'It's like Florrie herself. She will have to change the rules set down by Daniels's first wife and his sister and start doing things her way once she and Daniels are wed – if it ever happens,' he chuckled. To cheer her, he told her of Florrie's difficulties and ended by whispering, 'Did you know the man's name is Ponsonby? It's small wonder that he walks with his head in the air and treats us all as his inferiors! Imagine being given a name like that. At a few days old, hardly bigger than a two penny rabbit, to be called Ponsonby!'

Barrass stopped to admire the goat that Spider had chosen at the market, and went on his way happier, yet with a feeling of uneasy guilt for the night he had spent with the fisherman's wife, Charity. What was it about Olwen that made him want her yet hold back from admitting it? He knew that it wasn't the disapproval of Mary and Spider. They would be persuaded once he showed them how much he really loved their daughter. Perhaps, he thought, it was the memories of his childhood still giving him a feeling of inferiority. It must fade soon, he told himself. One day I will wake up and realize that it doesn't matter any more.

The following Thursday evening, Barrass sat on a wooden settle beside Olwen, her mother and baby Dic. Even Mistress Powell had managed to walk down the path to enjoy the entertainment Pitcher had arranged. Spider helped Arthur and Pitcher serve the drinks, running up and down the cellar steps until they were all red-faced and breathless. The place was full so it seemed there was room for no more.

The fire burned brightly sending out so much heat that the doors were propped open to release it. Clay pipes bearing the sign of a pitcher on their bowls, made specially for the alehouse, were on display on the counter and Barrass bought one and filled it. In the fireplace several pipes already broken had been dropped on to a pile for Arthur to remove when he had time. Throughout the evening the pile on the counter offered for sale decreased as the collection of pieces on the grate grew.

The smoke from tobacco, excellent, indifferent and poor, rose from dozens of mouths and settled against the ceiling. Night fell and the warmth and comfort of the room intensified. Friends exchanged confidences and even enemies forgot the reasons for their quarrels and talked in harmonious cordiality. Lovers slid closer and many a sly kiss was exchanged in the darkest corners when the music created a mood of romance.

Enyd sat with Dan and her mother, her father, Kenneth, having declined to come, insisting that he had work to do on the books. Enyd suspected that as soon as Ceinwen had left the house, he would run to the tumbled down cottage on the green lane to see Betson-the-flowers. She wondered if her mother also guessed and whether she cared.

Enyd was fuller of face than previously and looking at her, Mary thought her daughter-in-law would soon be announcing that a baby was on the way. Mary often knew before the mother had realized it herself, noting the altered face and recognizing the slight bloated feeling, a fullness that made a loosening of a skirt waistband necessary. As she thought it, she saw Enyd untie the girdle that held her dress to her small waist and knew she was right in her assumption.

Cadwalader was there when they arrived; he sat cross-legged

94

on the floor near the fire only jumping up once, to greet Olwen. He smiled freely but seemed unwilling to join in any of the groups who offered ale and a space at their table.

When he began to play, the silence was praise for his ability, the notes from the harp sending a sensitive harmony up into the room above and making Emma stop and listen with a rapt expression on her plump, rosy face.

When Cadwalader and Dan sang their rehearsed songs they were applauded until Pitcher and Arthur both shouted 'Order', to remind them all that they were there to drink. The encore waited until mugs had been refilled before Pitcher gave them the signal to continue. The shouts of Pitcher and the potboy were like a duet of their own even if less melodious, with Arthur's voice so high-pitched and Pitcher's, deep, almost gruff in his anxiety not to lose custom from the excellence of his entertainment.

A slight draught that made the lights gutter attracted Pitcher's attention. Surely there weren't more people trying to squeeze in? To his alarm, there were more than a dozen soldiers now standing near the door, ominously preventing anyone leaving. Among the soldiers, clearly with them, were men not in uniform but strangers to him. He felt his heart leap as he wondered if they were men from the excise. The silence that followed was not an easy one as more and more people saw them and nudged their neighbours to look.

'Don't stop the fun, landlord,' one of them said. 'We are only passing through on our way to Carmarthen. Continue, please do, and if someone could pass back some ale we'll be content to listen for a while and share your pleasure.'

Cadwalader stood and began to play a lively tune on his harp and, gradually, the tension eased, but the evening continued with less jubilation than there would otherwise have been.

But when Pitcher ran upstairs and counted his takings, he was more than delighted with the amount.

'That Cadwalader was a real find,' he confided to Emma. 'What luck he came here and not to one of the other places and asked to sing for his supper.'

'So long as it's only music and profit he brought and not the soldiers, Pitcher,' she replied. 'You never know with strangers and that's a fact. And since when did anyone come to Mumbles on the way from Swansea to Carmarthen?'

Thinking of the supplies arriving in a few hours' time, Pitcher shivered in apprehension.

'If they were expecting a landing they would surely have hidden, not shown themselves?' he said, but Emma only shrugged her fat shoulders.

'Bluff, double bluff, no bluff at all? Who's to tell? Just be careful Pitcher, please. I would be so devastated to see you harmed or thrown into gaol,' she pleaded.

Chapter Seven

Pitcher left Emma and ran back down to the bar-room. The sound of the singing and laughing filled the building and sounded as if most of the village had come to drink with him. But why had the soldiers chosen this night to call? He knew that unless the soldiers and the other men who were with them were kept away from the beach, the smugglers would walk into their arms. He went into the smoke-filled room and beckoned to Barrass. He led him through the door behind the counter, through to the passage beyond and whispered,

'Barrass, will you go and warn Markus that there are soldiers here?'

'Should he stop the boats coming in?' Barrass asked.

'That must be for others to decide – ' Both men turned as a shadow eased itself from the doorway and revealed the darkly clad figure of Cadwalader.

'Forgive me for intruding,' the man said, 'but I can guess your predicament and will willingly help.'

'Go back to your singing and keep your mouth well closed if you want to sing again for your supper,' Pitcher warned.

'I have an idea that would solve the problem of the soldiers being here *and* give you all a fine alibi,' Cadwalader whispered back. 'I am a stranger to you and know the risk you would take by trusting me, but, at least listen to my idea.'

Pitcher raised a lantern that had been standing on a small table and stared into the man's dark eyes. For no reason he could ever explain, he trusted him at least enough to listen.

'I think it is a trick you have used before but perhaps never so boldly,' Cadwalader began. 'You should go at once and call up as many men and women as you can, ask them to come here and exchange places with those who have to leave.'

'You mean for us to go out and hope that the soldiers will not notice?' Pitcher exclaimed.

'One by one, two at the most, some come in and take the places of those who have to leave,' Cadwalader explained.

'It might work, but if one of the soldiers should see them and guess – ' Pitcher said.

'I will help to amuse them and your potboy can ply them with enough ale to slope their eyesight.'

'You do not move from the place!' Pitcher warned after staring at Cadwalader for a few seconds as if making up his mind. He turned to Barrass. 'We'll do as he says.'

Barrass ran off to call on as many houses as he could in the short time he and Pitcher had allowed themselves, sending messages to others from the people to whom he spoke. Arthur was given his instructions and he, together with Cadwalader, concentrated on discouraging the soldiers from leaving.

A helping of brandy was added to the ale and served with frantic enthusiasm by Arthur, whose Adam's apple bobbed like a coracle on a wild river. Cadwalader sang and played but his melodies had changed from the beautiful and lyrical and sentimental to the more bawdy songs of the soldier's repertoire.

He moved to sit close to the soldiers and the men who had come with them, shielding those who were leaving and the newcomers slipping in to take their places. When a soldier did rise to go outside to the privy, he noticed nothing different about the over-crowded room.

After making the necessary calls Barrass went back to the alehouse only briefly, just to reassure himself that Cadwalader was in fact doing as he had promised, and that Arthur was coping. Then he set off up the sloping path and along the dark cliffs to the place where the boats were expected to come in.

Olwen saw him go with the wish that she could have gone with him, but the cliffs this night were no place for a woman. Then to her chagrin she saw Harriet slip out of the back doorway close on Barrass's heels. She stood as if to chase after them but Mary pulled at her skirt and frowned for her to be still.

On the way back from his visit to Betson-the-flowers, Kenneth was just approaching the village when he became aware of activity. People were moving in the fields around him. He stopped and wondered if, it being likely that this was to do with the smuggling, it would be better for him to stay where he was until those passing had gone from the area. His hesitation was his undoing. His movements became suspicious and he was seen by Edwin Prince.

Edwin ran to where Barrass, followed by Harriet, was just about to disappear into the trees that lined a section of the path, and called them back to where Kenneth had hidden. With few words spoken, Barrass and a masked Edwin tied the man's hands together then fastened them to his ankles so he could sit but not easily walk.

Harriet was given charge of him, being told not to let him go until she had been so instructed. She smiled in the dark as she sat beside her prisoner and began to tickle him.

'What will Ceinwen say?' Kenneth murmured.

'It's what I will say. That's what you want to be worrying about, my fine boy,' Harriet said with a low chuckle.

Barrass heard stifled laughs and groans and half-hearted protests as Harriet murmured, 'Ticklish by there, are you, Kenneth?'

That Barrass felt no jealousy might have been surprising, but although he and Harriet had spent many pleasant evenings together, there had never been a proprietorial feeling between them. Never on either side had there been a sense of belonging, although he knew that Harriet would marry him if he should ask her. He also knew that if Harriet's brother, Carter Phillips, found out just how close they were, a wedding would be the least of the threats he would offer to Barrass.

If it had been Violet he had left with Kenneth it would have been different altogether. Or if he had overheard Penelope laughing in that sensual way, jealousy would have consumed him. Or little Olwen he admitted to himself in surprise. If it had been Olwen, he would probably have killed Kenneth just for being there!

On the cliff path, shadows slipped out of the bushes and hurried with Barrass and the following form of Edwin but no one spoke. Ponies and donkeys trod through the deep grass on to the path and joined the silent procession. Too late, Barrass remembered he had been told to bring Jethro. Well, better he and the others arrived safe, rather than risk the soldiers hearing the sound of a horse setting off towards the cliffs.

One of the boats had already landed its cargo when he reached the small beach. Figures shrouded in sacks to conceal their identity moved up and down the rocks to where others waited to fasten the loads either on their backs on onto their mounts.

A man approached Barrass and he watched carefully, fearing to see the glint of a knife, but the man only asked in the accent of a Frenchman for 'The man who is called Pitcher'.

Cautiously, Barrass denied there being anyone of that name and the man thrust a small package into his hands and dissolved into the darkness whispering, 'For the man called Pitcher, from Jacques.'

Tucking the package inside his coat, Barrass ran to help with the unloading.

For safety and speed, most of the contraband was taken deep into a cave, and out into the grounds near Edwin Prince's piggeries, not carried across the fields to where they were usually hidden. The exception was the load destined for the underground rooms of John Maddern. He had recently discovered a disused basement below the house he rented. He insisted that his place was as safe as any could be and walked back across the fields urging the men and the animals to 'Shift your heels'. Not living in the village but visiting on occasions, he doubted if Daniels would give his small cottage a thought. Silently the figures dispersed again into the darkness, and the only sounds heard above the waves were the slap of ropes on masts and the pull of oars.

Barrass was the last to leave the beach. He was on edge and longing to run back to the safety of the alehouse, but some sixth sense bade him stay. He told himself it was simply that he would be unobserved once the rest of the group had gone and the night was still. Found on his own, anyone, even the suspicious Daniels, would believe he had been kissing a girl.

As the last sound faded and the night returned to its customary order, a faint cry disturbed the night. At first he thought it was an animal, but there was something about the cry that made his blood freeze. When it came again, slightly stronger, he realized it was human.

At first he did nothing, just sat there watching the area around him trying to see a movement within the blackness, then as the cry came again, he made his way to where it came from, and seeing a movement, reached out and grabbed at a man crouched in the rocks close to the tide.

'What are you doing here?' he whispered gruffly.

'I fell, I knocked my head and now the boats have gone back without me,' came the reply.

'You're from, over there?'

'Yes. I was unloading and the boat tilted and, with a barrel on my shoulder, I lost my balance.'

'You don't sound like a Frenchie,' Barrass accused.

'That's because I'm not.'

The stranger rose and offered a hand to Barrass for assistance in climbing up away from the lapping water. Barrass took the hand and pulled the boy up to stand beside him but there was something about the lightness of the step, the smoothness of the hand, that made him suspicious. He reached out and pulled the brimless hat from the boy's head and saw long, straight hair fall from beneath it.

'Yes,' the newcomer said unnecessarily. 'I'm a girl.'

At the alehouse Arthur was attempting to sing a sailor's working song, his high voice a parody of the words. His dog sat in a space at his feet and throwing back its head, howled a mournful accompaniment but out of pain or pleasure, none could decide. People crowded around to see the unexpected performance, the soldiers joining in the laughter.

Mary stood to leave, unable to stay longer, even though fear for the safety of Spider and Dan kept her eyes continually glancing towards the door.

'It will be more strange for us to stay after so many hours, Olwen,' she said. 'Go you and make sure there's someone else to fill our place.'

'Just a while longer, Mam,' Olwen pleaded. She shared her mother's anxiety for Dan and Spider and knowing Barrass was probably out on the cliffs added to her fears. Lifting the sleeping Dic from her mother's arms she settled uneasily with Mary to wait.

It had become extremely difficult for Arthur to keep the mugs brimming. The place was so full that there was no room for his feet and the people demanded faster and faster service. When

Daniels walked in, tall, imposing and dreadfully official, pushing several sleepers from behind the doors, panic rose in him and all but erupted in a scream. His Adam's apple did a frenzied jig and he felt like running away, hiding from the responsibilities he had been left to handle.

Instead, he ran up the stairs and asked if Emma could help him. Worried as she was for the fate of Pitcher out on the beach, she came at once.

She stayed behind the counter, with Arthur bringing fresh supplies up from the cellar, but their combined efforts were not enough to stem the demands that became louder than the singing and ended in a chant of discontent.

Arthur went first to hand a beaker to the Keeper of the Peace, who announced that he wanted to talk to Pitcher.

'Being kept busy in the cellar, sir. No time to spit he hasn't, come when he can, he will for sure. I'll tell him you want a word, but busy he is, never a night like this for ages,' Arthur babbled, wondering how long he could hold the man back from discovering Pitcher's absence.

It was Daisy who coped. From the little her mother had said and the frenzied attempts of Arthur to be three people at once, she guessed the true story and came into the room, carrying a tray of bread and cheese, people making a path for her miraculously and allowing her to reach the soldiers and Ponsonby Daniels.

Haughty, rude and as separate from the others as perfume after rotten eggs, she subdued the liveliest and even woke some of the sleepers, simply by standing there, beautifully dressed, a character from a different world, and throwing bread, cheese and insults.

To Daniels she smiled and asked, 'Are you comfortable standing there, or would you prefer to sit?' Without waiting for an answer, she raised her foot and pushed against one dozy-looking man and slid him from his seat. Then she gestured to the Keeper of the Peace to sit down. Bemused by her presence amid the unruly mob as much as her actions, he did so.

Pansy followed her sister down the stairs but could not face entering the noisy, unruly room. Arthur skidded to a stop risking dropping the foaming mugs he was carrying on a pewter tray when he saw her.

'No, Pansy, don't you go in by there! That lot aren't fit company for the likes of you!'

'But I want to help.'

'Help me by going back to the safety of your room, please my dear,' he whispered. 'Your sister being in there is bad enough but she's brave and can cope. This isn't for you, this hullabaloo.' Balancing the tray momentarily on a small table, he glanced nervously around and touched her cheek with his lips before hurrying back into the bar-room to satisfy at least a few thirsty mouths.

Pansy stood on the stairs for a while, listening to the riotous choruses below, sneaking glances in through the door to the smoke-filled bar-room where the colourful uniforms added a brightness rarely seen. But she didn't envy her sister's boldness in entering the rowdy place. The bar was not the place for her; she returned upstairs to listen to the distant noise and wondered how long it would be before Daisy came and they could go to their beds.

Horses passed close to the place where Harriet and Kenneth sat. They were oblivious of them as Harriet untied his hands and guided them to her body. A while later, a donkey slipped on a muddy patch and shook the bush under which they lay and they hardly noticed a thing. As the parade of men and animals became less frequent, Kenneth allowed his hands to be retied and he sat trying to look nonchalant when a messenger came to tell Harriet to free him. For long after she had departed he still sat there, a shattered man.

After a few moments, panic returned to his inert form and he gathered himself and hurried back to his house, arriving just moments before his wife. Longing for a drink to ease his dry throat, he dared not face her but pretended sleep, the thirst easier to cope with than her accusations and anger.

Pitcher arrived back at the alehouse, puffing and panting after his strenuous two hours' work and the run back, just in time to see his daughter Daisy turn away from Daniels who now sat with the soldiers, obediently facing away from the counter. He heard her call for Arthur to, 'Fill the man's cup, if you please,' and stared in utter disbelief.

Adam's apple wobbling like a snake half-swallowed, Arthur

nodded at Pitcher and went to do as Daisy instructed. Pitcher blinked, rubbed his eyes and stared after his daughter in amazement as she left the room and joined her mother behind the counter.

'You've come up from the cellar to talk to Daniels,' Arthur whispered from the side of his mouth as he passed him. Taking a filled pitcher from Emma, Arthur handed it to him and pushed him in the general direction of the Keeper of the Peace. Pitcher nodded and, still looking dazed, pushed through the crowd past Cadwalader still playing his harp, past the fiddler whose elbow was brushing the nose of a sleeper, to stand beside Daniels.

'You wanted to see me?' he asked, wondering if he were awake and beset with a fantastic dream.

'Yes, you've been a mighty long time coming.'

'You can see why I couldn't leave the cellar,' Pitcher said, his words coming seemingly of their own volition, without him having any part in their making.

'Well, the truth is,' Daniels said slowly and with the infinite care of the inebriated, 'the fact is, I've forgotten what it was I had to tell you.'

'Best you have another drink then,' Pitcher said and topped up the mug being waved about his face. 'Help you to remember for sure.'

With little disturbance, the men and women who had been called went out, one and two at a time, and their places were refilled with the previous occupants. The boats had come and gone with soldiers on the premises and none of them aware of what had happened. Pitcher urged Dan to sing, and Cadwalader seemed untiring as he accompanied the young man with voice and harp.

On the cliff path the blackness made it impossible to see a foot in front of them as Mary, Mistress Powell and Olwen walked home. Relieved as she was to have seen Dan and her father safely returned, Olwen had left reluctantly as Barrass had not yet appeared.

'There would have been a word if there had been any trouble,' Mary reassured her. 'He probably went straight to his room. It's almost dawn and we all have to rise as usual in the morning.'

The two people suddenly in front of them were impossible to

make out, so very dark was it still.

'Olwen? Mary? Is everything all right at the alehouse?' a voice asked. 'I was delayed, er – this is Lowri.'

Olwen gasped. It was Barrass! And, he was with a woman!

'Worried about you, we've been, everyone back and you not –' she stumbled to a stop, afraid that her angry words would lead them all into trouble. 'I might have guessed you'd found yourself a way to idle away an hour with a woman.'

'Hush, Olwen.' Both Mary and Barrass warned her.

Pushing him aside with a growl of anger, Olwen ran. Tripping over trailing bramble branches, not feeling them tearing at the skin of her legs, she burst into the house, climbed the ladder and threw herself on her bed. Even on a night when danger filled everyone's mind, Barrass still managed to find himself a woman!

Barrass led the girl to the alehouse and bade her wait while he went inside to explain the situation to Pitcher.

'One of the Frenchies was hurt and left behind by the boats,' he said after telling him that he had someone seeking shelter.

'Best to tell Emma,' Pitcher said with a slightly hysterical laugh. 'Funny night this has been, boy. What with my Daisy being seen in the bar-room and my Emma actually serving ale. Never seen a night like it. What's a lost Frenchie beside all that, eh?'

Barrass beckoned to the girl and led her upstairs to where he expected to find Emma and begin his explanations all over again. From the door behind the counter, Pitcher turned to watch as the girl followed Barrass upstairs.

'It's a woman!' he gasped. 'A *woman* from the boats?'

Emma appeared at his side, swiped him and told him to hush his nonsense. Arthur shushed him and pointed madly towards the soldiers and Daniels. Pitcher gave a groan and took a long swig from the tankard in his hand.

Once Emma understood the situation, she woke Polly, who had managed to sleep through most of the noise. Whispering explanations about how Lowri had arrived, she sent the girl with Polly to accompany her, to spend what was left of the night with Mary and Spider.

'No sense taking chances with that lot still on the premises, even if they haven't the wits of a baby!' she said firmly.

It was almost four a.m. before Arthur was able to relax and look around him. Still crowded, with only the local people beginning to go to their homes, the room looked like a battle-field, which, he thought wearily, it was. Men and women were sleeping across benches and tables and each other. Red coats surprisingly gay amid the more sombre colours worn by the rest. Daniels sat in a formal, upright position against the wall but was snoring peacefully with Arthur's dog curled up on his knees, also snoring.

More and more people dispersed until eventually only Daniels and the soldiers were left. Leaving them to sleep until morning, a confused-looking Pitcher and a popeyed Arthur beckoned to Cadwalader, who was still strumming the strings of his harp, to follow them.

They went to their beds even though they were too wound up to sleep. Cadwalader was given a corner of the passage, with some blankets supplied by Emma in which to wrap himself. The exhausted dog stayed where he was until the gap between Daniels's legs widened and he fell through.

Over the sea, the sun rose and shone on the quiet alehouse and a slight onshore breeze swung the open door, its squeak an echo of the music that had died with the dawn.

Morning broke too early for all the participants in the previous night's activities. Some distant sound disturbed Barrass and he moved stiffly and wondered vaguely why he was sleeping in the passage behind Pitcher's bar-room. Realization came slowly. The sounds of groans and muffled snores seemed to come from all around, puzzling him almost as much as his location. He turned to a crawling position and moved until he could peer around the counter.

The bar-room was full of bodies! He stood up, forcing his eyes to stay open and feed information to his stunned brain. What had happened? Then he saw the tall figure of Daniels rise from among the sprawling redcoats and it all came back.

The first memory was of the young woman who had mat-erialized on the beach. Where was she? Had he dreamt her?

'Morning, Daniels,' he said with difficulty, his sluggish brain matched by his still sleeping tongue. 'Quite a good night, wasn't it?'

'Why wasn't I woken?' Daniels demanded. 'Allowing me to sleep here amid all this stink!'

'I'll find you a mug of tea – supposing Pitcher has such a thing as the makings,' Barrass offered.

'Just go and find my horse!' the man insisted.

Barrass went to the cellar door intending to rouse Arthur when he saw his friend's head appear above the flap door.

'Daniels wants his horse,' Barrass announced, and falling back on the area of the passage he had made his own, he fell back to sleep.

Later, when the world had righted itself and the day was underway, albeit in a half-hearted manner, Barrass asked what had happened to the girl.

'I sent her to stay with Mary and Spider,' Emma told him. 'There's no room here for vagrants and it will be some while before we can get her back where she belongs. Her with no money and only the clothes she stands up in.'

Barrass went up the path to see if he could see the girl, curious about her and half suspicious that the 'accident' that had forced her to stay had been planned. In this he was correct.

'My brother is somewhere in Wales and I want to find him,' Lowri told Barrass and Mary a while later on that Friday when they sat beside the fire drinking a cup of the tea that had already been delivered to the house. 'His name is Cadwalader and he earns a crust singing and playing his Welsh harp. Have you heard of him?' Lowri asked.

'He's here, in the village, staying at Pitcher's alehouse,' Barrass explained. 'Come with me now and I'll take you to see him!'

'There's a bed here for you, Lowri, remember that,' Mary said as the couple set off down the path. 'Olwen doesn't mind sharing with you, sure of that I am.'

'Now she knows I am not Barrass's new friend,' Lowri said.

Mary chuckled as she remembered the fuss her fiery daughter had made when Polly had brought the girl up the previous night. At first Olwen protested that she wouldn't share the same field with one of Barrass's women, let alone her bed! But when it transpired that Lowri's arrival with Barrass had been innocent, she relented and hearing of the girl's dilemma, willingly shared the small, narrow bed and was glad of the company through what remained of the night.

'She was too afraid of being late for work to sleep,' Mary explained to Mistress Powell, 'there only being a few hours left of the night before she had to rise.'

'I wonder if she *is* a sister to that Cadwalader,' Mistress Powell mused, her knitting needles clicking as she began another row of the sleeve she was making.

'They look alike,' Mary said. 'Thickset, sturdy, and they have the same colouring, so dark they've something of the foreigner about them. She even has the same white flash in her hair, strange that, isn't it?'

'Not so strange as this sleeve for your Spider,' the old lady sighed. 'No matter how many rows I knit, the length is still not enough. He's a long shanks that husband of yours, Mary. Easier it is to knit for baby Dic and that's a fact!'

Barrass remembered that the package given to him on the beach to be handed to Pitcher was still in his pocket. He patted it to remind himself to hand it over, but first he went back to the alehouse with Lowri, to find Cadwalader.

'Gone, he has,' Arthur told him. 'When we finally roused ourselves to wakefulness his corner was empty. The blankets were there, all curled up as if around a man but of Cadwalader there was no sign. Taken his pack and gone he has.'

Barrass explained that Lowri was his sister and needed to know his whereabouts but Arthur shook his head. He took Barrass on one side and whispered,

'Worried Pitcher is. Afraid the man has gone to report what he knows of last night's activities. Sharp eyes he has, see, and could probably tell who was missing and for how long they were away.'

'There's nothing to prove his story now. Everything is hidden safely away and I bet there's not even a mark on the beach now there's been another tide.'

'Except her,' Arthur said, glancing at the young woman, who, dressed in trousers and having replaced her cap, looked very like a man.

'Her we'll have to watch,' Barrass agreed.

Barrass gave Pitcher the package from the boat. He was curious to see that it contained a box of dominoes from France.

Pitcher had been told about the new game by Edwin Prince and William Ddole, and on a visit to his friends in Bristol, William had arranged for one of his cargoes to include a set.

'Will you ask William to come and explain the game?' Pitcher asked, as he replaced the oblong pieces in the wooden box. 'Can't see how they'll catch on without a couple of experts able to explain the game.'

'I expect these new visitors you're going to attract will know it. London's the place for things new,' Arthur said wisely. 'Everything starts there it seems to me.'

Hidden in the newly sprouted leaves, high in the branches of a tree, Cadwalader sat and watched as the soldiers set off to rediscover the road to Carmarthen. Their marching left a lot to be desired, and he thought with a wry grin that if their officers could see them they would all be whipped – and probably be too insensible to feel it.

He could see the road outside the alehouse and saw Lowri arrive with Barrass. He guessed she must know by now that he had been at the alehouse the previous night. Thank goodness he had seen her arrive and had been given the chance to get away. Pity he had to move on. Just when he had the feeling that his search for a place to settle was almost over.

Behind him, the sea murmured sleepily as if it too were exhausted after the previous night's revelry. To his right he saw the line of soldiers fading from his view. On his left, the outside of the alehouse was being brushed free of the sand and small stones that constantly appeared, by a sleepy-looking Arthur. The chairs and tables were being placed in the shelter of the porch wall out of the rising wind. In the doorway, as if undecided whether to go out or stay, he could just make out the shape of Arthur's dog, head drooping as if he too wondered what day it was.

When he had seen Lowri making her way back up the steep path to the cliffs, he jumped down, and shouldering the pack he had hidden among the sand dunes, he set off inland, towards the town.

All through the day, people could be seen crossing and recrossing the outskirts of the village delivering packages.

Tobacco and liquor and small quantities of tea were transported casually, as payment to those who had taken part and those who had helped.

At the shabby house in which the Morgan family lived, there was no reply to Oak-tree Thomas's call when he arrived with the share of the cargo. Although none of the family actually helped, they were paid as compensation for the loss of their parents during one of the deliveries some years previously. He called again, and pushed open the broken door.

At once chickens escaped into the field cackling their disapproval of some unknown misconduct. A goat butted against him playfully and frolicked off to find food. He called again, staring into the stale-smelling room trying to penetrate the darkness.

'Anyone there?'

In the darkness something moved and he stepped back, half expecting trouble from the wild, ill-tempered Madoc or Morgan. But it was Seranne who stood up and came to the door. Her face was white and in the loose gown she wore that was partly covered by a ragged blanket, she looked so thin that he was afraid to touch her in case her bones snapped.

'Sorry to disturb you, Seranne,' he said. 'I've brought you some – Look, I think I'd better go and fetch someone to help you. You look sick.'

'I have caught a chill again. It seems that for me the winter ails will never end.' She smiled and shook her head. 'No need for help, Vanora looks after us all. She has gone to tell them at Ddole House that I won't be in today. Polly will call later when she has finished her morning's work for Mistress Palmer, and Morgan and Madoc aren't far away.'

'I'll be back with some food,' he promised, and handing her the packages he had brought, he went along the stream and back on to the track. He glanced back and could see her pale face in the doorway, and saw her hand raised in farewell.

When he returned less than an hour later with a knuckle of pork, two roasted rabbits he had had cooking near his fire, and a loaf of bread, Seranne was dressed, her long hair was combed neatly and she looked like a different person.

'It's only the mornings,' she explained. 'Once I get up and set about the day's tasks, I shake off the aches and tiredness.'

She thanked him for his gifts and assured him that by the following day she would be well enough to go to her work. Oak-tree Thomas returned to his house feeling a great anger against Seranne's brothers, who at seventeen and nineteen, should be able to take better care of her. He did not know that as he and Seranne had spoken at the doorway, they were lying in their beds, weaker and more sick than Seranne.

Chapter Eight

It was several days before Seranne returned to Ddole House and when she did, it was to be met by a smiling Annie who told her she was no longer required.

'But why?' Seranne gasped. 'Isn't my work satisfactory?'

'I'd hardly know would I, you being away more than you're here?'

'I want to talk to Florrie.'

'I'm sorry, but Florrie is no longer responsible for the running of Ddole House. She will be marrying soon and until then, she is assisting me.' Annie smiled again, but closed the kitchen door firmly in Seranne's anxious face.

Dozy Bethan looked at Olwen, sharing with her a look of consternation, but neither said a word. They both knew the risk was great of them losing their place too. It had become a constant threat since Florrie had given notice that she intended to leave.

'It's all right for you,' Bethan said later, when both girls were safely out of hearing from the house. 'You have a home to go to, however crowded it is. I have nowhere but here. This house is all I've ever known, being a small child when I came here.' It was a long speech for the slow-thinking Bethan and an indication of her anxiety.

'I'm sure you and I will be kept on,' Olwen said, to cheer her friend.

There was something else to worry them later that morning. It had long been Florrie's habit to leave their money on the kitchen table every Sunday morning. A few hours after the dismissal of Seranne Morgan, both girls went to collect their wages; Bethan to put in the small metal box she had in her bedroom, and Olwen to hand over to her mother when they met briefly in church.

The two piles of coins were there but instead of the one shilling and four pence Olwen was expecting, there was only a shilling. Bethan's shilling had been reduced to four pence.

'This must be all mine,' Olwen said. 'She's forgotten yours, or perhaps she's gone this very minute to find the coins to make it up.' When Annie came into the kitchen smiling as always, Olwen hesitantly asked if either was the case.

'Good heavens above, no! You were late on Friday morning and so tired that all day you only worked at half speed. How can you expect to have a full wage when you didn't give Master Ddole a full week's work?' She turned to Bethan, who held the four pence in her hand like a beggar asking for more. 'And you, Bethan. What about the best china dish you dropped? How will that be paid for unless you contribute? We can't expect the master to be as generous as he is *and* pay for our mishaps, now can we?'

Olwen's temper flared but, glancing at Bethan's stricken face she held it back, swallowing it, looking down so Annie wouldn't see the rebellion in her blue eyes. She forced herself to nod agreement and willed herself not to cry in frustration.

Straight from work she would go and talk to Florrie, see if something could be done. But, as she confided in Bethan later on, it was a poor hope. Annie was now in charge and what she said was law so far as Ddole House was concerned.

There would be no point in her mentioning it to William Ddole himself and there was no one else. If only she dared to write to Penelope. But that would surely lead to her dismissal. She picked up the hated coal buckets and carried them outside to the coal store. Best she gave Annie no opportunity for complaint, or next week she would have nothing to hand to her mother.

Madoc was waiting for Olwen when she finished work that evening. He was standing against a tree, chewing a blade of grass and he smiled as she approached, but Olwen sensed that he was unwell. There was a transparency in his skin, a look about him that was like the fine porcelain cups used at Ddole House.

'Olwen,' he called in greeting. 'I have a mind to walk with you and see this goat of yours.'

Olwen was startled by the suggestion, but more startled by the breathless way the words were spoken. Was the whole family to be struck down with disease? He was obviously in pain too, she noticed as they walked together across the fields to the cliffs.

He admired the young goat and said, 'I'll lend you one of our billies when she's old enough for mating and you'll soon have a young kid and a supply of milk to sell. A year later another. Before you know it, you'll be rich.'

He didn't stay long and when he left, Olwen followed and saw him stop and rest several times before he reached his house. Fearing the hidden illness that was threatening his life and those of his brother and sisters, she ran along the cliff path, down on to the sands of Longland, taking joy in the health and strength she took for granted, thanking her parents for them.

Madoc fell on to his bed and panted with exhaustion. His eyes shone with fever and fury as he thought about the need for money that would take them from this house and give them good food and warm, dry beds. It was so little to ask of life, but the attainment of it was beyond their combined strength.

When Seranne went home to tell her brothers and sisters she no longer had work, Madoc rose from his bed and, coughing between almost each word, threatened to make William Ddole pay for his cruelty.

'Robbing us of the means to earn an honest wage and threatening us with prison if we do anything the law frowns on,' he growled. 'What justice in the law? How can people like Daniels uphold a law that says we must starve?' He settled back on the bedding, and turning restlessly, almost delirious in his fever and anger, he muttered that he was determined the food and medicines they all lacked would come, if not from William Ddole's purse, then from his woods and fields. 'Better be hanged for poaching than die of hunger and cowardice,' he muttered. Beside him, Morgan whispered his agreement.

Once she realized that her brother had moved on, Lowri decided that until someone told her she must leave, she would stay on in the house of Spider and Mary, and share Olwen's bed. To earn her keep she offered to help with whatever work was on hand.

'Come on the boat if you like,' Dan offered. 'Dadda has to go into the market and if you will come with me, we can land a harvest we'd otherwise miss.'

Lowri tried unsuccessfully to wriggle out of the invitation and when she had been on board the small fishing boat a few minutes, Dan guessed why.

'You've never worked on a ship,' he accused. 'I doubt your feet have ever left the shore. You certainly didn't come off the boats from France the night Barrass found you.'

Lowri looked at him standing beside her as he stepped up the mast, skinny but threatening and strong. She knew that at that moment she was in danger of being pushed overboard and held under. The smugglers rarely took chances.

'I'm not from France, and I didn't come off the boats. I was sleeping not far from where the boats came in and was curious. Foolishly so, I'll admit, but curious enough to crawl along and see what was happening. I fell rather badly and I was caught between the men with their unloading and the safety of the fields. When Barrass found me I said the first thought that filled my mind.'

'Who are you?' Dan demanded.

'Who I said I am, Cadwalader's sister.'

'Dressed as a boy?'

'It's safer sometimes than showing yourself to be a girl travelling alone.' She pointed to the southeast. 'It's Bristol I've come from, before that, London. I'm searching for my mother. But please, don't tell anyone. She – she doesn't want to be found.'

'What about your brother?'

'He's looking for her too, but we have different ideas about what happens when she is found.'

'Are you brave enough to go on with our fishing?' he asked. 'Even a small boat like this one needs an extra pair of hands to pull in the nets.' When she nodded, he unfurled the sail and allowed the small craft to glide swiftly on the shining water.

She soon found her sea legs and Dan was able to teach her the minimal skills needed to hold the boat steady while he leaned over and released the nets. The sun was bright and Dan managed to catch very few. The net was easily seen and the fish wary. But, he admitted to himself, he was more interested in hearing Lowri's story.

He would have to tell the others about her, and leave it to them to judge the story. He looked at her while she stared across the water apparently at peace with herself. She was probably about thirty years old, and the white streak in her dark hair gave her a youthful look rather than adding to her age. He wondered who she was and, if she were Cadwalader's sister, why they were searching for a mother who didn't want to be found? He had lots of questions, but Lowri, although very polite, was reluctant to give him any answers. Best I leave it for Blind Markus to sort out, he decided, and he altered the sail and set the boat towards home.

At the Swansea market, Spider and Mary had a good day. Mary sold all of the woollens and woven cloth she had managed to make, and the fish, caught that morning and on the previous evening by Spider and Dan, were almost gone. Mary left a sleeping Dic with Spider and wandered around the few remaining stalls looking for a last-minute bargain, when she saw Seranne.

'Are you having a day off from Ddole House?' she asked in surprise. 'I thought this Annie Evans was overstrict about the hours you worked?'

'Not with me anymore. Told me to go, she did, and after the extra hours I've put in to show my willingness too.'

'Why?' Mary asked.

'I got sick again. Not that I didn't hurry to get back to work the minute I could stand, mind. No, I was off for three days only and when I went back she told me I was no longer required. Your Olwen will have to watch out or the same will happen to her,' she warned.

'I sometimes think it would be best if it did,' Mary sighed. 'She's so unhappy there.'

'Can I walk back with you and Spider?' Seranne asked, and she looked around her at the few rabbits hanging on a bar against a wall, the line of small, plump partridge and the pheasants, their long tails waving in the rising evening breeze. 'I would like to wait a while longer, there's still a chance that these will sell.'

'I'll buy a rabbit from you,' Mary offered, and while they discussed a price, two others came and bought, and within moments others had scented a bargain, the wall was emptied and Seranne's pocket jingled with coins.

'I'll go to the apothecary's stall to get something for Morgan and Madoc's coughs,' Seranne said. 'And some foot rub to ease the aches poor Polly suffers.'

When the three of them set off for home, Seranne had bought fresh vegetables and an assortment of bottled medicines, each with a label proclaiming its efficaciousness in disagreements of the lung.

'Isn't it unusual to find pheasant for sale, now, in the breeding season?' Spider queried hesitantly.

'Culling the weakest,' Seranne said, and quickly changed the subject.

Annie was jubilant. Already she had disposed of several of the servants who gave the impression they might be troublesome, and Florrie had been made to understand that, having given William her intention to leave, she no longer had any say in the way things were run. She knocked on the door of William's study and stepped inside. In her hands were the accounts books and in her pocket, the money she had saved him from the allowance he had given her for the first month.

'Forgive me for disturbing you,' she said in her quiet gentle voice. 'But I would like your approval on the figures for my first month.'

'Mistress Evans,' he said, raising his eyes from the book he was reading. 'What you do with the money is your concern. As long as I am comfortable and well catered for, and you have adequate arrangements to entertain my friends when I ask it, I leave the small matters to your good self.' He wanted to add that neither his wife Dorothy, nor his previous housekeeper Florrie ever bothered him with the details of the household, and he found it a trifle irritating.

She put her hand in her pocket and drew out a handful of coins, which she placed on the table before him.

'This is surplus, sir. Shall I keep it and take less for the month to come, or would you take it and allow me to begin afresh?'

He looked at the glinting coins as if seeing money for the first time, then up into her small fascinating eyes, half hidden in a nest of thick lashes and eyebrows.

'How should I know,' he said, uncomfortably aware that he had been staring at her. 'Do what you will, just don't bother me with it.'

'I see you are used to someone taking complete charge, sir,'

Annie smiled, her eyes almost disappearing yet giving the impression of deep interest and concern. 'With a wife that can happen. Such a sadness for you to lose her so young. And Penelope, whom I have yet to meet. Gone without a thought for your comfort, such is the independence of young people today.'

'Penelope is the dearest and most considerate of daughters,' William said. 'It was I who sent her away, and I regret it with every passing moment.'

'I'm sorry, I didn't understand. I thought, if you had lost your wife, then your daughter's presence would have been necessary to you.'

'It is.' William, soothed by her gentle tone and quiet solicitude, told her of how he had sent the girl away to save her from the attentions of an unsuitable young man, although not how lowly was the man's position.

'Loving is a pain as well as a pleasure,' Annie said. Leaving the coins on the table, she glided softly from the room.

The pattern began then. Every afternoon, except when William was otherwise engaged, Annie would knock on the door and stand quietly and listen to him. He began to look forward to her visits, confiding, at her subtle invitation, all his inner sadness, especially regarding the absence of Penelope.

'Sir,' she suggested one day, 'why don't you take a few weeks away from your work and visit your daughter? It would be a tonic for you both, deprived as you are, one from the other.' As he hesitated, she smiled and patted his shoulder daringly. 'You need not fear for anything going amiss. I will run the house exactly as if you were here.'

'I don't want to miss Florrie and Daniels's wedding,' he frowned. 'I promised to be there.'

'Then go soon, sir, and be back in comfortable time. I understand there is no date yet fixed so it cannot be until the autumn.'

Florrie frowned at these tête-à-têtes, but with diminishing authority in the household she had once commanded, she could say nothing. Gradually, and with more and more firmness, she was being separated from the duties she had once called her own.

'It isn't that I don't understand her need to change things to the way she wants the house run,' Florrie said to Emma when they met in Swansea one market day. 'I know it's my fault for not leaving promptly, but I find it hard to let go.'

'Hard to let go of the reins of Ddole House? or *take* hold of the reins of Daniels's household?' Emma asked shrewdly.

Florrie did not reply; instead she said, 'And there's that daily chat. Never been allowed in Dorothy Ddole's day! We all knew our place in the household and that was best for everyone. Even little Olwen knew what was expected of her and although she was always a bit forward, treating Miss Penelope as almost a friend, she knew her place. Didn't always like it, mind, but knew it. Now this Annie woman takes on the role of loving friend, listening to all his thoughts and opinions as if she were a wife rather than a paid servant!'

'Perhaps that it what she intends?' Emma said thoughtfully. 'With both Dorothy and Penelope gone he is very vulnerable to a bit of sympathy and flattery.'

'Now there's a thought!' Florrie said. 'And her only here five minutes!'

Seranne saw the two women approaching her and put forward her remaining goods in the hope that they would buy. She was tired, and longing to be home. They smiled, commiserated with her about losing her post at Ddole House and moved on. Emma turned back and enquired about Polly.

'Will she be back to work soon, Seranne?' she asked. 'I am finding it difficult to be without her.'

'She's mending nicely, Mistress Palmer,' Seranne said encouragingly. 'Back she'll be in a day or so for sure.'

She watched as the two women separated, each having several purchases to make, and she heard them promise to meet again and travel home together in the wagon that Percy the stable boy had driven in with Emma aboard. Seranne watched them go with something approaching envy. There was such a small increase in her funds needed to make life for herself and her family reasonably comfortable. Funds which the two women probably wouldn't miss. She thought of them riding contentedly home with their purchases, to homes where warmth and good food were the norm, and hunger something they read about in storybooks.

With only two rabbits left to sell, she decided to give up. The extra meat wouldn't be wasted; her brothers were not yet sick of the taste of rabbit although it was their only source of meat and had been for a long time, with the unknown kindness of William Ddole! She picked up the handles of the simple cart and trundled off towards the Sketty road.

She had passed Sketty when the wagon overtook her. She had strung the rabbits about her neck and occasionally, when she saw a likely purchaser, called 'fresh meat' in the hope of a sale. After passing her, the wagon drew to a stop, the horse snorting, impatient with the further delay. Emma turned and called for her to climb up.

'Plenty of room and I'm sure you would be glad to reach home a bit earlier,' Emma said, and after helping Percy to put her handcart on the back, Seranne gratefully took a place on the bench seat beside them.

With the well-dressed and reasonably sweet-smelling ladies, Seranne was aware of her own state. Setting out before seven that morning in the hope of finding work, she had wandered through the streets asking if there was a job for a scullery maid, knowing that her appearance would now discourage anyone from employing her as a cook. Then, with the cartload of produce, she had stood all the afternoon in the market.

Morgan Morgan and his brother Madoc were slowly recovering from the illness that had kept them in bed for days. Hollow-faced and thin, they dragged themselves into the fields and along the river banks to find illegal game and wildfowl for Seranne to sell at the market.

As well as the stock being stolen, Seranne's very presence at the market was illegal, not have paid for her space to set up a stall. But she waited until a seller had finished and left his spot, and quickly spread her own rabbits and birds, and began shouting her wares, hoping people would think she had been there all day.

It meant selling for a much lower price than she would have received in the early part of the day, but the risk of setting up without permission was too great. Once the majority of the traders had packed up and left, the inspectors were less diligent, and the chance of her being questioned unlikely.

At home, her brothers sat in the weak sun of late afternoon, making nets for another foray into William Ddole's woods.

Between two broken chairs weighted down with rocks, Madoc had tied the head rope and with the aid of a shuttle-like netting needle and using a sheet bend knot, the end result was a square net of some eighteen inches. He threw it on to the pile already made and sat to rest when Morgan set up another head rope and started the process again with a row of evenly spaced clove hitches. Armed with a dozen of these small nets, they would throw them over the entrances of a rabbit warren to catch the frightened animals as they escaped the small terrier they sent down the holes.

'I wonder how Seranne has done at the market,' Madoc said.

'She'll have earned enough to buy some food and some medicines with luck,' his brother replied. He gestured to the doorway with a nod and lowering his voice, added, 'Best we get some warmth into young Polly there or we won't have her come another winter.'

Sitting on a wooden chair, wrapped in a thin blanket and dozing in the rays of the sun, Polly heard their remark and sadness filled her. She knew what they said was true. Her face was rosy so she looked pretty, although the flush was not a healthy one but a sign of the fever that raged in her. She wondered vaguely if she would ever work at the alehouse again, and felt only a brief regret that she wouldn't.

'I have an idea for making better money,' Madoc said. 'Dangerous, but if it's successful, it will bring us enough to feed and warm Polly and the rest of us and see that the doctor will treat us properly.'

'Vanora does her best,' Morgan defended. 'But I know what you mean. Money would give young Polly a better chance.' He finished the row of clove hitches and watched as his brother began the first row of the net. 'What did you have in mind, Madoc?'

'Robbing the King's Mail, that's what.'

They said nothing more as their sister came into sight, having left the handcart near the alehouse, the rabbits strung around her neck threatening to pull her to the ground with their weight. She smiled at them, ignored the food Vanora had prepared and went to bed.

Pitcher's plan to take the letter-carrying from Kenneth seemed to be at stalemate. Unwilling to go and complain about the man's idleness and of how he was passing the work to a poorly paid Barrass, Pitcher dithered and wondered how to set about it. Taking a part of their livelihood from Kenneth and Ceinwen was not easy even though he was consumed with anger at the way they used Barrass.

'I can't just go into the sorting office and say, I wants the job because I can do it better and I wouldn't take advantage of a boy like Barrass,' he said to Emma. 'All I can do is wait and see if an opportunity arises. Be sure that if it does, I'll be ready and a-waiting.'

'I see your predicament, Pitcher,' Emma said. 'And I like you for your concern, but if we are to make this Posthorn Inn pay for all the expense and trouble, we have to get the extra custom.'

'We could report Ceinwen for selling ale, I suppose,' Pitcher mused. 'She uses the house like the tipple houses I've read of in centuries past, buying a barrel and selling it for retail, and that the law frowns on.'

'That's difficult too, her being my friend,' Emma sighed. 'You're right, best we wait and see if something turns up for us to take advantage of, my dear.'

'Meanwhile, there's the building work to busy myself with.'

'And the sooner that's done and finished with the better I'll be pleased,' Emma said sharply. 'I haven't been able to arrange a single dinner party or an entertainment of any kind, since you began it. How am I to find husbands for Daisy and Pansy without even a room that's free of dust, Mr Palmer, tell me that?'

Seeing that Emma was back on her old complaint, Pitcher hurriedly made his excuses and ran down the stairs calling for Arthur to get a move on and get the bar-room floor washed while there was a spare moment. His anger with the boy was not real but an echo of Emma's criticism.

Saturday evening was always one of the busiest. Those who worked on the small farms received their money, and those lucky enough to have something to sell at the market had extra money to jingle in their pockets. Pitcher and Arthur replenished mug after mug, running up and down to the cellar filling the large pitchers they used, laughing and joking with the customers to build up a jovial atmosphere.

Around the fire men sat discussing their daily existence, the long clay pipes nodding with their heads as they agreed on the unfairness of life. The collection of broken stems was already growing, and a few of the older, poorer men had only the abandoned stumps in their mouths, their moustaches and noses brown from the smoke which rose close to their faces from the well-used bowls.

Barrass was absent. His Saturday letters kept him away from the village until mid-afternoon on a Sunday. Pitcher wished he were there, he missed him. The boy was like a son, his partner in all his hopes and ambitions. Pitcher sighed and his thoughts wandered to the time when he could pay someone else to take the letters on the occasional day and leave Barrass free to help him.

Barrass was sitting at another alehouse, talking to a young woman who served there, eyeing her and considering his chances of spending some time in her bed. She was about his own age, but experience glittered in her greeny-grey eyes and hardened her expression. He knew that for her, he offered only a few moments' excitement and perhaps some money spent on food and drink. But, he thought ruefully, that was all he was looking for too. The thought saddened him. An image of Olwen grew before him, her young face smiling with deep sincerity, with none of the calculation of the serving girl.

He stood up and walked outside into the coolness of the evening. Shivering in the sudden change of temperature after leaving the fire-warmed room, he was angry. Angry with himself and with Olwen, who, although far away, still managed by her innocence to make him feel ashamed.

It was worse than when she followed him everywhere, watching him and preventing him from kissing a girl he had been attracted to. He remembered with a smile how he had become so used to her shadowing him, he had watched with the edge of his sight for her to appear when he should have been looking into the girl's eyes as he kissed her and murmured sweet endearments. Small wonder that some had begun the rumour that he was absent-minded and vague!

Abandoning all thoughts of a few hours of loving, he walked to where a small stream flowed and sat on its banks and thought of Olwen. When he had eaten his supper, he went to bed, alone.

Olwen had tried without any success to find out more about
Lowri's past. All the girl would tell her was that she had
worked at alehouses and inns. She wasn't rude or apparently
offended by Olwen's curiosity, but she smilingly evaded her
questions.

'It's as if she's just been born!' she complained to Mistress
Powell one morning as she dressed to leave for Ddole House.
'There seems to have been nothing at all before the moment
when she was found by Barrass. It's a-w-f-u-l strange.'

'Not everyone is as open and friendly as you are,' Mistress
Powell laughed. 'And, not everyone's life is as free from
unpleasantness.'

'Nothing very unpleasant can have happened to her,' Olwen
said in a whisper. 'When she had owned up to have come from
Bristol and not France, she brought her clothes from where she
had hidden them and a fine lot of clothes they are. And look at
her, well fed and used to bossing people about if you ask me. No,
I suspect that her life has been far from unhappy.'

The object of their discussion was on her way back up from
the fishing boat with Spider and Mary. Since her arrival she had
been no further than the village and appeared in no hurry either
to find her missing parent or set off again on her travels.

She was enthusiastically helpful and Mary had been pleasantly surprised at how easily she had slipped into their
life, handling baby Dic one moment and the next, scouring
the boards of the boat to clean them of the fishy smell. Whatever
job she was given she did willingly and when she was offered
none, she found one for herself. Rarely idle, she even helped
Mary and Mistress Powell with their woollens for the market,
sitting with them long into the night to finish off a consignment.
She listened, asked questions but always managed to avoid
telling them anything about herself. Like Olwen had said, it was
as if her life had not existed until she came to Mumbles village.

When she had been there for almost two weeks, she asked
Olwen if there was a possibility of work for her at Ddole House.
Olwen was inexplicably unwilling to help her. She did not dis-
like the woman, but knew she did not want to work for her.

'I don't think that would be a good idea,' she said quickly.
'Best you find somewhere else. This Annie Evans is not nice to

work for and in fact, I think I'll be thrown out on my ear soon just because my face doesn't fit.' She shook her fair head so her hair waved about her face like a spiky golden flower. 'No, best you ask in the village, or perhaps in Swansea. Now there's a place to work. Plenty of houses looking for servants in Swansea for sure.'

'I think I'll ask at the alehouse,' was Lowri's unconnected response. She offered her hand to Olwen and invited her to go with her.

Pitcher shook his head. Much as he liked the idea of having an extra pair of hands for serving the ale, he neither knew nor trusted this newcomer.

'No new serving maids wanted here,' he said, guessing without seeing how Arthur's face would drop at his words. They did need help and it was becoming more and more apparent that they would have to have more help, but not this woman. Best if she was made to feel unwanted and encouraged to go away. Life was difficult and dangerous enough with the boats due again in a few days, without untried people watching and listening.

'Swansea, now that's the place,' he said. 'Plenty of work for willing hands there.'

To everyone's surprise and relief, Lowri took his advice and went. She carried her bag of clothes on her back and with a hug for Mary and Olwen and gushing thanks for their generous hospitality, she waited at the door of the alehouse until someone offered her a lift into the town.

'Cardiff. That's where I'll try next,' she shouted as Pitcher watched her go.

But it was in Swansea that she stopped and found herself a place, as a maidservant at the small house of which one room was the sorting office for the post. The postmaster seemed to hint at a more than friendly welcome and her dark eyes gleamed at the prospect of some forbidden fun. There was nothing like a bit of forbidden loving behind the back of a suspicious wife to lighten the heart and blank out disappointments.

Once she had unpacked her things, she stood at the edge of the tide behind the castle and stared for a long time across the six-mile sweep of the bay at the distant houses of Mumbles and silently decided that one day she would go back.

125

If her mother could not be found, then she would make a new life for herself, and Mumbles with its friendly, generous people would be a good place in which to do it.

Chapter Nine

When Barrass reached the Swansea sorting office one Monday morning in early June, he saw at once that something unusual had happened. Two men were standing outside the door forbidding anyone from entering. One was Daniels and the other his counterpart from the eastern side of the town. Barrass went to Daniels and asked what was wrong.

'A death,' Daniels told him. 'The Deputy Postmaster has died and until some word has come telling us what happens next, we are not allowing anyone to touch the mail.'

'Where's Ben Gammon?' Barrass asked, feeling sure that if anyone knew anything, it would be Ben.

'Inside the Voyager Inn, spinning out the little he knows to entertain his audience.' Daniels was clearly disapproving.

Barrass went to greet the sixty-year-old postboy, who had ridden the end of the route from Monmouth to Swansea for more than thirty years, and when he looked into the dark interior of the drinking house he knew that where there was the biggest crowd of people, he would find Ben Gammon. As if he knew he was there, Ben turned and said,

'Ho, I says to myself, who will that be but but my friend Barrass come to hear the news?' Ben's voice boomed out as Barrass walked through the inn doorway, and he raised a hand in greeting. 'I says to the barman, Ho! I says, draw a quart of your best ale and he'll quaff it in less than a wink of your barmaid's saucy eye.'

Barrass smiled as he took the offered ale and found a place beside the postboy.

'So the Postmaster is dead? What happened?' Barrass asked.

'Taken in his sleep and him not a day more'n forty.'

'What will happen now?'

'I've told them slow-worms of Peace Keepers to let his wife sort the letters, she's done it often enough while he's been sleep-

127

ing off a bellyful as you and I well know.' He raised his voice as he went on, 'Slow-worms they are as are given authority. Now you and me, Barrass, we could have got this all sorted and everyone on their way in the time they take to ponder the correct procedure.'

The crowd shifted and they looked up to see Daniels in the doorway.

'Pausing to make sure his entrance was noted,' Ben whispered hoarsely.

'We have decided to allow the Deputy Postmaster's wife to set the mail on its way, so if you please, Master Gammon, will you come along and see that all is correctly done?'

'Well, as I says to Master Barrass here, he and I would have done so long since if you'd taken the thought to ask.'

Barrass listened to the chatter between the locals and the officials, gathering up as much information as he could, asking questions of everyone who seemed even remotely likely to know the answers. He had some news for Pitcher that needed immediate action.

Not stopping for more than a brief word of comfort for the widow, already draped in black clothes, and a more cheerful fare-thee-well for Ben, he mounted Jethro and hurried back to the alehouse. Kenneth was standing on the doorway of his house, tapping his foot, impatience reddening his face.

'Come on, Barrass, you should have been back an hour ago!' he shouted. The crowd around him, waiting for letters and news, added a chorus of agreement. 'There's work to be done, and you are slowing up the start to everyone's day.'

'The Postmaster's day started slowly enough and that's a fact!' Barrass replied, but he darted into the alehouse without explanations.

'What's that?' What did you say? What d'you mean? Where are my letters? Let me have them before any more time is wasted, boy!' Kenneth shouted in vain and had to admit defeat and sit back on the chair provided by Ceinwen, to wait until Barrass reappeared.

'Dead you say?' Pitcher smiled. 'Then this is the chance we've been waiting for!'

'Once a new Deputy Postmaster has been appointed, we must get to see him fast and apply for the right for me to deliver Gower letters,' Barrass said. 'Everyone will need to reapply and if we're quick, well, he won't have any loyalty to Kenneth, will he?'

'Not when I tell him about how Kenneth tackles the job!' Pitcher said firmly. 'Go you, and get your deliveries done and be back as early as you can tomorrow. I'll go straightaway into town and see whoever's in charge. If I don't talk the new Deputy Postmaster into using the alehouse as a collecting office then my name isn't Pitcher Palmer!'

'Daniels was in charge when I left!'

'Pity. Such a one for doing things the right way he's sure to hold everything up. But a new appointment will be made quickly for sure. The King's Mail can't be held up.'

They separated, each pondering the event and how it might give them the chance they had been waiting for. Pitcher ran up the stairs and explained briefly what had happened then set off to the stables, calling for Arthur to 'do what he could' until his return. He had hardly fastened his coat when Daisy came down the stairs, fully dressed in a redingote, carrying a stock and wearing a tall, small-brimmed hat, insisting she went with him.

'I heard what Barrass said and I want to help,' she said, a firmness in the tightened lips and the slight frown warning of determined arguments to come should it be necessary.

'But Daisy, this is man's work. And what would a young lady like you want with listening to your father arguing his case with a lot of shouting and accusations – no, it isn't for someone like you. Stay with your Mamma and I'll hurry back to tell you what happened if you're really curious about such matters.'

'Dadda, I'm coming.'

In too much of a hurry to argue, Pitcher nodded defeat and helped her to mount one of the ponies, which the stableboy had already harnessed, knowing from past experience that Daisy would wear her father down. Glancing proudly at her riding beside him, elegant, smartly dressed, and rather beautiful, Pitcher had to admit silently that her involvement could hardly jeopardize his case.

Barrass stood near Kenneth on the grassy mound in front of his door and after hurriedly whispering the news to Kenneth, told it to the waiting group.

'Dead in bed he was,' Barrass said, not adding the news that it was the new maid's bed he was found in and not his own.

'His poor wife went to call him as usual but found he was deep in his last sleep.' Again he refrained from pointing out that the maid whose bed he had chosen was severely beaten with the china pot from under the bed, the only weapon easily to hand, and sent from the house before the sun was up. He also withheld the spicy information that the maid was Lowri, who had so recently shared Olwen's bed.

'So what will happen now?' Ceinwen asked when the crowd was satisfied that Barrass had told them all he knew or could guess. 'Who will see to the appointment?' She looked at Kenneth, her dark eyes shrewd and added, 'What if you go and apply? The wages are poor enough and not that regularly paid, but it's a position you and I could manage.'

That was not news Barrass wanted, so he suggested they wait for a day or so.

'Best you give the poor widow a chance to recover her wits,' he said. 'Then write a letter to the Postmaster General in London. It's to him all appointments must go.'

Kenneth nodded. 'I'll compose a letter for you to take in on Wednesday,' he said.

Satisfied he had done all he could to delay Kenneth, Barrass set off with his letters. There was an urgency in his manner, he was impatient to be finished so he could learn more of the interesting situation.

When he had gone, Kenneth reached for his cloak and the wig he wore only on special occasions.

'I'm going to take the horse and go in to town at once,' he announced. 'I don't trust that Barrass, he's too friendly with Pitcher and if there's something to gain, I want to make sure it's we who gain it.'

Barrass was surprised to find that he had a letter for Olwen. So far as he knew, the family had never before received one. Few of the humbler homes had anyone who could write, and those who did had no business that would involve any dealings other than those contracted by word and a handshake. The handwriting on this one was unmistakable. It was from Penelope Ddole.

The letter, although not addressed to him, had the effect of wiping the excitement of the proposed new Deputy Postmaster from his thoughts. He normally set off through Sketty and to north Gower, leaving the local letters and those inland of the village for the following day when he returned.

Pondering this he wondered why he had continued with the routine when he had taken over the route from Kenneth. He knew that for Kenneth the convenience was apparent. Kenneth had a few local calls where he stayed longer than formal politeness required. To be seen around the village when his calls were almost completed was a convenient cover for his amorous meetings.

Today, Barrass decided, he would change things around and go first to the fisher family's house on the cliff. If Olwen was not there, as was likely to be the case, he would then go to Ddole House and interupt her work to give her the letter. With a bit of good fortune, he would be asked to stay for a bite and learn the contents of the note.

In both hopes he was disappointed. Having learnt from Mary that Olwen was at Ddole House, he hurried there and asked permission to hand her the letter. Dozy Bethan opened the door and Barrass saw at once that she had been crying. Her face was red, the eyes swollen and stricken with dismay.

'I'll see she gets the letter and, thank you for it,' she said. 'Will you call back for the money? I daren't stay and talk, Annie will be letting me go without a recommendation if I offend her further.' So saying, she closed the door.

Trying not to howl his disappointment, Barrass wrote the transaction in the unpaid column of his book and set off on Jethro to the north of Gower and a return to his normal route.

Watching him go from an upstairs window where she was brushing the walls of a rarely used bedroom, a frilly mobcap covering her hair and falling down over her eyes, Olwen sighed. She would love to have been going with him, astride the gentle pony, across the fields where they could talk without restraint about anything that came into their minds. Just as it had once been, day after day.

Curious about his visit, she made an excuse to go downstairs to fetch water to wash the already scrubbed paintwork and whispered to Bethan.

'What did Barrass want?'

Bethan took the letter from her apron pocket and handed it to her.

'What was that, my dear?' Annie's sharp eyes had noticed the exchange and Olwen showed her the letter.

'A letter and it's for *me*!' she said gleefully.

'Not while you're working, it isn't.' Snatching the letter but managing still to look pleasant and gentle, the precious paper was tucked into the folds of her dress and hidden deep in a pocket.

When her day's work was finished, Olwen hung around waiting for the letter to be returned. When it was made clear that she would have to wait until tomorrow, for William Ddole to see it and approve its delivery, Olwen ran home and told her father what had happened.

Spider and Dan walked to Ddole House and knocked loudly on the front door. They demanded of a startled Annie that they be shown in to see William Ddole and, as William had already seen them coming, Annie had no alternative but to obey.

The letter was handed over and Annie told politely and firmly, that should any other letters arrive, they must not be withheld. As compensation for the girl's upset, William took a few coins from the pile left month by month by Annie, from the wooden bowl on the sideboard, and handed them to Spider.

'This is to pay for the delivery,' he explained. 'I doubt my daughter thought, when she wrote, about the four pennies plus Kenneth's fee, or that such an amount might be impossible for your daughter to find.'

When Annie had left them, William checked that she was not behind the door listening, then in a whisper, the three men discussed the arrival of a cargo due in a few days. William walked with them to the end of the drive, and said casually,

'Should the letter contain any news other than the chatter young girls so enjoy I would be glad to know.'

'I'm sure Olwen would keep nothing from you,' Spider assured him.

Olwen took the letter up to her small room and sat on her bed. In the light of a tallow candle she read the words which in deference to her early skills in reading, Penelope had printed.

My dear friend Olwen, whom I miss most terribly [it

began]. Life in this big and noisy city is terrifying. I fear for my life every time I go on the streets, yet I find it exciting too. The ladies are dressed with such skill and elegance that I am made to feel like a poor country maiden who has never left the safety of her nursery. How I wish you had come with me, together we would have had so much to talk about and so many sights to enjoy!

The letter went on to describe some of the new clothes the Thomases had bought her, but under the excitement of shopping in the large and expensive London shops and full descriptions of outings and new friends, Olwen sensed a loneliness. She had promised her father that she would show the letter to William Ddole and she sat on her bed, thoughtful and wondering if she dared to hint that Penelope would be far happier at home.

She suggested as much to Mistress Powell and that old lady shook her head firmly.

'It's none of your business, my girl,' she warned. 'Penelope was very kind to bother to write to you and I don't think you should abuse her generosity by causing trouble.'

'But I think that is why she wrote to me,' Olwen argued. 'Just so I *can* cause trouble, and make her father see how mistaken he was to send her away. After all,' she added, a scowl shadowing her face, 'it's because of Barrass that she's gone and I'm sure he's learnt his lesson, and won't go near Penelope again.'

'There you go again, interfering!' the old lady laughed. 'How can you speak for Barrass?'

'Because he's my friend, and if I explain, tell him he must keep away from the likes of her, he'll – '

' – laugh at you!'

Olwen's scowl deepened and she tucked the sheet of paper away, angry at Mistress Powell's words, even though she knew they were probably correct. The following morning, she handed the letter to William Ddole and said no more than, 'If you please, sir, can I have it back once you have read it? I haven't had a letter before and would treasure it for always.'

'Sit down,' she was bidden, and she sat on the edge of a wooden chair while he studied the page, apparently reading it several times before handing it back.

'Why should my daughter write to you?' he asked.

'Because she taught me to read and thought that a letter would be a sort of reward, sir. At least, that is what I think.' She crossed her fingers and with a beating heart added, 'Unless, she wants to let me know how brave she is and how well she copes with the loneliness of being away from you, sir.'

'She says nothing about loneliness,' he said with a frown.

'Not in the words, but I think she writes a brave letter not a happy one, don't you?'

'Here is your letter, Olwen. I would be obliged if you would show me any others you receive.'

'May I write back, sir?' she dared to ask.

'If you have any news that would interest her, I'm sure she would be pleased to read it.'

He smiled as she scuttled out of the room, tucking the letter into a capacious apron pocket, but the smile faded as he thought of his daughter so far away. Olwen's words had added to his increasing opinion that sending her away had not been the wisest move. He sat for a long time, wondering how he could word a letter suggesting she could now return. Olwen was probably right in that Penelope was unhappy, but if he left her there much longer, she might begin to enjoy city life and then he might lose her for always.

Kenneth set off to discuss the new arrangement for him to be responsible for Gower letters, feeling confident. After all, he had never been reported for holding up the mail, whereas many of his counterparts had been repeatedly warned for lax timekeeping, slowness and missed connections. No, there was little chance of his application being refused.

He went across the sands to the town, the tide being a slack one and almost fully out. He did not hurry, but enjoyed the ride, knowing that with Barrass on his deliveries and Ceinwen at home to take in any letters that might arrive, everything was well ordered. Really, he thought as he approached the town, his life was a good one.

There was the usual gathering outside the receiving office and he handed his horse to a boy to look after and pushed his way importantly to the doorway. The widow of the Postmaster was still there, draped in heavy dark shawls, her face almost hidden in the depths of them, and behind the counter a new face.

'My son Walter Waterman,' she said by way of introduction. 'The new Deputy Postmaster for Swansea.' She gestured to the young man who sat behind the counter gazing at a page in a large ledger, apparently uninterested in the new arrival.

Walter was pale-faced, with washed out freckles on his nose and forehead. His hair was fair with a touch of redness and the moustache he wore failed to give the impression of the soldier he had once been. He wore a slightly bored expression and this alone was enough to annoy Kenneth, who liked to feel he was someone to whom others gave their full attention.

'I am the letter-carrier for Gower,' Kenneth said with an authoritative sharpness.

The young man looked at him and with an offhand nod said, 'Who's who and what's what in the world of His Majesty King George's Royal Mail, well now, that's for others more important than ourselves to decide.'

'I think perhaps you do not understand, being new to the office. I am Kenneth, and I have held the position of letter-carrier on Gower for many years.' Kenneth was put out by the young man's attitude; he was used to being treated with politeness as befitted the position he held.

'However long you've held the post doesn't matter. It's whether you hold it *now* is the question and that's a question as cannot be answered until we hear from London.' Walter Waterman lowered his head and with a finger keeping his place, he read out the entries for his mother to check against her list. Kenneth had been dismissed.

He went out into the warm sunshine and walked around like a farmyard cockerel who had been confronted with a rival. Without feathers to ruffle and a comb to waggle, he managed to give the same effect by puffing out his cheeks and flapping the cloak which hung loosely around his shoulders. He tutted to anyone whose eye he caught but said nothing to explain his agitation. He needed time to think. Should he go back in there and tell them again who he was? Walter Waterman might be a dullard and his mother refusing to face the fact? Or was it best to wait until Ben Gammon arrived for support?

He was so put out by his reception he was unable to wait and after a few more minutes spent strutting up and down outside

135

the receiving office door, he flung it back on its hinges and marched back in to demand that he be given an assurance as to his position.

'I didn't come here to beg leave to continue,' he spluttered, 'but simply to introduce myself!'

'Your name will be considered with the rest,' Walter said calmly, 'but I must warn you that the other names have already been sent forward. You'll go in as a latecomer.'

'A latecomer?' Kenneth glared at the young man but when Walter stood up and with some apparent difficulty, limped around the counter, he backed off and quickly found himself outside the door and it being closed firmly in his red face.

He rode into town every day for more than a week. Each time he went to the office and saw Walter Waterman, he was told that so far there was no confirmation from London about his appointment.

Ben Gammon met him there one day some eight days after his first meeting with Walter Waterman, and to Ben, Kenneth poured out all his anger.

'Why, I have the very letter here in my bag as you be awanting to read, Kenneth of Gower,' Ben said, having listened to Kenneth's complaints at the way he had been treated. He delved into his leather bag and waved a single-page letter in front of Kenneth's worried face. 'I seed that it was addressed to Walter Waterman the new representative of the Royal Mail for the town of Swansea and I thinks to myself, Well then Ben, I thinks, there'll be a few who will value the speed with which you gets that one to its destination! So I ignores the urge for a rest and a draft of ale at the middle of the day and continues on so as to arrive just a few minutes earlier to put you out of your misery.' He laughed, and jumping down from his horse, pushed his way through the waiting people and into the office.

Kenneth sank down on to a bench and waited for the door to open and his name to be called. Pitcher appeared from inside the inn and sat beside him. Kenneth muttered something about treacherous friends and turned his back on the alehouse keeper.

Ben Gammon came out after several minutes had passed without a word spoken between them, and nailed a notice to the outside of the door. Kenneth wanted to run quickly and read it but he deliberately waited until Pitcher had reached the door, expecting to be able to sneer at the man for the impudence of applying for his post.

'So then,' Ben's voice boomed across the open space. 'The decision is not yet made?'

'What?' This time Kenneth could not be still. He bounded across and demanded to know the reason for the aggravation.

'Him as is called Walter Waterman being the son of his father, has now to write a report on the suitability of each and every applicant,' Ben reported for the benefit of those who could not read the notice. 'And he says as how he can't see anyone today, him being fatigued and ready to drop. And,' he grinned, his mouth opening to reveal stubs of black teeth, 'talking about drop reminds me that I have a strong need for a drop meself if one of you would be so obliging.'

Kenneth watched as the postboy walked through the inn doorway with the crowd gathered around him to ply him with drink and listen to his specialized version of the news he had brought.

With Pitcher standing beside him, Kenneth read the notice. Walter had stated that those who had applied for the post should call on him on the following day to discuss their suitability. Kenneth went for his horse and giving the boy who had looked after it a halfpenny, set off home to discuss the development with Ceinwen. The only pleasant episode in the whole day was when he saw Pitcher walking beside his limping horse. Pitcher asked for help and Kenneth gleefully ignored his request to send Percy to meet him with another horse.

'I hope your boots rub 'til your feet split!' he muttered as he hurried past.

'There's nothing definite,' Pitcher warned Emma later that day as he sat with his sore feet in a bowl of water to which Emma had added some leaves and flower heads of ragwort. 'I think we must go together, my dear, so this Walter Waterman can see for himself how respectable and morally upright we are.'

'I think I should come as well,' Daisy said. 'For if there's a young man involved, then who better to deal with him than a young woman?'

Daisy sat silently as her parents gave her a dozen reasons why she would not, could not, go. Then a smile, that was hardened by a steely look in her blue eyes, lightened her features and she said firmly, 'I will be ready to leave with you, Dadda. I think I will wear the newest of my bonnets. Mamma, will you help me to fix the decorations more firmly?'

Pitcher sighed. He recognized in his daughter something of the determination he frequently met in his wife. Daisy was the only one to inherit it, he thought, Pansy being the gentler of the twins and Violet altogether more pliable and conventional. If only one of his children had been a boy, then he would have had a partner to work beside him and see the dream of a smart and successful inn materialize before them. Pitcher and son. Yes, that was what Emma should have given him, a son.

Pansy smiled at him and he had the startling realization that she had been reading his thoughts as she put down her sewing and said, 'Daisy might not be the son you wanted, Dadda, but she's as close to you and your ideas as many a boy, don't you think?'

'Rubbish!' snorted Emma. 'A boy is a boy and a girl is a young lady and that's how it will always be!'

In defiance of Emma's outraged arguments to the contrary, Daisy was with Pitcher when he went once more into town to discuss his application for the alehouse to be a receiving house for the King's letters. She had spent a lot of time on her appearance and everyone they passed stopped to look at her.

She sat in their wagon, the seat of which had been covered with Welsh wool blankets fringed extravagantly with red and green. She wore a dress of cream cotton, with a neckline lower than Emma thought permissible, but Daisy lifted it to a more decorous height before they left and was amused to see Emma nod approval. Her straw bonnet was large and held in place by ribbons of cream and green, and on it were huge flowers made from the same cotton as her dress.

Pitcher wore a suit of cinnamon-coloured wool, trimmed with light brown. His leather hat was brown and his boots were of the same fine quality.

'What a pity that the fine waistcoat Pansy was making for me was not a good fit, being a bit tight,' Pitcher sighed. 'With that on I'd have looked so smart they'd have taken me for a man of the city.' He frowned and asked, 'What happened to it, d'you know?'

'Put aside for Arthur I think, Father,' Daisy replied vaguely. She wasn't interested in Pitcher's clothes, only her own, and the effect of them on the new Deputy Postmaster in Swansea.

Pitcher was very proud to have Daisy beside him and although he knew she would not be able to add anything to his persuasions, business being the province of a man, he was glad he had given in and allowed her to accompany him. He smiled and waved at everyone they saw, and he called out good wishes almost, he thought with a chuckle, as if they were like those wealthy people who arrived in grand carriages and walked along the seashore breathing the sea air like it was a precious commodity discovered by themselves!

There was such confidence about the well-attired couple that people made way for them as they approached the door of the sorting office. Despite his intention of leaving Daisy at the inn while he attended to his business, he did not insist when she headed for the Postmaster's house after he helped her to alight. She went before him, her skirts held up out of the dusty earth, and stood while a young boy jumped up and opened the door for her. Inside, she stretched to force the neck of her dress to its intended low line and smiled at Walter Waterman. Pitcher pretended not to see.

'I,' she said with a dazzling smile, 'am Daisy Palmer, the daughter of Pitcher Palmer of Pitcher's alehouse in Mumbles.' She offered him a small, delicate hand and smiled as he stuttered his greeting. 'My father wishes to see you on a matter of business. May I stay and listen? Please?' she added, pouting prettily. She looked around for a chair and frowned at the dusty one that stood in a corner of the small room.

Still stuttering, apologizing for the awful neglected state of the chair, he dusted it with a stock hastily unwound from his neck and begged her to sit.

'You are most welcome to my humble room,' he managed to say. He shouted to a boy standing at the doorway to fetch a second chair and offered his own to Pitcher.

Pitcher had difficulty not to smile as he watched his daughter flirting and making the young man aware of her attractions. He knew he should stop her, and send her back to the wagon to wait for him, but he could not. The possibility that her presence might sway Walter to decide in their favour was too tempting.

'Lucky for you that your mother can't see the way you're behaving, Miss,' he managed to whisper.

'I understand you have a proposition regarding the managing of Gower letters?' Walter said when they were all seated and ale had been sent for. 'Can you tell me exactly what you had in mind?' He spoke to Pitcher, but his attention was on Pitcher's daughter, who sat staring at the young man with admiration and full attention.

'I want to offer the use of my alehouse as a centre for the collection of the letters,' Pitcher began, wondering how much of his explanation the bemused Walter would remember. 'The house of Kenneth is small and inconveniently placed up on a high bank where some of the older messengers can hardly climb. The alehouse is in the process of being improved and soon the house will be one of the most excellent in the village. Where better to distribute the letters of the King's Mail?'

'Oh, I agree with you, sir,' Walter said. He shuffled a few papers as if searching for something, then stood up. 'I think if you and your daughter will spend an hour with me at the inn, going into details of your argument, I can make a good case for your application being accepted.'

Smiling demurely at the ex-soldier who offered her his arm for the short walk to the inn, Daisy managed to turn her head briefly and looked knowingly at her father. Pitcher raised his eyes heavenward and hoped none of this would be reported to Emma. She would kill him!

Chapter Ten

William Ddole almost ran into the house after dismounting and handing the reins of his horse to David. His face was white and his hair looked unkempt and wild. He said nothing to Annie, who met him at the door, but went at once to the study where he poured himself a brandy with a hand that shook.

Annie hesitated outside the door but was afraid to knock. There was obviously something wrong, but now was not the time to enquire. Instinctively she knew it was wiser to wait until he had calmed down. She went into the kitchen and warned the very subdued Olwen and Dozy Bethan to make as little noise as possible as the master was upset.

There was no need for such a warning, threatened as they both were with the end to their jobs; neither girl showed a tendency to display high spirits. Olwen had seen William arrive home and she was curious to know what had upset him, hoping that it had not been bad news about Penelope. But she said nothing of her fears to Annie. The less that interloper was told the better.

William sent for Annie after a second helping of brandy and she glided silently in and sat in a chair behind the door as she usually did when she expected him to discuss something with her. Today there was no friendly approach.

'I understand you have told Seranne to leave?' he said, and his voice was so stern she at once stood up as if preparing to defend herself.

'I did. She is obviously unfit to work and even when she did feel able to attend, she didn't give a reasonable day's work for the money you pay her.'

'She is to have her job back.' His eyes were full of something akin to anger, yet she saw distress there as well. 'I also want you to make sure that, as Florrie always did, you see that she is given any spare food that is left, to take home.'

Surprised, Annie could only nod.

William dismissed her with a wave of his hand. At the door she hesitated, and asked,

'Master Ddole, about another matter. Do you really wish to continue paying Florrie? Now she has been replaced it seems an unnecessary waste. And,' she added softly, 'I'm sure the woman has plenty to do preparing herself for her marriage to the Keeper of the Peace.'

'I will decide what and whom we can afford,' William said. 'Florrie stays and does as little or as much as she wishes. And Seranne is to be given back her place now, today, and I want you to make sure that if she is tired, then she will rest. She will not be made to feel that her money is dependent on the amount of work she does. Neither Seranne nor Florrie will be allowed to feel anything less than useful and needed. Do you understand?'

Annie closed the door behind her and stood in the passageway wondering how best to manage this sudden change of attitude towards her. To her surprise, she heard the sounds of sobs coming from the room she had just left.

William left the house again a while later. He did not use the main door but walked through the kitchen, where he stopped and watched Olwen chopping up vegetables for his meal, and Bethan, nervously looking at him through the edges of her eyes, washing the slate floor.

'Are you both happy in your work here?' he surprised them by asking.

Bethen whispered an anxious, 'Yes, Master William,' convinced that the moment had arrived and she was going to be told to leave.

Olwen was, as usual, more outspoken.

'Happy, yes sir. But not so much as when Florrie was in charge of us and that's for sure. And when there were more to cook and see to,' she added, looking at him to see if her words were angering him. 'That was a busier and happier time too, sir.' She lowered her voice and whispered, 'I know you miss them, but we miss them too.'

'Olwen! Get to your work and don't be impertinent!' Annie appeared at the door and her arm was raised in a threatening gesture. 'I'm sorry, sir. I have been too lax with the management of this one.'

William shook his head. 'There is no strong servant and master atmosphere in this house. I asked Olwen a question; she would have had to be very dull not to reply with honesty.'

William went out, a strange, absent-minded look on his face, his eyes suspiciously reddened. He went to the stables and set off to see Edwin Prince. He had to tell someone.

Annie waited until the sound of the hooves on the hard surface of the drive had faded then she slapped Olwen in a body-swinging blow across her head.

'If the master, in his unhappiness, allows such behaviour, I do not!' Leaving Olwen holding her head and blinking to recover from the knock that had sent her staggering, she left the room.

'What's got into this house!' Bethan whispered. 'If I had somewhere to go I'd be off like a shot from Master Ddole's gun!'

Stunned as she was from the strength of Annie's punishment, Olwen couldn't resist a weak smile at the thought of Bethan resembling anything fast!

'Best we don't think about it too much, just get on with our work,' Olwen said, holding her ear to ease the pain.

A few moments later, Annie returned to the kitchen and she was wearing her outdoor clothes.

'I will be back in a little while, so be sure you don't relax into idleness,' she warned. When she did return, both girls were surprised and very pleased to see that she had Seranne with her.

William found Edwin sitting under a tree in his garden with some papers on his knee. Beside him was Violet, the nurse and the baby Gabriella. The scene was such an attractive one he held his breath and did not reveal his presence for a while, soaking in the atmosphere of contentment. He wished he could reclaim the years when his children were small, wondering with regret why he had not made more of them.

Seeing him, Edwin jumped up and placing the papers on a small table with a stone on them to still their fluttering, hailed him and walked to meet him. Violet whispered a few words to the nurse who went into the house presumably, William guessed, for refreshments. Picking up the baby, Violet followed her husband.

'William, I hope you aren't just passing?' Edwin said.

'I would like a little of your time if you are free,' William replied as a boy took charge of his horse. 'But first, let me look at this baby. How she has grown!' Talking the expected small talk, they made their way back to the chairs and table under the trees.

Violet guessed it was Edwin that William had called to see. Making the excuse that Gabriella was in need of an extra coat she went into the house. William watched her go with something akin to envy. If Penelope had married John Maddern as I had hoped, I might have been a part of a scene similar to this, he thought regretfully.

When a servant girl had provided them with refreshments, Edwin asked his friend what was troubling him.

'For I saw in a moment that all is not well with you,' he explained. When William didn't speak, he went on, 'Is it Penelope? She hasn't chosen to stay in London, has she?'

'It's something very different but in its way even more frightening.' He paused, looking around as if preparing to divulge a dangerous secret. 'I have seen death on the face of Seranne.'

'Will you explain?' Edwin asked, startled.

'Three times in my life I have seen something on the face of someone and have known instinctively that it portrayed their death. I saw it on my own mother a few weeks before she died, and again when I looked at my dear wife, Dorothy, before she too left me.'

'They are relations and loved ones. But Seranne?' Edwin asked.

'I know it is inexplicable, but it has happened. It's like the image of a skull, which intensifies so I can't see the features at all, then it fades and the person is there, staring and wondering what is wrong with me. Edwin, what can I do?'

'Have you spoken to the vicar?'

'I have tried, and to the doctor. They both agree that it's an outward show of the love and affection I have for these people, a love which I don't easily reveal. With my mother and my wife I can see how they might think that, but Seranne?'

'There is nothing you can do, you have to try and forget it and treat the woman as normally as you can.'

'Annie had sacked her. I insisted she brought her back. At least I can see she has enough food and money for medicines.

Although Vanora is good with herbal remedies, a visit from the doctor might help.'

'She is ill then?'

'Of the morbid lung. Her brothers too, I suspect. Oh, Edwin, I am afraid to meet them in case I see the same early death in them too!'

'The morbid lung is likely to carry them off to an early grave whether you see it on their faces or not.'

'I walk with my head down as I pass people I know, this thing is so terrifying, the more so because I know I can do nothing.'

'Stay a while and play with Gabriella. She is such a cheerful child I'm sure you will not find a better tonic.'

During the afternoon, while the baby alternately slept and chortled happily, William explained to his friends why he continued to pay the wages of Florrie.

'There have been so many changes in my life and I cannot bear another. Florrie disappearing from the house and Seranne being sent away was more than I could face. That was why I went to see her and ask about her health.' His face again became troubled. 'That was when I saw the sign of her impending death.'

'This Annie Evans, is she satisfactory?'

'Apart from an overriding determination to save me money, yes. She does her work calmly and with an ease I can only admire.' There was reservation in his remarks but Edwin did not delve.

The two men discussed the payments to come from the people inland whom they supplied with contraband goods, and when William left, the family stood to wave him off. He looked back at Violet holding her husband's arm, the baby safely curled against her, and decided that he would forget his pride, and write to tell Penelope she could return.

The house should be filled again. Young Olwen had seen more clearly than he had the problem with Ddole House. It had once been a home for a family and a dozen servants. The death of Dorothy and the departing of Penelope had changed everything, and, since Florrie decided to marry Daniels, the servants had been reduced by Annie so the place rattled about him like the lifeless branches of a dead tree.

When he reached home, Annie served his meal, having sent

the others away. She was solicitous of his comfort and he was too tired to think of her attentions as anything but normal.

'I am writing to my daughter,' he told her when he pushed away the last plate. 'I will tell her it is time she came home.'

'Is that wise, sir?' Annie asked quietly. 'She has hardly had time to find her feet in the society of the city. Wouldn't it be less cruel to see her there and decide whether or not she wants to come back here?'

'Of course she wants to come back!' Fear that the woman might be right gave an edge of anger to his voice.

'Of course you know best, sir,' Annie said. 'But perhaps you should give her at least until the end of summer?'

William was confused. Perhaps Annie was right and Penelope would not thank him for taking her away from friends she was just beginning to know? Then he thought of Olwen, whom his daughter had befriended. She thought Penelope should return. Young and inexperienced as she was, she had sensed his loneliness, showing understanding beyond her years. Young, and only a servant, yet he took comfort in her opinion because it was what he wanted to believe.

He took out all Penelope's letters and read them through, the pleading to be allowed home more apparent than when he had not wanted to see it. He took out his pens and the bottle of black ink Florrie made for him, and began to write.

Annie never went out, preferring to send one of the servants to collect anything she needed. One Friday she pleased Olwen by telling her to go into town and buy some material for new curtains.

'The material is chosen,' Annie explained. 'The woman came with samples and I explained to her exactly what I needed.'

'She didn't explain how I am to carry it!' Olwen confided to Dozy Bethan. 'Heavy it will be and me with arms like bits of unravelled wool!'

'You will be back to help clear after luncheon,' Annie warned as she handed Olwen the sample of material and the money, together with the measurements for the seller to check.

A morning of freedom was a luxury and Olwen thought carefully about getting full value from it. Then realization came and she was hard put not to shout her delight. It was Friday, the one day on which Barrass was free. He had no deliveries or collections and he must be persuaded to go with her!

She lifted her skirts high and ran down the drive and through the fields towards the village, her bare feet dancing. She was singing aloud her hopes and prayers that he would be at the alehouse with Pitcher. She reached the alehouse breathless, rosy-faced and full of hopeful excitement.

'Barrass?' she called. 'Barrass, are you there?'

Pitcher came to the door and invited her inside.

'Down in the cellar sorting out the empty barrels for washing. Best you go down and see him. It seems you are in too much of a hurry for him to come to you!' he laughed.

Olwen ran down the stone steps into the chill, gloomy cellar and, hearing the sound of voices, went into the cavernous room beyond.

'Barrass,' she burst out, 'I have to go into town and carry home a bale of material and it will be a-w-f-u-l heavy. Can you come with me and help?'

Barrass straightened up from the barrel he had been inspecting, his head almost touching the curved ceiling.

'Olwen!' He looked pleased to see her, his smile revealing even teeth, his eyes crinkling with delight. 'I thought it was a storm coming up the Channel to engulf us all, you sounded so driven!' he teased. 'But a welcome sight you are and no mistake.'

'But can you come?' she asked.

'Come? I was so startled at your flurried appearance I didn't listen to what you asked,' he grinned.

'Oh Barrass.' She put her small hands on her hips and bent slightly into a scolding position to say, 'You are a-w-f-u-l irritating sometimes.'

'All right, I'll have a word with Pitcher and if he can spare me for a few hours I'll go with you to carry your heavy load.'

Olwen's eyes glowed as she preceded him back up the steps to find Pitcher.

Barrass's horse, Jethro, was stabled behind the alehouse and he was unaffected by the extra weight as the two people mounted him. The luxury of the ride instead of the long, six-mile walk was an added bonus, although Olwen hoped it did not mean she had Barrass's company for less time.

'Could we eat at the inn?' she asked.

Barrass nodded and she hugged his arm. Being seated in front of him she feared to fall off if she tried to hug his body. She leaned back against him and decided that this unexpected morning out was the most wonderful thing that had happened in many a day. She looked up at Barrass and hoped it was the same for him.

It was one of those days when everything seemed right. The inn was busy, but without the usual crowd who waited three times a week for the letters to arrive with Ben Gammon. So although many knew Barrass, they did not at once surround him and involve him in their questions and general chatter.

Having left Jethro at the stables, they walked to the shop, paid for the material and arranged to collect it after they had eaten. On the way back to the inn, they walked through the busy market surrounding Island House. In a corner, half hidden by carts and wooden, wheeled stalls, they saw Madoc Morgan. He was standing beside two full sacks, the contents of which were almost completely hidden. Occasionally he would touch the opening of the sack with his foot so someone passing close to him could see what he surreptitiously offered for sale, then the foot would reach out and close it again when a stall holder attempted to look.

'He has no permission to sell,' Olwen whispered.

'And what he sells is probably not his anyway!' Barrass added grimly. 'Best we keep away. To be seen talking to him should he be caught, might bring us trouble.'

There was a young girl selling flowers, and Barrass bought a large bunch and handed them to Olwen. She stretched up and kissed his cheek and hugged him.

'Thank you, Barrass! Mam loves to see flowers in the house.'

'There's no flower lovelier than you, Olwen-the-fish,' he replied.

They ate roast pork in sorrel sauce for their lunch, with chunks of freshly baked bread. Olwen thought she had never tasted anything so good. She was so light-hearted with the plea-sure of the unexpected treat that her mood imparted itself to everyone they met. Laughter followed them and was reborn at every encounter.

The old woman selling sweetmeats encouraged them to stay

at her stall, seeing that their presence brought a cheerfulness and an inclination to buy to those who stood near. A man selling medicines begged her to take a bottle so he could use her as an example of how others would look once they had drunk his elixir. Barrass pulled her away with a laugh.

'They could drink a thousand bottles and not look as fresh and young and beautiful as my Olwen,' he told the man proudly.

When they went to collect the material for Annie, they saw that the sacks at the feet of Madoc Morgan were almost empty. Madoc smiled at them and nodded, touching the sack with a foot to conceal the feathers that showed. Olwen thought he looked tired and was reminded how fortunate she was not to have to face the long walk home.

On impulse she begged a coin from Barrass and bought Jethro a bunch of small new carrots. Hardly bigger than quills, she knew they were only the thinnings from the crop, a mere mouthful for the animal, but one he would relish.

When she slid off Jethro at the end of Ddole House drive, Annie came out to scold her for being so long. Whatever time she had arrived, Olwen knew she would have complained. The fact she had ridden and saved more than the time they had wasted in town was not relevant. She didn't bother to make an excuse, but was glad when Annie's tirade was shortened by the appearance of William, with a letter.

'Run after Barrass will you, Olwen, so this can go into tomorrow's bag?'

Olwen did so, dropping the bale of cloth to the ground. She handed the letter to Barrass and when she returned, William was directing David to carry the heavy parcel into the house for her. She wondered briefly about the interest he was showing in the servants' wellbeing. She had carried heavier loads than the curtain material without a thought of expecting help. He's almost treating us like a replacement for his lost family, poor man, she thought.

For the rest of the day Olwen worked hard, carrying in water and coal, doing jobs without waiting for Seranne or Annie to point them out. At the end of the day she ran home full of the prospect of reliving her morning with Barrass, every wonderful moment remembered, revived time and again, and then stored.

*

149

On the following evening when Barrass went with the local letters into Swansea to receive the newly arrived ones from Walter Waterman, Pitcher went with him. When Ben Gammon had arrived and handed over his leather, baize-lined bag, Pitcher sat at a table outside the inn and watched the scene. It was raining and most of the people who waited to ply Ben with drink and hear his news were inside the inn. In the partial shelter of a large chestnut tree, Pitcher huddled under his cloak and waited for the crowd to disperse.

Barrass put his letters into his bag after examining them and planning his route to deliver them, before rejoining him.

'I've told Walter you want to have a word, Pitcher,' he said. 'Do you want me to wait with you?'

'Best if you do,' Pitcher replied. 'I think we need to use all our persuasions to get him to give us what we want.'

When Ben had passed them on his way into the inn, with a cheerful greeting, Pitcher stood and tilted his head for the rain to run out of the brim of his hat and walked towards the sorting office. Walter limped towards him when he entered and smiled a wary welcome.

'Come to state your case yet again, Pitcher Palmer?' the man asked. He looked exaggeratedly behind Pitcher and seeing Barrass, reacted in mock surprise. 'What, no daughter today? Perhaps a trifle early for her to be about I suppose.'

'Daisy is at a music lesson this morning,' Pitcher explained.

'Pity, she has a far prettier face to plead than either of you!'

Pitcher ground his teeth in silent rage. The man was rude and unpleasant.

'It is not my daughter's place to plead with anyone, sir.'

'Of course not, but her presence gives me the mood to listen with deeper regard for your opinion,' Walter replied.

'Have you considered my case?' Pitcher asked. 'Barrass here will tell you honestly of the way Kenneth has treated the honourable and favoured task. Giving the work to others casually and carelessly while he dallies with unsavoury people, ignoring the comfort of those he employs and giving the Royal Mail a determined lack of dignity.'

'Yet Kenneth has been the letter-carrier for many years. Why should I take it from him when I have had no complaints about the service he gives?'

'Because it's Barrass you have to thank for the fine manner in which the service is carried out.'

'And Barrass has helped Kenneth for – how many years?' Walter asked sarcastically.

'A matter of months only,' Pitcher admitted.

'Perhaps you can come and see me again, when I have made my final decision. And – ' Walter added, limping towards the half-open door to see them out, 'perhaps you will come on a day when your daughter is free to accompany you. We could eat together at the inn, on Friday perhaps?'

'Haughty young beggar!' Pitcher grumbled as they went to where they had left their horses. 'Thinking I'd use my Daisy to advance my chances.'

'And of course you wouldn't – ' Barrass smiled.

'Tell me, Barrass,' Pitcher grinned, 'what should we tell Emma?'

They watched as Ben set off on his return, waved off by the familiar faces who greeted his every arrival and departure like a pack of affection-starved puppies. Barrass noticed that his bag was lacking its strap. When Barrass mentioned it to him, Ben said, 'I says to my wife, I says, ho, wife, you will have me accused of carelessness with the Royal Mail if I should let one of these letters slip to the ground. "Ben," she says to me, "I will fix it for sure this very morrow." But the morrow comes and at once it's today! So I fear I will have to find myself a pretty little sewing maid afore I get it all made safe. And soon!' he went on, unable to resist making a story out of a simple remark. 'I shall have to talk urgent and soon to some sweet maid. Can't have Ben Gammon accused of being careless with his letters,' he laughed. 'Daren't risk no complaints, dare I?' He rolled his eyes and added, 'I thinks to myself, I thinks, plenty of folk willing to step in and do it for me, eh, Pitcher?' he teased.

Grumbling at the impudence of the man, Pitcher turned away and he and Barrass rode back to the village.

When Daisy heard what was expected of her she agreed at once. Pitcher was pleased but rather surprised that all the arguments he had prepared to persuade her were not necessary.

'I want us to have that letter receiving office,' she said. 'Kenneth doesn't deserve it and Ceinwen is the sort to make money from something or the other, and neither will starve.'

'Daisy!' Emma remonstrated. 'This is no way for a young lady with your schooling and position to talk!' She turned to Pitcher. 'Really, Mr Palmer! What are you thinking of that you allow your daughter to become mixed up in business!' She spat out the last word as if it were something with a sour taste.

'Business is what keeps us warm and with full bellies and never forget it,' he retaliated, although he knew that Emma appreciated the importance of the alehouse and his plans for enlarging its success. Her protest at involving their daughter in appealing to Walter Waterman was for appearances and not a strongly felt dismay.

'Why shouldn't we all go in,' Pansy surprised them by suggesting. 'If we went as a family, he couldn't fail to see how important we are in the community.' She put down the sewing with which she spent much of her time and smiled at them. 'I would enjoy a visit to the town. I need some new cotton and silks for the cushion I am making for Violet's baby.'

'Cushion?' Pitcher said. 'I thought you were working on a shirt for me?'

'The shirt is finished, Dadda, and it was for Arthur, not you,' Pansy smiled.

'Hand sewing shirts for the potboy!' Emma gasped. 'Whatever next!'

Pansy did not tell them that, unnoticed, she had made three shirts and several stocks and two embroidered waistcoats for Arthur, which he had hidden away in a box beside his bed in the cellar.

One waistcoat was specially fine. Made of a snuff-coloured velvet, Pansy had neatly covered it with small stitches in soft greens and lemon and cream. The back and the pocket linings were taffeta and generously pleated. She had carefully wrapped it and hidden it at the bottom of her deepest drawer.

She and Arthur rarely met for more than a few minutes, yet their affection for each other grew by the week. There was nothing to show to any but the keenest observer that they were any more than daughter of the house and servant, yet when they did manage to find a few moments to be together, the nature of their relationship was clearly as relaxed and comfortable as an old and well tried friendship.

When Pitcher and Barrass were occupied in the rebuilding of the rooms above the newly enlarged stables, and Daisy and Emma were busily writing letters to friends, when Edwin and Violet Prince came to tea with their daughter, Gabriella, with Emma fully and happily occupied, Pansy took the opportunity to run down to the bar-room, which was mercifully empty of customers.

'Arthur, come up, I want to talk to you,' she whispered from the top of the cellar steps. Arthur appeared behind her, attracted her attention with a cough and she gasped with shock. 'Oh! I thought you were Mamma!' She unfolded the paper-wrapped parcel she carried and showed him the new cushion she was making. 'I told Mamma this is for Violet,' she said, 'but it's for me, to keep for when I have a home of my own.'

'It's perfect,' Arthur said in his oddly pitched voice. 'I don't know how you can do something as perfect.' He frowned as he sat beside her on the top step. 'I don't understand, how d'you know where the needle will come up when you push it from beneath the cloth? It looks so impossible to me. I manage to miss the shank of the button every time when I try to repair my coat!'

As he examined the delicately stitched material, he gradually slid closer to her until his thin, bony jaw was close to her smooth, rounded face. Turning slowly, he kissed her cheek.

'So clever, so full of beauty and yet with time to spare for the likes of me,' he said in wonder.

'You make me *feel* clever and full of beauty, Arthur,' she replied.

She told him in a whisper of the material she had bought to make trousers for Pitcher.

'But I know already they will be too small and will fit you to perfection,' she laughed.

Ben Gammon sang loudly and with a distinct lack of talent as he approached the end of his day's ride. He was in no hurry and allowed the horse to walk at its own pace. The day was damp and humid after the rain and a mist was rising from the warming earth. He had only a few miles to travel when he crossed a field where hares were often seen. Today he was not looking for them, although it gave him pleasure to see the powerful animals making a run for freedom when hunters disturbed them.

The regular path leading diagonally across the field was wet, and when his horse slipped and staggered in a deeply muddied patch, he steered it to one side to walk on the grass where the ground was firmer. A few traces of mud showed that he was not the first that day to decide on a slight deviation from the marked path.

Unseen, some distance in front of him, a hare lay in its form, ears back, listening to the horse approaching. It wasn't worried. It knew that the path lay well to one side of it and that the animal would pass as others did, without making it run. It crouched lower, eyes wide, brain assessing the situation, preferring to stay put rather than risk showing itself in flight.

The hare realized that the sounds of the horse's feet were closer than was usual and tensed its muscles ready for flight. When the hoof dropped within inches of it, it darted from cover almost under the horse's belly. The horse, startled out of a daydream, saw the sudden movement and shied. Ben, also startled out of semi-sleep, slid down and landed in an undignified position, shoulders on the hard but muddy ground, foot still entangled in one of the stirrups.

The horse ran, dragging him for several yards until his foot came out of the boot and freed him. He thought his head must have been pulped as it had been bounced along the ground and he warily touched it with his gnarled hands. There was no blood to frighten him, and stretching his muscles to test them he realized that he was unharmed.

'Damn all horses to hell!' he shouted. 'There never was a one that you can safely say – now that's a fine and trustworthy animal!'

He picked himself up, groaning as he bent to retrieve the boot that had fallen from the stirrup a few yards further on. He rubbed his head and neck and looked about him for the bag he had carried, moaning and repeating his favourite swears. When a voice began to repeat them with him, he stopped and banged his ear, convinced that the fall had caused him to hear double.

'A damage that will confound the doctors and have me locked away!' he shouted in rage. He wandered around, thumping his head and muttering to himself, convinced he was seriously damaged. It was with relief that he heard someone call his name.

'Ain't that Ben Gammon I can hear swearing and carrying on like a wronged husband?'

Ben turned and groaning with renewed agony, held his neck and demanded, 'Who's that tormenting me, a poor injured man, then?'

A young man came towards him hesitantly.

'Is it safe to approach you, Ben Gammon? I'm not looking for a fight, for sure.'

Ben groaned theatrically and said, 'I couldn't punch a hole in a cobweb. I haven't the breath to blow the seeds off a dandelion. Thrown I've been and I can't find my bag. Help me will you, Madoc Morgan? I have the feeling that my head will leave my body and land at my feet if I bend down to find it myself.'

Madoc agreed to help and while Ben sat on the ground trying to put his boot back on, the young man kicked around in the long clumps of purple moor grass and sheep's fescue, tripping occasionally over the uneven ground and the high clumps of the swaying grass.

After a moment he called and showed Ben that the bag was found.

'It's empty, mind,' Madoc informed him. 'I think your leters have fallen out.'

The letter written by William Ddole was apart from the others, falling to where it was hidden by a rotting branch of a birch. The rest were gathered and as he handed them one by one to Ben, Madoc felt them, assessing the likelihood of there being some coins inside. Three he slipped into his pocket. The letter from William remained unobserved, and Madoc's boot slipped on the branch and pressed it, unseen, into the mud.

For several weeks William waited impatiently for a reply from his daughter, then he sadly decided that Annie had been correct and he had been wrong. Penelope was settling into life in the city and no longer had the desire to return.

He was proved correct in another matter: after a week of coughing had exhausted her, Seranne died in her sleep.

Chapter Eleven

Before Pitcher and Daisy could make their Friday visit to call on Walter Waterman, he called on them. One rainy afternoon, when Pitcher and Barrass, their shoulders protected by sacks, were putting the finishing touches to the extended stable yard, Polly ran out to tell Pitcher he had a visitor. The girl hurried back to the shelter of the house before telling him who his caller was and, grumbling at the interruption, he threw down the hammer with which he had been fixing up a sign, abandoned the sack and followed her.

'Well, I didn't expect to have you calling to see me, not yet anyway,' Pitcher said as he recognized the Deputy Postmaster from Swansea. 'Can I take this as encouraging, you coming to look over my fine premises?'

'I had an idea to call on you and see for myself, yes,' Walter said. 'I had a mind too, to see Miss Daisy, if she is at home.'

Pitcher called Polly, and the girl told him that Miss Daisy was with her mother and sister, and they were preparing to join them. When the three women appeared, they had dressed themselves in their best dresses, and over their arms they each carried a light cloak.

'We thought to go for a walk in the rain. We feel the need to freshen ourselves before we take tea,' Emma announced. 'Perhaps you would like to walk with us?' She smiled then turned to glare at Pitcher, daring him to argue.

'I think Walter has come to see for himself the suitability of the house –' Pitcher dared to say, but Emma's eyes, almost popping from their sockets, stilled his tongue.

'You can talk later, Dadda,' Daisy said, taking Walter's arm. 'First we must steal him from you.' As she went through the door she slyly gave her father a wink that shocked him. He hadn't seen a better one from the sauciest of the women who strolled the dockside! What was his family coming to?

Walter was entertained and persuaded to stay for food and then taken to the bar-room where Pitcher plied him with some of his best drinks. Fortunately it was a busy night and with Dan singing, and Oak-tree Thomas not singing, the evening was a very pleasant one. Prising Emma out of her precious parlour was difficult, but Pitcher persuaded her to bring the girls down to sit in the room behind the bar where they had once lived and which would soon serve as a kitchen to cook the food they planned to sell.

It was there that the last hour of his visit was spent, and from there that Daisy left him to go to her bed, a wistful and demure expression on her face as if parting from him was a bravery she could hardly sustain. Walter went home a slightly drunk, but very happy man.

A few days later, a notice displayed on the big tree outside the sorting office announced that application had been made for Pitcher to handle the letters for Gower, and for the alehouse – soon to be The Posthorn Inn – to be the receiving office. Kenneth saw the notice and rode home to tell Ceinwen and decide what was to be done.

'Without I ride with the letters and put my own case forward in person, there's nothing I *can* do,' he wailed.

'I'm going to talk to Emma,' Ceinwen decided. 'Friends we are, or so I thought!'

Their daughter, Enyd, stood up from the table where she had been entering the payments into her father's ledger.

'I am going to talk to Olwen!' she said. 'She's my husband's sister and should be loyal to us, her extra family, above her friends! If anyone can persuade Barrass against this move, she can.'

Neither Ceinwen nor Enyd were successful in their attempts to persuade Pitcher and Barrass to change their minds.

'Pitcher is the best man for the work. His premises are in by far the best position,' Emma insisted when Ceinwen told of her disappointment.

'But,' she whispered surreptitiously behind a fat hand, 'if we should be granted the change, and so far it's only an application backed by Walter Waterman, then I will pay you a few shillings each week to compensate you for the loss of it.'

Ceinwen was strongly tempted to complain that she had no

daughter to use in the fight for her living, but decided against it. Best she kept Emma on her side, if only to receive the few shillings she had offered, which Kenneth would not hear of.

Kenneth walked the fields and fumed over the way Pitcher planned to steal his business. The letter deliveries were not over profitable, but the people who waited for Barrass bought whatever Ceinwen could find to sell, and he enjoyed the position of importance in the community. Now Barrass did the actual walking, his life was a very pleasant one. He also enjoyed the gossip.

He tried to think of a way to get the position returned to him. His reputation was good, he had only three times been robbed in all the years he wandered across Gower, he was rarely late, and everyone knew he was trustworthy. If only he could show that Pitcher was less capable than he. A robbery perhaps? Or if the letters were lost –

His anger quelled by the possibility of revenge, he walked more slowly, making his way to discuss his chagrin with Betson-the-flowers, and tried to think of a way to persuade the Post Office to revert to the old arrangement.

Olwen was afraid to argue with Enyd and said little when her sister-in-law asked her to intervene and persuade Barrass not to support Pitcher in his unfair application.

'Barrass has never had anything good happen to him,' Olwen began, but at once she was shouted down.

'Never had anything good happen to him? What about my mother giving him a room and a meal every night of every month? And what about my father allowing him to help deliver the letters? If it hadn't been for that generous act Barrass and Pitcher wouldn't have stood a chance of their application even being read!'

Olwen pleaded for Enyd to sit.

'Please, Enyd, think of the baby to come. It isn't good for you to get angry. Sit next to Mistress Powell and I'll make you both a good cup of tea? Or coffee? We have a little if you fancy a change?'

'The only change I want is for you to change Barrass's black heart.' But she sat in the small room and allowed herself to be pampered a little. She knew that Olwen's loyalty was with

Barrass, but she was determined to change her mind.

Enyd had always been a rather sulky girl and marriage to Dan had not changed her. She seemed always openly looking for a reason to complain and this loss of her father's work to Barrass was irresistible. When Dan returned from the sea, she was in the new room alone, quietly sobbing.

'Enyd, my love, what is the matter?' Dan knelt beside her, at once alarmed.

'Your sister is disloyal to me. I am her family now and she chooses to favour Barrass before me,' she sobbed, clinging to him.

When he gradually unfolded her story and got the facts clear, Dan was in a quandary. Love for Enyd fought in his honest mind with the fact that Barrass and Pitcher had been given the letter deliveries by the Postmaster of London. He tried to explain that.

'Local people might offer their opinions, but the decision is not theirs to make.'

She was not comforted. 'My father deserved it, Pitcher stole it from him!' she insisted.

Knowing it was useless, Dan promised his wife that he would make enquiries. He had no intention of wasting his time and feared the thought of dealing with 'officialdom', but his words comforted her and calmed her, and that was what he wanted to achieve.

The funeral of Seranne was a small one. The Morgans had lived outside the village both geographically and in their attitude. They rarely visited anyone and seemed to buy what they needed in the town without coming into contact even with Spider and his fish selling. The people from Ddole House were present at the simple service with the exception of Annie, who pleaded that hardly knowing the young woman, they would be better served if she stayed to make sure there was food and warm drinks for the others when they returned.

The two sisters of the deceased, Polly, who worked for Emma, and Vanora, who attempted to care for the rest of the family, held hands and wept as the body of their eldest sister was carried along the path to the church. The brothers followed behind, their faces cold, eyes showing the anger that helped them cope with their distress, and ignoring the comments of those who had come to watch.

Olwen was an exception. Madoc stopped beside her and said, 'You were her friend, she was yours. If there is ever anything you need, Olwen-the-fish, you only have to ask.'

His eyes were wet with tears. He looked a vulnerable young boy, and she felt a sudden sympathy for him. She felt herself blush as the eyes of others stared speculatingly at them. Stuttering words of consolation and her thanks, she left him and went to kiss Polly and Vanora who were being supported by Morgan.

William looked at the sad group and shared their grief. The sight took him back to the funeral of Dorothy and he relived the pain. He walked with the others, head down, afraid that he would see the portent of another funeral, in the faces of Seranne's family.

At the fisherman's cottage on the cliffs, old Mistress Powell searched among her belongings for the grave clothes she had made some years before. A long white gown, which fastened with ties at the back, and a bonnet, both embroidered with white cotton. She was smiling as she smoothed them out before refolding them.

Life was good, the ending of it far happier than she had ever imagined it would be. Widowed when only a few weeks a bride, working for several of the farms at any job she was offered, she had lived a life of near poverty and had expected to end her days in the poor house, not sharing joyfully in the family life of Spider and Mary. When her house collapsed and she lost even the roof above her she had despaired. But, rescued by Barrass and Arthur, then taken in by Mary and Spider, life had become happier than she had dreamed of.

Among her belongings were some coins, more than she had remembered. Mary and Spider refused to accept them for her keep, insisting she more than earned the food they gave her and her place beside their hearth, and she had almost forgotten they were there. Now she sat and stared at the half-full box and wondered how best to dispose of them. For a long time she sat perfectly still, gazing into the fire, until an idea came to her. She smiled as she found a pen and some paper and began to write.

*

The servants returned to Ddole House on foot, and William rode with Edwin Prince.

'Come and take a bite before you go home,' William offered and Edwin agreed. They dismounted at the stables and left the horses for David to attend to when he returned from the church.

Annie greeted them sorrowfully and asked politely if all went well.

'No one had hysterics, or threw themselves into the grave, if that's what you mean,' William said sharply. 'How can a funeral be expected to "go well"?'

'I only hoped that there were no mishaps, sir,' Annie said, smiling. 'If it's a gentle affair, then people go home comforted and less sad.'

'Of course you're right. I'm sorry,' William muttered. Then he asked, 'Have you decided whom you will take as cook, now Seranne is no longer with us?'

Edwin watched the way William behaved with Annie and was curious. First being unfairly angry with what was only a polite comment, then, surprisingly, apologizing to the woman! When they were alone he asked,

'This Annie, you are still satisfied with her?'

'Oh yes. She does her work and involves me only a little. I can't complain.'

'She doesn't – er – do more than her work, does she, William?'

'I loved Dorothy and have no need of another! I don't see her as a woman.'

'But perhaps she sees you as a man,' Edwin warned. 'It happens, a lonely man and a scheming woman.'

'Really, Edwin!' William snapped, refusing to admit to himself that there was some truth in his companion's words. The way he looked forward to talking to Annie, the way he confided in her some of his thoughts and even some of his plans was a weakness, he knew that. The relationship was becoming less servant and master and more friend to friend.

'The letters of commendation, William. You have heard from the people who wrote them?'

William shook his head impatiently.

'No I have not and there is no need. I am capable of deciding whether or not the woman is honest, Edwin.'

'What a pity Penelope isn't here,' Edwin said. 'She would be best running this house, then, with Annie relegated to the kitchen you would be well served I think.'

'Penelope is content in London with her new friends. I wrote and told her she could return,' he confided sadly. 'There has been no reply.'

'John Maddern will be with us again in less than a week,' Edwin said to cheer William. 'He will surely have news of her.'

'And until then, I have persuaded Florrie that we still have a greater need of her than Daniels, who is well cared for by his sister!' William smiled and forced himself to shake off the gloom that had surrounded him since the death of Seranne.

Emma watched as Polly polished the new table and chairs in the parlour. She had heard that John Maddern was returning from his business in London and she was determined to impress him with the quality of her home and the excellence of her two daughters.

'If he does not choose one of them for a wife then I'll send them both into the nunnery!' she threatened Pitcher. 'They might be twins, Pitcher, but with a difference in their personalities that's more apparent as they grow. Daisy is the boldest and most confident. Far too confident for a young lady of prospects!'she added with a tightening of her mouth. 'Pansy is quieter with every day that passes. Do you know she has given up her dancing lessons?'

Pitcher grunted something in reply, his eyes never leaving the news sheet he was reading.

'She frequently refuses invitations to visit friends, except when Daisy insists she accompanies her.'

'Don't worry, my love,' Pitcher said, hoping that was the right response.

'Don't worry! Don't worry! What else can a mother do with two beautiful girls refusing to take an interest when I am trying to find them a husband?'

It was late in July. Polly and Emma were putting the finishing touches to the table being set for thirteen people. The dinner party had been filling Emma's thoughts for days. Besides William and John, she had invited Edwin and her daughter Violet, Dan and Enyd, Florrie and Daniels and, after careful consideration, Walter Waterman.

Her face was red and covered with a film of moisture as she rushed from room to room, up and down the stairs to check on the food and make sure everything was in readiness. She trusted no one. Polly, and Olwen, who had again been hired to assist for the day, were exhausted with her constant accusations and interference.

Emma ignored their assurances that everything was as it should be and checked again and again. Nothing must go wrong on this occasion. John must be shown how well either of her daughters would manage the home of a gentleman. She ran to where Daisy and Pansy were dressing, pulling their waists tighter, their necklines lower in a way that startled them.

'Pigs at market couldn't be better presented,' Daisy giggled, straightening her dress after Emma's ministrations. She grunted and curled up her nose to make her sister laugh.

'She is determined we shall find a husband, isn't she?' Pansy smiled. 'Poor Mamma, we are her life's work.'

Dressed alike, the twins settled on their bedroom chairs to await the arrival of the guests. Emma insisted they enter the dining room only after everyone else had arrived.

Their hair had been curled in rags the previous evening and both girls had slept uncomfortably, sliding their fingers among the bunches in an attempt to ease the pulling. The result was, they both grudgingly admitted to their mother, well worth the pain.

They wore dresses of gingham generously trimmed with bands, bows and trailing strands of satin ribbon. On their feet were slippers of buckram. Mauve and summery, they both looked like artist's models posed for a dreamlike portrait of the country life imagined by those who lived in a town.

Polly was ill, Emma could see that. But she tried to ignore the way the girl had to stop and regain her breath halfway up the stairs with even the lightest load. And the way she held her hand to her thin chest to ease the obvious pain. Tomorrow she would give her a day off to recover, this afternoon she was needed. Unreasonably, she felt irritated with Polly. The girl could have taken better care of herself. To inconvenience me now, when I need all the help I can get is – ungrateful, she decided with a frown.

When the guests were gathered, Emma sent Olwen to call her daughters and was gratified to hear the gasp of approval as they stood in the doorway as she had instructed, before entering and finding their places. Daisy and Pansy were seated one either side of John, flanked by William and Walter. Emma's beady eyes watched to see if the conversation was directed as she hoped and was pleased with the way that John seemed to share his attention between the two girls.

Walter seemed at home in the company and his eyes rarely left Daisy. He talked to John, but it seemed to Emma's sharp eyes that he did so simply to be included in the conversation with her lively daughter. He asked about London life and seemed to share an interest in the theatre of which he had seen plenty in the city of Bath. With two daughters and John Maddern the only likely prospect of a husband for one of them, she looked with greater interest at the Deputy Postmaster, who was more worldly than she expected and almost gentlemanly in his manners. Before an hour had passed he was firmly fixed on her list of last-hope-possibles! She was less pleased to see the animated way John's eyes lit up when the subject of Penelope was raised.

'She is well content, William,' John said in answer to Pitcher's query, 'but still thinking of home, and wishing to come back to her father.'

'I think not,' William said, lightening his voice with an effort. 'I suspect she is more than happy to be feted and spoilt by the young gentlemen she has met in London and rarely thinks of us at all!' He turned to Emma and Pitcher. 'For all our care and however generously we treat them, children soon forget us and go their own way, I fear.'

Emma shook her head firmly.

'In that we are fortunate, Pitcher and me. Our children have been devoted, obedient to our wishes and ever grateful – as I am sure Penelope and Leon are to you, in spite of your words to the contrary, William,' she added quickly, a smile suffusing her red face as she covered her *faux pas*. 'Penelope is a dutiful daughter for sure. And Leon, well, isn't he a son to be proud of? Wearing the uniform of the King's army? Fortunate you are in your children as we are in ours.'

She gabbled the words, afraid she had offended him by agreeing that his children were less than good to him. Seeing in his face the loneliness he suffered, she wanted to comfort him. Instead she offered more food.

At the doorway, Olwen watched and listened. Unaware of the lost letter, she tightened her lips in disapproval of the thought that these people would not be truthful about their love and need of each other.

'Love is something to be proud of not to hide in shame as a weakness,' she confided in Mistress Powell later that evening when she returned from her day's work. 'They seem afraid to admit that they have need of each other or are lonely for them. It's as if caring and needing were things to be ashamed of. I can't understand why people make trouble their companion, just for want of a truthful word. Just think how much happier William Ddole would be with Penelope sharing his life, yet he pretends not to miss her.'

The following morning when she was on her way to start her day's work at Ddole House, Olwen saw Polly. Arthur was with her, the dog a few yards in front of them pausing occasionally to look back as if showing them the way. She called and ran to join them.

'Polly's been given the day off,' Arthur explained. 'Not feeling too well, like.'

He was carrying a basket in which Olwen could see bread, meat and cheese besides a few apples and a rather sorry-looking unripe pear.

'Mistress Palmer gave me some food left from yesterday,' Polly said, gasping after the few words. 'There's kind she is.'

Olwen walked with them for part of the way, talking for the three of them, wondering at the paleness of her friend and the slowness of her walk. That she was ill was in no doubt. She cast surreptitious glances at the girl and wondered with dread if she too were suffering the same sickness as Seranne. There was a similarity about the pinched expression and the slight bloom of colour high on the thin face. She chattered more brightly to fend off her fears.

She went to find Annie for instruction and found her with William Ddole. She told Annie that Seranne's sister was sick and although Annie showed sympathy, Olwen guessed it was for the benefit of her employer.

'Pity for her, what can we do to help?' She gave Olwen an old blanket as she left for home and asked her to deliver it to the house near the stream.

Olwen was pleased with the gift, knowing it would be very welcome, but she did not want to take it to the Morgans' home. Madoc had given a gift of a piglet that had been stolen. Other gifts sporadically arrived, but she always sent Dan to thank him. There was always a wildness in his eyes that unnerved her. The risk to her if she had been found in possession of the pig was great, so she was apprehensive of meeting him again.

To her joy she met Barrass who was walking back late from his deliveries as Jethro had gone lame.

'Come with me, Barrass,' she pleaded, when she had explained her errand.

'I'm so late, another few minutes will hardly matter,' he smiled. But their visit was longer than either of them planned.

There was no smoke coming from the chimney when they approached the field in which the house stood. At once Olwen thought that meant they had no hot food. The door stood open and a large dog lolled across the threshold. Barrass called to it and tied it up while Olwen stepped inside the fetid room.

'Polly? Are you there?' she called and a shadow eased itself from a corner and revealed itself as the young girl. She was wrapped in a blanket that smelt of mildew and Olwen took it from her and hung it over the door.

'Best you have this one, sent by Annie,' she said briskly. 'That one smells as if it's been used to dry the dog and bed the goat!'

While Barrass gathered sticks and logs and started the fire burning, Olwen dragged the bed on which Polly slept out into the fresh air. She managed to raise it high enough to drape it over the line and saw to her consternation that the sacking which had been filled with straw, was rotting, discoloured with mould and beginning to tear.

There was a cauldron suspended on a chain near the fire and she saw that it contained some vegetables and joints of rabbit. She turned it so it hung over the slowly strengthening fire and soon it was sending out the pleasant smell of meat, carrots and leeks.

She and Barrass stayed for two hours and by the time they had finished, the room had been emptied of the foul bedding and replaced with fresh bracken, green and scented like mountain pastures.

'You will have to dry some heather later in the summer,' Barrass said. 'It makes the best of beds. For now this greenery will be an improvement for tonight, tomorrow Olwen and I will find you something better.'

Polly did not reply and when Olwen investigated, she saw that the girl was fast asleep wrapped in the clean blanket on her sweet-smelling bed.

There had been no sign of either Vanora or their brothers. For the absence of the brothers Olwen was thankful. But Barrass insisted they waited until the brothers returned.

'I think they should be made to care better for Polly and Vanora,' he whispered, not wanting to disturb Polly.

Olwen would have preferred to avoid them, but the chance of a few more moments in Barrass's company decided her. Barrass prowled around the house and the surrounding, carelessly worked field.

'Something could be made of this place if only Morgan and Madoc would make a little effort,' he said. 'They spend too much time in William Ddole's fields from what I hear. Best they stayed home and made better use of what they've got.'

When Morgan and Madoc arrived, Vanora was with them. They had been to the market. Vanora among the family was the only one without the feverish and thin-faced look of the morbid lung, Olwen thought. She wondered why some households seemed so unfortunate, while others who were taken far less care of than Vanora's family, seemed strong and robust.

Madoc seemed very pleased to see Olwen, and he threw down the empty sack he had been carrying and sat beside her outside the door, calling for Vanora to bring them all a drink. Olwen moved away to tell Vanora about her sister. She felt ill at ease with his wild-eyed admiration that somehow seemed insincere, and the way he seemed to disregard Barrass, and treat her as his own personal guest.

Vanora went inside and tucked the new blanket around the sleeping Polly and looked at the fresh bedding and the glowing fire with gratitude.

'What a surprise! Thank you, Olwen, and you Barrass. It's a treat to find the fire burning and the pot of cawl simmering on the hearth. I expected it all to be cold. Thank you 'til you're better paid,' she said. She brought out a pitcher of ale and poured some into an assortment of misshaped pewter tankards. She chose the least battered one and handed it to Olwen.

'Sorry I am that you had to find us so lacking in comfort. With Seranne gone and Polly not very strong, I'm hard put to get through all the tasks of the day. Now, I have to go to the market as well.' She leaned towards Barrass, and behind a hand said, 'Best you don't ask why, us not having paid for permission to be there.' She sat and leaned against the green-stained wall near the doorway. 'Things will be better soon,' she said, half to herself.

Madoc stood up and putting his hands into his pockets, drew out handfuls of coins which he threw into Vanora's lap.

'Getting better by the hour! There you are, all that from selling good fresh rabbits and a couple of duck from the round pond. Not bad for a day's work, eh?'

'A day and a night more like,' Vanora said, again in a whisper. 'It's so dangerous, you taking from the woods. If you were caught you'd be taken from us and where would Polly and I be then? At least the herbs and potions and vulneraries I sell are honestly acquired.'

'You worry too much,' Morgan laughed.

'We can move about at night with no more sound than the gentlest breeze, and our shadows wouldn't disturb the nerviest bird,' Madoc added, smiling at Olwen.

'You know how dogs are soothed by Madoc,' Morgan said. 'He walks right up to them and they wag their tails and never show the keepers he's there.'

Olwen said nothing. She wished she and Barrass had not been privy to such talk.

When Madoc had taken the money from his pocket, a piece of paper had half escaped with it. When Madoc removed his coat and threw it across to land on a pile of logs, the paper fell to the ground.

At once Barrass picked it up and before Madoc managed to snatch it back he saw the name – Henry Glan Preece, Bristol – written across it. It was a letter he had personally taken from the Rector of Rhossili only a few days previously and handed in to the Swansea sorting office. It should have been put into Ben

Gammon's bag and taken on its way.

'That letter,' he said. 'How did you get it?'

'Oh, I found it on one of the bridle paths across the fields. Must have been dropped by someone for sure.'

'Can I see it?' Barrass's dark eyes were issuing a warning that he would not be dissuaded and Madoc casually threw the letter back to him.

'It was opened when I found it, mind,' he said. 'I didn't tamper with the King's Mail. Know better than that I do,' he said belligerently. 'So don't you think different!'

'I think I'll take it to show Walter Waterman, he'll need to know that a letter has gone astray.'

'No, I won't let you do that.' Madoc ran in through the doorway and dropped the letter into the flames of the fire. 'Best we don't start any enquiry that would bring that Daniels around here,' he explained. 'Now, let's pretend we never saw it, shall we?'

'I can't!' Barrass exclaimed.

'Best that you do,' Morgan said. He looked pointedly at Olwen and slowly back to Barrass before adding, 'Innocents can be harmed if there's too much said about things best forgotten.' Barrass hung his head. He was in a turmoil. He knew that any information about missing letters was important. But, he admitted with a pang of conscience, not more important to him than Olwen.

'Come on, Olwen,' he said, rising and offering her his hand to rise. 'Time we went home.'

'What are you going to do?' Olwen asked when, almost breathless at the pace he led her along, they were at the edge of the village. 'Report it, will you?'

'No. Not without the sight of it to show what happened,' he said.

She knew he was angry, but not seeing the threat Morgan had issued about her safety, she could not understand why. Perhaps it was simply that by Madoc burning the evidence he had been outwitted. Barrass took seriously everything to do with his occupation and would hate not being able to tell what he knew.

'I don't want you to tell what we saw, either,' he told her as they reached her house on the cliffs.

'If you say so, Barrass,' she said. 'But only if you will give me a kiss!' She was relieved to see the anger smoothed from his dark face with a smile and as he bent to kiss her cheek, she turned so he kissed her lips instead.

'Thank you for coming with me,' she called back as she skipped happily into the house.

When Barrass next went into the Swansea sorting office, Ben Gammon was full of the much embellished story of his fall from his horse and the scattering of letters.

'What's this, I says to myself, me with a sore head and a painful ankle and faced with crawling about trying to gather my letters? Thanks be that some kindly passerby stopped and helped or I'd be there still searching for 'em, painfully doing my utmost for the responsibility I carries.'

'Who was he?' Barrass asked, coming in on the seventh telling. 'Do you know him?'

'Name of Madoc Morgan. And him so far from home, why, it was a miracle for him to be there when I was in sore need of help!' Ben said, raising his voice for the crowd to hear like an actor on a stage.

Barrass asked him where the accident had taken place and, when Ben left, he went with him to see for himself the exact spot. Leaving Ben to continue on his way, Barrass went around the area leading Jethro, circle after widening circle. As he kicked a birch branch aside, he saw, almost buried in the now dried mud, a piece of paper, which, when it was partially cleaned, revealed itself to be William Ddole's letter to his daughter.

Hurrying back to Mumbles, Barrass told the story of the burnt letter to Pitcher and told him how he had found the one written by William.

'I think you should go there at once and tell William. He might be waiting for a reply to a question Penelope hasn't received.'

William received Barrass ungraciously. He disliked the boy and showed it without reservation. But after easing open the page of his letter, he surprised the carrier of it by smiling widely, calling him a fine fellow and telling him to go into the kitchen and find refreshment while he rewrote it and sent it again on its way.

Chapter Twelve

Annie was on the landing between William's bedroom and that used by his daughter. From the landing window she looked out at the front of the house, where in the distance she could see the line of willows bending their branches like long hair into the stream. The stream followed the road for some distance and as she watched the gently swaying trees she noticed someone walking along with only his head visible above the hawthorn hedge.

She waited, curious to see who it was. Since she had begun working at Ddole House she had made no effort to meet any of the local people, but gradually she had begun to recognize those who called at the house. Tradesmen mostly, those who sold things at the kitchen door or called to offer some service.

The figure reached the end of the drive where he struggled to unlatch the long gate. With a gasp of dismay she recognized the young man. She was transfixed, unable to decide in her panic whether to run down to try and stop Olwen or Bethan inviting him in, or to hide somewhere until he had gone. Making up her mind, she lifted her skirts and ran down the stairs and into the kitchen.

'There's a strange person approaching. I do not want you to invite him in!' she announced to a startled Olwen. 'Whatever he wants, whatever story he tells you, he must not enter this house. D'you understand?'

Before replying, Olwen went up on her toes to look out and see for herself who it was that had upset Annie so much. Then she turned and smiled.

'It's Cadwalader! He won't do any harm. He looks ungainly but that's on account of the harp he has strapped to his back.'

'He mustn't come in!' Annie insisted. 'Send him away or I'll report you to Master Ddole for impertinence!'

'But he was allowed to sleep in the barn and – '

'Tell him to go!' Annie's small eyes were almost lost to sight as she glared at Olwen, defying her to argue further. Olwen shrugged and went to the door. Annie disappeared into the passageway, but Olwen knew she would be listening to make sure she was obeyed.

'Cadwalader!' she greeted the visitor. 'Sorry, but I can't even offer you a bit of food, me being in the middle of – er – cleaning out the fireplace! Good day to you!'

She closed the door on the surprised expression on Cadwalader's face. Through the door, he said, 'Olwen? What have I done that I am received like a murderous looking beggar? I've done you no harm.'

Olwen stood behind the door and bit her lip. It was against all her instincts to refuse a caller a sup of ale or a mouthful of food. She heard him scuffling his feet for a moment, then he began to move away. He called back, 'The grate you have emptied for cleaning must be a magical one as the chimney smokes so richly without a fire in the hearth!'

Olwen stretched and watched as the small, cloaked figure returned to the road and disappeared.

'Why did you make me do that!' she demanded cheekily when Annie re-entered the kitchen. 'If you wanted him gone you should have told him yourself!'

'Hurry with those dishes, Olwen,' was the only reply. 'You must have slept half the morning away for them still to be stacked unwashed!'

Another glance at the gate showed that Cadwalader was gone but someone else was approaching.

'Here's Florrie, d'you want me to send her away too?' Olwen shouted after the retreating housekeeper. Annie turned and slapped the girl hard across her face.

'Howl and you'll get another one,' she warned. Straightening her skirt nervously, she went to greet Florrie.

'I saw that harpist, Cadwalader, in the lane,' Florrie said as she entered. 'He said Olwen had sent him on his way without a polite word!'

'Girls!' Annie said. 'Never two minutes the same. Some imagined quarrel I expect. Come and share a drink of tea. Olwen!' she demanded of the girl who was rubbing her reddening face. 'Fetch us the makings of tea and some of those cakes Bethan took all morning to bake.'

172

There was a third caller at Ddole House that afternoon. When Annie and Florrie were sorting out cupboards and chests to decide whether the household linen needed replenishing, the Keeper of the Peace knocked on the door. Olwen was tempted to leave him standing without an invitation and say it was Annie's instruction, but she dare not. In any case, Daniels was not the sort to wait for an invitation. He walked in, sat in the wooden chair near the fire and asked for Florrie.

'I'll go and find her,' Olwen said, handing him a mug of ale. 'She and Annie are deep in discussion about bed sheets and covers for pillows.'

When Florrie had joined Daniels, they settled to talk in the kitchen and Olwen thought it wiser to leave her work and find something to keep her out of the way. There was something in the expression on the man's face that suggested all was not well between him and his intended wife. She went out to the stables and on the pretext of looking for eggs among the scattered straw, passed an hour away from the house.

When she returned to the kitchen door she was startled to see Florrie and Daniels standing glaring at each other like cockerels about to commence battle. They were unaware of her entrance and she quickly slipped back out of the door.

She stood there, wondering what to do. If she did not get on with the meal soon everything would be delayed and that wouldn't please Annie. If she interrupted the couple inside, they might be even more annoyed. She settled for the simplest: waiting for a few more minutes while Florrie and Daniels finished their bickering. She leaned against the door, ear to the gap, listening with the hope of hearing enough to decide when it was safe to go in.

It was clear that the problem was the date for their wedding, Florrie insisting that she was still nowhere near ready, and Daniels insisting that she make up her mind.

'But I want to see first that things are settled here,' Florrie said. 'I owe William Ddole that.'

'And what about me, the man who has asked you to be his wife? What do you owe me? I am being made a laughing stock! Friends ask when I am to be wed and I have to tell them that you still haven't arranged a day.'

'You are hardly uncomfortable, with your sister running your home so smoothly,' Florrie said.

'And that is why? You think I have no need of you? You think my life is complete?'

'I think you need me, yes. But your need is hardly as urgent as it would be if you and your children were without someone to look after you.'

'I see. So if I sent my sister away and allowed us all to fall into neglect, then you would condescend to come and rescue us, is that it?'

'You will never need rescuing, Ponsonby,' Florrie countered. 'You will always be comfortable, you aren't the kind of man to be otherwise.'

'Well, share that comfort with me. What is there here to delay you? Come with me now, this moment and talk to the vicar. We can see this settled today and I can sleep easy tonight.'

Florrie bent her head and Daniels said, 'There's something you aren't telling me. What is it, Florrie? This isn't a very good start if there is something you can't tell me!'

'I'm used to having servants to do the heavy work and from what you say, I will be expected to run your house unaided. Once we are married, it's your sister's intention to move away, find a place and an occupation of her own. I don't think I could manage the house, the children, care for you and be happy.' She looked at him to see how he had taken her words, but he was not watching her. As if to himself, he said quietly, 'For that I'll need promotion unless we're to be abysmally poor. Florrie, if only you'd help me catch the smugglers.'

Florrie waited until he looked at her, then slowly and deliberately she said, 'Smugglers? What smugglers?'

Olwen darted away from the door, but the couple didn't appear and she crept slowly back. She did not hear footsteps and was startled when a voice close behind her whispered, 'What is happening here today? First you tell me I am unwelcome and now you eavesdrop on two people talking of their love.'

'Cadwalader!' Olwen grabbed his arm and pulled him to where they were out of sight of the door. 'Annie, the new housekeeper, will not have you near the place. She is a little feared of strangers, I think. Why did you come back?'

'Only to be sure that it was not you who was against me,' he smiled. 'And to ask if I could sleep in the barn for one night.'

'If you promise to be gone before cockcrow. I'll try and bring you some food before I leave tonight,' she said. 'Now, if I don't break up the argument in by there – ' she pointed to the kitchen, ' – I'll be sent home and won't be able to help you at all!'

Singing loudly, to let Florrie know of her approach, she slowly walked back into the kitchen with her basket of eggs to find both participants sitting calm and apparently at ease one each side of the fire range. She nodded cheerily to them and began to attend to the meat.

The following morning, Cadwalader did not rise and disappear as he promised. He was curious to see the woman who feared him without exchanging a word with him. He hid from everyone but Olwen.

'You promised to go!' she hissed when she went to the barn to make sure he had gone. 'Now you'd better stay and I'll bring you some food to see you on your way.' Her disobedience alone was reward enough, but Cadwalader's grateful thanks gave her satisfaction too.

It was late evening before he departed, taking with him a pack of food supplied by a nervous Olwen. What he had seen of the comings and goings of the house was of great interest to him and there were a few surprises. For the rest of the day and throughout the night he pondered on them.

Emma was pleased with the result of her dinner party. Both Walter and John called again and they both seemed interested in Daisy. She sympathized with Pansy, but warned, 'Pansy my dear, you must be more amusing, more light-hearted. I won't have either of you being too familiar with young men, of course, not even those whom we know well like John Maddern, but you must try and – shine, dear.'

'I don't mean to take everyone's attention from you, Pansy, I really don't,' Daisy said anxiously. 'In fact I give Walter to you with my best wishes!'

'Daisy!' Emma warned. 'Don't be so condescending to your sister!'

'I was joking, Mamma, Pansy knows I was joking,' Daisy protested. 'Pansy would be too discerning to take someone like him!'

'Of course she would, but,' wondered their mother, 'when I

have arranged for so many young men to meet her and she finds none to her liking, I am curious to know what kind of person she *would* choose! I confess that sometimes I despair of ever finding out.'

'Don't worry,' Pansy smiled, 'I really am most content here with you and Dadda.'

'And we are happy to have you both with us – at an age when most girls are flown the nest, building homes of their own.'

The barbed comment didn't go unnoticed by either of the girls and they shared a secret smile.

'We love having you here, never think different but,' Emma went on, 'we don't want you to settle so deeply into a world arranged by us that you miss the opportunity of a husband and beautiful daughters of your own.'

She spoke to both of them, but it was at Pansy she looked as she spoke, believing that Daisy's ability to attract men was lacking in the quieter, gentler sister.

'You must recommence your dancing lessons before winter keeps us in for weeks on end, Pansy,' she said firmly. 'And I'll have no arguing.'

The gifts of food continued to arrive at Olwen's door and although her parents would not offend the young man by refusing or returning them, they knew that the sign of affection did not please their daughter. Enyd too found the idea distasteful.

'He is such an aggressive looking man I don't like to think of him wandering about here at night, especially when Spider and Dan are at the alehouse enjoying themselves, and I'm here in this delicate condition, with only Mistress Powell to protect me,' she whined.

Dan promised that he would not leave her to sing at the alehouse even though it meant a few extra coins to put into their small savings.

'You only worry because of the child,' he said. 'A woman fears more when she has another life to think about. Brave you'll be when the baby is safely with us.'

Olwen listened to the complaining and the reassurances and wondered what Enyd would find to complain of when the baby was no longer an excuse. She thought that for Dan, the years ahead might be less contented than he had hoped when he had taken Enyd to the church to make her his wife.

It was to Daisy that Walter gave the news that Pitcher's application had been approved by the Postmaster General in London. She had agreed to go to Neath with him and take tea with friends of his. On the way home, sitting in a coach he had hired to take them, he told her that the letter had arrived that morning with Ben Gammon.

'But why didn't you say earlier?' she said after telling him how pleased she was and thanking him for putting her father's case so successfully.

'I wanted to delay the pleasure of seeing your delight,' he said. 'It was like holding an unopened parcel, knowing what was inside, wanting what was inside, but stretching the anticipation until it was impossible to wait a moment longer.'

'Dadda will be so pleased,' she said.

'I wouldn't be upset if you showed your pleasure by kissing me,' he said, looking deeply into her eyes.

She touched his cheek in the merest brush of her lips and turned away.

'I think I will do as you did and wait until Dadda is sitting quietly with Mamma and casually tell it,' she said.

'Daisy, will you come with me to church on Sunday morning?' he asked, soberly.

'That I cannot,' she shook her head with earnest regret. 'We worship as a family; even Violet, who is married, still comes with us.' Then she took pity on him, and added, 'But you could perhaps come with us?'

'I will call for you on Sunday, and until then, I will dream of you,' he said.

Daisy could not keep the news to herself for a moment. She burst in through the door of the alehouse and called excitedly for her parents.

'Mamma, Dadda, come quick I have such news!'

Emma ran down the stairs her hand over her heart. Surely the stupid girl hadn't said 'yes' to a man like Walter? No, she couldn't! When she saw Daisy's flushed face her worst dread seemed to have become a fact. Through her disappointment, in a kaleidoscope of fractured images she thought of the choice between Daisy marrying Walter or staying a spinster. Of how she could build him up to sound more important than he really was. Of how she could best discourage Daisy before people had heard of how the friendship was growing. Of how far below her aspirations for her daughters she had fallen. With a fixed smile on her face, she held her breath.

'Dadda, you have been granted permission to collect the Post!' Daisy said, holding out the letter and hugging her father.

Emma cried, loudly and in an unladylike howl. The relief of not having Walter to explain to her friends was such a joy that she hardly took in the real reason for Daisy's excitement. When she did, she cried again.

'My dear daughter! Now you can say goodbye to that common person and we can forget all about him!'

Kenneth was most upset when Pitcher went over to tell him the change of address for the receiving house. He gave vent to a long list of expletives that startled even Pitcher, who had been an alehouse keeper for most of his life. Pitcher stood there while the man attacked him verbally, and thanked heaven that Kenneth was a small man and unlikely to attack him physically.

'I won't say I'm sorry,' Pitcher said when he was given a moment to speak. 'The way you've taken advantage of Barrass would make that a lie. And the fact that I wanted this for myself and went all out to get it would make an apology nonsensical. But if I can help in any other way to make up for your loss, then I will. I can't say fairer.'

'Barrass won't be sleeping with us any longer, mind, you can tell him from me that he's a traitor!' Kenneth said as Pitcher walked down the bank and towards the alehouse. 'And tell him he won't get any more food either!'

'All right, man! I'll tell him! That's if he hasn't worked that out for himself!' Pitcher shouted back. 'You damned old fool!'

'Ungrateful louse!'

'Maggot of sour apples!'

'Friend of traitors!'

Emma went across later that day, and she stepped back as the door opened, unsure of her reception. But Ceinwen just nodded and gestured for her to enter with her usual vague welcome.

'Can I come in?' Emma asked hesitantly.

'Of course come in. I thought to come and see you,' Ceinwen said, 'but decided it's best to let things between our men cool down a bit. Glad to see you though.'

'I'm sorry we've taken the bit of weekly money from you, Ceinwen, truly I am,' Emma said, inspecting the chair for dust before sitting down. 'There was no choice really. Pitcher and I want to build our business up and we needed the post to increase our trade. It'll make a greater difference to us than it did to you, you must see that?'

'For sure,' Ceinwen nodded. 'I don't think badly of you. I'm certain that Kenneth would have done the same if he was wearing your hat. The truth is, Emma, it's a good chance for me to make him find a job where he has to work! Never did much, especially not since young Barrass took to helping him. Just strutted around looking important and getting under my feet.'

The two women chuckled and spent a pleasant hour discussing the uselessness of men, and when Emma left, she slipped a few shillings into Ceinwen's hand.

'I'll see you have that every week, to make up for your loss,' Emma said. 'Even if we did do you a favour!' Still chuckling, she hastily hid her face when she passed Kenneth walking up the bank.

'Dared to come and say you're sorry?' he said sarcastically. Unable to trust herself to speak, visualizing some of the stories she had just heard from Ceinwen, Emma tightened her lips together to hold captive her laughter, and nodded.

On the first day that the letters were collected at Pitcher's alehouse there was trouble. Barrass handed the leather bag to Walter as usual but instead of letters sliding out on to the desk, when the bag was uptilted, it was empty.

'The mail, Barrass?' Walter asked with a raised eyebrow. 'Don't tell me that there were no letters for today's collection? Seems I needn't have bothered to transfer the business, the need has competely dried up. In your pocket are they? That's against regulations, mind.' Walter looked at Barrass when there was no response and saw that the lack of letters was a complete surprise.

'But – I put them there myself,' Barrass gasped at last. He took the bag and stared into it as if by sheer belief he could make the mail appear. Walter began to demand explanations but Barrass ignored his questions and frowning, tried to visualize a point at which the letters could have been taken. It was Kenneth. It must have been Kenneth. A revenge for having the business taken from him. But when?

Taking the rest of the Gower mail, he left Walter assuring him the matter would be resolved immediately, but with no idea where to begin. When he set off on his journey, he left Pitcher organizing the local children into a search party that showed every sign of becoming a fun day for all.

The children and those who had nothing better to do set off with clear instructions on the area in which they were to look, but within moments of leaving Pitcher, groups began to gather and many did nothing more energetic than sit just out of sight of the alehouse and play games before returning with pretended exhaustion to claim the money Pitcher had promised them for their help.

The letters were found in the quarry, held down with a large stone and unharmed. When Barrass went to tell Kenneth they had been found he thought the man showed no surprise and a lot of satisfaction.

'There's no point in telling Daniels, but I am sure Kenneth did it to try and show Walter you aren't capable of managing the mail,' Barrass said.

'Watch him, boy,' Pitcher warned. 'Watch him.'

For the first time since she began work at Ddole House, Olwen was glad of the rule which made her walk to church with the family when they were there, and the rest of the staff. Without that protection, she could see no way of preventing Madoc from walking with her, boldly and openly declaring his interest in her. The plan of sending Dan to thank Madoc for his gifts no longer kept him away. He began the habit of meeting her as she left Ddole House and walking her home. He attempted to take hold of her hand but this she avoided by the simple expedient of gathering flowers and filling her hands with them.

To his comments she answered as briefly as she could, never adding anything to extend a conversation.

'Surely anyone else would see at once that his attentions were unwelcome?' she sighed to Mistress Powell. 'Besides the uneasiness which I feel when I'm with him, there's the added problem of Barrass,' she went on gloomily. 'If the gossip makers begin to talk about our regular meetings, Barrass might believe that I've stopped loving him and doing as Mamma and Dadda want, looking elsewhere for a husband!'

'Love is always a mixture of gloom and melancholy as well as happiness, dear child,' Mistress Powell said with a chuckle. Lowering her voice she added, 'As you see if you bend your ear in the direction of Enyd.'

'I would never be such a complaining scold if Barrass were my husband!'

'No, Olwen, I don't think you'd ever be that.'

With the summer bringing long days and short nights, deliveries of goods from across the water arrived long after midnight. Even after they had been landed, there was still the problem of getting them to the customers. In winter few ventured out of doors except to visit the alehouses and inns. In summertime, children spent hours after their work was done wandering through the fields and woods, adults sat and enjoyed the warm evenings, and the result was that movement, without everyone knowing what you were at, was all but impossible.

Markus called at Ddole House one day to discuss with William and Edwin the best way of arranging deliveries and the collection of money.

'We've never used the post,' William said. 'With Kenneth's sharp eyes watching and him so disloyal to his neighbours it was always too much of a risk. Kenneth, and the fact of so few letters making ours too obvious. But with Kenneth gone and the increase in the number of letters of late we might reconsider. Barrass has in his bag sometimes as many as thirty, and I have been writing regularly to some of our – friends – with the intention of creating a habit. I think we can send money inside a letter.'

Markus was not sure, but he agreed that starting with a few, they could at least try it.

'Barrass would have to know,' he said, 'and that boy I do not like. Refused straight out to carry our letters separate from the rest. Such impertinence for one so young. The boy wears his morality like Emma Palmer wears a new hat; with the price still attached! Yet morality and young girls is something aside. Who does he think he is?'

'He's young, and that isn't a crime, it's something he will out-grow as we all have,' Edwin said. 'And for myself, I wish he would go somewhere else to do his growing!'

'If we do it, it will have to be as normal post and that is very risky you must agree. He would have to be given a false name on his book for the sender, or the money could be traced back.' William disliked Barrass too, but was honest enough to know that they needed his cooperation.

'I had in mind a false name for the recipient too!' Edwin said. 'Don't worry about Barrass. I think we can be sure of his loyalty.' Together the men worked out a way they could deal with the plan safely.

'Next we must talk to Barrass and explain how he will help,' William said. 'He will have to be told everything so he can be prepared for any trouble.'

Barrass had long ago decided that if he wanted to be an accepted member of the small community he had to support them in all their activities and that meant accepting that the extra income from the boats was essential to the comfort and financial stability of most of the families. Without the shillings earned by taking part in the deliveries, most families would have been hard put to survive on the small wages the men and women could earn from the local farmers.

Barrass had never directly benefited from the illegal trade, re-fusing both contraband and payment when he had been forced to assist them, but rather than be an outsider, he had agreed to support them with his silence. Carrying the payments from customers was a step deeper into involvement. But he agreed.

Markus walked the cliffs with an ease that surprised sighted people. He had spent a childhood scrambling over them, ex-ploring every bend and fold in the grassy slopes and learning the shape of the rugged shoreline better than most knew their near-est field. When he had been blinded, the scene had become etched on his mind and from memory alone he walked without hesitation, carrying a stick which he appeared not to need, an ill-tempered expression on his face that prevented all but a few foolish strangers offering him assistance.

His servant, who sat outside his porch until instructed to follow him, usually knew the moment there were any changes in the cliff paths. During his free time, he would walk the paths and places used by Markus and note any slight alteration.

Weather broke up the hard earth and rain sent it tumbling down the slopes. Rocks were sometimes removed for building or during children's play. Holes appeared and became deeper. Every change was reported and the servant, who was known only as, 'him by the door', would take his master and allow him to examine the alteration to the terrain so there would be no need for further help.

The fine weather had meant that children had been out in the evenings, allowed by their parents to have an hour or two of freedom before going to sleep, and several of them had begun to make a den high above the gulleys where Dan and Spider set their traps for lobsters.

Not knowing about this, Markus walked briskly across the top of the steep slope at the edge of the small fields where crops waved like a reflection of the sea below. He fell over an abandoned stone, crashed awkwardly against a pile of rocks and lay, stunned, for several minutes.

He crawled across the stones and branches the children had gathered for their play, disorientated by the fall, his head bleeding profusely where he had caught it on a jagged rock. He lost his walking stick and was afraid to risk standing in case he was closer to the edge of a further fall. Fearfully, he stayed on his knees and gradually made his way towards his house. The breeze rising from the sea on his left was his only clue to his position, and it wasn't until he was on the narrow path, with hedges of blackthorn on either side of him, that he found his place in the dark world he inhabited.

When he reached the porch where the watchman sat, he was aware of a lightness around him. The pain in his head was lessening, but the brightness was more frightening. What was happening to him? Was he dying? The need to reach his house before death claimed him was an urgency that made him run stumbling through the gate and along the path.

The watchman heard him coming and saw at once that all was not normal. He took hold of the man's arm and guided him into the house and to the chair near the fire.

'Open the curtains!' Markus demanded. When this was done, he sent the watchman away and stared at the oblong of light with fear making him tremble, but with hope gradually taking its place.

Emma delighted in the crowds that resulted from the relocation of the post. The usual poor, whom they were pledged to supply with food and comfort under the agreement of keeping an inn, were always there, news of a good place travelling like lightning across the skies. But there were others, usually too busy to stand and wait for the news from the town, who came to sit at Pitcher's tables and eat Emma's food. The room was like a waiting room for the long distance coaches, she thought, with tension rising as Barrass was due to arrive. And for the village, just as important.

The only irritation to Emma was the fact that Daisy ignored her entreaties to avoid Walter Waterman. Neglecting his duties shamefully, the Postmaster took Daisy out more and more frequently.

Although Daisy was not as attracted to him as he obviously was to her, she found his company both flattering and pleasant. With Pansy less and less inclined to accompany her to the various entertainments and parties to which they were invited, Walter was a useful partner.

He was more and more often not to be found in his office, as tea was a popular time for Daisy to meet her friends. Even when he was reminded of his duties as Deputy Postmaster of Swansea, he shrugged off the objections and pointed to the open window through which letters could be dropped and assured the complainants that the service was well run and they could have no fear that their letters were not being given his best attention.

At first he had been ably assisted by his mother, but she had soon grown tired of the responsibility she had expected to lose at the same time she had lost her husband, and shrugging off her widow's drapes, she had gone to live in Bristol with her sister. Walter carried on alone, offended by her abandonment but too involved with his newly discovered love to care over much.

It was not uncommon for either Ben Gammon or Barrass to attend to the sorting of the letters received, and Barrass had on occasions even entered the late arrivals in the ledger which Walter filled with his spidery writing. One morning the office remained firmly closed and Barrass first of all banged on the door, then, with Ben's assistance, climbed up to the bedroom above the office and peered through the window.

Walter was fast asleep. He stirred when Barrass threatened to break the glass with his fist, and looked startled as his bleary eyes focused on the face surrounded by long black hair, momentarily convinced he was seeing the ghost of his dead father.

'Wake up, you dozy dreamer!' Barrass shouted through the pane. 'There's an inspector below!' His untruth had the desired effect and he laughed to see the man jump from his bed and grab a maroon dressing gown which he wrapped around him as he headed for the stairs. To Barrass's further amusement he saw, when Walter opened the door, that the man had added a tall silk hat to his attire, believing no doubt that it added dignity to his dishevelled, unwashed appearance.

Unfortunately, Barrass's jibe about there being an inspector present was not far from the truth. Two gentlemen who stood outside the door of the inn watching the proceedings with disapproval were indeed representatives of the Royal Mail. The taller one nudged his partner, and asked him to write down the morning's occurrences in detail.

It was Barrass who helped Walter to share the letters between the outgoing and incoming bags, and it was Barrass who arranged for Walter to be supplied with breakfast and ale from the inn and a man to shave him. Passing the two curious watchers, he laughed and told them that Walter Waterman was 'A joy to have around for the stories he provides'. Neither man looked remotely amused.

Before setting off on his return to the village, Barrass went to make sure Walter was sufficiently recovered to manage the office.

'I'm not ill,' Walter assured him. 'Just bemused to know why I slept so soundly after being awake for most of the night.'

'A girl, is it?' Barrass asked. 'By the name of Palmer?'

'Perhaps,' Walter grinned. 'She fills my thoughts, and – '

'And you'd like her to fill your bed?' Barrass's smile reflected Walter's but his eyes were less cheerful. Pitcher would not be pleased at how far the man's thoughts were taking him.

Daisy listened to her mother and sighed.

'I understand how useful it has been for you to have a partner, my dear daughter,' Emma complained, 'but consider how easily it has become accepted that you and Walter are a couple. Only today you and he have been invited to attend a wedding! A wedding! My dear, think where this might end! Daisy, you are missing opportunities by keeping company with this man. Best you tell him goodbye before you find yourself with no friends but he.'

Daisy dared not tell her mother that besides walking out with Walter with a proprietorial hand on his arm, she had actually sat with him in the sorting office and entered items in the ledger in her own hand. Her lettering was boldly formed and larger than Walter's, whose writing was hesitant and spidery in style. She had made sure the visits had been at a time when there was no chance of being seen by Barrass, and so far, no one had reported the occurrences.

It had been fun, pretending she was a woman with a business to attend. Daisy thought, not for the first time, that she had been born into the wrong family. Her instincts were those of a lady, reinforced by the training and schooling her parents had provided, but deep inside her was an excitement that only the dealings of commerce could satisfy.

On her visits to Swansea and the once only time she had gone with Emma and her sister to stay with friends in Bath, she had looked with envy at the women who served in the smart shops, imagining the delight of accounting, and of deciding which among her wares were the most profitable and which the ones she could abandon.

She even imagined running the alehouse with her father, although that was completely out of the question. She smiled at the thought of Emma's face if one of her expensively schooled daughters should even mention such an idea! But wistfulness soon replaced the smile. Such a nuisance to have been born a girl!

When Daisy told Walter, so sadly, so tearfully, that she would not meet with him again, he was devastated. He had begun to consider himself one of the family, even calling her father Pitcher, like everyone else. Perhaps, he wondered, that was my undoing? To refer to him as Mr Palmer would have perhaps been more respectful.

He took to coming to the alehouse every evening, and he would sit where he could see out into the passageway in the hope of seeing Daisy pass through. Pitcher watched the man warily, afraid that the drink would soon change him from a reasonable man to a nuisance. But Walter seemed content to sit and sup, share a conversation with others and then leave to ride the six miles home without his presence being an embarrassment.

The way Walter did show his unhappiness was in the way he ran his office. Abandoning all but the most irregular entries, the books became less and less an accurate picture of his transactions. When a man arrived to check that the procedures were being followed, he found chaos.

The report sent by the men who were passing through Swansea on their way to Carmarthen had been serious enough for them to investigate. What they found was far worse than had been suggested. One evening there was a letter for him from the London office. It threatened that unless he organized himself swiftly and thoroughly, he would be replaced.

Chapter Thirteen

The alehouse had become increasingly busy once people knew that the post was collected there. Those who had gathered outside in all weathers to hear Kenneth pontificate on the latest news and gossip, revelled in the comfortable, relaxed atmosphere of Pitcher's bar-room. The doors were opened in time for Barrass returning with the letters from Swansea, and even at that early hour, the bar was rarely without someone sitting and drinking his ale.

Markus surprised everyone by becoming a regular visitor. He was guided in by his watchman, who then sat far enough away to be unable to listen to his rare conversations, but close enough to help if his master needed something. Markus always chose the darkest corner, sitting facing into the room, his head still, the eyes staring at one place on the distant wall, whatever went on in the room. He made people nervous at first but so regular was his attendance that they grew accustomed to him and hardly noticed he was there.

Pitcher was up early yet customers began arriving before he and Arthur were ready to receive them. They both ran about with Arthur's dog trotting after them, to and from the cellar, trying to clean floors and wash tables while they were in use, Pitcher undecided whether he was pleased or irritated when some who spent the day in his bar-room told him how comfortable he made them feel.

'I don't mind them that drinks steady, they pay well for the comfort of a fire and a decent chair, but there are those, like Oak-tree Thomas, who sit without a drop in front of them and pass the hours in conversation and idleness that pays me nothing at all!' he grumbled to Barrass. 'Seems some don't have a home to go to!'

A man waved a hand irritably at Arthur and called for him to go and take an order. With a sigh, Arthur put down the wood with which he was replenishing the fire and whispered to Barrass, 'Being polite all day long to people who think they're your betters is killing me!' He prepared a smile and went to see to the gentleman's wants and Barrass reminded him that, 'Being subservient is what Pitcher pays you for.'

Two well-dressed gentlemen entered the room, one about fifty, the other one younger and carrying a large saddlebag. Arthur pushed Barrass forward to serve them.

'Go on, see how well you do at being subservient,' he whispered. 'Good for your soul it is, so Mistress Emma always tells me.'

Barrass looked at the newcomers curiously; they seemed rather familiar. 'Gentlemen?' he queried.

'Some of your best ale if you please,' the elder of them asked. 'And some information.'

At once Barrass was on the defensive.

'I don't work here, sirs,' he assured them. 'If it's information you want, then I'll call for the proprietor, Pitcher Palmer.'

'No, it's you we want to talk to,' the younger man said. 'You are the letter-carrier known as Barrass, aren't you?'

'That I am.' Barrass frowned at them trying to remember where he had seen them before.

'We are paid by the Postmaster of London,' the younger one explained, dropping his bag. 'There have been some discrepancies in the accounting of the Swansea office and some of the writing in the ledgers is believed to be yours.'

'More than likely,' Barrass said. 'I have often helped Walter when he has been busy. The people who bring letters often wait until the very last moment and then there is a rush to get the bag ready.'

'There is the writing of a third person.' He opened the canvas and leather bag and showed a page to Barrass. 'Know this writing, do you?'

Arthur, who had crept closer, curiously gasped and said, 'I do! That's Mistress Daisy's or I'm a parson's cat!'

'Fetch them their drink, Arthur, I'm going to find Pitcher,' Barrass said. He hurried to the cellar where Pitcher was clearing out some abandoned barrels and empty boxes and quickly explained the situation. Pitcher ran up to the bar-room and introduced himself.

'My daughter is from home,' Pitcher explained, 'but I can tell you what happened. My daughter was very concerned over Walter Waterman who was greatly grieved by the death of his father. Daisy helped him until he was recovered.' He stood as if dismissing them. 'That's all. Now if you'll excuse me, I have to prepare for the small service I give and deal with the letters brought in to my own sorting office.'

'We will wait if you please,' the elder one said. 'We wish to see for ourselves how well you attend to the task.'

When the wagon drew up outside, Pitcher went to help Emma and his daughters down, managing to explain that there were inspectors on the premises, by words spurted out from the side of his mouth.

Daisy went at once into the bar-room to greet them, her cheeks rosy, her eyes a bright summer blue, her hair a shower of gold. She spoke to them like an obnoxious queen dealing with peasants and they abandoned their superior attitude, stuttered, backed away and apologized for disturbing them. They were on their way before Barrass could tell Arthur to come and look.

'I hates to say this, daughter,' Pitcher whispered, 'and your mother would have my heart for a pincushion if she heard me, but you are a great asset when it comes to business and no mistake.'

'I know,' Daisy smiled. 'I know. And, Mamma would be even more horrified to know that I like it!'

Daisy felt rather mean when she thought how she had used Walter. She had deliberately set out to attract him with the sole intention of winning the change of address for the sorting office. Now, knowing he was in trouble, she wanted to help. The following morning, she decided, she would go into town and talk to him, persuade him to make an effort to get his business back and running as it should.

Barrass was pleased that he no longer had to waste time at the end of his Thursday round. With Jethro he finished early most days and set about helping Pitcher and Arthur with the last minute finishes to the new rooms.

One Thursday he was disappointed when, at his last call, he was given a letter to be delivered to Markus. For a moment he was tempted to take it back to the alehouse, where he could hand it to the man when he next visited, but the temptation was denied. Turning away from the village, he rode along the narow cliff-top path to the dark house.

The watchman wasn't there. Damn me, he thought, I expect he will be at the alehouse and I could have saved myself a journey. But he knocked in case and expecting to see the door opened by a servant, was surprised when, after a stick-tapping approach, the door was opened by Markus himself.

'Who is it?' the man demanded.

'Barrass, with a letter for you.' Barrass pushed the flimsy pages into Markus's hand. 'Shall I wait for the money, or will I call tomorrow?' he asked, presuming that, if Markus opened the door, the servants were out in the fields.

'Wait,' the man gruffly said and disappeared, tap-tapping his way along the dark corridor.

After several minutes had passed, the tapping returned and Markus waved a hand in his direction, with a letter and some coins in it.

'Take this reply, will you?' Before Barrass could answer, the door was closed, and there was only the faint, fading tapping of the man's stick.

It was on the following day that Barrass was reminded of the unusual occurrence of Markus opening his own door.

'Seems Markus had sent all his servants away,' Arthur told him. 'There was money missing and as no one would own up to taking it, he sent the lot of them on their way and has sent for Sally Ann in the town to find him new ones.'

For a while Barrass thought nothing of the news, then he felt cold shivers threading down his back. With no one to read the letter and write the reply, there was only one explanation. Markus could see!

Barrass made cautious enquiries convinced he must have been mistaken, that the watchman had in fact been there, but no, the man had been in Swansea with the message for Sally Ann to find replacements. The watchman was the only one not dismissed and he had been six miles away.

When Markus next came to the alehouse, Barrass watched him carefully and there was only the slightest movement to follow a moving object to reveal it, but he was certain he was correct; Markus was deceiving them. Whether it was a recent or long-standing situation, Markus was no longer blind.

While Daisy was considering how she should approach him on the following day, Walter was sitting in his upstairs room, reading through the day's transactions and trying to rouse some enthusiasm for what he was doing. While his father had lived, he had been able to do a little to help and go out to meet friends when the tedium was too much.

He was naturally a lazy man, and after his father had left the post office in his mother's hands, he had expected to continue the same as before after a few weeks of artificial concern for her and a pretence of helping. When she had seen what he expected, she had written her intention to the head post office in London and gone to find a new and more interesting life in Bristol. Walter had been devastated.

Then Daisy had appeared in his life and he had believed that the life of the idle gentleman could after all be his. He spent the little money he had put by on new clothes and in courting her and it had all been for nothing. He gazed unseeing at the thick, leather-bound book in front of him and wondered what he should do next. Work, he did not consider.

A knock at the door surprised him. Of late, having spent all his time with Daisy and her friends, his own companions had neglected him. He went down the stairs and opened the door. A young woman stood there smiling, a bag stuffed untidily with clothes beside her.

'Hello, Walter,' Lowri said. 'Can I come in?'

Daisy decided that to ease any embarrassment when she called on Walter, she would take her sister. For once Pansy agreed to accompany her and the sisters, driven by Arthur, who had some business to see to for Pitcher, went into town soon after Barrass had left with the letters for Gower.

'If you wish, I'll leave you to talk to Walter while I look at the shops,' Pansy offered.

'No, that's what I do *not* want,' her sister said. 'I don't *want* to talk to him at all! But I feel he is unhappy and I am the cause. The least I can do is assure myself I have done everything I can to comfort him in his misery.'

The wagon pulled up in front of The Voyager Inn and Arthur

helped them both down. He tied the horse to a convenient post and after seeing he was out of the sun and with a drink nearby, wandered to sit under the big beech tree, on the bench.

From an upstairs window, Lowri watched the girls approach. Walter was lying on the bed drowsily watching her.

'Customers,' she whispered. 'Go and see to them, shall I?' She didn't wait for his agreement but slipped a gown none too neatly about her stocky form and went down the stairs. She pulled at her hair to make sure she did not look tidy, loosened the neck of her gown even lower and yawned as she opened the door.

'Why, Mistresses Daisy and Pansy!' she said in feigned surprise. 'Have you brought something for the post?'

'No, I – that is –'

' – we wondered if Walter is well,' Pansy added swiftly. 'We were told he was incapacitated somewhat.'

'Fine and handsome he seems to me! Sleeping like a babe he is, and with such a smile of contentment on his face. Pity to wake him – if it isn't nothing urgent –'

'No, please don't disturb him. And there's no need to tell him we called,' Pansy said, and hurried her sister away.

Arthur watched as Daisy and Pansy entered the office, then stood up in surprise when they turned and hurried back to the wagon.

'What is it?' he asked, seeing their tight-lipped expression.

'Don't ask!' Daisy said grimly. 'Just take us to where we can sit and drink a glass of cordial and forget we came!'

From the sorting office, a face stared after them. Lowri smiled. They were unlikely to call on Walter again. For the moment, she had a place to sleep and a man to feed her. It would do, until she was ready to move on.

Daisy wanted to buy some beads to match a dress she planned to wear when they went as a family to dine with their sister Violet, Edwin and their little niece.

'I think I'll stay here and sip another cordial,' Pansy said. 'Take your time, I won't be impatient.'

'Are you sure you're well, Pansy?' Daisy asked. 'You seem loath to do anything, go anywhere or even take an interest when I do! You aren't feeling sick, are you?'

'The summer weather is a bit trying, but no, there is nothing wrong that a cooling breeze will not mend. Go and find the beads you want and I will sit here until you come back. Bring me some sweetmeats, and some to take back for Mamma.'

When Daisy had disappeared, Arthur and Pansy hugged each other and left the front room of the house where they had bought refreshments.

'A whole hour at least!' Pansy said, as, taking Arthur's hand, she ran with him towards the edge of the sea behind the castle.

Like children released from confinement, they took off their shoes and ran at the edge of the tide, laughing with delight at the sensation of the rippling water. They waved to the men who worked on some upturned boats, talked with the urchins who wandered along the line of the tide looking for treasures. They aimed pebbles to skim across the waves, earning their cheers when their missiles touched the surface more than twice.

They searched for seashells and Arthur found some large shells which he gathered for Pitcher.

'He uses them for the tables,' he explained to a curious Pansy, 'for the men to empty out their pipes into, and to use as trays to rest the pipes on to cool.'

Pansy laughingly helped him to fill his pockets, then stopped and gasped with admiration at the rockroses growing in profusion on the dunes, their yellow petals as fine as silk.

When they felt they had been there long enough to become invisible to those nearby, they found a place amid the dunes and sat together with their arms about each other.

'Such a pity we have to go back,' Arthur said. 'But I don't want us to have to explain our absence. A brief walk along the shore, that is easily explained, but it's best we go now.' He kissed her lightly and stood to help her rise.

'How can I explain the brightness of my eyes? I know it shows when I have been with you, Arthur,' Pansy sighed. 'How no one has guessed I can't imagine.'

They walked back to the small room, pleased that their return was well-timed as, within a few minutes, they were joined by a jubilant Daisy.

'I have found exactly what I want,' she told them, holding up the beads she had bought.

'How wonderful,' Pansy said with a secret glance at Arthur. 'To find what you want makes the world a beautiful place.'

*

Annie still refused to leave the house. For a while she had begun to relax, thinking her time for caution was ended and she could begin to explore the neighbourhood and its people. Seeing Cadwalader had made her withdraw again like a snail whose shell was touched. Unaware that he had seen her, she thought that with extra caution, she was safe.

It was from Olwen that she gleaned the news. Because Olwen was gregarious and belonged to a family who were familiar with all the inhabitants of the village, she knew what was happening as soon as anyone. Her mother sold fish both locally, knocking at doors, and in the Swansea market. Spider and Dan were regular visitors to the alehouse, where, it seemed to Annie, all the information of the world filtered. Anything she needed to know, she asked Olwen.

One afternoon, when William was in Bristol with John Maddern and Edwin, Annie suddenly needed something from the village. She called for Olwen, then remembered that both she and Dozy Bethan were out helping with the harvest in the cornfield. She stepped outside into the warmth of the afternoon and called for David and the other stable boys. None appeared in answer to her demand. She stamped her foot irritably.

Should she take a chance and go as far as Ceinwen's house to buy the vegetables she had forgotten she needed? She looked around the kitchen and the small garden close to the house, but there was no alternative. William would be home either that day or the following and after four days away, would be expecting a decent meal. The risk was a small one, the thought of not giving William the best meal she could provide, unacceptable.

She put on the thick, unsuitable cloak she had not worn since her arrival at Ddole House and adding a hat which, she hoped, might mislead anyone who saw her, set off across the fields. She was not even sure of the way and with only Olwen's vague, half-remembered instructions to go on, she found herself walking along the green lane. She stopped at the house of Betson-the-flowers and asked her way.

'It's vegetables I need,' she explained crossly. 'The girls I depend on have forgotten them. They are most unreliable! If you could direct me to the house of Ceinwen, who I understand sells them, perhaps I can get what I need.'

'Don't worry yourself to walk all that way on such an afternoon,' Betson smiled. She beckoned the woman inside and from a shelf gave her a bundle of pea plants on which full pods still hung. 'Have these, and welcome. There are plenty more where they came from. Some parsnips too.' She picked up a paper-wrapped bundle. 'With plenty of butter they make a tasty meal even tastier.'

'You must let me pay you – ' Annie took her purse that was hanging from the chain around her waist and opened it.

Betson shook her head, making her long red hair shimmer in the sunshine.

'Take them and welcome,' she said, pushing the purse away from her. 'I've plenty more. People are so kind to me, I'll never understand why.'

Relieved that she had managed to avoid a visit to the outskirts of the village, Annie hurried back to the house.

From a position close to the house of Betson-the-flowers a figure watched her go. He was wrapped in a black cloak and sat cross-legged against the trunk of a tree on a high branch. When Annie passed close beneath him, he did not move.

When she had disappeared from sight, he climbed down and began to walk back to the town. He did not want to go, but having promised to play and sing for supper and a barn in which to sleep, he felt obliged to keep his word. There would be other times and being reliable was important. Tomorrow he would return.

Lowri spent several days with Walter, and with a bit of coaxing, managed to persuade him to part with a few pounds which she told him she needed for clothes. Taking a few items from her pack and paying for them to be pressed, she paraded them for his benefit, making the demonstration of her purchases a flirtatious dance, and explained that the money was spent.

When he was sleeping beside her later that day she crept down and counted her hoard. Soon there would be sufficient for a coach journey to Cardiff, where, she suspected, her mother might be.

She knew her brother was still in the area, and for a while thought that meant he had found her, but he was showing no sign of it, wandering around, singing at the market place, and at alehouses and inns, to keep himself fed and warm. Cadwalader, she thought with relief, had given up the search and was staying in the town because of some woman.

When she went out to buy food, she saw him, sitting with his cloak around him, in his usual position, legs crossed, his bundle and his harp beside him. He was eating the flesh from a pig's trotter, and almost on his knee, a paw raised in pleading gesture, was a dog waiting for him to abandon it.

Cadwalader was smiling and at first she thought it was at the anxious expression on the dog's face, its head to one side, its brow furrowed like a row of cigars. Then she realized that he was unaware of the dog and the smile was one of satisfaction not amusement. Instead of greeting him, she decided to watch, just in case he had stumbled on a clue to the whereabouts of their mother. She retraced a few steps and stood at the corner of a house, where she could secretly observe him.

When he moved off, she followed. The shopping she had done was abandoned near the corner and, allowing him to get well ahead, she carefully moved along the street keeping him in view and ready to dart for cover if he should turn around. She guessed he had something on his mind as he did not once glance back, but walked steadily and with a clear indication that he knew where he was heading, back to Mumbles.

Lowri was getting tired by the time she and her quarry reached Pitcher's alehouse. At first she thought he was going inside, but he seemed to change his mind and walked past. Wearily, Lowri followed. Her shoes were broken and they were cutting her toes, so once they had left the road and taken to the fields, she threw them into a hedge.

The grass was cool under her feet with the approach of evening, and the occasional stream a welcome, soothing pleasure. She gradually discarded one idea after another about where he was heading as they went through the village without stopping, and once or twice she felt disappointment at the thought that he knew she was there and was leading her on a long, fruitless journey. But she knew she had been very careful, keeping him close enough to see if he looked in her direction, and being far enough back for him not to hear her.

Then she saw him walk through the gates of Ddole House and her mind filtered the information she had on the household. William Ddole a widower, and – 'Yes,' she said aloud. 'A new housekeeper!' Keeping well back now, she darted past the drive and through into the field beside it, then down to where she was near the house but sheltered by a thick hedge of hawthorn.

For a while she listened, then, hearing a door close, she pushed her way painfully through the hawthorn, her excitement such that she did not feel the pricks of the cruel branches. The kitchen door was open and she boldly went inside. Cadwalader and her mother were facing each other across the table.

'Hello Mam,' Lowri said into the sudden silence. 'Glad I've found you. I want my share of the money you stole.'

'Cadwalader!' Annie wailed, 'you promised me that she hadn't followed you!'

'I didn't see a sign of her,' Cadwalader said. 'How did you know to follow me today of all days?' he demanded.

'Saw a smile on your face like a pig with a full belly and knew that it was more than food to make you look like that.'

'What are you going to do?' Annie asked. Her small eyes had lost their smile, and her jaw was tight and jutting. She would not give up all her hopes without a fight.

'I want you to come home,' her son said simply.

'I want my share of the money,' Lowri said firmly. 'You sold the boarding house that was our home and had us all evicted, Dad, Cadwalader and *me*!'

The emphasis seemed to suggest to Cadwalader that if she had been included in their mother's plan she would not have had any righteous or moral objections to the act. It was not the selling of their home, their abandonment and their eviction, but the fact that she had not been a partner in her mother's crime.

'You've survived,' Annie said coldly.

'Would you like me to tell you how?' Lowri demanded.

Annie ushered them into the sitting-room out of sight and looked at the big longcase clock. Ticking away the seconds, marking the passing of her brief freedom. William must return soon. She had to get rid of her children, but how? She did not want to run away and start looking for a place now, when William was beginning to depend on her, but if he came back and heard what they had to say, she would be told to go anyway.

'Come back tomorrow and we'll discuss what's the best for us all,' she said. 'Go now or you'll spoil the best chance of bettering ourselves we're likely to have!'

'I'll sleep in the barn,' Cadwalader decided.

'And so will I,' Lowri said firmly. 'Don't think of running away again, we'll find you, and next time it will be with the law!'

Annie didn't waste time wondering how Cadwalader had found her, but thought of all the choices she had left. To do as Cadwalader wanted and go back to her drunken husband was out of the question. To run away, when she was just beginning to make a home for herself, seemed hard. But how could she stay put with them at her heels?

She wondered if it was too soon in their relationship for her to confide in William. By missing out the fact that she was still married, and make the man she was running from her drunken brother, he might just believe her. But there were still Lowri and Cadwalader. Nothing she could say would make *them* go away now they had found her! With an unaccustomed frown on her normally gentle face, she put finishing touches to the meal she had prepared and looked anxiously along the drive for the return of the servants. Yesterday she railed against the inconvenience of having to tend the cooking while the others helped in the fields, today it seemed a trivial chore.

The following day, after a sleepless night, Annie rose early. The household was silent and still when she called Dozy Bethan. With the girl's sleepy assistance she prepared all the food for the day, so she would be free. When the servants, including Bethan and Olwen, had gone to their work in the fields, and William was eating his breakfast, she went to the barn to find Cadwalader and Lowri.

'I can't stay long,' she whispered. 'You must go from here. Give me time to decide what to do. I won't go back to your father, Cadwalader, and you can take that as definite! As for you, Lowri, why should I share my hard-earned money with you? Grown up you are and well able to work. Go and find some like I always have!'

'Dad is devastated and ill,' Cadwalader said. 'Surely you have some sympathy for him?'

'None! He had a good business as a printer and spent all his dwindling profits at the alehouse.'

'Then give us a share. As a family we did our bit to keep the boarding house going, why shouldn't we benefit from the sale of it?' Lowri demanded.

'I can't talk now. You'll have to give me a couple of days. No, don't worry,' she said as Lowri began to protest. 'I won't be running off. This place suits me fine and if you'll give me a while to consider, I'm sure I can satisfy us all. Now go, before William comes out and sees you here.'

After more discussion, in which Cadwalader showed regret and Lowri showed consternation and aggression, Annie persuaded them to leave. With a sigh of disappointment showing on her face, she went back to see if William needed anything further before she cleared the table.

When she thought William was watching her, she allowed the faintest sob to escape her lips.

'Is something wrong?' William asked. 'Is something worrying you, Annie?'

With her back to him, head bent into a handkerchief, she shook her head and opened the door to leave.

'Annie, a moment if you please.'

He rose from his chair and came to where she stood, touching her shoulder and making her face him. Her fascinating eyes were barely visible in their thickly-curled lashes. The strong eyebrows looked as if a comb had just passed upwards through them. The eyes looked reproachful, as if some dreadful wrong had been witnessed by them. He felt his heart race as he tightened the arm which he had placed on her shoulder and led her to a chair.

'It's nothing for you to concern yourself about, sir, best I go now before I bring some trouble to your house.'

'Trouble? What sort of trouble?' His first thought was that she had overheard something to do with the boats and he straightened in preparation for some damning revelation. 'You can tell me,' he coaxed, half afraid that what she had to say would condemn her to death. If she had learnt something of their activities and felt morally bound to report it, then she would be dealt with efficiently and in haste.

'I am here because I ran away from a problem, sir,' she began. 'I have a brother who spent most of each day drinking and then he would come back and treat me badly.'

'Oh, you poor woman.' William's relief that it was something less sinister than he had expected showed in the way he greeted her revelation.

'I ran away from him and I also ran away from my children. They being more than twenty, I thought them able to make up their own mind.' She allowed another whispered sob to punctuate her words as she went on. 'I regretted leaving them within hours, and on the following day I went back, but they were gone. Only my brother was there and he so furious that I ran off again and didn't even look back. Oh, sir, I feel so guilty about my behaviour and wish I could go back and help them all, but, sir, I daren't. Not now, I really dare not.'

William's arm had tightened and pulled the woman closer to him. She smelt sweet and feminine and her skin, close to him, was smooth and unblemished. Those deep set eyes looked up at him, the lips parted and for a moment he was lost to everything but her nearness and her need of him. He lowered his lips to hers and she gave a sob as she clung to him.

'Sir!' a sharp voice demanded. 'Will we get no lunch today for the men working in your fields?'

William turned so fast that Annie almost slipped to the floor. He stumbled away from her and glared at Olwen, who stood, hands on hips, bending slightly towards him, disapproval on her freckled face. 'Olwen. Please go into the kitchen. Annie has had a shock and is distressed and quite unable to see to food. You and Bethan must attend to it.'

'Thank you, sir, for your concern,' Annie said weakly, 'but I must see to the servants.'

'No, Annie, first I must hear the rest of your story.'

Watching the door, wondering if Olwen was listening, she said softly, 'Sir, my children, Lowri and Cadwalader, have found me and they want me to return to the house where their uncle lives. Oh sir, what can I do? I need to get away for a while. Perhaps, if you know of a house in London?'

'Why so far?' Suddenly, he did not want to lose this woman. In his loneliness he clung to her presence like a child will cling to even the most careless mother, her importance due to the absence of anyone else. 'Surely they won't force you to return?'

'I feel I have let them down, sir. They argue strongly in favour of taking me back.'

'Go to your room. I will ride over to see the doctor and get a sleeping draught. Tomorrow we will discuss this further. Until then you must rest.'

Olwen darted back from the door and busied herself with the lunch baskets that Annie and Bethan had put ready. She filled large stone flasks with water and put them with the food and the cider.

She left them ready and went back to the fields to find someone to help her carry it, taking only a basket of bread and cheese. When David and Bethan and several others had emptied the kitchen of the supplies, she picked up the last stone flask and tiptoed to peep into the study where William and Annie had been talking. William was alone. He sat at his desk, with papers spread out before him, but he was not working, he was staring at a drawing of his wife, a sad expression on his face.

'Do you need anything before I return to the fields, sir?' she asked. There was a stern disapproval in her voice, not the tone he expected to hear from a servant, and he glanced quickly at her.

'Nothing,' he said.

She continued to stand there, her coarse apron and the striped blouse she wore emphasizing her youthfulness and her smallness. Her expression was bold.

'Was there something else?' he asked.

'Just that what you and – she – were doing was what you sent Penelope away for, and it seems to me that you are – '

'Olwen!'

'Sorry, sir.' There was no apology in the words, only more defiance.

She was crying as she ran out of the kitchen door. She knew she had gone too far, and it was likely that when the day was over she would be told to go. Tears in her eyes prevented her from seeing the figure that stepped out in front of her as she hurried down the lane.

'Olwen, whatever is the matter?' Cadwalader asked. He stopped her hasty steps and took the heavy flask from her. 'Tell me, has someone upset you?'

'Only myself. I've just been a-w-f-u-l cheeky to Master Ddole,' she sobbed. Then swallowing her tears she glared at him and said aggressively, 'And it's *you* have the fault not me!'

He laughed and asked, 'What have I done that could upset you?'

'Annie, she's your mother, isn't she? Run away from your

drunken uncle. And you and that sister of yours let her go! Why couldn't you keep her away from us, causing nothing but trouble she is and her trying to persuade William Ddole to look after her! Marriage is what she has in mind for sure and from what I just witnessed, she's well on the way to persuading him!'

'Persuading who? Olwen, slow down and tell me properly what you know. I promise I will tell you the rest.'

They sat down under the hedge and she told him of how difficult life had become since Annie arrived. Then of her fears that Annie intended to persuade William to see her as a replacement for his wife, Dorothy.

'She'll send us away, even Dozy Bethan who has never known any other home, and everyone will be miserable.'

'Stop your worrying, Olwen,' he said grimly. 'There's no marrying for my mother. My father it was who she ran away from, not my uncle. She is still married.'

'But we must tell William Ddole!'

The relief was brightening Olwen's face and on impulse, Cadwalader leaned over and kissed her.

'Perhaps we should also tell him that she sold the boarding house bought with my father's money which she ran with our help. Sold it without a word. The three of us were evicted, thrown into the street, with only what we wore, while she set off with the money and searched for a new life.'

'What shall we do?' Olwen asked, looking to him for guidance.

'Wait until this evening, and you tell him what you know. That way he might overlook your impertinence. Then, I will be waiting outside to corroborate your story if he doesn't believe you.'

Their plans made, Cadwalader walked with her to the field, where, lunch time spent, she went back to work without tasting the food she had helped to carry down.

William sent for her as soon as the party of weary workers dragged themselves back from the shadowy fields. The sun was below the horizon, but while there had been light enough to see their feet, the men insisted they continued. Glancing at him, Olwen saw at once that his anger had remained with him. There was no sign of Annie.

'I'm sorry, Olwen, but you will have to go,' he said grimly. 'I have been lax in not sending you on your way before and it was only my daughter's affection for you that saved you. Before you leave, I wish you to apologize to Annie for the unhelpful attitude that has made her work less than pleasant.'

'That I won't, sir!' she said at once, 'and if you will listen for just a moment, you will understand my reasons.'

'No Olwen, I won't give you a moment!'

'There's no drunken uncle,' she said quickly. And before he could stop her she added, 'There is a drunken husband though.'

'You don't know what you're talking about. Go home before I whip you.'

'Sold his boarding house she did and ran off with the money and if you don't believe me, ask her son, Cadwalader. Outside he is, shall I call him?'

'Where did you hear this nonsense?' William demanded.

'I'm sorry to have to tell you this and I know you will make me leave because of it, but I couldn't just do *nothing*, sir, even if it means losing my place.' Olwen hung her head, very frightened, half expecting him to hit her, although unlike many masters he never had before.

'We will talk about this in the morning. First I need to hear Annie's story. I have to be fair.'

He was shaken and bitterly disappointed. There was little doubt in his mind that the girl was telling the truth, unless Annie's son spread this version out of spite and jealousy; such things had been known to happen, he consoled himself.

He watched through the window as Olwen walked up the drive and saw Cadwalader meet her there. With a sigh he went up the stairs and opened the door of Annie's bedroom. Looking in he saw that she was fast asleep. He had no heart for facing her and closed the door again.

Annie opened her eyes and raised herself in the bed; beneath the covers she was fully dressed. Having heard all Olwen had said, she made her plans. When the house had settled into the darkness of the summer night, she crept down the stairs and to the saucepan which was standing ready filled with milk for his regular evening drink, and she added the sleeping powder

204

which William had obtained for her use.

Two hours later she left the house, carrying a heavy case in either hand, and hurried across the fields towards the town to find her daughter.

Chapter Fourteen

Olwen was dismissed by William on the following morning. He had woken up to find the house empty apart from Bethan, who, having heard of the events of the previous day from Olwen, tapped cautiously on his door with water for him to wash and said nervously, 'Seems it's only me and Olwen to do everything.'

'What d'you mean?'

'She's gone, sir.'

Without being told to whom Bethan referred, William knew it was Annie. He felt bitter regret and wondered sadly what she had taken with her.

'Olwen no longer works for me,' he told a startled Bethan.

'Then there's only me!' she gasped, sitting down with the bowl and jug still in her hands. 'Can't do it all, sir, now can I?'

'Get me some breakfast. First things first,' he said. 'The rest we'll sort out later.'

'About Olwen, sir, gone to the fields she has.'

'I will go and see her as soon as I have broken my fast,' he said grimly. 'And let this be a lesson, Bethan. No one is allowed to be impertinent, not even those who feel that this is their home.'

'No, sir.' Bethan put the bowl and jug on the washing stand and left the room in what was, for her, great speed.

William washed and dressed and by the time he had reached the dining room, Bethan had brought cold meat, bread and cheese, a bowl of fruit and was pouring a tankard of ale. She was at his elbow to refill his glass and to cut him fresh pieces of the previous day's loaf and he was able to smile, wondering how long she could keep up the pace. When he turned to ask her for a fresh plate for the fruit he had chosen, she was sitting on a chair, fast asleep.

William walked to the fields and called Olwen to him. She ran smiling, her blue eyes glowing with good health, her face bronzed by the sun, the freckles standing out giving her a mischievous look. When she ran to him, there was no anxiety in her expression; a smile added a glow to her lovely young face so he hated himself for what he had to tell her.

'I'm sorry, Olwen, but I no longer want you to work at Ddole House,' he said at once. Guilt swept through him as the smile faded.

'I know I was rude, sir, but I thought, when you realized I was telling the truth you would forgive me. Someone had to say it, sir.' Her voice sounded breathless, the unexpected announcement having shocked her. 'I thought I'd have a telling off, or that you would cut my wages like Annie often did, but – I'm a-w-f-u-l sorry.'

She bent her head and he guessed that tears were filling her eyes. He almost relented but knew he would be a fool to allow a servant girl to get away with such behaviour. Why was life so difficult? Why was he more and more alone? He turned away and walked back to the house. Trailing behind him, he knew without turning around, was the dejected figure of Olwen. A small, unimportant child, straw in her hair, an oversized shabby apron tied about her tiny waist, a look of utter despair and sorrow on her face. He hardened his heart and increased his pace.

When he reached the open door he saw Cadwalader sitting comfortably against the step, his bundle beside him, his arms around his knees.

'What do you want?' he demanded gruffly.

'Please may I beg a moment of your time, sir?' he asked.

'No, you may not. Your mother is no longer here and I have no idea where she may have gone.' William was curt as he walked past the seated young man.

'My mother stole the boarding house that belonged to my father,' Cadwalader said to the retreating back. 'What Olwen told you was the truth. The first we knew of it was when the new owners came and threw what few items that were ours into the road.'

'It's no longer my concern,' William answered. 'Now go, before I set the dogs on you.'

'As you please, sir. But forgive Olwen, she was guilty only of telling my story for me.' He rose to his feet and gathering his belongings around him, walked back to the gate.

William watched him go, his jaw tight with anger, not aimed at Cadwalader, but against fate that seemed to treat him so badly since Dorothy had gone. He went to the stables and mounted his horse. Riding with no real aim, he found himself near the house of Daniels. Outside, washing clothes in a big bath of soapy water, was Florrie.

She looked flustered when she saw him. Her hands flew to her hair, patting it as if to create a miracle of tidiness in seconds. Her face was red with the effort of scrubbing the clothes and around her, on bushes, were other clothes drying, the result of many hours' work, he guessed.

'Florrie, forgive me for delaying you,' he said. 'If you've a moment, I must tell you what has happened to Annie.'

'The wicked woman, sir!' she exclaimed when he had briefly told her what had occurred. 'To think that you were willing to put your comfort and wellbeing in her hands!'

'Have you an idea where we can look for a replacement?'

'I will sit and think about it, but I suppose we will have to go to the town and ask. Perhaps, if Daniels can spare me for an afternoon, I might go there and see what I can find?'

He looked at her face, red and moist, but white near the hairline, and wished she did not have to work so hard.

'Is there any need for you to do this?' He waved his hand at the washing surrounding them.

'I confess it's vanity,' she admitted, going on to explain, 'Daniels's sister is constantly reminding me of how ill equipped I am to be his wife, having been used to having others around me to do the worst of the work. I am foolish enough to try and prove her wrong.'

'I suppose Daniels would not spare you for a while to help me out of my difficulty? I have told Olwen she must go, and with the others having been dismissed by Annie, I doubt I will get any food, let alone have someone to wash my clothes!'

'She has "left you in the lurch" as the crib players say. In the circumstances I think Daniels would be willing for me to come back until you are suited, sir.'

'Tomorrow?' he asked tentatively.

'Now,' she said. 'and with your permission, I'll call and gather a few of the servants who have left, so we have something to build on.'

Within twenty-four hours, the house was humming with the conversation of the returned servants. William tried to forget that Florrie's presence was temporary and he relaxed to enjoy the sound of cheerful voices around him again, something he had sorely missed.

Two people were unhappy with the new arrangements, one being Olwen.

'I know I deserved it, Mamma, and that makes it worse,' Olwen told Mary. 'I know you have warned me often about holding my tongue, but the house had become such an unhappy one and my thoughts burst out unbidden when I am vexed.'

'Don't I know it!' Mary wailed. 'Best we forget it now. Perhaps there will be another position for you. In the meantime you can help me with the work here, there's plenty for an extra pair of hands for sure. We want to have a good supply of garments to sell at Neath Fair.'

'Can I go and tell Barrass?' she asked, and she looked so disconsolate that Mary agreed.

Daniels was less easily comforted. He had been met by his sister telling him of Florrie's return to full-time employment at Ddole House and had at once ridden over to talk to her.

'What does this mean, Florrie?' he asked, as, smoothing his clothes after his ride, he settled in front of the kitchen fire. 'Don't I even justify a discussion before you hare off to help out your employer?'

'William Ddole is in trouble. You can't expect me to ignore the fact that the woman I approved to replace me has left him without a soul to run his house.'

'Am I unreasonable to expect that your loyalties change now you and I are to be wed?'

'It's only for a week or so, just time to find servants to replace the ones Annie dismissed, or treated so badly that they left.'

'Or until the next crisis!'

'No, Daniels, this will be the last time, that I promise, only – '

'Go on?' He watched her as she neatly cut slices of the meat she was about to serve, her hands dealing with the bony joint of pork with a dexterity that fascinated him. Filling a plate with the thin pieces of meat she added a few sprigs of herbs to enhance it and went on to tip the strained vegetables into a large tureen.

She would be such an asset to him and his family, if only she could be persuaded to name a day. Efficient and always looking her best, the children would soon learn to be obedient to her. Then he looked from her hands to her face and saw that there was something troubling her.

'There's something else, isn't there, my dear?'

'Daniels, your sister is right, I will find it hard to cope with a household of five on my own. The washing alone took me all day, then the iron threatens to keep me a captive at the kitchen table for a further day. I am used to having servants to do these things and, well, it would be hard for me to do them all. I admit that it is these thoughts that make me hesitate to become your wife.'

Daniels was thoughtful as he rode home. He was content in his work, in a small community like Mumbles the task was not an arduous one, and he had plenty of time to sit and enjoy a book. But he had long hoped for a promotion. With promotion would come extra money and privilege and then he would be able to pay for a servant to come in and deal with the time-consuming, and the tedious.

The smugglers! If only he could catch those responsible, then he would be considered for a higher position. It was ironic that to persuade Florrie to be his wife he would have to catch her friends in the act of carrying illegal cargo. An act hardly likely to endear him to her. But she knew of his occupation *and* his determined intention of capturing the locals involved in the trade. She wouldn't help him, she had made that clear and he dare not ask again, but surely she would understand the necessity of his hunting them down?

Much as he hated the idea, he was going to have to spend time out on the cliffs, and sitting at the alehouse listening for a careless word. The alehouse was to reopen as an inn in a few days' time. There would be celebration and that meant tongues loosened by drink. A good time to begin his intensified efforts.

First of all he needed an assistant. Someone who was a familiar face, yet willing to earn some extra money for reporting what he heard. He sat for a long time in the evening sun, considering the most likely candidate.

He went first to find Kenneth and found him still bemoaning his lot with a blank-faced Ceinwen who was seemingly deaf to his complaints. From Kenneth's small cottage, he rode into town. At The Voyager Inn he soon learnt the whereabouts of Annie and her daughter. The conversation he then had with these two was most interesting, although he had to persuade Annie to tell him what she knew about her ex-employer's activities, bound as she was by what he considered false loyalty. The man had sent her packing for chastising one of the servants, she told him, and sent her on her way without even a letter of recommendation. Yet she had felt the strong need to protect him.

He thought of Florrie and mused sadly that loyalty to husbands came far below that to an employer! He could not help anticipating the moment when he told Florrie he had arrested William Ddole. Perhaps then she would remember what the words of the marriage ceremony meant and consider how she must support him against all the rest. With William Ddole behind prison bars sharing the tribulations of the lowest criminals, perhaps she would give his calling its rightful respect. He rode back to Mumbles a more contented man.

The gifts from Madoc still appeared at Olwen's door on occasions. It amused Olwen to think that while Madoc was giving food to her, others were supplying the Morgan family with food of a different kind. The generous villagers, having heard of the sickness affecting the poor family, were leaving fresh fruit and vegetables to improve the family's diet.

A grouse, a partridge, a hare were left at the door of the cottage on the cliff. Then, to Olwen's surprise and Mary's and Spider's alarm, a haunch of venison.

'We can't keep it!' Mary gasped. 'It's stolen for sure. What is he thinking of? He could get us hung!'

After urgent discussion, they decided to give it to Pitcher, who had ordered several meats for celebrating the opening of his long awaited Posthorn Inn.

'Among all that he's bought it won't be noticed,' Spider agreed and, at midnight, having agreed the arrangement with Pitcher, he walked down the steep path carrying the sacking-wrapped parcel on his shoulders and praying that no one would meet him and ask what his heavy burden contained.

He moved silently and carefully, his feet hardly disturbing the grass. At the bottom of the path he hesitated, looking up at Kenneth's house and across at the alehouse, where a faint light showed. Taking a deep breath, he stepped out to cross the open space and had amost reached Pitcher's doorway when a voice called,

'What you got by there then, Spider? Fishing in the dark is one thing, but knocking at doors after midnight to sell it is another altogether, isn't it?'

'Kenneth! Couldn't you sleep either? No this isn't fish, just a bag of winkles I forgot to bring for Pitcher. Couldn't sleep, and when I remembered it I thought a nice stroll down would settle me off. Smell they will, by tomorrow, if they aren't salted.' He looked up at the dark window above the door and then at the doorway. As Kenneth moved towards him, he called through the door, 'Got the winkles you asked for, Pitcher. Sorry it's so late, boy.'

Pitcher came out and seeing Kenneth, speedily took the sacking-wrapped joint from Spider's shoulder and carried it inside. Emerging again a moment later, he said, 'Sorry I can't invite you for a drink but it's ready for bed I am. Thanks, Spider, goodnight.'

Inside the dark building, a high pitched voice called from the cellar, 'What's happening? Who's throwing dead animals down on me? What have I ever done to you?' Arthur's face wore an offended frown as he drowsily hugged his pillow and drifted back to sleep. The dog came out of his barrel and sniffed at the parcel. He peed on it to claim ownership and went back to bed.

On the cliff path, Spider hurried home, wondering why Kenneth was watching at such a late hour. He had betrayed them once and might do so again. He would need to be watched.

Olwen had been unhappy working for Annie at Ddole House, but now she no longer had to go there each day she missed it. She had become accustomed to the chatter of the other servants and even when the number had been reduced by Annie's attempts at economy, there had been Dozy Bethan with her gossip about what went on in the house, and the people who worked in the yard, stables and farm. To be told to leave for impertinence had been a disgrace and it was this as well that made her wish to be back there.

Mary and Mistress Powell were busily filling basket after basket with goods to sell at the big September Fair, and Olwen was expected to help them. Enyd was asked to add her skills to the ever growing pile of work, but Enyd always managed to find a good reason for avoiding the crafts which would help to keep the family during the winter months.

'Why do I have to do so much while Enyd sits on her chair and stares out to sea?' Olwen demanded one morning when she had finished sewing up the neck of the seventh jumper. 'It isn't fair!' She stamped her foot and threw the offending garment down.

'If you hadn't been so badly behaved, you would be working at the house and earning the money for us to buy more wool!' Mary snapped. She too wondered how Enyd could be persuaded to do her share, but she said nothing, knowing that with a baby on the way, some women acted oddly. She hoped that the baby was the cause of Enyd's idleness. If it were not, then Dan would have a lifetime of problems ahead of him.

'Mamma, can I go and see Madoc? I think we should tell him not to bring any more gifts.'

'He must be reminded of the danger to us all. I'm sure he doesn't realize we were at risk,' Mistress Powell said.

'Go then, you aren't much use to me today,' Mary sighed. 'But won't you wait until Dan or your father can go with you?'

Olwen had already decided that it being a Friday, she would search out Barrass and ask him to accompany her.

'No need,' she said, hiding her joy. 'I won't be long, back in time to help gut the fish.'

She found Barrass helping Pitcher and Arthur to move old and new furniture into the recently finished bedrooms. Emma, leaning over the banisters, was calling instructions as Arthur, wearing a chair like a snail's shell, was trying to ease himself up the first flight of stairs without touching the banisters.

'Careful. The paint is hardly dry and you're shaving it off like skinning a rabbit!' she wailed. 'Oh, Mr Palmer, can't you see to it before the place is wrecked and we have to start all over again?'

Olwen found herself carrying up bed linen and hanging curtains and before she realized it, half the day had gone.

'Best I go now,' she said, when they had all eaten a scrappy lunch at one of the tables set outside near the shore. 'I told Mam I would be back to help with the fish.'

'I'll come with you,' Barrass said. 'There's still plenty to do, but I can't let you go to the Morgans on your own.'

'If it's the Morgans you're visiting,' Emma said, 'You can ask about Polly, see if there's any chance of her coming back. Take her these,' she added, and handed Olwen a bunch of flowers and a basket of small turnips and carrots.

They set off across the field on foot; the distance was not great and Olwen was glad to have the chance of more time with Barrass.

'Never see you these days,' she scolded. 'My father must have been very insistent that you don't spend any time with me, and you must be as soft as an overripe plum to do as he says! I doubt you'd keep away from that Harriet if Carter Phillips asked you to!'

He laughed and put an arm across her shoulders, pulling her closer.

'I haven't seen anyone apart from Pitcher and Arthur, except when I'm delivering the letters,' he said. 'Too busy getting the place ready for the grand opening!'

'Not even Harriet?'

'Not even Harriet.'

They managed to hold hands while carrying the gifts for Polly and sauntered through the fields chattering contentedly about small, unimportant things, and their mood when they reached the house was light-hearted. A glance at Polly changed that to one of concern. The young girl was in great pain and obviously very ill.

Olwen stood outside having glanced at where the girl lay, taking deep breaths to help her overcome the shock, preparing for what she would say. Barrass went to the sick girl and knelt down beside her pallet mattress. Olwen slowly approached and knelt beside him.

'Polly, we hoped to find you a little more improved,' Barrass said. 'Emma is in quite a state without you. Never knew how much she depended on you, that's what she told us, isn't it, Olwen?'

'More fussed than usual with you away,' Olwen agreed.

Unable to sit and look at the thin, wasted face, Olwen busied herself in the room. She found a teapot minus its lid and with a broken spout and into it she put the flowers they had brought.

'Put them where I can see them,' Polly asked. 'I love to see bright colours around me.'

Olwen did so, wondering how anyone could live with such drab surroundings without crying. The room was tidy, with shelves to hold the many bottles and jars filled with medicines and ointments made by Vanora. The fire, although low, burned well enough to keep the big cauldron simmering above it.

But the ground around the cottage was bare and churned up as if someone had spent a demented day digging it then changed his mind about completing the job. Tufts of grass and a few sad roots of corn were all that could be seen. The soil was poor, filled with stones, and rubbish was strewn all over the place with no attempt to disguise it.

She cut up the few vegetables and added them to the meat that was simmering, washed the plates that littered the rude wooden table and then stood, anxious to leave. The place depressed her, yet with the desolation of the place she felt an urge to sweep out the poor contents and refurnish it with clean, properly made furniture, and in her mind's eye she imagined it warm, cosy and neat. All things it lacked at present.

She went back to Polly and forced herself to sit and talk to the girl. She exaggerated all the happenings in Ddole House to amuse her, and added some items of news about Emma and the new inn. Polly only made brief replies and when a time passed without even that much, Olwen looked and saw that the girl was sleeping.

Barrass and she were just about to leave when Madoc and Morgan arrived. They greeted them then went at once to their sister.

'She's sleeping,' Olwen said unnecessarily.

'Best for her,' Barrass added.

'It's you we came to see,' Olwen said when the brothers came out again into the sun. 'I want to beg you not to leave any more gifts of food. Get us caught by Daniels you will! What would happen to us if he found us with a haunch of venison?' She stood in her usual scolding pose of arms on hips, bending slightly towards Madoc as she spoke. 'Besides,' she added lowering her voice, 'you'd show better sense if you sold it and spent the money getting the doctor to call for Polly!'

'We have,' Morgan told her. 'Nothing he can do except tell us to move from here and where would we go?'

'Can't you get the place made safe?' Barrass asked. 'It only needs a strengthening wall beside the stream and a good raised floor to the house to make it dry. Perhaps I could – '

'What business is it of yours!' Madoc shouted. 'Go on, clear off from here, telling us how best to look after our own!'

'I only thought – ' Barrass didn't move away from Madoc, and standing his ground seemed to inflame the man. Madoc shouted abuse and the dog who had followed him began barking and growling his support. But the cough that was ever present with the whole family brought the flow of words to a halt and Madoc bent over and was comforted by Morgan.

'We do plan to do it,' Morgan said. 'But it takes all our time feeding us all and getting money to pay what we owe to the doctor.'

'All their energy more like,' Olwen said sadly as they walked away.

'I won't bring you anything more that would endanger you, Olwen,' Madoc managed to say before once more succumbing to the coughing.

'And thank you for your call,' Morgan added. 'Our Polly values a visit.'

When Olwen returned home her mind was full of two things; the first was the seriousness of Polly's condition and the second, the possibility of working at the alehouse, or the inn, as Pitcher now called it. She planned to discuss the second idea with her mother, but the voice of Enyd complaining took it from her head.

'Olwen! Where have you been? I've had to see to the meal and bake the bread, and look after baby Dic!' Enyd complained.

'Where's Mam then!' Olwen asked, looking with dismay at the small, hard loaves Enyd was taking out of the oven.

'She's gone selling fish. Dan and Spider are off after mackerel. Seen out in the bay the shoals were, the water boiling like a cauldron with their numbers so they said.'

'You didn't go and see?' Olwen ignored the complaints Enyd

shouted after her and ran to the cliff top to see the boats gathered for the rich harvest of summer.

A few mornings later, a strange sound greeted her when she opened the door. She looked out and saw, tethered to the fence, a young sheep. It was injured, having a previously broken leg that caused it to limp badly.

'Mamma!' she wailed. 'Madoc has done it again!'

Spider promised that this time he would go and see the Morgans and taking the creature under his arm, he set off to ask them to take it back. He found the two brothers attempting to clear the weeds from a patch in which to plant some straggly-looking cabbage plants.

'Honestly got!' Madoc assured him breathlessly. 'We are grateful to Olwen for befriending Polly and we thought it proper to give her a real gift to comfort her after the fright of the stolen ones. Ashamed we were for our thoughtlessness.'

'Where is Polly?' Spider asked, and was shown the bed where the girl was lying. He gave her some sweetmeats Mary had made and offered to bring a thicker blanket than the one spread over her.

'Ask Olwen to bring it, will you,' she pleaded. 'She makes me laugh with her tales.'

'She'll be glad to,' Spider promised.

Still carrying the small sheep, he walked home, saddened by the plight of Polly and wondering how long before the brothers too were confined to their beds. Only Vanora seemed free of the sickness that had laid them all low, and she looked tired and without the spark of youth although she was only twenty.

Olwen went every day to visit Polly and each day found her weaker. She took broth and many other tempting dishes made by Mary and stayed with her while Vanora went into the market to sell her medicines or searched the fields for the plants with which to make them. With Barrass's help, she found wood to raise the sick bed off the damp earth floor and brought blankets and pillows to make the girl as comfortable as was possible.

She tied the sheep to the fence on a long rope and ran back each day to play with it and feed it. One day she arrived home to find Barrass there. With Dan's help, he had enlarged the goat's pen and made a small house for it to shelter in at night.

'Large enough,' Mary said, 'to hold several fully grown ones!'

217

'Now there's an idea!' Olwen said, looking at Barrass with a frown of concentration on her freckled face.

One Friday, Barrass met her as she approached the Morgans' cottage.

'I am getting from under Emma's feet,' he explained. 'She's so frantic getting everything in readiness for the guests they hope to attract, there's no sharing a house with her!'

'Barrass, I thought to ask Emma if I could work for her. They will be needing extra hands now, won't they? Not yet, mind. I think I would rather be free to spend time with Polly while she needs someone. But later, when she is recovered, perhaps I will ask Dadda to talk to Pitcher.'

Barrass declined to comment on the passing hope that Polly would recover and said instead, 'I mislike the idea of you serving at an inn, even with someone like Pitcher to look out for you.'

'But why!' she frowned. 'Why have I got to be treated different from everyone else? Other girls choose what they will do, I am always told "no, you can't!"'

'Ask your father, but I can tell you what his reply will be.'

'I'm beginning to wish I was back at Ddole House. At least there even with Annie I had *some* choice, even if it was only whether to get the coal first or carry in the water!'

Barrass decided to suggest to Mary that she go to see Florrie in the hope that William might have relented. To Olwen, he said, 'Let's pick some flowers for Polly, you know how she loves them.'

That Polly was worse was at once apparent. She was bright red, and tossing about on the bed, throwing the covers off in fever one moment and the next, shivering like the ague. Olwen bathed her forehead and talked soothingly to her while Barrass ran to find the doctor. Before the doctor could be found and informed by the dozen or more people Barrass sent in search of him, Polly had died.

When the brothers and Vanora returned from the market, and arrangements had begun for another funeral, Olwen and Barrass went back to the village to try and find the mood to join the rest of the village in celebration at the opening of The Posthorn Inn.

Chapter Fifteen

The opening of The Posthorn Inn was marred by the loss once more of the letters from the postbag. Barrass went to Swansea with the money he had collected the previous day and the letters he had been given for sending along the route with Ben Gammon, and when Walter opened his bag it was empty.

'I shall have to report it, Barrass,' Walter said. 'This is the second time you have lost the King's Mail. Pitcher is clearly failing in his duty.'

Barrass took the letters for Gower and hurried back to Pitcher. On the previous occasion the letters had been found in the quarry and it was there they went; Barrass, Pitcher and Arthur followed as always by the dog. They found them under a bush with a heavy rock holding them down and a quick glance showed none missing when compared with Barrass's notebook which was also under the rock.

'Best I take them at once into town, while you go on with your deliveries,' Pitcher said. 'Perhaps I'll take Emma with me.'

'Yes,' Arthur agreed at once, 'Mistress Palmer will be happier to be involved in the explanations and excuses.'

Returning to the stables for Jethro, Barrass set off. All day, his thoughts were on the perpetrator as he rode across the beautiful, sun-drenched peninsular, through narrow lanes and across downland richly coloured with myriad flowers and grasses. For once he did not stop and admire the small ponds which fish and frogs made into larders for herons and eagles, or watch the soaring kestrels and mewing buzzards riding the wind, heads moving from side to side as they watched for a movement below them that would disclose the presence of a meal.

Even from the highest point at Cefyn Bryn, where the shimmering sea was in view on both sides within a few short paces, he did not stop to marvel. He was unaware of the impressive rocky bays, the long stretches of sandy beaches and the small, secret

coves where seals basked in the sun, and gannets dived dramatically for fish, and the showy little puffins dived and filled their
bills neatly with small fish. His mind was distracted from the
beauty he so enjoyed, by worries about the post.

He tried to think who would be foolish enough to interfere
with the Royal Mail. Trying out every possibility with questions
and answers in his mind, he decided eventually that there was
only Kenneth, and he vowed to face the man on the following
day when he returned to the village.

Emma dressed in her smartest clothes for the interview with
Walter. Her wig was firmly fastened with a deeply-brimmed hat
which in turn was fastened by a flowing scarf. She needed to look
her most impressive; she was embarrassed by the way Daisy had
taken up with Walter only to drop him once Pitcher had what he
wanted from him.

'Clothes,' she reminded Pitcher as she dressed him in his
brown trousers and waistcoat over a full-sleeved shirt and long,
neatly tied stock, 'clothes give a man confidence as well as
making him appear cleverer than those less smartly turned out.'

'But it's so hot I'll boil!' he protested. She conceded only that
he need not wear his gloves.

To their chagrin they had to deal with Lowri as well as
Walter. Emma tightened her lips; she did not intend to behave
meekly in front of someone like Lowri! She glared at Pitcher,
warning him silently not to interfere and, instead of the apolo-
getic speech she and Pitcher had prepared, she launched into a
complaint.

'Really, the way you went on at Barrass, Walter!' she said.
'You'd think it was a fault with Pitcher and me! Stolen, those
letters were, and it was only through dedicated effort on the part
of my dear husband and our devoted staff that we found them
before snails made a meal of them!'

Walter backed from the room and Lowri opened her mouth to
respond, but Emma did not give her a chance to speak. She
glared at the young woman and ignoring the startled-looking
Walter, went on, 'You can tell your – master – or whatever – '
she said pointedly, raising a quizzical eyebrow, 'that we take the
greatest care of the letters in our hands and any complaints
should be directed at Daniels. The man is obviously not doing

his duty as well as we do ours.' With her nose in the air she left the office, leaving Lowri still trying to formulate a reply. Pitcher meekly followed her.

'D'you think Lowri *is* Walter's – er – "whatever" – ?' he chuckled.

Going into the inn for refreshment, they were surprised when Walter joined them. He had not given up hope of a reunion with Daisy, and he needed to explain the presence of Lowri. He apologized for his sharpness with Barrass, and assured them that he would indeed report the matter to Daniels without fail.

'No!' Pitcher shouted in alarm. They didn't want to attract the attention of the Keeper of the Peace! 'Don't make trouble, boy. We'll sort it ourselves. I have an idea who it might have been.' He leaned forward and whispered, 'Jealousy, Walter, and the trouble not aimed at us but you, due to the attraction you hold for – some beautiful young woman – and that's a fact.' He didn't name Daisy as the cause of the jealousy, but hoped it was implicit. He hid his face from Emma with a hand and nodded and gestured to explain his unwillingness to say more.

On impulse, Walter called for a boy standing near and sent him to buy flowers that he gave to Emma for her daughter.

'Just tell her they are from a devoted admirer,' he said, glancing back at the window of his sorting office where Lowri stood watching him. 'I hope one day to have the pleasure of calling on her again.'

'Of course,' Pitcher said, wincing from the sharp kick from his wife.

'That, Pitcher, was going too far!' she admonished as they set off again for home.

They were absent from the house only four hours but the time was enthusiastically enjoyed by Arthur and Pansy. In the pretence of needing a fresh breeze on such a hot day, Pansy set off with a parasol bought from a second-hand clothes seller who occasionally visited the town. She went down the stairs and stood where her voice would carry to the cellar, from which she could hear Arthur busily engaged in brushing the floor.

'Goodbye, Daisy,' she called up to her sister. 'I will be but an hour. I will walk along the edge of the tide and perhaps cool my toes.'

Arthur's thin face appeared over the rim of the cellar door and he quickly jumped up beside her.

'Meet you near The Ship and Castle,' he whispered before darting back down the stone steps.

They did not walk on the beach but kept to the drangways that traversed the hillside to serve the groups of houses built at odd places on the steep rocky slope. Breathless after a particularly steep climb, they stopped and rested on the slate threshold slab of an abandoned cottage hidden deep among summer-heavy trees. The sea was close but far below them, an indistinct susurration.

'This is like heaven,' Pansy sighed, leaning towards him for a kiss. 'So quiet, yet the air is filled with sound.'

'Welcome sounds,' he smiled, hugging her close to him. 'Birds pouring out their wonderful melodies. Love songs they are for sure! And the accompaniment to their song is the gentlest movement of the branches around them, keeping the birds in tune with their rhythm.'

'And the sea a soft murmur,' Pansy added. Then their lips grew closer and touched and words were superfluous.

Barrass hurried through his calls on the following day, anxious to face Kenneth with his accusations, the conviction that the ex-letter-carrier was the guilty one growing each hour. He raised the horn to his lips and blew to announce his arrival, threw the letters at a surprised Pitcher and went to the house on the green bank.

'I know it was you, Kenneth,' Barrass said at once when the man opened the door to him. 'If you touch the letters again it won't be Pitcher who will be in trouble. Daniels will hear of it.'

'How dare you accuse me! How dare you *talk* to me like that? You, a penniless beggar that I pitied and took in and fed!'

'If you want me to tell about your kindnesses, if you want me to broadcast the whole truth about you, Kenneth, like the seeds scattered in the spring, then just touch those letters again,' Barrass warned. He felt a pleasant satisfaction in the way Kenneth lowered his gaze and retreated into the house without a blustering denial.

Having told Pitcher of his suspicions and of Kenneth's lack of argument, they both thought the matter would end.

'Emma and me, we told Walter what we suspected, at least Emma did! I could hardly squeeze in a word. There's no man has lived who's more determined than a woman set on sorting something! We said that some jealous person was at the back of it, jealous of Daisy's attraction for him I implied, if he was sharp enough to understand my hints. I think he believed us. Anyway, he promised to hold back his complaint for a week, and if there were no more incidents he would forget it.' He lowered his voice and added, 'Watch your back, boy, watch your back.'

The opening of the new style inn was in difficulties due to the shortage of extra servants. When Emma discussed this with Florrie and found that Florrie's problems at Ddole House were the same, the women decided to go into town together and try to solve their difficulties.

'David will drive us in the carriage,' Florrie said. 'I've been told that it's for my temporary use as there are such problems.'

They went early one morning and at the market filled the carriage with extra food, both to fill the sadly depleted store cupboards of Ddole House and to add to Emma's supplies for the grand opening of The Posthorn Inn.

When their shopping was completed, they went to the house of a young woman who kept a list of names. In her house not far from the castle walls, she was regularly visited by both those in search of good servants, and by servants in search of a place. She charged no fee for the service she supplied but always managed accidentally to rattle a tin containing a few coins as a reminder that she was not too proud to accept a small 'generosity'.

Sally Ann was dressed rather smartly in a dress of pale mauve linen that was trimmed with bows of purple and pale green ribbon. Trailing strands of the same colour were woven through her hair. She sat just inside her door in a house that had been separated into individually rented rooms. A kettle simmered on a small fire and she made them tea in a china dish as they sat down.

'It's servants you need, is it?' she said, summing them up and deciding that they were both too well dressed to be looking for a place. 'Can you tell me first why the previous people left you? I like to know how best to please you and it saves time to get a few things straight.'

'I don't think you'll find any complaint in the way we look after the people working for us!' Emma said, puffing out her ample chest.

'My friend is the owner of a newly opening inn and needs people to help run it,' Florrie quickly explained. 'There has never been any complaint that led to her servants leaving her.'

They spent a while explaining their needs, then a small girl was summoned and sent to find the people named by Sally Ann. Before an hour had passed, they had both found the staff they needed and there was only one surprise. A door opened further along the passageway and Annie stepped out.

'What are these people doing here?' she demanded, her face smiling politely so they wondered if they had heard aright. 'Show them out if you please, Sally Ann, unless you wish to lose your room before nightfall.'

'What is *she* doing here?' Florrie asked of Sally Ann.

'Mistress Evans owns the house,' Sally explained, one eye on Annie to see that her words didn't cause complaint.

Emma began to argue but was ushered out by Florrie.

'Best we don't indulge in arguments with the likes of her,' she said. 'We've got what we came for and be thankful for that.'

Annie watched them go and as they approached the sorting office of Walter Waterman, she smiled. Now she owned a boarding-house again, and with a little money to spare, there would come a time when she could repay Florrie and perhaps Olwen too, for interfering in her plans to become mistress of Ddole House.

Kenneth was also watching the sorting office, wondering if a plea to Walter Waterman would persuade the man to reconsider his decision to give the handling of the Gower letters to Pitcher. Sitting quite near him was Markus. The man's watchman was muttering, telling his master who was there, describing the scene, blissfully ignorant of the fact that below the wide-brimmed hat Markus wore, the man's eyes were seeing for himself. Annie caught his eye and beckoned him. Without a movement of his head to reveal his interest, Markus saw him go.

'You are an ex-post-carrier, I believe?' Annie said, having been primed by Sally Ann.

'I carried letters all over Gower until Pitcher cheated me of

224

the privilege,' Kenneth said. 'But I'll get them back one day, be sure of that.'

'Perhaps I can help,' Annie said, smiling her kindly smile. 'Supposing you are a law-abiding man, I can perhaps share with you some information.'

'If you will walk to the inn and take a little light refreshment?' Kenneth smiled back.

Leaving town an hour later, Kenneth headed not for Mumbles village but for the house of Daniels. What Annie had told him about the arrangements to send payments with the assistance of the post was most interesting.

Taking a short cut back by Betson-the-flowers, he stopped a while and then walked past the shabby home of the Morgans. Madoc and Morgan were sitting outside their door listening to Vanora singing a hymn. Inside, he guessed that the body of Polly lay in her coffin awaiting the journey to the churchyard.

'Sorry I am for you in your sadness, boys,' he shouted.

'Someone will be!' Morgan sobbed. 'Two sisters gone and only for lack of a bit of money to provide a decent home.'

Kenneth declined to point out that they might have both home and money if they had not been so lazy. They were so distressed that even he could not speak his thoughts so unkindly. Then, as he was about to pass on, he had an idea. He waited until Vanora had finished her singing and had disappeared inside, before saying, 'Such a shame, when there's plenty of money to be had.'

'Not for the likes of us,' Madoc said.

'Perhaps not for you,' Kenneth shook his head in utter agreement. 'But for someone less honest, more careless of the laws of the land, well, it's there all right.'

'What do you mean?'

When they approached him, Kenneth abandoned his intention to tell Daniels, and explained.

The grand opening of The Posthorn Inn was planned to begin at midday, but others thought differently and the free drinks that Pitcher had promised to those who took the trouble to call and see what he had to offer, began to flow before Barrass had begun his journey across Gower. By evening, the place was littered with comatose bodies, which Arthur and Pitcher, in desperation, dragged out into the yard, there to lie in untidy heaps until they should recover.

Daniels came soon after the place opened officially and by using his authority, found himself a place near the fire, a mistake as he soon realized as the crowded bar became unbearably hot. Emma was so busy preparing the food that was an immediate attraction to both local people and visitors coming to walk beside the sea, that she was not aware of how much time Daisy was spending at the desk in the corner of the bar-room. Pitcher had bought a desk which he had set up near the door and at which letters were received and collected. The bookkeeping had slipped casually and swiftly into Daisy's enthusiastic hands. Her bold writing and figures covered the pages in an orderly way that had needed no teacher to describe.

Her superior attitude remained. She was rude to the people who came for her services and they loved it. Something about her appealed to men and women alike. Those she was polite to adored her. Pitcher wondered curiously what it was and decided that in their dull lives, the loudly confident Daisy was something to talk about, to complain about and on occasions, about which to boast.

Her rudeness was discussed and chuckled over by those who overheard the sufferers and loudly complained of by the recipients. Everyone who visited the inn had their turn, to laugh and be laughed at as Daisy inflicted her sharp wit on them all.

The wealthy travellers were soon made aware of the fact that she was no servant, but a lady with an education and an intelligent mind. Towards these her attacks were the most cruel and they too came back for more and brought their friends.

Soon it had become the normal procedure for her to dress early and be at the desk in time to receive Barrass and help him sort the letters for his route. Barrass stopped being surprised at Emma allowing it and was grateful for Daisy's efficiency. On the day of the party to celebrate the long delayed opening, Emma suddenly realized what was happening.

'Mr Palmer! A word!' she demanded as red-faced she threw down the bread she had been cutting up and walked from the back kitchen, puffing breathlessly up the stairs to the parlour.

With a sigh and a heavenward glance, Pitcher followed.

'I understand why you needed help while we were so low in

bodies, Mr Palmer,' she shouted. 'But now the need has gone, we have servants in plenty and I want you – I demand you – to send your daughter back up here where she belongs!'

Pitcher, who had been making tables and benches with Barrass and Arthur in the yard behind the house, just glared at her.

'Mrs Palmer, here upstairs and your children is *your* domain. Below is *my* domain and right now, my domain is in desperate need of my presence.'

'Mr Palmer!'

'Mistress Palmer!'

Glaring like dogs with a disputed bone they stopped talking. Their eyes were popping, their mouths shrinking to a small collection of wrinkles, until, first Emma then Pitcher burst into laughter, stepping towards each other to support themselves.

'Best we leave it until later, Emma, then, if we're still of a mind to, we'll persuade Daisy to give the desk to you,' Pitcher said with his tongue in his cheek. 'We must have someone there we can completely trust.'

'To me? I don't want it! I'll have far too much to do in the kitchen!'

'And Arthur and I will be as frantic and speedy as flesh and blood can be without catching fire. In the bar, the cellars, the stables and seeing to the renting of rooms. So?'

'I can't stand chattering to you,' Emma said, backing from the argument and the room. 'Sort it yourself. Three persons I'd have to be to satisfy you!'

'Satisfies me well you do, Emma Palmer, and never think different.' He reached for her and hugged her, while she pretended to escape. The new maid, a shy young girl called Megan, saw them and ran back down the stairs in embarrassment. Grown people behaving in such a way. She'd never thought to see the like!

Ben Gammon was on his way towards Swansea. An evening mist filled the hollows of the fields and poured into the low-lying lanes shrouding everything and making his journey tedious. There was always someone to share a word with, or something to see and weave into a story for those waiting for him at the inn. But this evening, although it was a long time before the sun would set, it was like riding through a nightmare.

Trees dripping their branches in front of him were unseen until they touched him. The horse was nervy and shied at half revealed bushes and trees. When two men stood out in front of them Ben was almost unseated.

'That's very unfriendly, looming up and setting the horse to throw me off in fright. Why, there ain't a day without I says to myself, this old world is afull of thoughtless and unthinking people!' He waited, pulling at his mount to steady it and asked, 'Well, do you want my help? Stranded are you, or lost in this soup of hell's kitchen?'

The men did not speak and as they stepped closer, Ben saw that their faces were covered with scarves. In their hands they both held a 'Brown Bess', long land service muskets used by British soldiers worldwide. The gun had been given the nickname 'Brown Bess' owing to the dull brown of the forty-six-inch long barrel which had been treated so as not to gleam and give away the soldier's position. To Ben's alarm the guns wavered as if the weight was too much for the arms that held them. Ben shivered as he thought that if the hands also lacked control he would soon be no more than a problem for his wife, her having to find the money to bury him.

Beads of sweat burst through his skin and he tugged at the horse to turn it and escape, but the horse's head was held and Ben was told to dismount.

'But that I cannot do. I need my horse to get me to Swansea,' he protested, believing them to be horse thieves. 'Spare an old fella from a long walk on such an evening.'

'You can keep your horse, friend, but hand over your bag.'

'But it's letters, being transported in the name of the King!' As he protested verbally, Ben hurriedly took the bag from his shoulders and handed it to the nearer of the men. The contents were swiftly removed and pages of the notebook torn out, then one of the men slapped the horse's rump to make him run and they both disappeared into the mist.

Ben listened for a while but there was hardly a sound from the men's retreating footsteps. He waited for what he guessed was long enough for them to have got well away, then he raised his horn to his mouth and blew.

Olwen was sitting on the cliffs watching the mist pour down

from the hill behind her. It was as if a great jug were tilted allowing the stuff to escape to fall and settle across the sea. She felt the chill of it and ran back to the house. She was wearing a dress of bright, buttercup yellow and over it she wrapped a shawl.

'Going far?' Mistress Powell asked, looking up from her knitting.

'Olwen, fetch some water for me before you go, will you? I'm that tired the bucket would pull me over,' Enyd complained from the room.

Fingers to her lips, Olwen tiptoed from the house.

She stopped to admire the goat, which came to greet her, its coarse, hairy body quivering under Olwen's stroking. The sheep was less friendly but it too came to see what was on offer. She admired them both and guiltily thought she ought to go and tell Madoc again of the pleasure the sheep had brought her. It wasn't far, and at this time of day, with the weather closed in, Vanora would be there. She did not fancy visiting when the brothers were alone.

The cottage looked gloomy when she reached the gate of the field and she almost turned back. The mist was thick here, in the valley where a stream ran through. The building could have been melting, she thought, its edges were already vanishing into the thickening mist. She wondered fancifully if the building was dying with the family it sheltered.

She approached the doorway which, as always, stood half-open. There was no fire, not even a smell of smoke, and from what she could see in the darkness of the cold room, no occupants either. With relief she turned to leave.

She was almost at the gate when she heard voices. They weren't coming from the house but from the field beyond it and she walked towards the sound, hoping that Vanora was there. Gradually she made out two figures and again she wanted to run. There was something frightening about the ghostly shapes, bending about some unseen task. Then a light flared, and a torch was lit. In its yellow light she saw that Morgan and Madoc, because it could be none but them, were burning some papers.

Her curiosity was greater than her fear and she stepped a little closer. Then she gasped. The paper they were burning consisted of letters, several dozen from what she could see. She turned

229

then and ran back to the gate. As she touched it, footsteps sounded behind her and giving a faint scream of fright, she tried to unfasten the latch. Failing to release it she climbed over and as she swung her leg over, it was caught in the grasp of two strong hands.

'Morgan, let me go!' she gasped, kicking out with all her strength. She could hear his panting breath, the short run had weakened him, but the power of his grip was unaffected. She did manage to escape, using her weight to fall from his grasp, but her yellow dress was like a beacon in the mist and he soon caught up with her again. This time Madoc was with him.

'Madoc! Tell him to let me go!' she said, trying to sound angry. 'I only came to see you, and thank you again for the sheep! Where's Vanora? She won't see me treated like this! What is the matter that you chase me away like a thief?'

'I think you had better come back to the house,' Madoc said sadly. 'You can't be allowed to tell what you saw.'

'I saw nothing, except two ill-mannered people who treat a visitor like an enemy!' Her protests were ignored and she was made to walk back to the cold, empty house.

Shutting her inside where she leaned on the door and shivered, they discussed their situation in undertones before releasing her and saying, 'We want you to help us dig a patch of the garden, Olwen.'

'All right, I'll come back tomorrow and help you. Perhaps Dan will come as well, strong at digging, Dan is,' she babbled, but she fell silent when Madoc shook his head.

'Now, Olwen.'

'But why?'

'So the law will believe we have been working all day and not moved from the house. Poor at turning soil we are, and if you do a good piece then Vanora will convince them we have been at it all day.'

'Hurry,' Morgan warned. 'If you don't help us, then you and Barrass will be blamed for the robbery. Easy it would be for us to put one of the missing letters in his pocket or in his bed. Easy to persuade Daniels you and he are partners.'

For three hours Olwen dug and cleaned the patch the brothers indicated. Beside her they also worked, but with far less result. Looking at the turned soil through the mist, she could see with ease which had been her work and which theirs. She hoped others wouldn't see the difference and wonder at it. For Barrass's sake she must do as they wanted.

The warnings were repeated when she set off at last to go home. She would help them or face the knowledge that Barrass was in prison, and she was responsible for his plight. They made no attempt to hide the fact that they had robbed the Royal Mail, boasting to her about the ease with which they persuaded Ben to hand over the letters.

She was holding back tears with difficulty as she walked home. The threats of the Morgan brothers seemed to fill the air around her, as if they had followed her with their intimidation. She decided that as an extra precaution against Barrass being implicated, she would stay away from him. To be seen together might mean he was accused too if she should be revealed to be an accomplice to the Morgans. Because that was what she had become, she thought with a sob. An accomplice to thieves.

Ben reached the inn near the sorting office three hours late. Walter, who himself had only woken from an evening nap just before he arrived, walked impatiently to meet him, complaining, threatening, and announcing that if Ben couldn't find a more reliable mount then he must give way to a younger man who could.

'It wasn't the fault of the horse,' Ben panted, hoping to give the impression he had run all the way. 'Attacked by gunmen I was and the horse sent away crazed with fright.'

At once a crowd gathered to hear his story. But it wasn't until he was seated comfortably at one of the tables beneath the tree with a mug of ale in one hand and a brandy in the other, that he began. He told it as he told every incident, setting the scene like an actor, beginning with how the mist came down and enfolded him, persuading his audience to feel as he had felt, the imminent danger in the air.

'A foreboding of evil,' he called it. 'I was helpless when they set upon me,' he told them. 'Two big strong men armed with guns materialized out of the fog, and so threatening I was at once afeared for my very life. I tried to fight them off and hold on to the bag, mind, but I couldn't. Ben Gammon was out-fought there in the fog of a summer's day with no one to say, "Ho, there, leave that man be or you'll have me to see to as well!" No, I was alone and although I says to them, think careful what you're doing to a poor, hard-working, Christian man, they went off with me letters and threw the bag at me without a word.'

Daniels had arrived by the time his story and several drinks were finished and he sent the crowd away and told Ben to begin his story again. 'This time without any fancy additions. I want to know everything that happened and nothing besides.'

Ben borrowed a horse from the inn and went with Daniels to the spot where the men had been waiting for him. Although the area was now dark as well as misty, Daniels dismounted and bent to search the ground. He found a letter, showed it to Ben and between them in the fading light they read the address as being 'To William Martin, of Llanelli, to be collected at his convenience'. Daniels shrugged; he had never heard of the man. He looked at the address again and saw that, written small, a few numbers and letters had been added. Frowning, he tucked it into his pocket.

There seemed little he could do until daylight assisted him, but Daniels went back to the inn and talked for a long time to Ben, getting as full a picture of what really happened as possible from such a wildly fanciful storyteller.

The news had travelled fast and the inn was full of those interested in hearing Ben's story and those who had similar stories of their own to relate. Lowri was sitting with Walter, and Daniels was surprised to see both Annie and Kenneth appear. They beckoned to Walter and Lowri and when they were in a huddle, Kenneth told the Keeper of the Peace quietly, 'I knew this would happen, see. Using as public a place as an inn leads to too much being known of the workings of the post. Since Pitcher had the letters in his place there have been two lots of letters lost and then found carelessly thrown away, and now this. It should be returned to my house where it belongs!'

'I doubt if anything Pitcher has said could have resulted in Ben being attacked, Kenneth. It isn't unknown for carriers of letters to be robbed, why, you yourself were beaten and tied a while back as I remember,' Daniel reminded him.

Watching silently from a corner, Markus saw a brief but unmistaken glance of understanding pass between Kenneth and Annie Evans. He did not move a muscle but knew that unless he

232

were very stupid, that look meant collusion. Information was passing between the woman who still called herself Annie Evans although shown to be of a different name, and Kenneth, the bitter, ex-letter-carrier of Gower.

Leaving Ben still regaling his audience with details of his adventure, Daniels left the town. He badly wanted to catch the thieves. He needed some successes to support his application for promotion. With Florrie insisting on servants, the increase in salary was urgently required.

He gripped the letter he had found. The numbers and letters on the front of the folded pages were worth an hour's study. They might lead him to the smugglers as well as the thieves. More fortuitous things had been known. The men had to communicate somehow. Why not by the post? He touched the horse's side with his polished boots and trotted on.

Next morning, the tall figure of Daniels knocked on the door of the fisherman's cottage. Stooping as Spider and Dan had to get inside, he sat near the fire and asked Olwen a lot of questions.

'You see a lot of Morgan and Madoc Morgan?' he asked.

Olwen nodded, glancing at her mother, her face stiff with fear.

'Yes, I visit them sometimes.'

'And walk with Madoc after church?'

'Yes.' Olwen's voice was a whisper.

'Did you see them yesterday?'

'Digging their garden they were,' she replied at once, glad to have the lie spoken and rid of it. Now she was committed to helping them. If she went back on what she said, the Keeper of the Peace would never believe her again.

That evening she lay on her bed listening to the droning complaints of Enyd and the accompanying voice of Dan, through the open windows. She had never been so unhappy. Sent in disgrace from Ddole House through the treachery of Annie Evans, forced by her love for Barrass to protect thieves, and separated from Barrass by the need to protect him. How would she ever return to the happy life she had once enjoyed? She wanted to run away. But that would only add to her misery. There was nothing she could do, only wait in the hope that the bad things would somehow end and better things return.

Chapter Sixteen

Daniels's first decision after the attack on Ben Gammon and the loss of the letters was to alter the route along which Ben travelled. He sat beside Ben with a map in front of them and they drew out a new course. This was written out and sent to London with a request for the change, but while they waited for approval, Ben used it. Avoiding the area where he was attacked didn't completely ease his fear of a repeat, but it helped not to pass the actual spot. Daniels felt happier having done at least something towards avoiding another robbery.

The letter he had found at the site of the attack seemed determined not to give up its secrets. Illegally, he kept it and sat for a long time studying the numbers and letters on the corners of the folded pages. 2 A 2, were printed faintly and half hidden by the writing of the address. It was probably nothing. Just an idle scribble while the writer's mind was elsewhere.

He wished he could discuss it with Florrie, but although she was betrothed to him, he knew regretfully that her loyalties were with the smugglers. Having lived in the village all her life, and probably knowing at least a few of those involved, she was unlikely to change to his way of thinking overnight.

It would take time for him to persuade her to think of the law as an absolute necessity for peace and tranquillity. He imagined a life where no one broke the law except under great emotional strain and knew that it was only a dream. But a dream he wanted at least to bring closer to the people in his care.

He gave up the letter to Barrass without telling him how long he had kept it, and explained how it had come into his hands.

'I looked at it for a long time in the hope of learning something,' he told the letter-carrier, 'but it remained dumb.'

'I will keep my ears and eyes alert for anything that might help catch the thieves,' Barrass promised, aware that the Keeper of the Peace was thinking more about the smugglers than of the armed robbers. When he left Daniels,Barrass went on an unscheduled call to Ddole House. There he discussed the recovered letter with William Ddole for some considerable time before continuing with his deliveries.

Ben liked the new route. It took him past two isolated alehouses that broke his journey in a pleasant way, and the extra time he took was easily explained.

'Damn me, there's a long way I have to travel now,' he announced. 'I says to myself, Ben Gammon, you'll have no seat in your breeches with all the extra riding you're doing for to get the mail to its destination in safety! And as for my poor horse, well, he thinks I'm daft, going such a way when he can end his journey far sooner following the way he knows, like a cow knows the quickest way home at milking time.'

Barrass soon allowed the thoughts of the robbery to fade from his mind. Something else began to puzzle him. Olwen was treating him like a leper. For all the years he could remember, Olwen had been there like a shadow attached to his heels. Unavoidable and frequently a nuisance, she had tormented him and caused him to lose the attention of many female admirers. He had always been very fond of her but she had been something of a trial. But now all that had changed and she seemed to dislike him so much she wouldn't stop for a friendly word.

He tried to think when the change had taken place. Was it after seeing her in town, when she had gone to help Mary with her market stall? Perhaps she had seen him talking to Lowri and in her childish manner had become jealous of the woman. But no, Olwen was not the sort to sulk, she was far too outspoken. He smiled as he imagined her scolding him for his flirtation, her small hands on her hips, like a nagging, gnawing wife.

Perhaps she *was* considering herself as a wife? Perhaps she had found someone whom she was learning to love? The smile faded from his dark face; the thought of someone loving Olwen brought surprising aches to his heart. His stomach twisted, a sick feeling enveloped him and he realized that the jealousy he felt was real and quite painful.

He saw her as he was heading back to the village on Thursday, the second of August. He was in a hurry to finish as the boats were due that evening and he was probably needed to ride out again with messages. Olwen was walking slowly through the fields towards him and he pulled on the reins and dropped them to allow Jethro to crop the grass. He didn't call, afraid she would walk away from him, but waited beside a bush, half hidden by the shadow of it against the evening sun.

The day had been a dull one and it was only as the sun began to set that the clouds revealed it and allowed it to give a short but beautiful glow to the day's ending.

'Where are you going, Olwen?' he smiled. 'Want a lift, do you? Jethro will be more than pleased for you to ride.'

She turned, startled, and began to walk away. Barrass dismounted and followed her. Taking hold of her arm he asked, 'Olwen? What has upset you? My truest friend turning from me? What have I done to deserve such a thing?'

'You have done nothing, but I want you to keep away from me.' She ran from him and he watched as she pushed her way through a weak part of a hedge and disappeared.

Tethering Jethro to a convenient tree, Barrass followed. He peered through the hedge in time to see her crossing the next field and once she had pushed her way through the further hedge, he followed. He soon realized where she was heading: the Morgan family's house. He felt hurt that she had not asked him to accompany her; she had admitted that the brothers made her uneasy.

He watched as she went through the door and he stood for a long time waiting for her to re-emerge. When she did it was with Madoc. She was carrying a dead rabbit. So, Madoc was still giving her presents, and Olwen was accepting them. Unable to go away, he watched as the girl left the cottage and wandered idly back towards the village. To his surprise she threw the rabbit into a hedge.

When she arrived back at the place where Jethro was tethered, he ran and caught up with her.

'Come on, Olwen,' he said firmly, shocked by the sadness in her eyes. 'You are riding home with me.'

'No, Barrass. No!' Her voice had the edges of a sob in it as she once more ran from him.

Startled and hurt, Barrass waited until she was out of sight, then remounted and rode home.

Between delivering messages to Markus and William Ddole, and the time to go and assist on the beach, Barrass walked to the house of Carter Phillips and his sister, Harriet. He had gone with the intention of losing his miserable mood with Harriet's generous attention, but he could not. The vision of the young, fair-haired girl with the sad eyes crept between him and everything else.

The activity on the shore, hauling in the boats, carrying the heavy cargoes up to where the horses, donkeys, men and women waited to disperse them, had never been more welcome. He revelled in the physical exertion, stimulated by the need to forget his rejection, energetic and enthusiastic in the way he helped. He ran from each completed task to help with another, a frenzied energy kindled and rekindled until the work was done and the beach empty of sight and sound of the night's business.

Even the frantic hour that exercised every muscle didn't help him to sleep. He was overwrought and completely unable to relax. He tried to deny it, but his body was crying out for love and the woman he was so desperately in need of was Olwen.

The straw with which he had recently refilled his mattress made a gentle, scratchy sound and eventually Arthur sat up and asked, 'Barrass, you sound like your bed is filled with fleas! Can't you sleep?'

'No, but I'm sorry if I woke you.'

'You didn't. I too have something on my mind.'

'A woman?' Barrass teased, knowing that although he was past his sixteenth birthday, Arthur had never walked out with a girl. He was surprised when his friend said, 'Yes.'

'Who is she?'

'Someone I love more than my life.'

'But who?' Barrass demanded. 'You can't tantalize me with such a small part of a story!'

'Someone whose parents would not have me for a son-in-law,' Arthur replied. 'That must be sufficient for you.'

Barrass sifted through his knowledge of all the likely young girls whom Arthur would know but failed to find a candidate for the boy's affections.

'I fear we are in the same predicament,' Barrass said. 'I have loved too many girls too often – '

' – and too well,' Arthur interjected.

' – but now I think I am to be punished. I have been rejected.'

Arthur chuckled. 'I can't help thinking this is something you deserve, Barrass, but sorry I am, all the same.'

The dog crawled out of his barrel at the end of the cellar and tapped his way to where Arthur was lying. He crawled up on the bed, slowly sidling up until he was in Arthur's arms.

'Seems I must get myself a dog. It's all we'll have, unless a miracle happens,' Barrass sighed.

Olwen went to visit the Morgan brothers each time Madoc told her to. She was so afraid of him doing as he threatened and telling the Keeper of the Peace that Barrass was involved in the robbery that she dared not argue. She didn't say anything to anyone, not even Mistress Powell who was the recipient of most of her secret thoughts. On the day Madoc asked her to walk out with him after church she thought she would die of despair.

'No,' she said, 'that I cannot do.'

'You will risk me telling Daniels that Barrass was at the scene?'

'I don't think you are really as wicked as that.' Her chin was out but she was quaking inside. 'I don't think Vanora would be pleased if you did that.'

'Leave Vanora to me,' Madoc warned.

The look in his eyes made Olwen want to run, but she stood her ground.

'I want you to find out where the new route takes Ben Gammon,' Madoc said.

'But I can't. I won't.'

She stared at him and he suddenly softened. 'Very well. We'll find out from someone else, but,' he added, 'in such a way that the information could have come only from Barrass.'

Madoc watched the girl walk away from him, saddened by the realization that no one had ever loved him as deeply and as bravely as Olwen loved Barrass. Perhaps, once he and Morgan were free of the sickness that troubled them, she might be persuaded to reconsider how she felt, although he doubted it.

The following Sunday, he called at the house on the cliffs, having brushed his hair down with water, and persuaded Vanora to tidy his clothes.

'Come to walk Olwen to church,' he announced to Mary when she appeared at the doorway with Dic struggling in her arms. Mary stepped back into the room and after a whispered conversation, she reappeared with Spider and Dan behind her.

'Olwen comes with us,' Spider said firmly. 'And after the service she will walk home with us.' The three of them turned and closed the door. Madoc stormed away so fast that when he was only a short distance from the house he was holding his chest and coughing until his face reddened and he was gasping for breath. He was sitting watching the top of the path as Olwen and her family set off down it to the church.

Annie waited at her front window, watching the sorting office in the hope of seeing Kenneth. She could not go to Mumbles to visit him and she had no idea how likely it was that he would come into town. He had no business now with the post, and as the days passed she tried to think of another way to get the information she needed.

On every morning and evening when the mail arrived and departed, the usual crowds gathered, those with business to see to, those who came to read the letters for people unable to manage their letters and those who waited to hear Ben spread the news that had filtered down from London and the other towns to intrigue them. When Annie saw Kenneth sheltering under the big tree outside the inn, she waited until all heads were turned towards Ben, then called for Sally Ann.

'Go and tell Kenneth I wish to see him,' she instructed and when Kenneth came she invited him to enter.

'Best we aren't seen talking,' she said, smiling pleasantly. 'Sally Ann will say nothing and I think those outside are too interested in Ben to have noticed.'

'What do you want?' Kenneth frowned.

'I want to know where the new route takes Ben.'

'Easy that is,' Kenneth said importantly. 'There's only one way he could go.' Taking the paper and quill she offered he carefully drew the new approach to Swansea, describing the journey with care. Annie politely invited him to take tea and food. He hesitated a moment, looking at the handsome woman and wondering if there was a chance of being invited to stay. Then he looked into the small, deep-set eyes in the smiling face. He quickly changed his mind, and left.

Daniels knew there had been a delivery on the previous night. With a rare carelessness, one of the silent workers had left a torn and crumpled news sheet on the cliff. It was written in French, and Daniels was convinced that it came from the boats. It would not have been part of the wrapping on some illegal import, they would never have been so foolish. Perhaps it had fallen from the pocket of one of the seamen, although he knew they usually did not leave the beach. Uninterested in how it came, he was convinced it had been brought with the illegal boats.

In his room where he wrote his reports, he studied the paper, willing it to give up its secrets, then he thought of the letter he had found. It had been marked, 2 A 2. Could it have meant the second day of August and two of the clock?

What if the post was how the smugglers communicated? He thought excitedly that he needed to glance at all the letters before they were handed to Walter. If the smugglers used the post once, they would surely do so again. He decided to do something that normally he would never contemplate; he would break the law in the hope that it would stop others breaking it more violently. Setting off on Saturday morning before it was light, he headed for the place where he could intercept Ben.

A mist had come with the dawn and clouded the land. It brought distant sounds closer and Ben hastened his mount through the more isolated area that lay to the north of the town. The birds were subdued, their cheerful song absent from the morning. The few twitterings and piped melodies were muted by the deadening, moisture-laden air.

To Ben there was an ominousness about the quiet. It was as if something were waiting, just out of his sight, for him to reach a certain point. To allay his fears and prevent panic from rising, he began to sing, loudly, suddenly, making a family of snipe flutter up from close by and give their scraping call as they flew away twisting and turning. For a moment the horse faltered and Ben thought it was the trap he dreaded. Then, when nothing further happened, he recommenced his song and patted the neck of the horse as if it were the animal needing reassurance, not himself.

He heard rustlings, the sound of men approaching, and steeled himself for a blow, trying to tell himself that it was only an innocent traveller, no one yet knew of his new pathway. He sang boldly, and only wavered on a few top notes, but the song was shortened as a man stood up and aimed a long stick towards the back of his head.

Daniels waited silently for a while, standing under a tree to which he had tethered his mount. He guessed that the time when Ben should have passed was long past. There had been a distinct unreliability about the man's timekeeping of late and he wondered idly if a woman or an alehouse were the cause of it. Leading his horse, he walked along in the direction Ben would appear in the hope of meeting him. Then he saw the horse.

Lathered and obviously frightened, the animal was panting, struggling to free its reins from a low branch. The saddle had slipped and there was no sign of its rider. Daniels approached the animal talking soothingly and was able to ease the saddle into the correct position and tighten the girth. Loosening the pistol in the holster on his horse's right shoulder, he walked slowly on leading both horses, listening for any sound to betray the presence of someone else. He found Ben lying across the path, his head covered in blood. To his relief the man was groaning. At least he was alive.

Having made the man comfortable, Daniels searched the area, but this time there was no carelessly abandoned letter to help him. The baize-lined bag was thrown aside and empty. He helped Ben remount and together they slowly made their way to the sorting office and the complaints from Walter at Ben's lateness.

When the two horses entered the square beside the sorting office, the murmur of voices attracted Annie's attention. She sent Sally Ann to enquire what had happened and watched as the man was helped from his horse and into the inn.

'There's been another robbery, and poor Ben Gammon silenced by the attack, would you believe? There'll be plenty of stories from Ben in a day or so for sure,' Sally Ann reported, 'but for today the waiting crowd will have to disperse disappointed.'

To Pitcher's delight, The Posthorn Inn had been full all day, with customers waiting for Barrass to arrive with the post and the gossip. Men and women with little else to occupy themselves came once their few chores were done to play chess and draughts, dice and the new dominoes; old people pushed out of the way by their family, those too old or too sick to work who survived on what their relations could give them, the wanderers who could for a few pennies feed well and spend the day in convivial company.

Besides these, there were the businessmen and those who came to spend a few hours taking in the fresh sea air. And for this high-class clientele Pitcher opened up the second room, where good upholstered chairs and a few rugs made the room that bit more like home.

It was there that William, Edwin and John Maddern sat wondering with the rest what had happened to the letters. When Barrass finally arrived and had only a few local letters for them, they were alarmed.

'Were they all taken?' William demanded.

'Nothing there but a wounded Ben and an empty bag.'

'Will you be going on your journey today?' Edwin asked the young man and on seeing Barrass shrugging and shaking his head he asked, 'Then will you do something for us?'

'Well, I did have a mind to enjoy my freedom and spend a few hours with Olwen,' he said. 'She's unhappy of late and I want to try and cheer her.'

William was silent for a while, then he mumbled, 'Wants to come back to Ddole House, does she?'

'I'm sure that will help!' Barrass said eagerly. 'She complained a lot before you told her to go, but it was mostly on account of the new housekeeper who treated her less than kind.'

'I confess I miss the cheeky young woman,' William smiled. He turned to Edwin and told him how she had criticized him for sending Penelope away. 'Impertinent she was, but she alone sensed my loneliness.' He suddenly looked at Barrass, remembering that it was on his account that his daughter had been sent from her home and growled, 'You can tell her she can come back, but I don't want to see you hanging around the house, mind.'

'I'll come only when there's a letter,' Barrass promised. His dark eyes were glowing with the prospect of telling Olwen she could return to Ddole House. Surely that would take the sadness from her eyes? Then he remembered that first he would have to deliver the messages for William.

'I'll ask Pitcher for some paper and pens, shall I?' he sighed.

The letters were brief, consisting mostly of one short sentence. None had a name on them or a signature and Barrass was told where to leave them. Some were left at houses but many on trees, bridges and in barns. Barrass hurried about the deliveries fearful that with Daniels determinedly seeking out both robbers and smugglers, he would be in a dangerous position if found with them on his person. The last letter was fully written and signed and was addressed to Markus.

The watchman was there as usual and when he saw the letter knew that no payment or reply was needed. He nodded briefly to Barrass and disappeared inside the gloomy house. Barrass waited a while to make sure Markus didn't need him, then turned Jethro and headed at last for Olwen's home.

She wasn't there. His disappointment was comic to Mistress Powell.

'Gone for a walk to see them Morgan boys no doubt,' she chuckled, 'and there's no use you looking so disappointed. You've never given the girl a hint that you cared what she does,' the old woman went on, 'or, things might have been different. Taken to them she has and all because of a few gifts and plenty of flattery.'

Barrass was very thoughtful as he rode across the fields to search for her.

He didn't have to go far. She was sitting beside a small stream, her feet in the clear water, watching a frog stretching its long legs and scooting across the surface to crouch, half hidden on the opposite bank. She had not heard him approach and when she did, she jumped up and the sad expression faded first to relief then to anger.

'Stop creeping about like that, Barrass!'

'Creeping about?' he laughed. 'And me with the biggest feet in the village and Jethro snapping twigs and warning all the neighbourhood that we're about?'

'Well I didn't hear you!'

'Dreaming, were you, little Olwen?'

'Don't call me that.'

'Growing up you may be but to me you'll always be little

243

Olwen.' He stepped nearer, cautiously. His loving shadow was his no more. She was like a frightened animal that might run from him at any second. 'I've some news for you,' he coaxed. 'Come and sit down and I'll tell you.'

'Another woman having your baby?' she sneered.

He was puzzled, the sneer on her face did not match the tears threatening to flow. She looked so utterly miserable he wanted to pick her up and hug her, let her cry the hurt away.

'I spoke to William Ddole this morning and he wants you to go back to work in his kitchen. I think he misses your beautiful lively presence, Olwen, as I do. Why are you avoiding me?' he demanded as she began to move away from him.

'You think that every woman must want to be with you! I for one can manage to survive without adoring you and waiting for a kind word. I'll leave that for the others. Plenty of them to please you for sure.'

'Olwen!' He stepped across the stream following her wild flight but after a few paces he stopped and walked slowly back to Jethro. Best to leave her, she was not the sort of young woman to be persuaded.

'Don't forget to go and see Florrie about returning to work!' he shouted after her. To his alarm the only response was a sob.

Wrenching himself away from her, he rode back to her house and explained to Spider and Mary about William's change of heart.

'I'll tell her,' Mary said sadly, 'but I don't think she will go. There's something frightening her and none of us can get her to tell us what it is.'

'She's too stubborn altogether,' complained Enyd, overhearing from her room. 'While she's had time to spare I've asked for her help many times and she's refused, and me not feeling well enough to cope.'

'Olwen is always willing to help where it's *needed*,' Mary replied pointedly.

'Perhaps that's the trouble,' Spider said. 'Those Morgan boys are in trouble and perhaps she has been persuaded out of kindness to do more than she wants to do for them.'

'No,' Mary said. 'It was only when Polly and Seranne were there that Olwen visited.'

Realizing that Olwen had said nothing to her parents about

244

her visits to the lonely cottage, Barrass quickly said, 'She once wanted to work at the inn with Emma and Pitcher. Would you be willing for that? I would see that she was not harmed.'

'Perhaps that would take her mind off whatever's troubling her,' Spider agreed. Barrass went at once to ask Pitcher. But when Mary and Spider told her there was work for her if she wanted it, again Olwen refused.

Cadwalader returned to The Posthorn Inn at that time. He asked Pitcher if he would find him work to pay for a bed in the stables and a meal each evening. Pitcher agreed but told Barrass and Arthur to, 'Watch him! Remember that although we know a part of his story we don't really know why he's here. His sister has found herself a place with Walter Waterman and his mother has bought a fine boarding house in the town. Now with Cadwalader here, they are all in good positions for finding out information. The family is a strange one but best we have him here where we can watch him and that you must do.'

Emma was not completely happy about the way the new inn was going. She had imagined herself sitting up in her parlour listening to the murmur of genteel voices coming from below, with an occasional visit from one of the better dressed visitors from the town. Daisy and Pansy would be sitting dressed in their smartest clothes and attracting the eye of those who came to take the air.

In fact, she was so busy cooking when the various girls she employed for the task decided the life was too busy and failed to arrive she hardly had time to talk to her daughters. She seemed unaware that Daisy had become more and more important to the collection and distribution of letters. Daisy sat at the desk in the corner, throwing insulting repartee to all and sundry, while her mother bustled to and from the kitchen behind the bar scolding her, telling her to behave, and to go upstairs away from the rabble.

'In a moment, Mamma,' Daisy said time and again, but a few moments later, when Emma looked into the bar-room she would see Daisy still sitting there, the big ledger in front of her, handling the money, keeping the books of both the post and the inn itself.

245

'I don't know how I'd manage without her,' Pitcher admitted one evening. 'You haven't time to see to the ledgers as you used to.'

'A fine situation you've brought us to, Mr Palmer!' Emma complained. 'Your beautiful daughters and your loving wife all made into servants for your greed and satisfaction!'

'It won't be for long,' Pitcher promised. 'I never dreamed it would be so different. The rooms are almost always filled, and the food you cook so well is famous already and brings people from far afield. A finer wife no man ever had, Emma Palmer, and that's a fact!'

'Hush your foolish chatter, and tell me what I am to do about Daisy!' Emma wailed. 'How can we expect a gentleman to look at her with any thought of marriage if she is sitting at that desk and burying her head in those ledgers like a paid servant? Tell me that?'

'She'll tire of it soon enough,' Pitcher reassured her. 'When has Daisy ever enthused about anything for more than a few weeks? All except parties and dancing and herself that is. And what about Pansy? She keeps away from it all, doesn't she?'

'All she does is sew, and goodness alone knows who for! Oh, was ever a mother made to suffer like this!'

'She regularly walks with Arthur's dog,' Pitcher smiled.

'And what good is that in the search for a husband, tell me that? What worse could happen to a doting mother but her daughters are indifferent to the need for a good marriage?'

That evening she thought she had found something far worse.

'Mamma,' Daisy said brightly, 'you are to be a grandmother again!'

'What? You wicked girls! Which one of you has disgraced me now? Oh, Pitcher, I think I am going to faint.'

Pitcher ran to catch his buxom wife. She leaned but didn't fall.

'It's Violet, Mamma,' Pansy explained. 'There's no disgrace in that!'

Emma slapped them both anyway, for the fright she had.

On Olwen's next visit to the Morgans' house, Vanora was there. She welcomed the girl affectionately not knowing she had come to see Madoc.

'How kind you are to come and see me,' Vanora smiled. 'I confess it's lonely with only two morose brothers to tend to. Both out at the market they are, giving me a day at home to cook and freshen the house.'

'Can I help you?' Olwen offered, and together they took out the damp bedding and replaced it, brushed and restamped the earthen floor. When Madoc and Morgan arrived home on borrowed donkeys, there was a meal simmering above the fire and the house was aired and sweet-smelling.

Madoc insisted on walking Olwen part of the way home and when he left her at the beginning of the green lane, he showed her a partly burnt letter.

'This will find its way into Barrass's pocket if you don't walk with me after church on Sunday,' he warned, and too frightened to argue, Olwen agreed.

Cadwalader sat in his favourite position, cross-legged against a tree, when the villagers came out of the church and he watched curiously as, with a stiff smile of welcome, Olwen walked with Madoc, leaving her family staring and unable to decide whether or not to intervene. Unnoticed, Cadwalader followed the ill-matched couple as they headed for the Morgans' cottage, trailing Morgan and Vanora, Olwen's hand on Madoc's arm.

In a large oak tree, hidden by its lush leafy green, Cadwalader continued to watch the shabby cottage near the stream. Olwen's unhappiness, reported to him by Barrass, had made him curious and he had the patience to sit and wait and watch and learn.

Chapter Seventeen

Madoc began to feel a stronger emotion than convenience in his relationship with Olwen. As days passed and he forced her to spend more and more time with him, affection for the small, fair-haired girl grew. His jealousy of Barrass increased at the same time and he wanted to drive the man from Olwen's heart. Absence was the only method he could think of. If Barrass were absent, then Olwen would be free to think only of himself. The half-burned letter hidden away under his bed, deep in the earth and fortunately not discovered by Vanora and Olwen when they cleaned the room, was once more taken out and considered.

When Madoc and his brother Morgan approached the inn the following day, a noisy game of fives was just ending and Cadwalader was serving ale at an outside table. They did not look at the players or the dark-haired man with the white streak who was wiping froth from a table. They ignored the glances from both curious and friendly patrons and called loudly for a tankard of ale and food.

Cadwalader continued to wipe the drips from the table, not appearing even to glance in the brothers' direction. Cadwalader was such a quiet man, smiling pleasantly and attending to customers with politeness and servility, but he rarely joined in a conversation. In the few days he had worked for Pitcher he had become a part of the scene, ignored by most except when they needed their tankards refilled or wanted a plate of food.

Having finished serving, he went back through the door into the overfull room and to the corner near the fire. An excited crowd pushed its way through the rest, arguing over the result of a game of fives they had played outside against the wall. Now they were each trying to persuade the others that the cost of the drinks did not rest with them.

For the convenience of the customers, a lavatory was placed

in the yard near the stables and when Morgan disappeared, followed by his brother, Cadwalader thought that was where they were heading, but a sudden impulse made him put down the pile of dirty plates he had collected and follow them. Morgan was indeed going outside, but he was in time to see Madoc slipping down the cellar steps.

Cadwalader ran up the first flight of stairs and in the gloom of the landing he watched. The players still argued good-naturedly, others called for more ale, Pitcher shouted an enquiry as to his whereabouts but if Cadwalader heard he gave no sign. He saw Madoc's head appear above the cellar opening and then watched the man quickly jump up and walk back into the barroom. Madoc was joined by his brother and gave him the slightest of nods.

Without giving the impression of hurrying, Cadwalader served the impatient drinkers and went between the kitchen and the tables with food. Only when he saw the brothers leave did he approach Arthur and tell him what he had seen.

'What could they have wanted?' Arthur asked in his high-pitched voice. 'They didn't steal anything, did they?'

'Nothing that I could see, so I wonder if perhaps they left something.'

'That's nonsense!' Arthur had one eye on the customers complaining about the lack of attention, and he frowned doubtfully as he made his way back to serve them. 'What sense is there in creeping into a place and risking a hiding without taking something?' He ran back to his work.

'That Madoc walks out with Olwen, who is very unhappy,' Cadwalader insisted as he followed the thin-faced boy towards the serving counter. 'And if he hates Barrass – well, Barrass sleeps in the cellar, doesn't he?'

Arthur stopped suddenly and stared at Cadwalader.

'We'd better look at once!' He thrust an overflowing pitcher into Cadwalader's hands and said, 'Me first,' and disappeared down the stone steps.

It was Arthur who found the torn letter. It was cleverly placed in a corner of the blanket, rolled and slipped slightly behind some large stitches. It hadn't fallen out when Arthur then Cadwalader had shaken the blanket, and it was only when Arthur had gone down for a second try that he had felt around the edge of each blanket and found it.

They said nothing when Daniels came in tall, impeccably dressed, and important, insisting that he be allowed to search the cellar where Barrass slept. They frowned with Pitcher as the man left having found nothing, and shook their heads and wondered with him at who or what had been the cause.

Later that night, when Barrass had returned, the three of them discussed the implications.

'It doesn't necessarily mean the Morgan brothers are involved in the robberies,' Barrass said. 'What it does mean is that they want me blamed.'

'Because of Olwen?' Arthur queried.

'But why? She clearly seems to prefer Madoc to me, so why would he have to send me to prison?'

'She doesn't prefer him,' Cadwalader said softly. 'I think she is afraid of them both, but especially Madoc.'

'Olwen is too brave to walk with him out of fear,' Barrass defended. 'She is brave and she speaks her mind. I can't think of a way he could make her do what she had a mind not to.'

'Yet she is unhappy,' Cadwalader pointed out.

The small portion of the letter was burnt and the ashes safely ground to powder. As they were sprinkled into the dying fire, Barrass was silent. Could Olwen have been forced into walking out with Madoc? Or had she been persuaded by his illness to keep him company out of pity? That she was acting out of fear he did not consider.

When he went out to deliver the Gower letters on the following day, Barrass stopped first at the house on the cliff to talk to Olwen. If there was something troubling her surely she would tell him? She refused to see him at first, but when Mistress Powell told her to offer him refreshment, she glanced into the room where Enyd was still sleeping and stepped back from the door to allow him to enter. When he told her what Cadwalader and Arthur had discovered on the previous day, the frightened look in her eyes intensified.

'Keep away from me, you are making me unhappy,' she lied. 'While you bother me and invent stories about Madoc, I can't enjoy a moment of contentment.'

'You mean it's me who is making the cloud that hangs over you?' he gasped.

'Who else?'

'Olwen, if you are in any difficulty, you would tell me, wouldn't you? I'm your truest and most trusted friend, aren't I?'

'People change, Barrass,' she forced herself to say coldly. 'I've grown up and away from fanciful dreams of you being true to me.' Stunned, he stumbled from the white cottage and mounted Jethro like an old man.

Ben's son had taken his father's place while the old postboy recovered from the latest attack, and it was he whom Daniels stopped, a mile or two from his destination of the Swansea sorting office.

'What I am going to ask you to do is against the law,' Daniels told him. 'I want you to allow me to look at the letters before you hand them to Walter Waterman.'

'First you'll have to tell me why,' the young man insisted. 'I can't go back to my sick old father and say, Father, what d'you think I did today, why, I opened the bag in the wilds of nowhere and handed the contents to someone wearing the uniform of the Keeper of the Peace! He would think I was dafter than the look on the face of a lovesick boy! You take one step closer and I'll sound this here horn 'til the end buckles!'

Daniels stretched himself to look down his nose at the angry young man.

'If I explain, I want your word that you will not repeat it. Lives may depend on it,' he warned.

As briefly as he could he described the letters and numbers that had appeared on a letter which, once returned to the sorting office, no one had claimed.

'You thinks as though it's messages about time and place?' Ben's son lowered his body as well as his voice, afraid of the knowledge he had been given and which he did not want.

'It seems too much of a coincidence to be wrong,' Daniels told him, irritated by having to confide in this gossip-mongering mouthpiece.

'Here, you take the bag and I'll shut my eyes as tight as a dead man's, then I won't open them until you put the bag safe back into my hands.' Closing his eyes into creases, Ben's son sat on his horse muttering prayers to himself in a monotone while

Daniels searched through the mail and examined every letter. When the younger man opened his eyes, Daniels was smiling.

Before the letter-carrier had reached Swansea, Daniels had sent messages to three people, the information was spread and plans were quickly set to cover the cliffs around the area of the small cove on the night. The sign on the envelopes Daniels had looked at was, 9 A 2. The night of August the ninth, at two in the morning. Next Thursday, a week after the previous delivery. It had to be the explanation, and this time they wouldn't get away.

Early on Thursday evening, Daniels walked into the busy inn. He bought one of Pitcher's clay pipes and sat contentedly puffing on it. The herbal smoking mixture sent its doubtful fragrance into the air, and around him he could smell the aroma of good quality tobacco. His thin nose quivered with suppressed excitement. After tonight few would be able to afford to pack their pipes with such quality filling.

He watched as people came and went, noting the absences and the arrivals, committing to memory who sat and spoke with whom. He could barely contain his excitement when William Ddole entered with John Maddern and Edwin Prince. He acknowledged them with a polite nod but did not attempt to join them.

The evening wore on, and by ten o'clock the room was so full that even the chill of the evening did not prevent the outside tables being used for the overflow. Smoke floated against the ceiling, the hum of many conversations flew with it. Daniels still watched, undistracted by the laughter and the occasional song, although he was good-humoured with those who sat near him. He did not want to show by the slightest innuendo that he was anything but a relaxed and comfortable customer.

On the cliffs it was as black as the August night could be. With no moon, and even the false light from the sea invisible under low clouds, figures moved silently and unseen into their positions. Well back from the cliff path, soldiers lay as still as the sleeping fields. Extra men gleaned from the towns further inland were dispersed among the red-coated soldiers, and all were listening for the first sound of oars, or the first sight of those coming to help land the cargo.

When midnight had passed and the room was still full, Daniels began to feel concern. Then, gradually, silently, people drifted out into the night. William and John Maddern seemed to be affected by drink and he heard them ask Pitcher if he could find them a room for the night. Surely it was an attempt to mislead him?

Within minutes he saw William and John being led away, then when Pitcher did not return he asked Arthur to find him. He was told by Arthur that Pitcher was nowhere to be found. He had been right! Tonight the smugglers would walk into a trap that was large enough to capture them all.

Up in the room above the door of the inn, Pitcher and Emma watched the dark street below. The men who drifted out of the doorway gathered for a while then scattered in ones and twos and made their way to their beds, noisily and with no attempt at concealment.

On the cliffs all remained quiet apart from the call of a vixen and the churring of a nightjar. Dawn slid through the horizon in splendid glory and lit the rocks and the grass above in all their beautiful colours. Rabbits hopped without fear around the recumbent forms, accepting them as harmless as the soldiers hardly moved and made no sound. When the officers in charge of the 400 men decided to abandon their watch, the wary creatures flashed their scuts and disappeared as men thankfully straightened their aching limbs.

Another colour was dramatically added to the muted greens and shadowy browns of the slopes above the sea as silently, the men stood and stretched their arms high above their heads. Red uniforms blazed in the incipient dawn, growing up out of the grasses and bracken like bizarre flowers.

Daniels was sitting in his armchair, dozing near a low fire when the officers knocked on his door to tell him of the failure of their ambush. His disbelief was absolute. He accused them of sleeping, and of surrounding the wrong cove. He had been certain that the numbers and letters were a clear indication of a planned landing. The officers dismissed their men and went wearily back to their camp.

To Pitcher's amusement, a large number of the soldiers sat at his tables and described to him their futile and wakeful night.

'Seems William Ddole's idea worked,' Pitcher whispered to

Emma. 'That should stop them bothering us for a month or two!'

Pansy crept down the stone steps and interrupted Arthur at his work. He was rolling the heavy barrels from one end of the room to the other, getting the fresh ale behind the old. Tilted on one side balanced against his left hand, he was rolling a full barrel with his right. He almost dropped it as Pansy gently touched the back of his neck.

'My dear Arthur, my dear love, how I long for your kiss,' she whispered and as she had closed her eyes to receive his kiss she did not see his own eyes flash a warning. From behind the partition wall stepped Pitcher.

'Pansy!'

The unexpected sound of her father's voice made her shout in alarm. Her mind fumbled for an excuse to explain her presence, but Pitcher did not give her time to speak it. He took her arm and marched her up the steps and up again to the parlour where Emma was taking a much needed rest.

'Mistress Palmer!' Pitcher shouted. 'This daughter of yours was interfering with my domain in a way I do not like!'

'Pitcher, what happened?' Emma, woken suddenly, her wig slightly tilted, sat up quickly recovering and frowned at Pansy. 'Pansy, dear, are you under your father's feet? Don't tell me I have two daughters who want to be involved in business! I couldn't bear it!'

'Business with my potboy!' Pitcher said. He was surprised to see his wife laugh.

'Don't tell me you expect your daughters to miss a chance of teasing the boy. I did a bit of that myself and no harm in it for sure!'

'Pansy, tell your mother your explanation of how I found you kissing my potboy!' Pitcher instructed and instead of a reply, Pansy ran to the top of the stairs and called for Arthur to join them.

He came and stood uncomfortably beside Pansy. His Adam's apple jigged uncontrollably, his eyes were opened wide enough to encompass the whole room, and as he began to stammer out a few incomprehensible words, it was Pansy who finally said, 'Arthur and I wish to be married.'

There was a moment's silence which was broken by a stifled sob from Emma. Pitcher finally said, 'Don't be a fool, boy, go back to the cellar and finish the job we was at. My daughter is behaving badly by you and don't think no more of it. We'll make sure she doesn't torment you again.'

'You don't understand, Pitcher,' Arthur blurted out. 'I love Pansy dearly and Pansy loves me.'

'Daughter, you haven't – ?' Words failed to come and Emma sank once again into silence.

'We want you to give your permission, Mamma,' Pansy said. 'I can't imagine ever wanting to marry someone as much as I want to marry Arthur.'

'But how – ? When – ? Oh, Arthur my boy, this is all beyond me!' Pitcher marched round in a circle, pulling at his hair. Then he turned to Emma and complained, 'Why did you have so many daughters, woman? It was sons I should have had, then there'd be none of this!'

Emma burst into loud and unmusical crying and Pansy and Arthur both ran to console her. All three grouped together and glared at Pitcher who threw up his hands and shouted, 'Stop it! What are you looking at me for as if I were the wicked one? Done nothing but work hard for to give my daughters the good start you thought they should have, Emma Palmer! That's what *I've* done! And where has it got us all, tell me that!'

Pitcher approached his wife and as they began to shout at each other, Pansy took Arthur's hand and ran with him down the stairs to tell Daisy of their announcement.

'Pansy, you can't mean it? You are giving Mamma a fright to persuade her to give in on something else, aren't you?' Daisy looked from the demure face of her sister to the thin, anxious face of Arthur and read something of their joy. She closed her ledger and stared at them in surprise. 'No, you *do* mean it!'

'Mean it or not. It will not happen!' screeched Emma from the top of the staircase.

Daisy saw a shared look between her twin and the potboy and wondered which side would win.

Emma was so upset that although she guessed the woman would gloat, she went across to talk to Ceinwen. Kenneth was sitting before the fire and he gave only a brief nod when Ceinwen ushered her inside. He was puffing his pipe at a fast rate suggest-

255

ing to Emma that he was fuming about something and that before she left, she would be told why.

As soon as Ceinwen had offered and served tea and a plate of small cakes, he fumbled in his pocket and brought out a few coins.

'I've discovered that my wife, who I am promised to support, has been given money each week to compensate us for your husband stealing our livelihood,' he said in his pompous way. 'Well, here it is returned. We won't be needing it. I have plans afoot to increase our business, in the same way Pitcher increased his!'

'There's glad I am.' Emma spoke softly, reasonably and the puff evaporated from the small man. He had been building himself up to say a lot more but her reaction had defeated him.

'Kenneth has applied for the house to serve ale,' Ceinwen said.

'Hush, woman,' Kenneth exploded. 'I wish you would keep a still tongue!'

'An alehouse? So close to the inn?'

'There, you don't like it when someone poaches close to you, do you?'

'It wasn't that, but I think you'll be disappointed, being so close to us and several others. There isn't the need.'

'It will go before the justices in September. They'll decide in my favour for sure.'

There were only a few people present in the inn that afternoon, but the news spread in the way that Emma and Pitcher dreaded, and at every opportunity they denied the story and begged the teller of it to report its untruth. Pansy and Arthur just smiled. Emma told Pitcher to send Arthur away, and Pitcher told Emma to control her daughters, so the situation remained static for a few weeks. Pitcher tried to cheer Emma by suggesting she had a dinner party to celebrate the news about Violet's new baby.

'And would we invite the potboy as a servant or a guest, Mr Palmer, tell me that,' she wailed.

Olwen's depression deepened as days passed without seeing Barrass. She had been told what had happened in the cellar of the inn and knew that Madoc's threats were real. The need to see Barrass kept her awake at night and inconsolably troubled during the day, but she said nothing to anyone. Not even to Mistress Powell to whom she told most of her secret thoughts.

One evening towards the end of August she gave up all attempts to sleep. She slipped out of her covers and went down the ladder to the living room.

The fire was low, little more than a red-edged greyness. She poked a few sticks into its heart to encourage flames and as she sat in its brief flickering saw that Mistress Powell was awake. The knotted hands were poised over a shawl and a needle had slipped from her fingers.

'Surely you aren't working at this time of the night, and with no light?' Olwen whispered.

'The candle died and I was too comfortable to move and replace it,' Mistress Powell sighed. 'But if you would light one I would like to finish sewing in the ends of this shawl.'

'Can't you sleep?' Olwen asked as she fetched a candle from the box on the wall and lit it from the burning stick.

'I just want to get this done and ready for your mother to sell at the big Neath Fair next month. I don't think I'll be starting another.'

Olwen looked at the old woman and saw with a shock how frail she had become. So used to seeing her, the gradual ageing had escaped her and now she hugged the shrunken shoulders and said, 'Don't worry if you are too tired to knit and sew. You don't need to work for your place with us. You are here because we love you and you are as much ours as any other member of the family – more than that Enyd will ever be!' she added in a whisper. She was pleased to hear the old woman chuckle.

'If I'm family, won't you tell me what is troubling you?' Mistress Powell asked softly.

'There's nothing wrong,' Olwen assured her, taking the needle and threading it with wool. 'Mam says all girls of my age get times when they are melancholy. It's nothing more than that.'

Partly to keep his mind busy and away from Olwen, and partly because the work interested him, Barrass took to riding into Swansea on the evenings he was free and helping Walter to sort

257

the letters. Most times Walter was absent and he found himself with the sole responsibility for arranging the post into the various piles for the different areas of the town.

The small room was usually in a muddle with unrelated mail piled in untidy heaps on the counter and the ledger open with letters sitting on it waiting to be entered. Barrass made shelves which he partitioned into spaces. The outgoing and incoming letters were then separated and when someone called to collect one it was easily found. If Walter noticed the improvements he did not remark on them.

When Walter was present, his first question was always about Daisy. When he was told that she was coming into town, he would abandon the office and watch the road for Pitcher's wagon to come into sight and invite her to take tea with him. Daisy always refused.

Lowri rarely appeared, although Barrass suspected that she shared Walter's bed. He wondered idly if Walter wanted her there or whether he was too vague to tell her to go. The man seemed obsessed with Daisy, yet unable to do anything determined enough to earn her respect. A bit like me and Olwen, he thought with a sigh.

He knew that like Walter, he spent a lot of time hanging about in the hope of just a glimpse of Spider's beautiful daughter. Olwen refused to give him even a word and the look on her face was mystifying. She wore the melancholy expression of a kicked dog, yet when their eyes met he saw anger. What had made her change so dramatically towards him? She had been adoring when he had not valued it, yet now her attitude seemed closer to hatred.

He tethered the patient Jethro under the large tree and went into the sorting office. There was no one there. The letters were strewn about for anyone to take, and he called up the stairs as he usually did, to rouse Walter from his sleep. He busied himself first with the scattered letters, then he began to enter the transactions into the ledger. The box under the counter did not rattle when he lifted it and he saw to his alarm that the clasp had been torn off. Someone had stolen the payments.

He ran up the curving stairs to the room above and shook the sleeping man. Of Lowri there was no sign.

'Walter! Wake up you fool! The money has been taken!'

Tousled and bleary-eyed, Walter sat up from among the tumbled covers and stared at Barrass.

'What did you say? Where's Lowri? She promised to call me.'

'Call you all sorts of an idiot I should think. If she's gone it's likely she has the money with her!' Leaving the man to wash and dress, Barrass ran back down and from the crowd waiting for Ben's son chose a boy to run for Daniels.

Annie watched from the doorway of her boarding house but she did not come out to see what had caused such a lively talk and excitement. Behind her, Lowri stood smiling.

'Now Mother, do I have a share of what you stole from us or do I tell Daniels you helped me?'

Without turning to face her daughter, Annie said, 'I don't think you would face prison just to punish me, Lowri. The money I took was mine. It was I who worked for it, I who kept the boarding house running while your father drank himself to the point of death.'

'But he isn't dead, he's being cared for by friends while he waits for me to find you and tell him where you are.'

Annie stared across the open space to where Ben and his son had just arrived. To an onlooker she was smiling, but her deep dark eyes were cold.

'Go away, daughter, and come to see me in a week from now. I'll have the money you demand of me.'

'For the moment, where shall I hide?'

'In the tall cupboard behind the dresses. Hurry now for here comes the Keeper of the Peace and he will be looking for you.'

Ben arrived amid cheers. His head was swathed in a large white bandage and his hat had been cut to accommodate it.

'I says to myself, Ben, where's the sense in being so brave as to have folks say, "He died a hero saving the Royal Mail"? No, friends. I'll have my son here to keep an eye to my back for as long as 'til the thieves is caught!'

Amid laughter the crowd gathered around him and half carried him into the inn to tell his story once again. His son joined Barrass and Daniels to investigate the situation within the sorting office. As soon as the letters had been examined, Daniels saw the letter-carrier on his way and went to see Annie.

'She isn't here, Daniels,' Annie assured him. 'That daughter of mine might be an ungrateful child but she wouldn't have

259

taken from the man who has taken her in and given her food and a bed. She's just taken it into her thoughtless head to go wandering off again. She isn't a one to settle. But it isn't at her you need to look for your thief.'

'It seems to me that your position here gives you the opportunity to see much of what goes on,' Daniels said.

'More than people imagine,' Annie smiled.

'Then can I ask that you take extra interest in what passes and let me know your thoughts and opinions, Mistress Evans?'

'I hope I know my duty as an honest citizen,' she agreed.

Once Daniels had returned to the sorting office where an anxious Walter was trying to find his way through the neglected routines, Annie called her daughter out of hiding.

'I'll go, Mother, but I will be back for what you promised within a week,' Lowri said.

'A week. No sooner,' Annie smiled.

When Daniels had departed and the area had returned to its usual quiet, Annie knocked on the door of Sally Ann's room.

'I am going away,' she told her. 'I want you to take charge of the house and act as my manager.'

'But of course. For how long will you be away?' Sally Ann asked.

'That I cannot say, but you must promise me that whoever asks and however urgent their business, you will not tell anyone where I am.'

Sally Ann agreed, and a few hours later Annie was packed and aboard the stagecoach for Cardiff.

At the inn the following day when Barrass had returned from his two-day journey with the letters, he was sitting in the bar-room playing nine-men-morris with Arthur, Pitcher and Daisy, when Olwen walked in. She hesitated when she saw him sitting there and for a moment, Barrass thought she would run back out.

'Welcome, Olwen!' Pitcher said and he beckoned for her to sit with them. 'Come to see me teach these how to play, have you?'

'I've brought some oysters and cockles for Emma to cook,' she said heading for the back room. 'Put them on the table, shall I?'

Barrass stood up and walked towards her. Taking the basket from her he asked, 'Stay a while, won't you? We see so little of you, less than when you worked all day at Ddole House.'

Olwen shook her head. She waved brightly to Pitcher and the others, but ignored Barrass and went out.

Following her out into the dullness of the late summer evening, Barrass caught hold of her arm to stop her.

'Olwen, let me at least walk a little way with you,' he pleaded. He thought she looked around as if to make sure no one could see them before agreeing with a brief nod. Once on the steep path they were partly concealed by bushes and tall grasses and he saw her shoulders relax. What could he say that would make her talk to him?

He was silent as they climbed higher towards the cliff top, considering several approaches to the subject of her misery but abandoning them all, afraid of saying a wrong word. He settled finally for not asking any questions but telling her about the return of Ben Gammon and his theatrical arrival at the receiving office. She smiled a little but showed none of her usual gaiety.

Mistress Powell sat outside the cottage door, a thick woollen shawl on her head and shoulders and a blanket tucked around her knees. She waved as they appeared, and Barrass went to talk to her. When he looked around for Olwen to share in his words, the girl had gone.

Olwen went across the fields to the Morgans' cottage and saw that smoke was issuing from the chimney. She sighed with relief. That usually meant Vanora was at home. Vanora must have seen her coming because as she reached the edge of the field, the young woman stood in the doorway and waved to her.

'Olwen, can you run at once for the doctor? Morgan and Madoc are both far from well.'

With guilty relief, Olwen agreed and hurried towards the house where the doctor lived, two miles away. The unexpected freedom from the summons to go and see Madoc was like sunshine bursting through a dirt encrusted window, surprising and utter joy. The four-mile walk was nothing, and when she reapproached the house she saw the doctor's horse outside and knew that as he had come as commanded, she could hardly be blamed for not being able to talk with Madoc alone. Almost light-heartedly she went to the door and sat to wait until the doctor had finished.

The two brothers were sitting against the walls of the house, covered with stale smelling blankets, obviously in pain. When Vanora went to draw some water from the stream, Madoc held out a feverish hand and forced Olwen to set beside him. The smell of sickness choked her so she breathed as shallowly as she could, but she knew she must not complain.

'Daniels is asking questions about some money stolen from the receiving office,' Madoc told her between bouts of coughing. 'We weren't there, but it's best he thinks we were miles away. He will ask you if you were with us all yesterday afternoon. You will say yes, won't you, Olwen?'

'Please, Madoc, don't make me come here any more. I'll tell Daniels anything you wish, but don't threaten Barrass. Please.'

'We walked together, you, me and Morgan, a way past Longland. You'll remember clearly, won't you, Olwen-the-fish? Come tomorrow and if you talk to Barrass, he will find it impossible to convince Daniels of his innocence. That I promise you.'

Olwen looked at the sickly brothers and wondered why it had been Polly and Seranne who had died and not them. Something of her thoughts must have showed as Morgan warned, 'My brother isn't one for idle threats, Olwen-the-fish. Think careful before you rebel.'

She felt unclean and when she reached the sea she bathed, throwing off all her clothes and letting the warm, silky water take away the stink of the Morgans' cottage and her own humiliation. Walking the cliffs until it was too dark to see, she returned home and went straight to her bed.

Chapter Eighteen

The September Fair at Neath was held on the first of the month and in the year 1781, this was a Saturday. Barrass was disappointed not to be able to attend, but his letters meant he would be travelling Gower and would not be free until late on the following day.

'Come with me to get the licence to set up my stall,' Spider suggested. 'It's best we do that on Friday, so we can get there early and begin selling as soon as the people start arriving.'

'At least I'll be able to see the start of it,' Barrass said. 'Although the setting up is not as exciting, seeing the travellers and entertainers arriving and practising their various tricks will be worth the long ride.'

Friday was the one day of the week Barrass was not involved with the post. He usually spent it helping Pitcher but the innkeeper willingly excused him. Setting off beside Spider on one of Pitcher's horses to give Jethro his usual day of freedom in the field above the quarry, he arrived at the middle of the day when already the town was in festival mood.

The streets were full of carts and wagons bringing the travelling tradesmen and entertainers. These were followed by processions of children already in the grip of the excitement the Fair Day brought. There was a long queue of people waiting to seek permission of the portreeve to erect their stalls, and Spider patiently joined it.

Barrass wandered through the streets and watched as people fought for the best sites, some even pulling down rival stalls and fighting for possession, rolling on the ground and cuffing each other. The roads entering the town were near to standstill on occasions when a cart overturned or lost a wheel, and everywhere there was shouting and arguing and bawled instructions.

Barrass had always enjoyed Fair Day, but this year the excitement failed to penetrate the misery that filled his heart. If

Olwen had been with him how wonderful the day would have been, he thought sadly. When she offered her love he had treated it like a joke, and now when he thought of no one else for every moment he was awake, she shunned him.

When he returned to the portreeve's office he found Spider tucking into some juicy roasted pork from a vendor who had set up a spit at the side of the road. Joining him, Barrass watched the hustle and bustle of the town preparing for a holiday, smiling with Spider at the scene but his mood was still far from cheerful.

The intention of Spider was to stay at Neath overnight and go and meet Mary, Dan and Olwen on the following day, but the houses which advertised rooms to let were all full, some having eight to a small room with beds lying side by side, wall to wall with another person given the place alongside their feet. With luggage firmly grasped in their hands it was unlikely any of them would sleep soundly.

'You either sleep under a hedge or ride back with me,' Barrass laughed when Spider had been offered a small, narrow strip of an unbelievably minute room, 'unless you can fold yourself up like some of these contortionists do and hide your long legs in your own pocket!'

Barrass was tired after the ride but insisted on working beside Arthur and Pitcher for the rest of the evening. He sensed an unusual excitement in Arthur and wondered what it was about a Fair Day that stimulated such expectation of pleasure. It must be more than a day free from work?

He went into town very early on the following morning and the road from Mumbles was already filled with those making the pilgrimage to the Fair. He searched the crowd of walkers and riders, most carrying goods to sell, all laughing with the prospect of the fun-filled day; but he did not see Olwen.

He had to wake Walter from his bed but it was he who once again entered the last-minute letters into the ledger and put the money he had collected into the new, reinforced box. He left Walter sipping a mug of coffee and trying to rouse himself sufficiently to deal with the day's activities and set off back to Mumbles. He did not notice the two inspectors standing watching the proceedings through the open door of the office. The rising tide of people heading for the town of Neath almost blocked the road and he rode slowly, the only one travelling westward, as he headed back to The Posthorn Inn and his breakfast.

Olwen walked beside her mother and took turns at carrying Dic. Now over a year old he was impatient of being carried and wanted to use his sturdy legs. He rode on Spider's shoulder contentedly for a while, laughing at the view he had over the heads of the rest. Olwen wished she too could ride at Spider's height in case Barrass had somehow managed to come.

A cart passed, the driver sounding a horn, the passengers accompanying the strident demand with shouted instructions to clear the way. She ducked down below her mother's shoulder, recognizing the voices of Morgan and Madoc. She did not want to be seen riding with them, increasing an ever stronger impression that she belonged to Madoc.

'There's a chance for you to ride,' Mary said as the cart pushed past close to them. 'Don't you want to be there before us and see the preparations?'

'No Mam, and please, don't let them see me.' Like a child, Olwen clung to her mother's thick serge skirt and lowered her small body to a crouch. Mary glanced at Spider and frowned. If only Olwen would tell her what was wrong. Philosophically she whispered to her husband, 'Tell us in her own time. There's no pushing that one!'

When they reached the town there seemed nowhere to go. Every thoroughfare was crammed with people pushing their way up or down. It was still early in the day, many visitors had left before dawn, and the crowd was still good-natured in its protests. They managed to find a place on the outskirts of the stalls to sit on the grass and take some refreshments from the many stalls offering every possible drink from 'Good fresh water drawn from Neath springs', to 'Chocolate, the latest London fashion.'

While Mary and Spider began to set up their stall from the boxes of goods Emma had brought for them on her overloaded wagon, Olwen was free to walk with Dic to see the sights. With such a confusion in the main streets she decided to begin at the edges of the town.

Beyond the houses amid the trees were dozens of gypsy caravans, each family bringing noise, colour and exotic beauty to the normally quiet green fields. From the caravans, brightly dressed children tumbled and ran towards the activities offered. Beside the wooden, horse-drawn homes, fires burned, sending smoke up into the clear blue sky. Shyly, Olwen approached a girl of her own age dressed in red, her dress and headdress trimmed with gold and said, 'You have come to sell?'

'My father is an entertainer who has appeared in the theatre at Bath,' the girl said proudly, but before Olwen could ask anything more, the girl's mother called to her in a strange tongue and she ran back to the caravan.

Working her way slowly towards the main streets, Olwen was fascinated by the variety of food being prepared and carried through the crowd. In one place a clay oven had been built and delicious smelling pies were brought from it. They were placed on trays hung about women's necks on brightly coloured ribbons and quickly sold. Olwen bought one and sat on the ground to share it with her brother.

It was in the street that most of the selling was done, with stalls selling a mixture of clothing, food and medicines, plus a wide assortment of household utensils made from wood and metal. Each bowl, brush and tool went with a promise that, 'it will double the housemaid's capacity for work once it has been placed in the kitchen'.

The gypsies promised to tell a person's future for the small offering of 'silver to cross my palm'. Olwen touched the coins in her pocket but would not risk being told she would marry someone other than Barrass.

Beyond the closely packed street many entertainments were on offer, the owners creating further din shouting of their 'good, safe rides full of excitement', or 'the sight of a lifetime for the payment of one penny'. There was a wooden roundabout pushed around a thick central pole by several small boys who, from their bright attire, were children from the caravans. Olwen paid a halfpenny for Dic to ride, her mood lightened briefly as she watched him shout with fear-filled excitement.

Rope swings were set up in convenient trees and were of varying heights to suit customers' bravery or lack of it. The ropes were garlanded with flowers, streamers that swung with the riders, spreading dancing tails of red and orange and green in rich profusion. Briar roses were included twisted around with lengths of ivy, but most of the blossoms were made from shaped and painted wood, dyed with colours from the countryside; again, the gypsies seemed to be the proprietors.

With Dic on her lap, Olwen sailed high above the crowd, her last extravagance before finding her mother and helping to sell the woollen garments they had all helped to make, and the home-made Welsh cakes, drop scones and biscuits Mary had cooked over the hearth on a bake stone.

She had just caught sight of the tall thin figure of Spider helping someone to load the goods he had bought from him onto his pack mule when a hand touched her and a voice she dreaded to hear said, 'Olwen. We have been searching for you, my dear.'

'Madoc. I thought you had not come,' she lied.

'With all this produce to sell? Why should we not?' He gestured to a stall behind him where eggs were piled into a wooden basket alongside apples, pears and an enormous amount of assorted vegetables. Olwen noticed that many of them were broken as if pulled in haste. There were rows of wild and domestic ducks and chickens and, displayed from hooks, hares, rabbits and pheasants. A sheepdog puppy was tethered to the front of the stall whining in fear as people crowded it against the wooden supports. Morgan was doing excellent trade, having lowered his prices to sell early.

'Where did you get these?' she gasped. The garden surrounding the cottage was empty of crops. She glanced fearfully around, dreading to see Daniels's sharp eyes watching them.

'From Barrass,' Madoc smiled, 'or that's what I'll tell the Keeper of the Peace if he should ask!'

Watching from the half shade of a nearby stall, Markus sat astride a small pony. At his side stood the watchman with his hand on the pony's bridle in case it was frightened into flight. Markus wore a hat with a floppy brim which hid his eyes but his head was towards Olwen and her companion.

Turning, Madoc saw the man and unaware of his returned sight, gestured towards him and said boldly, 'In fact, there's the man who donated most of what I have to sell today. Generous he is for sure.'

'You stole from – ?' Olwen gasped, not daring to utter the name.

Madoc's eyes glistened and he stared at the blind man and

said, 'There was a good shower yesterday morning. It made the ground soft and easy for pulling a man's crops when he isn't looking your way.' He leaned closer, gestured towards Markus and added, 'I'll swear it was Barrass who did the stealing, mind. Remember that. He's no favourite of Markus. The man will readily believe that he is a thief.'

There wasn't a movement of a facial muscle to indicate that Markus had understood what had been said as he watched Madoc handling the stolen vegetables and glancing his way with triumph on his thin sickly face. His face didn't display even the faintest hint that he understood, but the still eyes below the brim of the hat saw and digested it all as Madoc continued to look towards him from time to time, relishing his successful thieving. The crowd around the overfull stall thickened as customers offered coins for the fresh produce, and Markus touched his pony's flanks. The animal pushed its way forward and Markus was soon lost in the crowd.

Emma had come with Daisy and Pansy to buy more sheets for the regular visitors the inn was attracting but she was soon irritated by their suggestions on the best items to buy.

'Go you and look at the entertainment for an hour while I buy what we need,' she said and, leaving her daughters to wander around the stalls and amusements, she searched through the various linen merchants' offerings to compare prices and get the best bargain. Time and again she went back to each stall, pushing her way through to get the seller's attention, arguing with the proprietors, trying to persuade them with the size of her order to reduce their prices.

Hunger finally made her realize how much time she had spent, and with little hope she began to examine the faces around her for a sight of her daughters. It was Daisy she found first.

'Where is your sister?' she asked angrily. 'I've been looking for you for hours!'

'Mamma!' Daisy protested. 'You have passed me on three occasions, wrapt in your accounting, frowning over what to buy!'

'Well, whatever,' Emma muttered. 'You're here now and I want you to find Pansy so we can go and find some food, I want

Arthur too. He must collect the goods I've chosen, take them to the cart and guard them. As soon as we've eaten we will go home. This crowd and noise tires me so.'

The people pushing their way towards the area where food was being cooked caught them up in their inexorable determination and they found themselves a prisoner beside the stall where pork was sold. Unable to free themselves, Emma handed the owner some money and was handed a joint for each of them. Once they were armed with the proof that they had purchased they were allowed passage by those still waiting to buy and at last they were outside the throng, sitting on the ground chewing on the food.

'I expect Arthur and Pansy have money to buy themselves food. We'll soon find them.'

Uneasy at the joining together of the names of her daughter and her potboy, Emma threw down the remainder of the joint and stepped swiftly away from the dogs who quarrelled over ownership.

'I think we should search for them, Daisy!' she said firmly.

Once most people had assuaged their hunger, the crowd divided into circles around the entertainments. The dancing bear was taken from its cage and was soon surrounded by admirers. In a smaller booth geese were dancing, encouraged by the cruel practice of heating the floor on which they stood. Between the isolated knots of people Emma and Daisy walked, but although they travelled through and around the area several times they saw neither Pansy nor Arthur.

'Where can they be?' wailed Emma. 'It's your father's fault! He should be here with me.'

'How could he, Mamma, the inn can't be closed on a whim.'

They met Olwen and her parents, and soon they too were searching but without success, even with Spider's height enabling him to see above most heads. Emma told Mary of her fears that the young couple had stolen a few hours to spend together and wailed at the difficulties facing a doting mother when her daughters were both beautiful and wayward.

Olwen wandered away from them on the pretence of looking in the vicinity of the gypsy caravans and she found, not Pansy and Arthur, but Daniels and a group of men armed with heavy sticks. Beside them was Markus and his watchman.

She ran to where she could hear what they were saying and heard to her alarm that it was Madoc they were seeking. For Barrass's sake he had to be found and warned. The last place she had seen him was where a fire-eater was performing. She ran there, her heart fluttering, her eyes trying to look in all directions at once so she saw nothing but a blurr. As she reached the self-titled 'Prince of Fire', the crowd around him fell back and a huge gout of flame shot out above their heads amid screams. In the startled faces nearest to her she saw Madoc and Morgan.

'Madoc,' she called, 'it's Daniels, he's looking for you and he has gathered a group of ruffians to help him!'

The eyes of the fire-eater turned towards her, red, then blue as his flame was extinguished and in the awe-filled silence he heard what was said. Hands above his head, he signalled to others and the men who marched with Daniels at their head were balked at every turn.

It was a while before Olwen realized what was happening. Seeing the men about to surround them, she pulled on Madoc's hand and dived between two stalls with Morgan following. Squeezing through the narrow gap which took her to a pathway between one row of stalls and another, she found Daniels waiting for them; tall, severe and threatening. Before she could decide what to do next, she found herself being dragged into a tent and pushed out through a flap and into another, while Daniels and his assistants were besieged by instrumentalists dancing around them playing a lively tune. She realized that the entertainers were helping them.

'Why are they helping us?' she panted. To her alarm, Madoc could not reply; he was gasping for breath and holding his chest in obvious pain.

'A pretty face, why else?' Morgan said.

'Where shall we go?' Olwen asked. 'Daniels knows I am with you, he saw me plainly. We must get away. But where do we go?' She saw a terrifying future ahead of her, running from everyone she loved, hiding with the brothers, fearing every dawn would herald the day of her capture and imprisonment.

'We have to get back to the house, all our savings are there,' Morgan said.

'And there we'll discuss who told Daniels,' Madoc said quietly looking at her, his face white with exhaustion.

'It wasn't me!' Olwen told him, anger momentarily erupting. 'Who elso knows?'

'Look, we have to get ourselves away from here before we start arguing,' Morgan said. He looked at Olwen. 'Best you go out first and see if there are any of Daniels's men about.'

'How heroic!' she snapped with the last of her rage. Then she calmed down and concentrated on getting free from the situation she had been forced into by the Morgan brothers.

A number of young people had joined in the line of musicians and were dancing their way around the stalls. Daniels stopped in the middle of the pathway and held up his hands for them to stop. A formidable figure but completely ignored. Darting to either side, the merrymakers passed him jeering and imitating his pompous expression, leaving him frustrated and determined. Calling to some of the toughest onlookers, he told them to assist or be imprisoned for obstructing him in his duties. The band of men hunting two men and a girl grew to about twenty. In twos, Daniels sent them through the crowd.

'Report back to me at intervals,' he shouted. 'I will be at the tent where the fortune-teller has her stand.'

When he went there, the stand had disappeared. He stood in the vicinity of where he thought it had been, and was startled to see in the distance the conical shape of the canvas tent with its flags waving gaily at the top of it. Either he was losing his mind or the woman had moved! He strode angrily to complain but again he was obstructed by tumblers rolling about his feet, and sellers pushing their baskets of offerings up to his face, and the long line of dancers weaving to and fro. When he finished twisting and turning to escape them, the tent had again vanished, to appear at the spot where he had recently bought ale. The ale stall was nowhere to be seen.

It was only his innate regard for the dignity of his office and the importance of his standing in the community that prevented him from lying on the ground and kicking his heels like a frustrated child. When Florrie appeared, loaded with spices she had bought to take back to Ddole House, he told her what had happened and said, 'What is it about these people who will even protect those who have robbed one of their own?'

'It must be because of Olwen's pretty young face, and nothing more than that,' she said unconsciously repeating the words of

271

Morgan. 'These fairground people would have no knowledge of why you want the men, only that Olwen appears to be supporting them.'

They reached the large crowd watching the powerfully built fire-eater, who, head back, was lowering a lighted torch into his mouth accompanied by gasps of horror and admiration. He seemed to see them out of the corner of his eye. He waved a hand in signal to some unseen person and continued with his terrifying act. He licked a red-hot poker handed to him by an assistant who took it from the nearby fire, using only spittle to prevent his tongue being burned. Taking a pair of flaming torches, he casually rubbed them across his bare torso and down his arms with no apparent discomfort. When Florrie and Daniels pushed into the crowd and moved away, his eyes followed them.

In the tent where she had stopped to allow Madoc and Morgan to recover their breath, Olwen looked out across the still teeming crowds and decided that the best place to make for was the gypsy caravans. There were fewer people about there, but that might discourage Daniels from thinking of them trying to conceal themselves there. Telling Madoc of her idea, he just nodded and she was chilled at the realization that he was almost spent.

Wherever they went, it would not be very far. And – what then? She pushed aside the unwelcome thought and tried to think no further ahead than getting them away from Daniels. What happened to her then depended on whether or not she was considered an accomplice to them. And, whether or not they were caught.

The way they had to go was across to the furthest corner where the tents and hurdles hid the oddities for which the audience had to pay before entering. Queues of people stood waiting their turn to see the fattest man, the educated pig who could add and subtract, the pickled, two-headed chicken, and a dozen more of the country's marvels. As they made their way there, way was readily made for them to pass. Then the tall figure of Daniels spotted them as they wove through the cheerful gathering bent to below shoulder height and he shouted for them to be stopped.

The fire-eater who seemed to have made himself their

guardian angel, moved closer to Daniels and announced that he would cook an oyster in his mouth on live coals.

'Come and see this act of defiance against nature's cruellest element!' he shouted, and stepping to where his torch and equipment were in readiness, he took two pebbles from the fire his assistant had kept burning, and asked those close enough to touch them. One man, confident in the man's certain trickery, burned his hand fearfully when he squeezed the pebble between his hands in foolish bravado. He screamed in agony and as Daniels tried to extricate himself from the tangle of people, more joined the audience to see the performance and he was firmly trapped.

Olwen did not stop to see why Daniels was not chasing them but hurried to where the caravans stood. Weaving between the beautifully painted vehicles, she had to pause repeatedly for Madoc and Morgan to catch up with her.

Daniels fought to be free of the mob but he was forced to listen as the fire-prince explained that he would put hot pebbles onto his tongue then place an oyster on top of them and hold them all there until the oyster sizzled. He was deafened by the applause when the trick was achieved, unimpressed when the man showed his discoloured tongue to prove he had 'nothing in my mouth but what nature supplied at my birth'.

Once Olwen and the brothers were in a field with only the distant, muffled sound of the large assembly to be heard, she stopped, knowing from the look of them that the brothers could go no further. She looked around for some means of hiding themselves until Daniels had given up the search. There was only a broken-down barn, its wooden panels fallen and sloping up onto what had once been the low walls of the building. The ruin was partly overgrown with straggling grass, goosegrass and nettles. There was barely enough room for them to squeeze into the triangular-shaped refuge but, one after another, they did. Feet first they backed into the space; Olwen, last in, could look out and see if and when anyone came. She was sad to realize that she had taken charge of their safety.

Neither Madoc nor Morgan spoke but for a long time the sound of their breathing seemed as deafening as the calls of the vendors had been in the centre of the fairground. She hoped that

Daniels would delay exploring this far until the brothers were rested and quiet.

Daniels pushed his way through the audience as the fire-prince bowed and his assistant picked up the money being thrown by the appreciative audience. When Daniels had almost managed to reach the edge of the crush someone waved his own watch in front of him, and bowed as deeply as the fire-prince when Daniels snatched it in rage. But when the excitement died down and the fire-prince thought the runaways had had sufficient time, the crowd miraculously dispersed and Daniels gathered up the men he had instructed to help and made his way towards the gypsy caravans. Even then they were pelted with food as they walked away from the closely packed stalls to where a gypsy woman sat plaiting her hair.

A young woman came out of a caravan dressed in a red, gold-edged dress and headband. She assured Daniels that no such people as he described had passed her, but seeing the brief glance in the direction of the field where Olwen and the brothers were hiding, he mistrusted her and went on.

Olwen saw him coming, leading his small band. The sticks in their hands looked larger and more menacing now they were so close to finding them and their faces showed little sign of regret at what they were asked to do. She bit her lip and wondered why she had become involved in such a situation. If only she had told her father or Dan, she thought belatedly. They wouldn't have allowed anything terrible to happen to Barrass, not if they knew how much she loved him.

The steps came closer and she could hear the sound of their boots as they waded through the long grass. She looked through the screen of nettles that had hidden the way they entered the small space and hoped their keen eyes would not notice that some were broken. Then she saw feet standing within inches of her head, and a voice said, 'Olwen-the-fish, you and your companions can come out now.'

She felt a hand grip her ankle, warning her not to move. Behind her Madoc was hoping that the man had only guessed at their presence. She held her breath. She thought later that if Madoc had not tried to do the same they might have got away, but the effort was too much for his diseased lungs and his coughing soon filled the air. men grabbed the rotting wood and pulled the panels aside revealing Olwen still gripped by Madoc, head down, uselessly pretending to be invisible.

Morgan had vanished, taken his chance and left before Daniels had arrived. Under Daniels's instructions, two of the men hared across the field in pursuit. Olwen watched as they disappeared into a small woodland beyond where they stood. They all waited for a while in the hope that the men would return with Morgan, but when they did appear they displayed empty hands to show they had been unsuccessful.

Daniels arranged for Madoc, shackled at both ankles and wrists, to be taken to his own house, where a room was reinforced and occasionally used as a temporary prison. That he was obviously sick and unfit to face a long walk was to his mind irrelevant. The men were thieves and deserved little sympathy.

'You can go home, Olwen,' he told her after giving her a lecture about getting 'mixed up with the wrong persons'. She hesitated to clear herself, still fearing the brothers' threat to involve Barrass. If she remained silent perhaps they would keep their promise. Although with the threat of the gallows, she doubted if they would remain honourable to their word. They must surely try to exchange information, however false, for their lives? She walked back to the noisy fair with the gaggle of armed men who were discussing their plans to find Morgan and throw him in with his brother.

While Owen searched dejectedly for her parents, Daniels searched for Florrie. A tearful Emma, convinced of the worse, was looking for Pansy and Arthur, whom she had not seen since they arrived. Others too were looking for lost friends or family and they were easy to spot, their eyes ignoring the multifarious offerings and glancing head-height for the face they wanted to see.

With the approach of evening the fair had changed its character but had in no way diminished in size or volume. The food-sellers were doing good business, as those who had been kept away by their day's work arrived to swell the throng. The stall holders with goods left to sell were calling their bargains in a screeching attempt to out-shout the rest. Olwen passed the stall held by Madoc and Morgan and saw that the sheepdog puppy was still there, panting painfully for water, the whites of its eyes showing its distress, and she ran to find a receptacle to fill. It was there that her parents found her, sitting on the ground, with the puppy half on her knees, dipping her fingers in water and coaxing it to suck.

Olwen told her parents only a little of the story, about how Daniels had captured Madoc, convinced he was guilty of some crime, 'and him with not enough breath to think of such a thing. Yet he was dragged off to walk the long miles back to Mumbles in chains!' Spider wanted to go there and then to the Keeper of the Peace whom he could see stalking through the crowd searching for Florrie. He was confused over what had happened to his once happy child, but Mary persuaded him at least to wait until they knew more of what the Morgan brothers had told. Instinctively she knew that Olwen's behaviour was involved somehow with her affection for Barrass.

'This is something to do with Barrass, isn't it, Olwen?' Mary asked.

'Of course not!' Olwen almost shouted, but the expression on her face showed Mary she had touched on the edge of the truth. 'You love Barrass very much, don't you,' Mary said softly as she hugged her tearful daughter.

'He's a fool!' Olwen replied.

And so am I, Mary silently thought.

Florrie saw Daniels and asked where he had been.

'Looking for you for ages, I've been,' she said. 'I wonder if you would find David and tell him I am ready to leave, that is, unless you would like to stay a while longer and try some of the entertainments?'

'I'm sorry, my dear,' Daniels said taking some of her freshly bought packages from her. 'I have something I must do. I'll take you to the wagon and find David, then I must ride quickly back to the village.'

'Whatever for? Surely you can relax and enjoy a special event like a Fair Day?'

'Something about the Morgan brothers makes me think –' he began. He briefly explained about the events involving Olwen, then he looked at her as if trying to decide something. He sat her down near the wagon to wait for David to appear and asked, 'Do you really love me, Florrie?'

'Of course! How could I ever consider being your wife if the love I have for you is not great and undying?'

'Then I can trust you?'

She nodded, but crossed her fingers tightly, staring at him in anticipation of some trouble.

'I think the Morgan family are involved in the smuggling,' he said. 'I think that the gifts I've seen arriving at that poor cottage are payments. William Ddole is more than generous.'

'William Ddole is generous to everyone in the village!' she replied anxiously.

'More than is easily explained, my dear. And Edwin Prince, why should he help them? And I have seen Oak-tree Thomas calling there with small packages.'

'A sick family and everyone opens their hearts and their store cupboards,' she argued. 'It's nothing more than a good community looking after its own.'

'I found Madoc anything but loyal to the "generous-hearted neighbours",' he said. 'What he had to say makes me ride at once to the houses of William Ddole, Markus and Edwin Prince while they are away from their homes. From what that "grateful" young man told me, I think I will discover some very interesting facts. I'm sorry, my dear, but I will have to leave you to wait for David on your own. I have to gather men and go at once.'

Florrie tried to hide her alarm but her dark eyes widened and she looked around searching for a way to stop him. It was not the thought of him finding anything in the houses he had mentioned, the men were too experienced and careful for that to happen, but he might not live long if he were so determined to expose them to the authorities. A death to prevent many deaths would not seem unreasonable to them.

'Please, Daniels, won't you do one thing for me before you go? It's so rarely we have time together. Just a few minutes and you can go. Please?'

'What is it?' he asked, amused and flattered by her pleading.

'I want to go and watch the bear dancing but I am more than a little afraid of it. If you were with me then I could watch and forget my fear.'

'How can I refuse such a small request,' he said, smiling down at her, although every minute was important, and the delay tugged at his patience like a tethered bull.

Florrie led him to the edge of the fairground where the huge cage was standing open, the floor filled with droppings that smelled most unpleasant.

'Surely you won't find him here,' Daniels said. 'He would hardly be considered entertainment if he was locked in a cage.'

'I hope you won't be either,' she said as she gave him a sudden push and locked the door. She held out the key. 'I won't let you out unless you promise me you won't pester William Ddole and the others with this nonsense about smuggling! Rubbish it is, told for mischief.'

'Florrie! Open this door at once! I do not find this joke very amusing!' He had stumbled and almost fallen to the filthy floor, the near disaster making him white-faced.

'My dear, it's not for fun. If you go and search for these unknown men, your life won't be worth as much as the droppings on that cage floor! Promise me, please, that for your life's sake you will stop this search.'

'I can't do what you ask. I must do what is clearly my duty. If you can't see that then you aren't the woman I should marry!'

'So it must be then. Please believe I regret having to do this.' She held out the heavy key and with a flick of her hand, dispatched it into the pile of dung nearby, on to which a boy was emptying yet another steaming and noisome barrow-load.

Daniels fumed and shouted for someone to release him, but the few passers-by only stared, considering him to be a part of the entertainment. He didn't believe Florrie had done such a wicked thing to save his life. But if that were so it meant he was considered a joke by the local people. Tolerated because he was harmless. A fool who could be easily outwitted.

Being laughed at by his inferiors was as humiliating as the position in which he now found himself. They thought him a fool! The word echoed round and round in his head.

His fury increased as one then several boys started to search for the key. But angry and impatient as he was to be on his way, when he was finally released, he found time to stop at the nearest inn and demand that his boots be washed and re-polished before heading back.

Chapter Nineteen

While Neath Fair continued to throw noise and illumination into the night sky, Pansy and Arthur walked across country to the town of Bridgend. Directly, the distance was nineteen miles but overland, and having to take constant diversions for streams and hazards, they walked more than twenty-five miles. Pansy smiled bravely as they reached the outskirts of the town, trying to ignore the pain in her swollen and torn feet and the stiffness of her thigh muscles after the unaccustomed exercise.

The inflexibility of her legs caused her to turn sideways at each step and Arthur was worried that on the following day she would be unable to move. He decided that although they had planned to sleep on this, their first night together, under the stars, he would insist they spent some of their savings on a room. Pansy protested but Arthur insisted.

'I refuse to argue. Responsible for you I am and you do what I say, my dear. You'll spend the night in a comfortable bed,' he said in his high voice that made his scolding lose its authority. 'I'm well and truly used to walking with all the messages I do, and the running up and down those cellar steps. But you, well, I don't want you to suffer any more. Tomorrow we rest and after that we'll see about getting ourselves work.'

They found a room in a small inn half hidden in the shadow of the castle walls and neither stirred until the sun was well up on the following morning. The excitement of sharing a bed, far from anyone who would interfere, was ruined by their exhaustion. Hand in hand they fell into the bed with hardly a bite to eat, and collapsed into slumber.

In the morning, Arthur dressed and went down to find them some food and drink and some water to wash. When they had eaten, he slowly undressed again.

Pansy laughed with nervous tension and with the realization that she could barely move her legs! Arthur slid in beside her and slowly his hands began to explore her exciting body. But although he loved her to the extent that the room and everything else was a blur apart from desire for her that burned within him, they failed to consummate their love. To Arthur's relief, their attempt ended in laughter and before they fell once more to sleep, each had vowed to the other, that if the loving they had longed for never materialized, they would remain constant and true. When they woke, again, the need to try again overwhelmed them; this time they were completely successful.

On the following day, they sought work and Arthur managed to find employment and accommodation for them both at the inn where they were staying. Arrangements were going ahead for their wedding with such certainty that he knew God in His Heaven was in approval.

Emma and Daisy returned to Mumbles with Percy being urged to hurry. Emma dreaded telling Pitcher what had happened. She had no way of proving that Pansy and Arthur had run away together but there was no doubt in her mind that that was what had happened. She hardly spoke on the journey, trying to decide whether to go in attacking Pitcher and blaming him for employing such an ungrateful boy, or whether calmly to tell Pitcher her suspicions and let him vent his anger by accusing her of neglect. In fact, she burst into tears the moment Percy brought the wagon to a stop.

Pitcher ran through the door to help her down. It was clear he had been watching the road for her return.

'Emma, I know what has happened,' he said at once. 'There was a note propped up in the cellar, with a brief explanation. *And* a request for us to mind his dog!'

'I'll kill him, Pitcher, I'll kill him,' Emma wailed as tears, once unleashed, began to pour down her fat, red cheeks. 'My poor girl! The humiliation!'

They discussed the situation all through the night and decided that there was nothing they could do until the runaways decided to return.

'As return they will, my dear,' Pitcher assured his wife. 'But what will be happening between now and then, well, best we don't think about it.'

The loss of Arthur, the potboy who had been a reliable and

able member of the work force for years, was a more urgent consideration for Pitcher. With the inn regularly full, the boy would be greatly missed. As dawn coloured the sea and touched it with silver, grey, pink then gold, Emma and Pitcher made a list of those they could ask to help them.

'With Madoc Morgan captured and his brother on the run, Vanora might be willing to come and live here and work in the bar? Or serve as our cook?' Emma suggested.

'I'll send Arthur first thing –' Pitcher stopped and bent his head. 'Damn me, we'll miss him as much as we'll miss Pansy,' he sighed.

With Cadwalader and Vanora, the work at the Posthorn Inn simmered down to a comfortable routine. At first Vanora's cooking was a source of disbelief to Emma.

'You'd think she'd never seen an oven, Mr Palmer,' she complained when she found the girl boiling a fine roasting joint of beef bought for the weekend visitors.

'No more she has,' Pitcher said with a smile. 'I've been to that cottage of hers and when they were all living, there was hardly room for them all to breathe except in unison. The pot hanging over the fire was all they had. Even bread was a lack unless they bought some at the market.'

With patient teaching, Emma showed Vanora the skill of preparing good meat and fresh vegetables and the art of presenting it other than dropping it onto plates in untidy piles. The girl was quick to learn and Emma was pleased with her progress but Vanora herself soon found that the work was not to her liking.

'The cooking I enjoy,' she told Emma and Pitcher, 'but the walking through the diners and having them touch my skirts and even pinch my bum, well, it isn't for me. I've been offered a place at Ddole House with Florrie and I think I'll be taking it.'

With a sigh, Emma looked into the ground floor kitchen behind the bar. It seemed that for all Pitcher's determination to better their situation, and all the mess and inconvenience she had suffered in the preparation for it, that back kitchen was where she was likely to spend the next few years. She rolled up her sleeves and reached for the flour pot.

'Find Percy, tell him I want lots and lots of wood for the bread oven,' she sighed.

*

281

Florrie had hardly seen Daniels since the day of the Fair. That she had offended him beyond forgiveness by locking him in the foul-smelling bear cage was without doubt. She had heard from William that the Keeper of the Peace had not left the precincts of the Fair until long after darkness had fallen, the key conveniently eluding the searchers until sufficient time had elapsed for Markus and Edwin to be warned of his impending visit.

'I was told that although he was furious at the delay, he still stopped at an inn to get his boots cleaned and polished before riding home,' William told her. 'And the visits he planned were postponed.' He looked at Florrie and touched her shoulder in a kindly gesture. 'Florrie, my dear, I know what you gave up so we could be warned. I thank you for it and promise that whatever your future holds, you will always have a place here, at Ddole House.'

'Thank you, sir.'

William thought she looked melancholy. 'Are you very sad about the loss of Daniels? Is there something I could do to persuade him of why you acted the way you did?'

'Nothing, thank you, sir.' She smiled a little and added, 'Best really. I would have far less freedom than I have now, and suspect that I would have no more important a position. A housekeeper Daniels wants but a wife would be cheaper.'

It was on Thursday several days after the incident when Barrass heard about Madoc's arrest and Olwen's attempt to hide him. He hurried through the remainder of his calls, his horn blown impatiently at the village greens or the crossroads where he habitually stopped to collect or deliver letters. He was angry at her stupidity, wondering how she could have become so involved with the unsavoury activities of the Morgan brothers. The news that Morgan was still free made him want to begin looking for her at once to beg her to stop shielding him, if that was what she was doing.

'She's a fool!' he muttered angrily, not realizing that she had said the same about him.

His long, dark hair flowing about his broad shoulders and his deep brown eyes flashing angrily gave him a piratical air, and those watching him wondered at the depth of his fury but dared not ask the reason for it.

It was early when he returned to the inn and at once he demanded of Pitcher, 'Why didn't you tell me about Olwen?'

'I thought it best for her to tell you herself,' Pitcher said. 'And, to be honest, boy, we've enough to think about with Pansy gone and that Arthur with her. Haven't slept more than an hour at a time we haven't, jumping up at every sound in the hope they have come back. Nor *will* we sleep until we know what has happened to them.'

'Sorry, Pitcher. You haven't heard then?'

'Not a word, though I hope every day for a letter to come to tell us they're safe. Ben Gammon is asking everyone he sees, and in the town we've spent hours stopping travellers and asking if they've had sight of them.'

'Hiding they are,' Barrass said. 'But who would have thought it? Arthur and your Pansy? They hardly had a moment together to talk, let alone plan this.'

'Living in the same house, it wasn't difficult for you and Violet –' Pitcher said, staring angrily at Barrass. 'Seems I'm too trusting to have been the father of girls.'

Barrass hung his shaggy head but did not reply.

On Friday, with no letters to deal with, Barrass went at once to look for Olwen. Each time he called at the cottage on the cliff, Mary shook her head. Olwen was either out somewhere or refusing to see him. Frustrated, he settled near the top of the steep path from where he could see the cottage door and waited for her to appear. But he did not see her.

Mary came and spoke to him when the sun was beginning to set and brought him food.

'She's been out all this day,' she told him. 'Knew you'd be looking for her for sure, knowing it to be your day off from work. There's no talking to her. Tried we have, but she won't listen or tell us where Morgan is. She knows though, we're certain of that.'

He ate the food and after a brief talk to Mistress Powell, who looked as concerned as Mary about the girl's defiance of the law, he went back to the inn to fill the evening helping Pitcher. He was glad of the crowded room and the work of feeding the variety of customers. He found that like Pitcher, he constantly expected to see Arthur pop his thin face out of the cellar door, and he grieved for the boy's absence. As a reminder, should they forget, the dog followed them around in a confused manner, as if hoping for an explanation he could understand.

Daniels came and asked if he knew where Olwen was hiding Morgan. Florrie also came to ask if he had seen the girl, as William Ddole wanted to see her. To both he had to admit he was not in her confidence.

Cadwaladar seemed to fit into the work without a ripple of disturbance. He was quick and polite and Pitcher was grateful for his presence. He slept in the cellar with Barrass and Arthur's dog, rising early and setting about the chores without waiting to be told what to do.

'Lowri has gone with my mother, but I have no idea where,' he told Barrass as they settled to sleep on the Thursday night. 'It seems that people feel a touch of the same restlessness and go independent of each other, but called by the same mysterious need.'

'I think not,' Barrass argued. 'Arthur and Pansy have long planned to run away, even before they asked Pitcher's permission to marry and were refused, I think. Your mother is running away from trouble of her own making, isn't she? They don't compare.'

'And Olwen? How do you explain her running from you?'

'I can't.' Barrass turned on his side and pulled the blankets around him. He was silent for a while then said softly, 'I thought we were friends and trusted each other. Like so many things, I was wrong about that. It seems she prefers those wild Morgan brothers to what I have to offer her.'

'Offer her?' Cadwalader queried.

'Yes. Offer!' Barrass snapped. 'Marriage and my protection and love. That's what I have to offer and she won't even see me so I can tell her!'

'Write her a letter,' Cadwalader said. 'There isn't a woman living that would refuse to read a letter addressed to her and delivered by the letter-carrier of Gower.' He thought Barrass had not heard him as there was no movement from the bed alongside his own, but then Barrass sat up, pulled on his trousers and went up the stone steps. Cadwalader heard him go into the silent sitting room used by visitors, where paper and pen and ink was placed for the convenience of guests. He heard the striking of a flint and knew that in the light of a candle, Barrass was doing as he had suggested.

On Saturday morning, Barrass arrived in Swansea soon after six o'clock to collect his letters and found to his surprise that Walter was up, dressed and seemingly in charge of the office. The man had shaved, and before him on the wooden desk were ledgers into which he was adding rows of figures.

'Walter. You're abroad early?' Barrass greeted him, then something about the man's attitude puzzled him and he glanced to the bench behind the door and saw the two inspectors sitting there, dressed in black clothes with grey stocks; still wearing their tall, black silk hats they looked official and exuded solemn foreboding.

'Walter?' Barrass queried.

'Walter Waterman is no longer the Deputy Postmaster,' the thinner of the two gentlemen said. 'Today, we will take over and we'll stay until someone is appointed.' The other man coughed and added, 'If you wish it, you may apply.'

'For now, I think I will take my letters and deal with today,' Barrass answered in surprise. Me, an official of the King's Mail! His dark eyes glowed at the thought. A dream come true! He wondered why he even hesitated.

Then he knew it was Olwen. If she were here, he would only have to look at her to know she approved, and he would ask immediately for his name to go forward. Without her, even his long-held ambition to be a part of the world of the letter post was less than a mild thirst on a hot day.

He helped a subdued Walter to sort the letters he had brought and collected the ones for him to take, leaving his own to Olwen tucked into a pocket. With the prospect of running the sorting office to consider, he pushed thoughts of Olwen to one side and forced himself to deal with the day's work. Tomorrow he would be back in time for church. She would surely be there, with her parents? One decision made, the other to discuss when he eventually talked with her, he mounted Jethro and rode back to the inn.

Olwen hadn't seen Morgan since he escaped from Daniels at the Fair. She had determinedly avoided Barrass, in case some jealousy on the part of his brother made Morgan do what the brothers had threatened, and implicate Barrass in their deeds. She spent the days wandering around the fields between Mumbles and Swansea, thinking that he would avoid his home, but be drawn back to the places he knew.

It was a week since the day of the Fair and although Daniels had spoken to her and her parents several times, he seemed satisfied that she knew nothing. If only she could talk to Morgan, help him, in exchange for his promise not to involve Barrass.

The longing to see Barrass muddied her thoughts. Fear for him filled her mind so she could not think clearly about anything. Spider and Dan tried to persuade her to help on the boat but she refused. All she could do was search for Morgan and hope she found him before Daniels did, and be able to persuade him not to mention Barrass in his confession when he was caught. She ignored even the delicious food Mary prepared for her, unaware of the needs of her body, knowing only the need for Barrass. Pale-faced and thin, she knew Mary feared she was wasting away with the dreaded morbid lung disease suffered by the family of Morgans.

She had never searched near the damp old house, convinced that Morgan would never go back there, the most likely place for Daniels's men to watch for him, but something made her want to try. There was nowhere else and tramping the same fields day after day was becoming wearisome and futile.

As she walked past Betson-the-flowers's cottage and on up the green lane, she sensed that people were watching her. She saw no one but knew that Daniels had set people to lie in wait in case the wanted man returned to his home. She heard a horse, but although she stopped and listened, she saw no one. Nervously, imagining the eyes following her progress, she went closer to the house by the stream.

When Barrass stepped out and held her arms firmly, she tried to struggle free.

'Go away, Barrass, please!' she gasped, trying to keep her voice low for fear of Morgan hearing them.

'Looking for Morgan, are you?' he hissed. 'Then so am I!'

'Please, Barrass, leave me!'

'We can walk on with you struggling, or we can walk sensibly.

Which is it to be? For one way or another I am not letting go of you until we talk.'

'Not now,' she pleaded, her blue eyes full of fear, as she glanced around, expecting Morgan to appear. 'I'll meet you this evening, I promise, only go now.'

'Where you go, I go!' he said firmly. 'First, the cottage. That was where you were heading, wasn't it? Meeting with Morgan, were you?'

'No. Yes. I don't know. Oh, Barrass, why won't you leave me alone?'

'I have ridden here from the furthest end of Gower, Jethro thinks I have gone completely mad, and all so I can see you, Olwen-the-fish. Now I'm here, we are going to look at the Morgans' house, then we will talk.' His hand gripped her arm and he half lifted her so her toes were barely touching the ground.

'Barrass, you're hurting me.'

'Pity,' he said, urging her to move faster.

His jaw was tight with determination, but his heart was filled with compassion at the sight of her. She was dishevelled; her dress was torn and dirty, her hair, grown through the summer to touch her shoulders, was tangled and dull. It alarmed him to see her so neglectful of her appearance but he hid his anxiety, determined to settle the disharmony between them.

They both saw the house at the same time and a gasp of surprise escaped them both. The house was a ruin. The mud walls had been pushed in, the thatched roof was nothing more than a brown mess and apart from three hens pecking about in the debris, there was no sign of life.

Releasing Olwen's arm, Barrass ran with her to the ruin, and they tried to ease up blocks of the mud walls to search beneath them. It was soon clear that the place was deserted. They could see that an attempt had been made to burn it, but the thatch had been so damp, moss covering it like a soft green blanket, that the attempt had failed.

They stood looking at the pile of useless rubbish that had once been a home for a family of seven people and wondered what had made Morgan knock it down.

'He blamed the house for them all being ill,' Olwen said.

'How could that be?' Barrass asked.

'After their parents died, it became damp, cold, the stream

287

seeping in under the walls and soaking their beds no matter how many times they were changed. The doctor agreed with him, but he couldn't get the others to find a better place.'

They turned away from it, but Barrass took off his coat and gave it to Olwen to hold.

"We might as well take the hens with us. It's a miracle they haven't been taken by a fox.'

The hens were laying birds and as he held a hand over their backs they crouched and allowed him to pick them up. With one under each arm, he walked back while Olwen help open a sack she had found. Barrass carried the sack and Olwen led Jethro.

'Will you go and tell Daniels what we have done?' he said. 'I don't want us in trouble for stealing.'

'I'll leave them at Betson-the-flowers's,' Olwen said. 'I don't want to go home yet.'

Having done so, they stood outside the shabby cottage and Olwen began to walk away from him.

'Olwen. We must talk,' he began. Then something in her expression made him look in the direction of the small woodland' where she was heading. A movement amid the russet colours of the dying leaves made him run to investigate. He saw a crouched figure stumbling away from him and caught him easily.

'Morgan!' he gasped.

'Help me,' the man whispered, his face blotched and wet with perspiration. His eyes went from one to the other as Olwen reached Barrass's side. 'Hide me.'

Before they could recover their wits sufficiently to make a decision, men appeared from the bushes around them and Morgan was held. He was so weak he needed no restraining; two men had to support him. He looked at Olwen and shook his head.

'We'll be freed when we tell what we know!' he gasped. There was no roughness as he was led away after one last malevolent glance at Olwen.

'He believes I led them to him,' Olwen sobbed, unable to tell Barrass the meaning of his words. 'There's so much hatred in him.'

'I think he is dying,' Barrass said softly.

'I think you have been helping him, Olwen!' Daniels

appeared, immaculate as always, his tall imposing figure making her afraid so she clung to Barrass.

'What if I have,' she said defiantly. 'poor, sick and in debt, always in trouble. Someone had to care!' Before either Daniels or Barrass could stop her she ran back past Betson-the-flowers's house and disappeared through a hedge.

Daniels glared at Barrass as if it were his fault.

'What is it about you people?' he said. 'You'll protect your own even when they have robbed and cheated. When they have disobeyed the law and assisted the smugglers to deprive His Majesty King George of his excise money. Even the Morgans, who, I suspect, were behind the attack on Ben Gammon and who left him bleeding and battered unconscious. These you will protect?' He stalked off to where a man was holding his horse. These people do not deserve me, he thought angrily.

Olwen ran from Barrass, but she stopped as she thought of Vanora. Now working at Ddole House, she would not know of the capture of her brother. Changing direction, Olwen ran to tell her.

Feeling a bit uneasy approaching the house where she had worked so recently, Olwen knocked on the kitchen door and called for Florrie. To her amazement, it was Barrass who opened it.

'I thought I should come and tell Vanora where her brother is,' Barrass said in explanation. 'It seems we both had the same thought.'

Vanora came out of the house wearing a cloak and carrying a box which Olwen guessed would contain food.

'Barrass is giving me a ride to Daniels's house to see Morgan,' she said as she hesitantly approached the horse tethered near the stable door.

Barrass strode from the doorway as Olwen prepared to leave and gripped her arms. He bent to touch her cheek with his own. 'Olwen, you belong to me,' he said. 'Not to Morgan or Madoc or anyone else. You are mine.'

He looked into her eyes momentarily, his own liquid and large. Then his lips touched hers so briefly she thought she must have imagined it as he released her and went to where David was helping Vanora up onto Jethro.

'I will see you tomorrow, when I have finished my deliveries,'

Barrass called, as he jumped up behind Vanora and urged Jethro forward.

'And I will see you *now*,' Florrie said, having to speak twice before Olwen heard her. 'The master has said you can come back here to work. There's no time to go home. Clean yourself here. We can't have you here looking like that.'

'But –' Olwen protested.

'Hurry, girl. There's three extra for dinner and only me and Dozy Bethan to see to it!'

Bemused by the sudden change in her day, Olwen obeyed.

She was glad of the work to keep her occupied as she waited for the announcement to come from Daniels that Barrass was arrested. She told Florrie nothing although the woman guessed that something was troubling her. If Madoc or Morgan did what they threatened then all she had suffered to save Barrass had been for nothing.

Washing the endless dishes, her mind wandered to Barrass's brief declaration he had made with Florrie and Vanora close by. If only she could have thrown her arms around him, told him how much she loved him. But while there was a chance of protecting him, she must keep away from him. Association with her would confirm his guilt if the Morgans swore he was involved. A word from the imprisoned brothers and Barrass would be past anyone's help.

For five days she waited for news to come from the prison in Swansea, days of avoiding Barrass, hoping that if she did as Madoc had asked, and insisted she was their alibi for the days of the robberies, they would not accuse him.

She was beginning to believe her life would be spent avoiding questions, and keeping away from everyone who tried to make her speak. Then on Thursday Daniels came to Ddole House and asked to see her. He ignored Florrie as if she were lower than the simplest kitchen maid, and insisted on William Ddole being present while he interviewed the girl.

'I think you should tell me everything you know about the activities of Madoc Morgan and his brother Morgan Morgan,' he said when Olwen was standing before him in William Ddole's study. 'Before you say anything,' he added as the girl began to shake her head, '– let me tell you that I know a great deal already, and will know at once if you are lying.'

'Olwen doesn't lie,' William defended.

'I hope for her sake that is *not* true!' Daniels said. 'Now, on the day of the robbery, the brothers were supposed to have been digging their garden.'

'That's right,' she said.

'That's wrong. They were beating Ben Gammon into the ground with sticks and taking the letters he carried.'

'No, it couldn't have been them –'

For a moment, Daniels waited, watching the colour spread on Olwen's face. He slowly shook his head.

'How did they persuade you to say that?'

'They didn't persuade me. Ask Vanora. She would know how long it took them to dig such a patch of hard earth, sick as they are.'

'How did they persuade you, Olwen?' he repeated. 'Surely you didn't lie for them because of any affection for them?'

She didn't reply and after a pause, he took out a piece of paper and began to read.

'We the undersigned, do declare without persuasion, that we attacked several persons including Ben Gammon, with the intent to steal. We also declare without persuasion that we forced Olwen, daughter of Spider Fish, to support us, under the threat of involving her and Barrass, letter-carrier of Gower.'

'Is that true, Olwen?' William asked.

Olwen nodded.

'How did you find out?' William asked.

'You have Cadwalader to thank for the speed at which I solved this muddle,' Daniels said. 'He could see that Olwen was unhappy and by diligence that would make him a fine Keeper of the Peace, if he had some learning from someone as expert as myself, he observed that Madoc was the cause. What he knew, added to what he guessed and surmised, gave me sufficient information to persuade Madoc and Morgan I knew it all.' Daniels was unable to resist giving her a lecture about the importance of truth, and the need to trust in the law of the land. William could see the girl was trembling and he stood, implying that the interview was at an end.

'I think Florrie will spare you for the rest of the day, Olwen,' William said. 'Go home and tell your parents everything. They have been as confused as the rest of us about why you were so troubled.'

Daniels left the room beside her and waited until she had gathered her cloak before walking through the kitchen. Olwen saw that Florrie had placed some cake and a mug of ale on the corner of the big wooden table for him, but the solemn man ignored both refreshment and Florrie.

'I can't give you a ride, Olwen,' Daniels said. 'I have to get back to Swansea and complete my report on this case. But I will see you again, soon, together with your father and mother and we can get everything clear.'

'Yes, and thank you,' Olwen said, anxious to be away. She walked calmly and casually as he rode past her, but as soon as he was out of sight, she skipped, and shouted her joy. She was free of the danger! Now she could tell Barrass why she had been so indifferent to him. Singing loudly she ran through fields that were still rich with the colours of late summer flowers and approached the house, breathless, rosy and sparkling with happiness.

She heard the wailing of Enyd crying before she had come in sight of the front door. At once anger flared in her. There was always something wrong, something to make Enyd complain. Never a day when her crying or her criticism did not touch them all. Even on this day when Olwen's world had suddenly come right again, Enyd was threatening to ruin it.

'What is it now?' she demanded when she entered the room, off which Enyd and Dan's home was situated. In answer, the wailing grew louder.

'Where's Mam?' Olwen asked. The room was dark after the brightness of the outside, and she could see nothing.

'I don't know. I'm here, facing it on my own. Dan's gone, and your father, there's no one to help!'

At once Olwen was concerned. The baby, there must be a problem with Enyd's baby!

'Enyd, what is it?' she asked, pushing her way into the recently built, overfull room. Her sister-in-law was lying on the bed, curled up, hugging herself, tears streaming down her fat cheeks.

'It's terrible to be on your own at such a time,' she wailed.

'What is it? Please tell me. Shall I go and find Bessie Rees?' Olwen asked. It was Bessie who helped most of the village children into the world.

'Yes, you better had. It's Mistress Powell. She's dead.'

The shock was so great that Olwen did not feel immediate relief that it was not after all Dan's baby in trouble. Mistress Powell had been a part of their family for months only, but she had been so important to Olwen, that the loss of her stunned her. She ran back into the family room and saw what she had missed the first time; Mistress Powell had fallen forward from her chair and was crouched on the floor as if picking up something she had dropped.

So small had the old woman become it was easy for Olwen to lift her. She sat with the body across her, rocking, crooning comforting sounds, as if it were a baby she held. Enyd continued to demand attention but Olwen did not hear her any more. She had lost a dear friend.

She looked up when a shadow crossed the threshold and only then did she cry.

'Barrass, oh how glad I am to see you.'

He knelt beside her, hugged her and kissed away her tears and together they nursed the body of the old woman until Mary and Spider returned.

Before the burial, Mary and Olwen sorted through the old woman's few possessions. In a box they found thirty pounds in assorted coins. With it was a note.

These are for Olwen to start a business for herself so she need never again be unhappily employed.

Chapter Twenty

Olwen had blossomed in the knowledge that Barrass loved her. She still looked childlike, but there was a new expression in her blue eyes, a new awareness about her that seemed to add stature to her slim figure. As the days shortened and winter signalled its approach, she continued to work at Ddole House, but ideas for a change were brewing in her head.

'Barrass,' she said one day, 'I think I have an idea for a business Mistress Powell would approve of. Something I would enjoy.'

'As long as it doesn't take you far away from me,' Barrass smiled.

They were sitting in Mary and Spider's crowded living room. Dan and Enyd had managed to squeeze themselves in and the family were sharing a meal.

'*And* so long as you don't want to keep a lot of equipment in here!' Mary added with a laugh. 'Prisoners we'd be, unable to move an inch!'

'I want to use the money to buy some animals, sell milk, cheese and butter. I've even thought of a name for what I sell,' Olwen said. 'Olwen is my name and it's very like Olwyn the Welsh word for wheel.' She turned to her brother. 'Dan, could you make me butter pats and a beautiful sign with a wheel on it? I'll call my products, Olwyn.'

Dan agreed to carve the butter pats and make her a sign.

'I'll paint it so it will be readily seen and long remembered,' he promised. 'A big one you can put up when you display your wares at the market, or even the fairs.'

'I'll help with caring for the animals,' Mary promised.

'There's often stale fish which will help to feed them,' Spider added.

'What can I do?' Barrass demanded. Then he went silent, a frown creasing his brow. Mary's mention of prisoners had

294

brought the Morgans' home to his mind.

'Barrass? You aren't pleased?' Olwen asked.

Olwen, how would you feel about living in the field and re-building the Morgans' cottage? There would be plenty of room for animal pens and hen coops.' He looked at Spider. 'The field slopes nicely down to the stream, the soil looks good to me, and if we built at the highest point –'

'Barrass, I'm not sure,' Olwen frowned. 'With Madoc and Morgan in prison waiting to be hanged, we couldn't be happy there, could we?'

'I'll talk to Vanora, although she's made it clear she won't go back there even if she could rebuild her home. And I'll discuss it with William Ddole. It's he who owns the land.' His eyes shone with excitement, already planning the position of the house he would build. 'As for the house, well there's Pitcher to help, and Dan and Spider, and – if only Arthur came back – but there, we'll have plenty of willing hands. Oh, Olwen, to have a home of our own!'

Spider went with Barrass to see William, who did not welcome the sight of the younger man. For this reason, it was Spider who did the talking.

'Mistress Powell's left money for Olwen to begin a business,' Spider explained when they had given the reason for their visit.

'So, you want permission to use the field, build yourself a house, and take away one of my servants?' William frowned. Then his face relaxed. 'Very well. I'll go and look at the sorry place and let you know my decision in a day or so.'

Barrass and Spider were dismissed and they walked back to the cliffs with doubts over the generosity of William Ddole. He had not seemed too willing to allow what they asked. They did not know how pleased William had been to hear that Barrass was to marry. Surely now he could write a more pleading letter to Penelope and ask her to come home?

The next day, when Barrass called at the house with the account from the post office for William's monthly transactions, he was handed a two-page letter addressed to Penelope at the London home of Gerald and Marion Thomas. Barrass handled it and wondered whether he too should write to Penelope and explain about his wedding plans. But he did not. Best, he thought, to wait a while and see what happened. Although he loved Olwen deeply, passionately and possessively, he could not altogether abandon the hope of seeing Penelope again.

While Olwen was washing the slate floor of his kitchen, when the afternoon meal was finished, Vanora told her that William wanted to see her. She hurriedly removed the sacking apron she was wearing, and straightened her fair hair. He was sitting behind his desk and when she entered gestured for her to sit.

'I've been to see the property, Olwen,' he said.

At once she tried to read on his face whether he was in agreement with her having it or not. He guessed her agitation and lowered his head to tease her.

'I will let you and Barrass rent the field we discussed and the one beside it, five acres in all. Will that be sufficient?'

'Two fields? Thank you, sir,' she sat back in amazement. This was more than she had hoped. 'And the house, sir?'

'The house will be built where Barrass and your father suggested. It's by far the best place.' He looked up then and smiled at her. 'I'm sure you can't wait another moment to run and share your news! Florrie says you can go and find Barrass and tell him. You will find him at the inn I suspect; it being a Tuesday, he will have long finished his calls.'

There was another waiting for news that day, but this arrived by post. Barrass handed a letter to Kenneth, who hurriedly snatched it, called for Ceinwen and began to lift the seal with impatient fingers.

'It's from the General Session of the Justices. News about my application for a licence to sell ale. This is the start of –' His smile drooped and fell off his chin as the letter's contents were revealed.

'They've refused us?' Ceinwen said.

'They've refused us. The place is too small for an alehouse and the village has sufficient for the number of residents and visitors,' Kenneth reported sadly. He threw the crumpled letter onto the table and sat down in his wooden chair. 'What are we to do now, wife?'

'Well, the selling I do at the door is giving us a small amount. If we increased what we sell, perhaps it will be sufficient?'

'How can we increase what we sell? Fish and a few scraggy

vegetables, some eggs from the fowls, what else is there?'

'I have an idea that if we went to market early, and brought back supplies, there would be many people who would gladly pay a little extra to save themselves the bother of walking six miles to and from the town.'

'And it would be *me* who has to go in each morning, I suppose?'

'And that would still leave me with most of the work to do!' Ceinwen raised her voice only slightly, but it was enough to warn Kenneth that she was determined.

'We'll try,' he said without enthusiasm. 'I will get up in the cold and dark of the morning and trek into town for what I think we can sell.'

'I will give you a list.' Again there was an unaccustomed firmness in Ceinwen's reply.

He nodded, throwing the disappointing letter into the fire. 'And to think I refused to apply for the letter sorting office position because we were so sure of being granted a licence,' he groaned. 'Get me a mug of ale, will you?'

'No, Kenneth. I think you should go at once into town and buy what we need. Today is not too soon to begin.'

Kenneth foresaw a less than comfortable future ahead of him as he looked at the line of Ceinwen's determined mouth.

As Christmas drew near, the preparations for the performance of the *Interludes*, the short plays depicting scenes made from the Bible or stories with a moral message, were being made. The actors and musicians rehearsed at the back of the inn in a room that was still awaiting completion. When Arthur and Pansy ran away, Pitcher had abandoned work on the room, lacking the heart to do more than plaster the walls and sweep the floors free of rubbish. The room was large, having been intended for a sitting room for parties of diners needing to talk with friends away from the noise of the bar-rooms. It was empty apart from the barrels and wooden boxes brought by the performers to use as a stage.

Pitcher and Emma remembered a previous performance, when Arthur was a main character in each of the stories. The present preparations lacked excitement for them, although they helped willingly enough.

With only three days to go before the first performance, at Ddole House, Emma was helping to shorten the dress of Vanora, who was playing the part of an abandoned wife. A doll, sewn and stuffed with hay, was clutched in Vanora's arms and on her face Emma had painted lines to represent suffering.

'Abandoning me to my fate in the cruellest deprivations of winter,' Vanora wailed, practising her third speech. Her voice was strong, and Emma rubbed her ear and asked her to soften it. Then she looked at the girl and said wonderingly, 'It's a miracle that you have such strength in your lungs. I feared you would suffer the same as your sisters and brothers but it's not to be, God be praised.'

'The news of my brothers is not good,' Vanora said. 'I went to the prison yesterday but they were both far from well enough to talk. They are sleeping most of the day and night and refuse to eat, so the guard tells me. It's small comfort they are too ill to take the punishment waiting for them.'

They were both gloomily continuing with their work, Vanora reciting her part and Emma stitching the dress, when the door opened and the room was filled with a cold draught.

'Close that door,' Emma said irritably. 'D'you want my poor fingers to snap with the freezing wind from the sea?' She did not look up from her task, and Vanora ignored the interruption and went on muttering the words she was learning.

'I beg you, sir, do not leave me and our child to perish in the bleak snow and cruel winter winds –'

The wind blew towards the fire and smoke issued out making Emma cough. 'Mr Palmer, will you be so kind as to close that door!' The draught continued to pull the smoke but there was no response and she turned, gave a gasp and allowed the material she was holding to fall from her hands.

'Pansy!' She ran to greet her long absent daughter with a choking sob. 'My naughty, wicked girl, where have you been?' Then, over Pansy's shoulder, she saw the gulping, nervous Arthur. 'What do you want?' she demanded. 'How dare you come here after what you've done?'

'I – we – that is –' Arthur stuttered, his Adam's apple bobbing like an onion in a pot of simmering stew, his voice at last an octave lower.

'Mamma, we are married,' Pansy stated softly.

Emma uttered a strangle cry for 'Pitcher' and fainted. Arthur and Pansy managed to catch her before she hit the ground. Pitcher ran up the stairs having been told by Cadwalader that his daughter was home, and saw a sorry tableau, reminiscent of one of the *Interludes* they were preparing. He ran to Emma first and patted her plump face and called her name, then, with Arthur helping, managed to sit her in a chair and fan her face with the dress she had been sewing.

'Pitcher, I dreamed that Pansy was back,' Emma whispered.

'We are, Mamma, Arthur and I are visiting you for the whole of Christmas.'

'Visiting! Married? Are you really married?' Emma asked weakly.

Pitcher sat down and asked in a confused tone, 'Tell me, right from the beginning so I'm fully clear. What's happened? Where have you been?'

With increasing confidence, Arthur told him. Emma recovered and listened to him, looking at Pitcher for a lead as to how she should react.

'Glad we are, boy, to have you both back,' Pitcher said when the story was finished. Emma could only agree.

The work on the new house beside the ruin of the Morgans' old home went ahead whenever the weather allowed. The first stage of sinking a shallow trench and building a low wall of stone to support the mud walls was already completed before a week had passed.

Slowly, the mud walls rose, each day a further layer of mud was mixed, and tamped down firmly, making the walls thick and strong with deep set window spaces that would one day be filled with frames and glass. As Barrass had guessed, there were many helpers including children who revelled in the joy of playing with the mud as the wall rose, foot by careful foot.

The floor was to be of mud too, but prepared with such care that it would be strong, easily cleaned and long lasting. Four barrels of earth were mixed with a bucket or two of lime and a barrow load of manure. Barrass had brought animal blood from the butchers' stalls in the market and this, added to the mixture, gave the finished floor a shine.

After the stones were removed, the mixture was beaten firmly then spread, until a layer was several inches thick. It was thumped with a spade, trampled by feet large and small, until it was smooth and level. Every evening, either Barrass or Spider would go and dampen the floor so it dried without cracks.

Pitcher had little time to assist, but offered to buy the glass for the windows. Emma promised to give them a pair of pillows made from real duck down plus a pair of linen sheets for a wedding gift. Mary began sewing a quilt filled with sheep wool, to be embroidered with their names and the date of their wedding. Dan, when he wasn't helping with the building work, began to make the patterned utensils Olwen had asked for and promised Barrass he would help him make a bed and two chairs.

Many of the local families contributed to the wedding gifts with small offerings, sewing from the women and useful wooden pieces like shelves and boxes for candles and a wooden tub in which to do her washing, from the men. By the time Christmas preparations were well under way, and the wedding was arranged for early in March, Olwen was having to spread her collection of gifts between several of her friends. Some were in the room used by Florrie, at Ddole House, some at the inn in the care of Emma and some with Ceinwen and Kenneth. Meanwhile the house rose, was thatched and had windows shining in the late summer sun.

Christmas was a happy time. Emma and Pitcher celebrated the return of Pansy, consoled to the idea of their potboy being married to their daughter and Daisy becoming so essential a part of the running of the inn that they no longer questioned her being there.

For William the season was made joyful by news that when John Maddern returned next, he would be bringing Penelope with him. He had Florrie clean and freshen Penelope's room and ordered her to have new curtain and bed hangings made.

'I will leave the choice of them to you, Florrie,' he said. 'Just make sure that it looks as welcoming as possible. I want her to realize how much she is needed here, and how much she has been missed.'

When Florrie went into town to buy what she needed, she took Emma with her for company, calling for her at the inn on the Ddole wagon which was driven by David. The day was grey and bitterly cold, with a fog coming in from the sea and ice on the surface of the puddles. The horse made a fast pace to warm itself. The speed and the keen air made the faces of the passengers glow.

On the road they met Olwen and Barrass, aboard Pitcher's wagon. Barrass was driving, and looking as if he had been doing so for years, Emma thought. Reaching The Voyager Inn near the post office where they were to leave the horses, they went inside together for refreshment to warm themselves after the chilling ride.

'I hardly recognized you, Mistress Palmer,' Barrass smiled as Emma unfolded a blanket, then a shawl, then a thick cloak from her shoulders before revealing her woollen jumper and skirt.

'I've never known such cold,' she said, pulling the chair she had claimed closer to the roaring fire.

'Mulled ale I think, innkeeper,' Barrass ordered with a snap of his fingers.

Olwen at once began talking to Florrie about the animals they had come to buy.

'With winter feeding so expensive, many sell before the worst of the weather so we hope to have a few bargains,' she explained.

Emma sat warming her hands and watching the authoritative way Barrass dealt with the serving boy and remembering the request of Barrass for permission to marry her daughter Violet. She had peremptorily forbidden it, and wondered as she looked at him, tall, handsome and becoming more gentlemanly and confident by the hour, if she had been mistaken. She had had such dreams for her three daughters, imagining them married to fine, wealthy gentlemen from Swansea with huge houses to run and servants to command. She had spent money they could ill afford on their schooling, determinedly planting in their heads ideas and attitudes far above her own situation.

Why had it all gone wrong? Violet *was* married to Edwin Prince, a wealthy man and with a sizeable house; and with a second child on the way she seemed to be content, but there was a wistfulness about her that Emma suspected of being a secret longing for Barrass. Now the twins, her beautiful twins, had failed to find themselves respectable husbands.

Pansy was wed to the potboy, a most unprepossessing character who must have been a source of much amusement to their friends. She squirmed at the thought that she and Pitcher had been laughed at. And Daisy had abandoned all her fine friends and social attributes to work beside her father at the inn! Really, she railed silently, life was so unfair!

They were soon warmed and comforted at least bodily, and Emma stood up to rewrap herself in the layers of coverings before setting out for the shops and the stalls around Island House, to begin their business.

'I'm sent to buy fresh curtains and flounces for Miss Penelope's room. Coming home she is,' Florrie announced, unaware of the effect her words were having on both Olwen and Barrass.

Barrass felt a sudden flutter of happiness he could not deny at the prospect of meeting Penelope again. He tightened his grip on Olwen's arm and bent to kiss her as if to reassure them both there was nothing to fear, but his eyes were soft and moist as he thought of the red-haired daughter of Ddole House.

The flutter in Olwen's heart was fear. She had always known about the brief affair between Barrass and Penelope that had resulted in the girl being sent away. However joyfully she planned for her own wedding day, the spectre of Penelope had always been there, unseen but ever present. Hearing of the girl's return was a cloud that threatened a devastating storm.

With Barrass helping, Olwen chose several crates of chickens, a second goat and a cow with a calf. The pens Dan and Spider were making beside their new home were not quite finished and she had decided that until their wedding a few weeks hence, the animals would stay where Mary and she could look after them.

'Soon they will be taken to their real home,' Barrass said as they placed their purchases in the care of one of the boys at the inn. He hugged her before they set off once again for the market. 'Our life will truly begin on the day you become my wife.'

Olwen hugged him back, burying her anxiety against his strong chest. Surely the sparkle in his eyes is really for me and not the thought of meeting Penelope, she pleaded with the fates. Please don't let anything go wrong after I have waited for him so long. As if to swell the feeling of impending disaster, the day grew warmer and clouds built up. Before the two wagons set off for home with their passengers loaded with purchases, the rain had begun.

*

News arrived on Christmas day that the Morgan brothers had cheated the hangman and died. Daniels was at the inn when a messenger came to find him. He read the note and told Pitcher. No one had liked either Madoc or Morgan, but the end of their lives were so filled with misfortune that people felt sympathetic grief. Several went to call at Ddole House to offer their condolences to Vanora, the miracle survivor of the family, and Olwen felt inexplicable guilt that she had failed to save them.

'They forced me to help them,' she told Vanora, 'and threatened to accuse me and Barrass of the things they had done, but I still wish I could have saved them from prison. For the few short weeks left to them they could have been free.'

'Don't feel remorse, their fate was decided when they were children,' Vanora surprised her by saying. 'Spoilt to the point of stupidity they were, the pair of them. Mam and Dad refused to seen anything but good in them, and Seranne and I followed their lead. If we had been stronger then perhaps things would have been different.' She looked at Olwen, then her glance slid away as she added, 'I think Madoc was really fond of you, mind. I don't think he would have really done what he threatened.'

'I was so afraid.' Olwen thought it was kinder not to tell Vanora about the time when the torn and partly burned letter had been placed in Barrass's bed for Daniels to find.

'I'm sorry.' Vanora hugged Olwen and smiled. 'Best we forget it all now and look forward, you to your wedding and me to a comfortable existence here.'

Olwen shivered and listened to the knocking coming from upstairs where preparations were in hand for Penelope's return. With every passing moment, her wedding was further threatened.

Barrass met her that evening when she had finished her day's work. She saw at once that something had happened. She could see latent excitement in the depths of his dark eyes.

'I have news for you,' he said calmly as he kissed her. Then he shouted, 'I have been offered the position of Deputy Postmaster to Swansea!' He lifted her and swung her around in the air. 'Two dreams come true! You my promised bride and the position of an official for the King's Mail!'

'Barrass! That's wonderful!'

'Shall I take it?'

'What d'you mean? Of course you will! It's what you've always wanted, since you were a child!'

'Only if you agree, Olwen. We make decisions between us from now on. Everything we do, we decide upon together. If you agree after we have talked about it, then I will accept, and gladly. I will be away from home for long hours, and there will be need to pay someone to be there when I am not.'

'Perhaps poor Walter would help. Without the responsibility of the books, he would be able, I think.'

'No, I will need someone utterly interested in the work, not someone who sleeps long, and daydreams about Lowri or Daisy!'

'If Daisy were to befriend him again, that would brighten him up,' Olwen laughed. 'He is badly smitten. Lowri was only an impertinent interloper.'

'How d'you know so much when you rarely go into town!' Barrass laughed. 'I'll have to behave with utmost care if you are to know my every move!'

Having been sent to buy fresh fruit and vegetables for Florrie, Olwen was at the inn near the sorting office in Swansea on the day when Penelope and John Maddern were expected home. She knew from Florrie when the couple were due and waited anxiously for news of the coach's arrival. The day was wet, with thunder in the air and lightning flashing occasionally against the walls of Island House, around which the market was held.

Some stall holders packed their goods and hurried home, others shouted that bargains were offered for the brave souls who defied the storm and came to buy.

Olwen had been one of those making for shelter at the first drops and now she waited for Barrass to finish discussing his future employment with the men from London. When the Ddole carriage drove up and passed through into the stable yard, she gasped with alarm. Penelope and John Maddern were inside. She felt her legs weaken. However she tried not to feel afraid, she knew that if she were present when Barrass and Penelope met after the long absence, she would see immediately whether they were still in love with each other. It was something she was not ready to face. Writing a note to explain her departure, she gave it to a boy to deliver to Barrass, and began the six-mile walk back to Ddole House. Better tired legs than a broken heart.

If she had waited she would have known that the couple did not stop in town but made their way almost immediately back to the village. Having been away for so long, and suffered such an unpleasant journey over six days, Penelope could not wait to get home and see her father and be once more in her own room.

It was on the following day that Barrass and Penelope met. When Barrass called at Ddole House with letters, he was told that Penelope wanted to see him. Olwen's heart threatened to burst from her thin chest as she pretended to concentrate on the cakes she was making and not imagine what they were saying to each other.

Barrass saw at once that Penelope had changed. She looked the same, yet there was an elegance about her that was more pronounced, a carefully modulated speech that added an air of sophistication. Her dress was more luxurious, fitting – with an ease that spoke of expense – her perfectly formed figure.

'Penelope, it's been so long I thought you would have the look of a stranger,' Barrass said, stepping forward to greet her. He took the offered hand, wondering if she had given it to him for fear he might forget himself and kiss her lips. 'You enjoyed London?' he asked.

'Not at first,' she said in her new voice. 'I found it rather frightening. But once the Thomases began to introduce me to its pleasures, I found it a most agreeable city.'

'Then you will be sorry to return?'

'I wish to see my father, of course, and perhaps I will stay, for a while at least.'

The formality of her language, and stiffness of her posture unnerved him, but instead of making his excuses and leaving, he tried to persuade her to relax into their once contented friendship.

'I missed you when you were sent away,' he said. 'I blamed myself for it. If I could undo those precious days when we were loving friends I think I would, if only to keep you here, near me.'

'We were happy, weren't we?' she smiled. 'I don't think I regret one moment of it. But now, I hear you and Olwen are to be married.'

'I love her, but not more than I loved you,' he admitted. 'That is a terrible thing to admit so near my wedding day, isn't it?'

'I love John, but only as much as I loved you,' she said, offering both hands to him. She pulled him close and touched his cheek with her lips. 'I will be marrying soon. Let us both be happy, shall we?'

Ignoring the possibility of a rebuff, Barrass took her in his arms and hugged her close to him.

'We will always be loving friends, won't we, Penelope, even though we will be true to our partners.'

'Always, Barrass, my dear,' she agreed softly.

Olwen did not stay in the kitchen for Barrass to come from his meeting with Penelope. On the pretext of searching for eggs among the straw of the barn, she sat with hens clucking around her and watched the door for him to depart.

In the kitchen Barrass looked for her and when Florrie nodded towards the barn he walked slowly across the yard. He hesitated at the open door then stepped inside and sat beside her, his leather bag still across his shoulders.

'It was good to see her again, she is a kind and gentle lady,' he began. 'Soon to be married, like us. John Maddern, who has loved her for a long time, has persuaded her to be his wife.'

'Then it's truly over? You and Penelope?' Olwen dared to ask.

'It's never over, a love between two people, but we are both content to be apart. Knowing the other is happy is all we need.' He put his arms around her and realized she was shivering. 'Olwen. Are you ill?'

'Not ill, just a little afraid. If you love me, Barrass, will you tell me so often? I'll need an a-w-f-u-l lot of reassurance.' She also thought she would need to watch him with the dedication of a hound on the scent of a fox if she were to keep him out of the arms of other women!

The wedding of Olwen and Barrass took place on a breezy, gloriously sunny Sunday, the tenth of March. The procession began at the house on the cliff with Olwen and her proud father, followed by Mary with Dic, and Dan and Enyd who carried their small baby daughter, Marilyn. Once the party had walked down the steep path to the village, they were joined by Ceinwen and Kenneth, Emma and Pitcher, Pansy and Arthur, Daisy and Cadwalader, and Arthur's dog. Soon, the whole village was in procession.

Olwen wore a white cotton dress with a skirt that billowed out in the frisky breeze, a veil of lace made by Mistress Powell only months before she had died, and she carried a trailing bouquet of spring flowers made by Mary. Barrass looked so handsome she wanted to cry. He had on a brown worsted suit and shiny leather boots given to him by Pitcher, but the smart outfit did not lessen the impression of a buccaneer spirit within. His long hair had refused to lie flat, and the wind picked it up as wilfully as it filled Olwen's skirts.

Both Dic and baby Marilyn had bells on their feet and hands. Children who ran alongside the head of the procession carried hoops that were covered with flowers and streamers of ribbon which they waved as they danced along the rutted road. Boys from the village played on reed pipes and kept the feet dancing gaily as they walked.

The church quickly filled and those who could not get inside waited at the great oaken door, stretching to glimpse at least a little of the marriage ceremony of one of their favourite daughters.

Olwen forgot any nervousness she had expected to feel at being the centre of such attention. The joy of those around her was an echo of the happiness within her. Seeing Barrass smiling at her, devotion and utter contentment in his brown eyes, made her wonder if there was anything else in the world she could desire, and decided there was not.

Penelope was there with John and Olwen could see by the way they looked at each other that from that source at least she had nothing to fear. Violet stood beside Penelope, baby Georgina in her arms, and on her face Olwen was briefly unnerved to see tears. Mary saw, interpreted the look and whispered to her daughter, 'There are always some who cry at weddings, my dear. I do myself although I am utterly content with your father and have no envy for the bride.' She pointed to where Dozy Bethan was being consoled by Florrie, and Emma was crying inelegantly into Pitcher's shoulder.

The crowd of merrymakers squeezed into The Posthorn Inn

and without the need for persuasion, Carter Phillips and Oak-tree Thomas began to play their fiddles, Cadwalader began to strum his harp and Dan began to sing. Daniels arrived and sat beside Florrie, although he did not speak to her. Not far from them sat William Ddole. Penelope and John Maddern were holding hands and smiling contentedly. Markus joined them, still guided by his watchman, although many had now realized that his blindness was not as complete as it once had been. Thieves and thief catchers, servers and customers, rich and poor, all for a few hours as one, Pitcher thought happily, and all here, in my inn.

Arthur helped his father-in-law to serve drinks and Pansy helped her sister to hand plates of food to the guests. Mistress Gronow, the shy dressmaker from the town had been invited, and she found herself a place in the corner, beside a familiar face no one had thought to invite. Walter Waterman watched as Daisy drew nearer to him, then as she offered a plate of meat and cheese to the dressmaker, he asked, 'Can I stay and enjoy the company for a while?'

Daisy looked at him, a wicked smile on her face. 'No. That is, unless you offer to help me serve the guests.'

'Willingly.' He stood up and pushing his way through the revellers, began to assist in the formidable task of feeding most of the village out of one small kitchen. That they managed extremely well told of the efficiency of Emma and Pitcher, and augured well for the success of The Posthorn Inn.

Olwen and Barrass left the party without being observed and walked in their finery to their new home. The moon lit their path, the house, white and welcoming seemed to be waiting for them, its door open, a fire burning and a kettle hanging over it spouting a thin thread of steam. The animals were all bedded down, new pens and sheds keeping them safe from harm. The silence was absolute and Olwen had dropped her chatter to a whisper as if afraid of spoiling the magic of the moment.

Barrass lifted her and carried her inside, kicking the door closed behind him. Their bed had been placed before the fire and he placed her gently upon it.

Behind them at the inn, people began to gather, and a procession, far less orderly that the previous one, began to snake across

308

the field. Giggling broke out and was quickly subdued. Whispered instructions passed down the straggling line of well-wishers. The assorted items they carried clanged occasionally, causing more laughter hushed in cupped hands.

When they reached the newly built house, they began to bang with sticks on the tins and boxes they had brought. They rattled chains, they beat on saucepans. Some had brought handbells, borrowed from the church, and the silent night was silent no more, being filled with a cacophony of harsh sounds and raucous laughter.

Within the house Barrass held Olwen close and they waited for the din to subside.

'The devils have been truly driven away,' he whispered. 'Now there's nothing to worry us until morning, my dear wife.'

Just then, one of the new cockerels crowed and they both laughed. Morning had broken and it was time to rise and begin their first day.

Emma stood in the darkness of the greatly enlarged building towards dawn when the last guest had finally been persuaded to leave, looking down the stairwell to the shadowy rooms below. Snores emanated from the bar-room and she sighed; perhaps the last guest had not gone after all. She shrugged, tomorrow was almost here, no point in making a fuss.

Pitcher woke and finding her missing from his side, came to join her.

'What are you thinking about, Emma?' he asked, putting an arm around her shoulders and hugging her close.

'Pity for the lack of fine husbands for our beautiful daughters, Pitcher,' she said looking down to where sunlight was creeping slowly across the floor. 'I thought we'd be wealthy enough to attract some gentlemen by the time they were old enough, but it wasn't to be.'

'Arthur is kind, and he loves Pansy. Things could be a lot worse,' Pitcher said.

'Oh, I'm not complaining, my dear. In fact, I confess that life with a house filled with guests wanting my food and a stable full of horses being cared for, well, it's a far happier life than I had ever imagined.'

Pitcher took a deep breath and let it out slowly. Emma was a wife in a million. This fine inn was his own creation. He could smell the sea close to his door. Already Arthur and Cadwalader were beginning to stir, enthusiastic to begin the day's work. He was content.